THE MAKING OF A VAMPIRE

From nowhere, a hand, ice cold and powerful, grabbed my forearm with a bone-crushing grip. Almost effortlessly, my assailant sent me careening across the front seat of my car. With wild fury, I began kicking as the dark-clothed man flew over the back seat and landed on top of me, putting his hand across my mouth. His skin felt firm, like plastic.

I hadn't seen a knife, but now I felt its sting against my neck. A momentary warmth slid across my throat but his mouth clamped against it, bringing coldness again. I stopped squirming beneath him. My fear dissolved. This was heaven. The sound of my heart pounded in my ears, matching each pull as he drew the very life out of me. This was ecstasy.

He lifted his head and turned to look at me. Blood colored his lips like the grease paint smile of a clown. He smiled. The sight of the small, sharp fangs forced me back from oblivion. *This is death.*

Instinct drew my own teeth into the fleshy part of his palm that was still pressed tightly against my face. He screamed and tried to pull away. Unconsciousness ebbed around me. I swallowed. The unmistakable taste of blood trickled down the back of my throat. And the dead weight of his body slid away as darkness folded over me . . .

PINNACLE BOOKS

are published by

Windsor Publishing Corp.
475 Park Avenue South
New York, NY 10016

First printing: January, 1989

Printed in the United States of America

Blood Thirst

L. A. Freed

PINNACLE BOOKS
WINDSOR PUBLISHING CORP.

This book is dedicated to:

Mom and Dad, for understanding me.
J. Carter and A. Rosier, for putting up with me.
And the City of Charleston, South Carolina, for inspiring me.

CHAPTER ONE

Brilliant reds swept across the great expanse of sky on the last sunset of my mortality. I will never forget it. As the sun descended somewhere west of the Ashley I distinctly remember leaning over the cold steel railing that surrounds the Battery of Charleston, South Carolina. Here is the place where a true Charlestonian will tell you the Ashley and Cooper rivers join together to form the Atlantic Ocean. And here is where I waited to snap a last picture of an old sailboat cruising toward Fort Sumter. That picture is forever with me, although the actual film was destroyed by the vampire who attacked me.

The Battery was at peace that night. The cannons surrounding White Point Gardens still faced out to sea but they stood silent, their barrels now filled with cement. Pyramids of cannon balls were arranged neatly beside each to remind tourists of the War of Northern Aggression. Dark clumps of Spanish moss hung like great deformities from the heavy, gnarled limbs of the old live oak trees which flourished in the park. A young couple embraced near the bandstand. An old couple sat arm in arm upon a wrought-iron bench beneath the golden halo of a mock gas lamp.

Distant clip-clopping of a mule stirred the silence. The tourist carriages were heading home for the evening. Beneath me the tide was being ushered in, lapping lazily against the old stone sea wall. I took in a deep breath of briny sea air before heading across the street to my car.

The red half moon of the parking meter told me my time had expired and I quickened my pace, stumbled over the curb, and slid the key into the lock. With my body half in and half out of the car, I reached over the back seat to set my camera inside.

From nowhere a hand, ice cold and powerful, grabbed onto my forearm with a bone-crushing grip. My brain screamed, but only a gasp escaped my lips. I could not see the person assaulting me. Almost effortlessly, a slight flip of my assailant's wrist sent me careening across the front seat. There was no pain as my head slammed against the glove compartment. With wild fury I began kicking as the dark-clothed hulk of a man flew over the backseat and landed on top of me.

RAPE! My brain screamed again, but his hand was already clamped over my face. If the weight of his body wasn't enough to stop my struggle, his corpselike coldness was, and I sank deeper into the plush, overstuffed bucket seats. The center console dug into my spine, forcing me to arch my back against his cold torso. His face was pressed against mine, the smooth whiteness of his skin felt firm, like plastic. He moved his head to the side, and the dark curls of his hair dangled into my eyes, forcing me to close them.

I hadn't seen a knife, but now felt its sting against my neck. A momentary warmth slid across my throat but his mouth clamped against it, coldness again. I stopped squirming beneath him. Fear dissolved. This was heaven. This was rapture. The sound of my heart pounded in my ears. This was beauty. This was harmony. My heart matched each pull as he drew the very life out of me. Pounding. Pounding. Pounding. It would not stop. This was ecstasy. The sound of my heart began to grow fainter, but still he pulled against me. This was desire.

He lifted his head and turned to look at me. Blood colored his lips, like the grease paint smile of a clown, and ran in a jagged line from the corner of his mouth to the tip of his chin, where it hung there in a small clotted drip. He smiled. The sight of the small, sharp fangs forced me back from oblivion. THIS IS DEATH.

Instinct drew my own teeth into the fleshy part of his palm that was still pressed tightly against my face. His scream was reminiscent of a screech owl and he tried to pull away, snapping my head up with the motion of his hand. With every last ounce of life he had left within my veins, I stayed clamped to that fold of skin. He shook his hand, forcing my head to flail back and forth like a rag doll. Something snapped in my neck but I bit harder, threatening to rip away a chunk of his flesh. He changed his tactics and slowly began to clamp his hand down upon my jaw, pinching my face until the pain drained me. I let go. Unconsciousness ebbed around me. I swallowed. The unmistakable taste of blood trickled down the back of my throat. The dead weight of his body slid away as darkness folded over me.

My own groaning woke me. I was sitting behind the steering wheel, held there securely by the seat belt. Panic seized me once again and I struggled to look in the backseat. There was no one there. A gray murkiness floated outside the windows, like a thick fog that had settled quietly to conceal the evidence of attack. My senses began to clear, but I could not focus my eyes and knew the bump on my head had caused considerable damage.

An odd sense of being totally alone hit me at the same time my car lurched to the side and a rush of escaping air bubbles flew by the windshield.

"Oh my God." My words were weak, disbelieving. I screamed as the car tilted farther and water sloshed around my hips. I plunged my hands into the cold water and frantically tried to release the seat belt. My fingers were slow and awkward. This simple task seemed to take forever.

The car lurched farther now, but I was at last free of the shoulder harness. I tried the door handle, nothing happened. The windows were electric, useless. My whole body began to tremble as I pushed against the door. How deep was I? Could I swim to the surface? The door would not budge, and with a fresh surge of tears I braced my body against the seat and kicked with everything I had left in me.

The door blew off the hinges like a bomb had blown it apart, and water quickly filled the interior of the car. But I was out, swimming toward the surface, my lungs ready to burst, my eyes squeezed shut with the effort. I kicked hard and pulled the water away with my arms, but there was no surface. Perhaps I was disoriented and swimming in the wrong direction.

I opened my eyes and almost laughed as my contacts floated right off my eyeballs. My vision instantly cleared. It was lighter at the top, I was going in the right direction.

"Swim, damn it, swim," I coached myself. My lungs were burning, and the reflex was there to take in a deep breath. I wasn't going to make it. I couldn't stop the reflex. Cold water rushed inside me, snuffing out the hotness of my lungs. With a final, desperate surge I broke through, coughing up great waves of water.

The dark outline of a pier caught my attention and I swam weakly toward it, reaching out to grasp the barnacle-covered cement support column. Nothing but the sky looked familiar, and I stared a long time into the blackness that seemed to fold and roll around the stars. I picked out the Big Dipper, Orion's Belt, and the Big W in the heavens. That's what it looked like, so that's what I had always called it, the Big W.

A heavy weariness settled into me as I pulled myself on to the rough creosote planks of the small, rickety pier. The moon was full, riding high in the sky, looking insignificant up there. I guessed it was close to midnight. My surroundings gave no indication of where I had been thrown into the river, in fact, I couldn't even tell which river it was. I forced myself up, staggered a little, ignored the thumping pain inside my head, and slowly crept along the length of the pier.

Each step brought me closer to tears. The pain in my head was becoming intolerable, and I wished I had some Tylenol. Remembering the brutal assault and near drowning did nothing but deepen my misery.

There are no such things as vampires, I thought. "There ain't no vampires," I said quietly. "Hey, Angela. Ain't no such things as vampires," I yelled. But someone, something, had attacked me, plunged my car into the murky depths, and left me for dead.

"What are you gonna do now, kid? I told you not to go on assignment alone. How are you gonna get back to the motel?" My hand pried into the cold, wet pocket of my jeans. The motel key was still there, along with a few soggy dollar bills and a quarter.

The path I had been following along the river's edge turned

inland, snaking into the darkness beneath the tall, loblolly pines. The sound of a boat grew near, its engine purred steadily above the splash of its wake. I hesitated, deciding if I should yell for help or take the path through the woods. What would I tell my rescuers? I'd been bitten by a vampire and then thrown into the river for fish food? They would want to take me to the hospital, run tests, and, and . . . I didn't want to know.

Although the underbrush became thicker, the path remained unobstructed and I clung hopefully to the faint sounds of traffic. My sweatshirt hung down past by thighs, water steadily dripped out of it keeping the lower part of my jeans wet and heavy. The breeze had picked up and I was cold, but thankful for the numbness that masked my aches and pains. The sandy path I had followed through the woods opened on to a well-packed road. Ahead, the headlights of a car rushed by. My eyes were momentarily blinded by the streak of high beams, but began to clear. At last I got some bearing and headed for the highway.

I walked several miles, clinging to the white line that edged the side of the blacktop. Whenever a car approached, I ran back into the camouflage of the dark woods, not wanting to be offered a ride, not wanting to have to explain. It wasn't long until I stumbled upon a sign marking the Dorchester county line. Huge, thick branches made a canopy over the two-lane road that twisted and turned to avoid the removal of any sacred live oaks. This had to be Highway 61, the Ashley River Road. I must have passed Middleton Plantation and would soon be coming upon Magnolia Gardens and Drayton Hall.

I shoved my hands deeper into my pockets, hunched my shoulders, and leaned into each step, urging myself the estimated fourteen or fifteen miles back to Highway 17 and the security of the Best Western motel room which had been home for the past four days.

Every breath had become a shortened gasp; the long walk exhausted me. I slipped my room key into the door and turned the lock. The door swung in quickly, banging against the doorstop with such force the very frame shuddered. I stepped out of my soggy tennis shoes and onto the thick brown carpet,

11

relieved that it yielded some comfort to my burning feet. With the door securely dead-bolted behind me, I headed for the sink to quench the thirst that had robbed my mouth of saliva. Still gasping for breath, I downed three motel-sized glasses of water and sank into the smooth vinyl chair beside the television.

My breathing began to bother me, and I wondered if there had been some broken ribs or other internal damage. I was panting like a dog and my heart fluttered rapidly to keep pace. A cold sweat broke from the surface of my skin and the room began to grow dim. My stomach contracted violently and I dug my fingers into the armrest as wrenching heaves took hold, forcing the water back up. I began to tremble, my body racked with great sobs. But oddly, there were no tears, only bereaved cries which emanated from the depths of my soul. Pain now licked at every joint, making the slightest movement agony. A strange popping began in my ears, and I knew that I was losing consciousness before I made it to the bed.

Slow, rhythmic knocking woke me. One, two, three, pause. One, two, three, pause. Opening my eyes required too much effort so I kept them shut. In the dark solitude of my senses I heard the ice machine, located in the service alley outside my room, grumble. A fresh batch of cubes dropped into the freezer with a rattle.

Knock. Knock. Knock.

Muffled voices spoke incoherent words, and a car door closed. Footsteps scraped and shuffled up the metal stairway. A distant siren wailed softly.

Knock. Knock. Knock.

"All right, I'm coming." I struggled off the floor and to the door. For a brief instant dizziness whirled a threat to bring on another blackout, but I dropped my head and rested with my hands pressed upon my knees. I straightened and peered through the peephole. The distorted, magnified face of an old black man squinted in my direction. Without unhooking the security chain, I unlocked the dead bolt and cracked the door open.

"What do you want?" My tone was unintentionally haggard and nasty.

"I know what be ailin' you, missis," the black man said.

12

"I'm not well. Please, leave me alone." My tone softened, but I instinctively began to push the door closed.

"Ole Lijah seen such sufferin' befo'. You gonna die widout help. You let ole Lijah help."

Before I could protest further, his hand was inside the door. The security chain clanked uselessly against the wooden frame, and with a blur of speed he sailed by me, seating himself on the foot of the bed.

"Listen, old man, I'm just sick and need to rest. Now don't force me to . . ."

"Lijah never fo'ce you, never," he interrupted.

Cramps bit into my intestines, and I was sure that I was going to lose control of my bowels. I wanted him out of my room.

"Please, leave me alone." My plea now came like a beggar, and I groped for the chair, again forced to put my head down to avoid the onrush of blackness. The faintness subsided, and I raised my head to look at the old black man who sat on my bed.

He was not tall, perhaps five feet six. The bulge of biceps beneath the flimsy yellow windbreaker showed amazing muscle tone for a man I guessed to be at least seventy. His skin was black, not brown, but the dark black that characterized southern Negroes. Thick, tight gray curls encompassed his head and contrasted sharply with the dark wispy eyebrows that made perfect arches above the brown, liquid eyes. His nose was spread wide above full lips, and his nostrils were flared just enough to see a few gray hairs protruding from them.

I studied him, and in turn could feel him studying me. There was something about him that was unsettling, but I did not fear him. Without taking his gaze from mine, he got up, shut the door to the room, and returned to his spot on the bed.

The silence between us grew to the point that I thought I might explode. Finally I spoke.

"What do you want from me, Lijah?"

"E-Lijah," he nodded.

"Elijah," I corrected myself.

"Lijah want to know what decision you have come to. Lijah

13

know ain't 'nuff blood in you to bring 'bout change. Tell Lijah what you want."

"I don't understand," I said, burying my face in my hands. It had all been too quick, too unkind, too unreal. "I don't want anything from you." The sobs began again, and I rocked from side to side, trying vainly to dissipate my misery. Although my face remained hidden from him, I felt his presence hovering over me. His hands lighted upon the nape of my neck. The shocking coldness of them drove the reality home. He, like the man who had attacked me, was a vampire.

Instead of shrinking away from him, I leaned against his strength as he kneaded the tension out of my shoulders.

"Lijah sho' like to know what be yo' name." His words were melodic, his massaging hands a comfort.

"Angela," I said.

"Ainjul."

He whispered my name and I corrected him, "No, Lijah, Angela."

"E-Lijah," he corrected me.

I wondered if we were going to banter back and forth mispronunciations of our names. There was so much I wanted to ask him, so much I wanted to know. He stopped rubbing my neck and slid his hand beneath my chin, drawing my head up to meet his gaze.

"Lijah knows what you want, Ainjul." A smile crossed his face.

The pain I had forgotten sent a reminder through my gut, causing me to double over in agony.

"You're offering me something, Elijah." I groaned as another hot cramp shot through my stomach. "But you're not real, sweet Jesus, you are not real."

I saw his hurt expression turn to anger. With a swift lunge he had me out of the chair, trapped within the viselike grip of his arms. And now I was afraid.

Tuning out my protesting cries, he dragged me effortlessly across the room and turned me around to face the large vanity. He forced my face against the cool, flat surface of the mirror and released me.

"Po' Yankee buckruh," he said.

14

I didn't understand him and didn't ask for clarification, I was too distraught by the ghastly reflection that unbelievably was me. My skin was the gray pallor of death, and my once vibrant green eyes were now clouded and lifeless. A knotted mass of stringy hair hung down below my shoulders. The finely chiseled features of my once pretty face had become a replicant of a concentration camp survivor.

"I t'ink t'ree, maybe fo' day 'til you die. You have to make decision befo' den."

I turned to face him, not quite sure of what he was saying to me, and still trying to disbelieve that he was indeed a vampire.

"Lijah vampire fo' sho'." The anger had left his face and a glint of sorrow passed over him. "Lijah never do nutt'n like dis befo', understan'?"

Understand? I didn't. Was he telling me that he had never before made a vampire? Was he saying that he never talked to a white Yankee girl before? What the hell had happened here? I was a nice girl-next-door, a registered Republican, and proud to be an American. I graduated with honors from the University of Ohio and had a good job as a photo-journalist. My assignment brought me to Charleston to capture the new rise of the South. And now I was a would-be vampire? What exactly did this little black man expect of me? The mental turmoil agitated my breathing again, and I was forced to take in little gasps of air.

"Ole Lijah mus' go befo' daybreak. Ef you make decision you find Lijah down at de boat in de Cha'ston Landin'. You know dat place?"

"Charles Towne Landing."

"Dat be de place. Lijah be dere every night. Ef you don't come, I knows dat Gawd done called Ainjul home."

With that proclamation he was gone, and I was left alone to decipher what he had told me.

The intense cramping in my intestines had dulled to annoying discomfort, and I thought that a good, hot shower would ease the aches and pains of my misadventure.

River silt had made my jeans so stiff that they almost stood by themselves when I tossed them against the bed. I finished undressing and reached into the tub to start the water. When plumes of steam billowed above the plastic shower curtain, I slipped into the hot downpour and let the warmth invade my chill.

T'ree maybe fo' day 'til you die, I kept hearing Elijah's words. *Not 'nuff blood in you to bring 'bout change.* So why wasn't I dead now? I tried to remember everything I had ever read or heard about vampires. Did it take three bites on the neck to become undead? Did it take being drained of every last drop of blood and then have it given back?

The shower began to grow cold, and I turned the hot water up a bit, letting the tiny streams sting my flesh as I turned slowly around and around in the tub. I stopped and leaned my head forward under the pounding spray. My hair gushed with the white foam of shampoo. It spattered out and made a neat circle around the drain, refusing to go down easily. I destroyed the little white whirlpool with my foot and swung my head up. My hair made a loud swat as it slapped against my back. Once more I reached to adjust the hot water, but the knob would turn no further so I shut it off.

I stepped over the edge of the tub and reached for the bath towel that was hanging on the back of the door. The hot shower had made me weaker, but had helped to ease the soreness of my muscles. I flicked on the exhaust fan as I wrapped the towel around myself, and then opened the bathroom door. I began to think that I really did feel better. I dried the steam from a spot on the mirror above the vanity.

A purplish-blue mark was plainly visible on my neck, and examining it closer revealed two puncture wounds which had not yet closed. Although the skin was tender, I squeezed the wound, trying to coax some blood out, but none came. I panicked. I had always been an easy and profuse bleeder. Even my menstrual periods were heavy.

A kind of madness gripped me, and I spilled the contents of my makeup bag across the Formica counter. I usually carried a safety pin, but now could not find one.

Suitcase. Look in the suitcase, I thought. The bags were neatly stacked beneath the clothes rack, and with wild fury I threw all three of them onto the bed.

My towel had come loose and fallen. I stood there, naked, flinging the clothes out and around me like a crazy woman.

"Damn it, where's the fuckin' pin," I yelled. My hands searched into the corners of the first bag. Nothing.

The second bag was underwear, socks, bathing suits, and once crisp shirts. Out they came, across the bed, onto the floor, and against the wall. Again my hands felt along the corners and inside the little personal pockets. I finally found a small safety pin, and without hesitating I opened it and jabbed it into my thumb. With keen concentration I squeezed and stared, stared and squeezed, jabbed again and squeezed. Nothing. Not even a hint of pink would rise up out of my thumb.

This time I did not cry but let the anger swell until an inhuman wail issued forth from my throat. I fell onto the bed, dropped my hands to my sides, and clenched them into tight fists. Beads of water slid off my shoulders and down the sides of my breasts. The only thing I wanted now was revenge. I wanted the one who did this to me. I wanted the *thing* that had taken away my life!

Revenge made me aware I had made an unconscious decision to take Elijah up on his offer. But I was determinedly stubborn, and always had been. To prove to myself that this was the only alternative to death, I would wait. I still held onto the belief that I would recover and live.

A rim of light gathered around the closed curtains; dawn had broken. I dressed slowly, wondering if the sun would harm me. Elijah hadn't said it would, but then again he hadn't said it would not.

Outside, the traffic noise on Highway 17 increased. In the parking lot car motors cranked, doors slammed, and an endless stream of people prepared to check out. The Friday morning rush hour was running full steam ahead.

I had planned to spend the day in the heart of Charleston. My piece on the rejuvenation of King Street and the opening of the new Omni hotel was nearly completed, and I had hoped to go on a carriage tour of the city before starting out to the resort island of Kiawah. But none of that seemed important

17

anymore. My camera and my car were gone. I would have to report the car as stolen, and let the police take it from there.

An intense tiredness swept over me. I was temporarily free of any pain. I settled back against the headboard of the bed, pushed a pillow under the small of my back, and intended to rest for only a moment. All too suddenly I was sucked down into the torment of dreams which vividly replayed my night of terror.

A knocking on the door woke me. Startled, I leapt for the door, hoping to find Elijah there.

The full force of midday sun blasted me back into the dimness of the motel room, and I tried to hide my cringing from the petite young black girl dressed in a maid's uniform.

"I'm sorry to bother you, ma'am, but your car wasn't out front and I couldn't get in because the security chain was latched. I thought maybe you were ill," she said.

I saw the skeptical glance she gave me and offered her as much of a smile as I could. A Best Western logo was blazoned upon her name tag. It read, Elaine.

"My car was stolen last night," I explained, not bothering to tell her that I was also dying.

"Did you report it to the manager?" she asked.

"No. It was stolen when I was down at the Battery. I'll call the police about it. Can you please tell me the time, Elaine?" She was startled when I spoke her name.

"One-thirty, ma'am. I've been waiting to do your room." She looked around at the disarray, and back to me. "Are you sure you are all right?"

I started picking up my scattered clothing, stuffing it any which way into the suitcases. "Yes, I'm okay. Thanks. You can go ahead," I motioned toward the unmade bed. "I'll stay out of your way."

I finished picking up my things and watched as she busied herself with fresh linens and towels, new soap and water glasses. She headed out the door once more and returned with a vacuum cleaner. In one fluid movement she had it plugged in and roaring.

I took this opportunity to edge for the door. With my curiosity piqued as to what effect the sun would have on me, I

18

dared to stick my arm outside. Nothing happened. I stepped from under the threshold. The light of the sun fell upon me. The immediate effect was that there was no effect, and I stood a minute, soaking up the warmth. Then I noticed a slight tingle on my exposed skin. It was not unpleasant, and I pushed up the sleeves of my sweater, feeling the tingle spread along as I uncovered my flesh to the sun's caress. The longer I stood there, the more it began to spread. Now it was running from the top of my head downward, and from my hands to my shoulders and upward.

I was reminded of pigs. They don't sweat, and I've heard many a story that they bake in their own skin on a hot day if left to the mercy of the blazing sun. I was beginning to feel like one of those unfortunate pigs. The heat multiplied in intensity. I went back into the motel room, and bumped into the little black maid.

"Excuse me," she said.

I nodded.

"Beautiful day out. Enjoy it now. Weather forecast is calling for rain on Sunday." She pulled the vacuum cleaner out behind her and began to rearrange the stack of towels on her linen cart. "I'm finished in there," she said.

"Thank you," I said, and I closed the door while I rubbed my arms until the tingling died away.

I crossed the room and turned on the television. An old movie about King Arthur came on. I flipped channels: Soap operas, videos, *I Love Lucy* rerun, *700 Club, Sesame Street,* or news. I switched back to King Arthur and left it there. It didn't hold my interest for very long, and I got up and switched channels again. I don't know what possessed me to stop at the *700 Club,* but a woman was saying a prayer for somebody's eyes to be healed, and I knew then that my eyes had changed.

It wasn't a prayer for me; God had not healed my eyes. Some evil creature had done it, and I suddenly felt stained with sin so vile that even God could not cleanse me.

A line from the Bible taunted me. If thine eyes offend thee, pluck them out. My hands went to my eyes. I had no intention of plucking them out, but instead covered one and then the other, marveling at the sharpness of my vision. I remembered my contacts floating away in the river. The usual blur of images I would see without them, or my glasses, was gone. I had my glasses with me and reached for the nightstand. The thick lens guaranteed I was as blind as a bat, but when I put them on they changed the room into a kaleidoscope of magnified, fuzzy forms. I grew dizzy, and the strain against my eyes forced me to remove them.

The room came into focus again. With no blood in my veins, and a heart that beat furiously in my chest, I really should be dead. But something was keeping me alive. I still breathed, though labored at times. I could walk and talk and see. I could hear and smell and taste. Taste? What was it? Blood?

Yes, blood was what I tasted. His blood. That little swallow was keeping me suspended between life and death.

Not 'nuff blood in you to bring 'bout change.

A sick uneasiness spread through me. I hadn't brought God into this yet, but now I begged for Him to come to me and tell me what to do. And I knew what He would say. Die my child and come home. But I was not ready to die. I was only twenty-three years old.

"Lord, don't let this happen to me. Let me wake up and find that it is all a dream," I prayed.

A new pain gripped me, tightening around my chest with such severity that I fell to the floor. Was it God, forcing me upon my knees, bringing me home to salvation? The pain increased, and I heard a voice from the TV say, "God loves you, He really does."

"Heal me then, God," I demanded. The pain eased a bit, and I had hope. But it just released me a moment before it reared its ugly head in another blow against me.

No matter what I did to fight the pain, it remained. I tried everything to relax myself, to find a comfortable position, to find relief. Just when I thought it might break me and bring me down, it subsided. I became aware of a vague hunger growing inside me. Every cell, every fiber, seemed to need nourishment. I realized I was shaking. I had low blood sugar and occasionally got attacks like this.

"Whoa, wait a minute, low blood sugar, don't make me laugh, Angela. More like low blood volume." I did laugh, and it felt good. I was going to beat this thing. Coming or going, I was determined to win.

"Eat, you fool. If you eat, you will be able to build your blood back up." At least that is what I hoped for. It was worth a try.

There was a Po Folks restaurant nearby. I had eaten there the night of my attack, so I decided to walk over and get a shrimp dinner. I stood in front of the mirror and brushed my hair. Though there was no shine or body to it, it curled about my face and softened the gaunt look of death. I smeared on some makeup and blush, hoping to hide the gray tone of my skin. A quick glance satisfied me that I was passable as a terminally ill patient.

I paced the length of the motel room until dusk came. The hunger grew.

I wanted to get there and back before any more episodes of pain hit. I dug into the pockets of the stiff river jeans that were now in the wastebasket. There were only two dollar bills there, but I had some traveler's checks with me and I grabbed them from the dresser on my way out.

The restaurant was not yet crowded. The smell of fried everything was a bit overpowering, but I placed my order to go and waited. Only a few minutes passed before the cramps started in my intestines again. The wait for my meal became an agonizing ordeal, but I toughed it out. At last I had the styrofoam container in my hands and was running back to room 101.

I made a mad dash for the bathroom. An explosion of gas and feces poured from me. It crossed my mind that at that point I was dying. I never had the runs so bad in my life. Even once when I was a kid and ate a whole box of chocolatey Ex-Lax, I did not go like this. The expression, "You're full of shit" would forever hold a new meaning for me.

I had to flush the toilet four times before I was finished. Even then, my bowels seemed to have the dry heaves, forcing every last particle of waste from me. At last I dared to stand up. I was literally drained. And the hunger grew.

My shrimp was lukewarm and getting soggy, but I started to pick at it anyway. Getting it down was tricky. My lack

21

of saliva necessitated drinking a lot of water, but I managed and could already imagine the little red blood cells being born in my marrow and swimming out to fill my empty veins.

Before I could finish, it all came back up, and again I found myself in the bathroom, hovering over that big white microphone. If ever there was a time in my life that I wanted my mom, it was now. She would know how to take care of me. She would clean up this mess and help me to bed. But I was in Charleston, and she was in Pittsburgh, and I knew I would never see her again because I was going to die. One way or the other, I was dead. If I were to seek Elijah out this very night I would live on, but Mom would have to know that I died, and this thought unsettled me.

I clutched the cold porcelain bowl. Anger clouded the relenting waves of nausea.

"Damn you," I cried. "Damn you to hell."

Night fell again upon Charleston. This fact was only known to me by the fading light outside the closed curtains of my room. I sat alone in the silence, thinking about my folks. Finally I decided to call home. I played the scene over and over in my mind, and was so consumed by the staging of my own death that I was almost ignorant of the burning pain again seeping into my joints.

I would arrange an accident where the body would never be found, or, if found, would never be recognized. A drowning at sea was my first choice. A fire my second choice. At least one witness was needed to report the accident. But these details could be worked out later, and I told myself again and again that one final telephone call had to be made or I would never forgive myself. It would be hard enough on Mom and Dad, and I owed them this one final conversation.

I practiced out loud. "Hi, Mom, how ya been? You and Dad have to come down to Charleston. The weather is beautiful. Take care, Mom. I love you." I rehearsed it over and over. Each time I sounded stilted and choked on the words. But I had to do it. I picked up the receiver and dialed the phone.

On the third ring I hung up.

I started scheming again. I won't tell them. I'll just say I've taken a permanent job down here and will keep in touch. What if they want to come visit? What if they ask me home? How long can I stall them? A year? Two, maybe? Would it be better to let them think I had died, or to sever my relationship with them and cause them hurt and sorrow for years to come?

"You son of a bitch," I yelled. "You bastard. I'll get you for doing this to me, I swear to God, I'll find a way to destroy you."

I thought of the vampire who had attacked me, forcing these decisions upon me. I indeed would remember him, for I never forgot a face. I closed my eyes and saw his blood-soaked lips leering at me.

My stubbornness would not allow me to go running to Elijah, yet. I would wait one more day. I would keep control of my final days, hours, or minutes, and only when I absolutely could not fight it anymore would I go to Elijah. I prided myself on my ability to do things on my own, and my spirit was not ready to surrender.

The anger of what had happened stayed with me for the duration of the evening. I stewed in it until, exhausted, I fell into a fitful slumber and did not awaken until the third day was well past morning.

Pain woke me. My tolerance was reaching ground zero. When the cramps no longer relented, and the burning in my joints forever held me in tears, a new pain assaulted me. A searing spasm pulled along my spine and seemed to snap each vertebrae apart then violently pop them back together with such sudden convulsions that I begged for death to deliver me. But I did not die, or even pass out. My body was totally beyond control, and all I could do was wait and ride the waves of pain until darkness fell.

When the sun finally bowed beyond the horizon, I could not bring myself to step outside and confront my destiny. I was having second, or third thoughts.

Death.

It repelled me so much that I had never been able to bring myself to touch the dead body of any of my beloved pets when

23

they passed away. To touch them one last time, to say a final goodbye, was something I never accomplished, and it shamed me.

I began to cry again. The sobs tore inside my chest. My own death I did not fear, it was the sadness I would leave behind that troubled me.

Tears streamed openly, the warm wetness felt good and I did not wipe them away. I had only one explanation as to why they flowed now, because death was knocking on my door. Still, I was not ready to embrace it.

Some primordial instinct of survival took over and commanded my body to walk. I headed into the night aimlessly, but uncanningly directed. As I walked, I wondered how I would ever touch death. To be a vampire, I would be a bringer of death, but I knew damn well that I could never touch it, never.

Charles Towne Landing had closed its gates to the public by the time I arrived. I passed quietly through the bushes beside the road and walked until I came to the parking lot. Each time a spasm tore at my spine, I was forced to rest. And each time I rested I grew fearful that Elijah would not be there, that I would reach the boat and die alone.

In the soft glow of the moon, beyond the gentle slope of a hill, I saw the top of a mast. When I crested the hill, the outline of the boat loomed against the haze rising from the marsh. Almost magically, the form of a man joined that outline.

"E-li-jah," I yelled. My body was failing me. I dropped to my knees, and he was there.

He gathered me into his arms and carried me the rest of the way. He descended the steps of the deck.

I felt the gentle sway of the boat as the tide pushed it against the moorings. The old wood creaked softly.

Elijah sat down with me upon his lap, and our eyes met. He seemed to be studying my torment, and his expression held so much pity I guessed I had waited too long for his gift.

Without saying a word to me, he reached into the pocket of his windbreaker. The glint of moonlight on metal was all I saw before he slit his jugular vein.

The dark fluid spurted out in a pulsing fountain, and he gently began to draw me to it.

"Ainjul, drink," he whispered.

I recoiled with horror.

He made no move to force me.

The blood continued to spurt out at an alarming rate, and my horror turned to fascination. His shoulders and arms were dark with the spattering stain, and heavy with the smell.

He made no attempt to stop the bleeding, but sat patiently, waiting.

The smell.

The hunger.

Something within me was boiling with madness. A rush of pain burst through my chest, as if my very heart was exploding. There would be no more waiting.

I closed my eyes, and leaned toward him. He embraced me, and guided me, and the moment his blood touched my lips I became forever wedded to the night.

CHAPTER TWO

The first swallow anesthetized me. Emotions, hopes, and dreams floated into oblivion. Everything slid into a dark void where the world ceased to exist. Only the blood mattered. I drank steadily, increasing my pull as my strength grew.

Blood pulsed within me, every artery and vein expanded to receive the flow. A new warmth spread through my groin and swirled down the femoral arteries of my thighs. The dried husk of my body awakened.

Elijah moaned against me.

He tried to push me away, but his feeble attempts only stirred the hunger; my rebirth was not yet complete. He pulled away and I bent with him, forcing more blood from his offering fount, pushing it deeper, driving it to the very core of my being.

I had become a receptacle, and the current of life flooded me.

"Ainjul, stop," Elijah groaned.

I ignored his plea and took a deep drag, wondering where it was all coming from, and when it would end.

Now I was the one moaning and Elijah shoved me away, retreating quickly to the opposite side of the boat.

I convulsively sucked in air, reaching out for him. But he kept his distance and I fell onto the smooth planking of the deck.

He stared at me a long time, staying clear of my reach.

I had found Utopia.

I had blossomed.

I stood up slowly, shaking back the thick layers of my hair. I looked at Elijah and wiped the blood from my lips. The way he hung back made it clear to me that he indeed had never done this before. I was the first of his procreations. And I began to laugh, beckoning him to come to me.

He stood perfectly still, gaping at me. I could not tell if the look in his wide brown eyes reflected fear or awe.

As I approached him he fell to his knees, making me feel the perfect fool. I wanted to embrace him, give thanks to him for what he had done, but he knelt before me like I had become a goddess and his reaction made me giddy.

"Elijah, what are you doing?"

"Oh Lawd, oh Lawd," he said.

"Please, Elijah, stop this." I extended my hand to help him up.

He rose slowly and with a trembling hand reached out to touch my hair. "Oh, Ainjul, dat be blood in yo' hair."

I ran my fingers through the curly layers and felt nothing.

I pulled a hunk of it forward, held it to the moonlight, and saw the strange highlights spark with life.

My gaze switched to the stark whiteness of my skin. I studied my hand for quite a while before Elijah gently took hold of my raised arm and pulled it toward him.

"White like a stah in de sky, you my own Ainjul," he said. He grinned at me with the pride of a new father and led me off the boat.

The euphoric state I was in is hard to describe in mere human terms and conditions. My motor skills had changed tenfold, and the simplest movements could be performed with such fluidity that to the eye they appeared blurred, if not completely invisible. My reflexes, which had been marked the quickest in my Human Anatomy and Physiology class of five hundred students, fired off so rapidly I could almost feel the synapses as my muscles contracted and flexed at my will.

This so amused me that I became a puppet of animation, glibly testing the limits of my new, seemingly unlimitless, form.

Elijah became transformed also, delighting in the discov-

27

eries that sent me careening happily in a mock dance around him.

Why had I let myself suffer so during the past three days when this was awaiting me? I wanted the world to know what happened to me, and I let out a piercing "yahoo" that stilled the other creatures of the night around me.

"Missis, you gonna wake de dead a hollern' like dat," he said.

We stopped walking a moment and listened to the hushed silence around us. A lone tree frog dared to strike a note, and soon others chirped in to begin the melody again, joined immediately by the rest of the marsh critters. The night's harmony flourished, and I was charmed by the subtle quality of the song.

We reached the clearing, but instead of walking out in the open, Elijah hung to the shadows along the edge of the woods. Though he didn't say it, I could tell something was bothering him. His movement reflected caution. He motioned for me to be silent.

Desperately, I tried to tune in to what he obviously could sense. But my new body was too alive for such a fine tuning, and I had to rely on him.

He began to dodge from shadow to shadow, motioning for me to follow. Try as I might, I could not match the unearthly ability that melded him into the dark. Had it not been for the increasing keenness of my vision, I would have lost him beneath the large magnolia trees lining the field.

He was running, and I was running. His footsteps did not stir the leaves or twigs littering the underbrush, but mine fell awkwardly, and the rustling and crackling was an intrusion on the unerring passage of my old friend.

I began to concentrate on the sounds, and tried to make each foot land noiselessly. I was so intent on this task that when I glanced up Elijah had vanished.

I stopped and swept the darkness for any sign of him. My senses were overloading with information of the newness abounding around, and within me. My heart should've been pounding in my chest from this exertion, but it maintained a slow, steady rhythm that a few days ago would have been unnoticed.

A unique smell surrounded me. I sniffed at the air, trying to detect the direction it came from. It was strongest behind me but fanned out to either side. I had known this smell before, but stood dumbly, searching for the facsimile of its odor.

People. Yes that was it. People. The smell of a busload of people on a damp day. The cloying closeness of it caused me to bolt blindly into the underbrush.

My speed could not be equaled and I slowed, playing with my sensory reception, discovering how much I could detect of these people.

Seven. There were seven. And at least one was a woman. Even with the distance I had put between us, I could smell the blood of her period. They continued their pursuit, but it was in vain. I was too far away now for them to ever hope to catch me. But why, I wondered, were they pursuing us and how had they known we were there?

The woods opened suddenly onto the highway, and I would have bolted right out into the oncoming traffic had Elijah not stepped in front of me.

I crashed into him with such force that we both flew onto the gravel and slid nearly a hundred feet. It was remarkable, the sliding, it went on forever like a slow motion replay had caught us in action. Gravel ground into my palms and knees, and despite my attempts to avoid it, it finally burned into the softness of my chin and left cheek.

The wounds stung, but not as badly as I expected.

Elijah was up before me, and he helped me as I limped across the street to his car.

"Ainjul, meet 'Melia," he said. He actually caressed the front fender with insane gentleness before opening the door for me.

'Melia, I could tell, was his pride and joy. She was a meticulously refurbished '52 Chevy. A stylish car, befitting my old vampire friend.

He helped me in and closed the door. The old smell was overpowering, but pleasantly so.

29

The big bench seat bounced. Elijah settled himself behind the steering wheel. With just one turn of the key, 'Melia roared to life. The radio blared. The Gatlin brothers were crooning about talking to the moon.

We eased into the traffic flow.

"Elijah, what was that all about?" I asked.

"Old Lijah have trubble wid dem folk, but dey ain't nutt'n to worry yo'self 'bout."

I picked at the gravel embedded in my palms. The bleeding had stopped and the skin was already healing from the inside out, pushing the tiny bits of dirt and rock to the surface.

"They were chasing us, or you, weren't they?"

"I tell you, it ain't nutt'n to worry 'bout."

"Elijah, please. Are you in some kind of trouble?" I asked, realizing my question was absurd.

"Ainjul, look what you be now." He tilted the rearview mirror in my direction and smiled at me.

Even in the dim interior of the car's single overhead lamp, the fiery glow that danced within my green eyes startled me. My eyes had always been a brilliant green, and I had considered them one of my best features, but now they sparked with a new life, and it was hard to resist staring at them.

My naturally deep auburn hair was flecked with shimmering red highlights, giving the curly layers a mystical quality. And my skin, despite the injury I dubbed "roadrash" was pure china white, no blemishes, no freckles, no flaws. I looked magical.

I smiled. My teeth were white and perfect. Each one set meticulously in place by my orthodontist when I was twelve.

Yes, my teeth were perfect, too perfect. I inspected them closer, and despair crossed over my lovely white face.

"What be trubblin' you, Ainjul?" Elijah asked.

I turned to face him, edging the mirror back into position.

"Elijah, I'm deformed," I said. I ran my tongue around the nooks and crannies of my molars, bicuspids, and canines. There were no fang teeth in my mouth, and I grew concerned.

Elijah was amused by my perplexity.

"Dey come in time. Trus' me, Dey come in time, Ainjul."

The rain, as promised by the little black maid, began. A few big plops against the windshield first, then a torrential downpour. The noise was thunderously loud, and I found myself covering my ears to dull the crashing upon the hood of the car. The suddenness of the storm was almost painful to me, but after I calmed my new senses it was beautifully awakening.

I was hearing and seeing the usual things for a first time. The flapping of the wipers and the steady drumming of rain intrigued me. The muffled purr of 'Melia's engine and the chatter of the radio all became one magnificent harmony, but at my will, I could pick out one instrument, or even one chord of that instrument.

And what can I say to describe the lights. Oh, what a rainy night does to the effect of lights! They glimmered and shone, reflected back from the street and played in the showering spray of the puddles.

We stopped at a traffic light. The wind had picked up and the light swung precariously upon the thin wire strung above the highway. The red glow swept across the shiny pavement in front of our car making awesome arcs. Back and forth, swiveling and blurring, pulsing like life itself. I was in awe of everything.

The light turned green and we inched forward with the rest of the traffic. Gradually old 'Melia picked up speed and Elijah shifted gears gently, giving the old car time to respond. When we were no longer lingering behind the line of traffic, but roaring by, he leaned forward against the leather-covered steering wheel and patted the dashboard lovingly.

I found myself glancing at the round, illuminated speedometer and was surprised to see we were only going 60 mph. The highway stretched out into blackness as we left the lights of Charleston behind and traveled south. I could feel the speed pressing me against the back of the seat. It was the same sensation one gets when an airplane acceler-

31

ates for the lift-off, and I wanted to go faster. But this new exhilaration began to dim also, and my body adjusted to the changes with an unfortunate quickness.

I did not care where we were going. Elijah had proved himself to me and my trust was with him.

The soft bluish light from the instrument panel outlined his profile, and it was the first time I had really seen his hunger. I knew I must have taken a remarkable amount of blood from him. His black skin was wrinkled and pale. The hollowness of his cheeks gave a skeletal appearance to the once broad face. Even his lips, as full as they were, were pulled back in a stretched leer that was frightful.

A pickup truck pulled behind us, flooding the interior of our car with its bright lights.

Elijah quietly flipped the rearview mirror.

The truck stayed behind us, tailgating.

Elijah pressed the accelerator to the floor. The increasing velocity sent waves of pleasure through me and I turned in the seat to watch the truck become a small speck of light behind us.

We slowed.

I waited, breathless, knowing now that Elijah was baiting the truck.

I studied him, expecting to see some kind of expression change the monster leer of his withdrawn face.

Calm radiated from him. With cool calculation we sped up again. Behind us the bright lights stayed glued to our bumper, matching our speed, and the truck began to play Elijah's game.

We would slow, and the truck would slow. We would speed up again, and the truck followed. This continued for several miles before the lone occupant of the truck had had enough and began to race past us.

With skill befitting Mario Andretti, Elijah neatly cut him off.

A blare of the horn, the screech of brakes, and a wildly careening blur of white flew onto the median.

Elijah was pulled over and stopped before the truck finished the roll. It came to rest upon the passenger side, threatening to flip completely over onto its hood.

All of this bombarded me with mixed emotions; the human frailty of despair and sorrow for the victim, and the alarming knowledge of the vampire need for blood. These feelings aroused my curiosity and I quickly followed Elijah into the rain.

No traffic could be seen, but I stood guard, straining to hear if any approached. The splattering of rain against the upturned metal hull of the truck was all that broke the silence of the night.

Elijah caught hold of my arm and turned me to face him. He did not speak, but I knew that I was to wait while he fed, and I silently cursed him. My vampire curiosity wanted to see it, I did not hunger myself, but I wanted to see him do it. I began to pace outside the truck.

I did not turn to look as the creak of metal told me Elijah had entered the cab, and only a few beats of my heart passed before he was back beside me. The look of death was still with him, and I wondered why he had not taken his catch.

"Ainjul," he said. He motioned for me to look with him into the truck. "Two lessons fo' you tonight. Never drink from de dead an' ef you aim to take a life you gonna have to make it an accident."

I did not venture any closer to the overturned cab. Death was in there, and my human weakness of it remained. I could not, or would not, confront it if I had a choice.

The smell of blood drifted around me, and it was tainted. Liquor.

The pungent sweetness of it penetrated my sinuses and settled on the back of my tongue. I repulsively turned away.

A searing wave of dry heaves hit me.

Elijah put his arms around me and helped me back to the car. His body felt somehow empty, like he was only a shell of a man, an animated corpse. The strength I had encountered earlier in my motel room and when he had so carefully carried me to the boat was gone. I silently accepted my third lesson of the night. A starved vampire is weak.

33

"Yo' body still be dyin'. You be sick only lil' while mo'," he said.

I crawled into the car and curled up on the seat. My arms encircled my knees, and I shivered as I drew them to my chest, hugging them tightly there.

For the first time since I had taken Elijah's blood I felt weakened. The hunger was not there, just a wiped-out, drained feeling that often follows sickness. I let my head fall against the back of the seat and watched the little drips of water fall from the ends of my auburn curls.

We were moving again. The tires whined along the water-logged pavement. My physical pain began to dissolve, leaving only my own brooding to gather into a cloud of turmoil. I could not forget the death I had just witnessed.

"Every deat' touches me," Elijah said.

I glanced up to look into those liquid-brown eyes.

"You'd be a smaht woman to let deat' be paht of you. Don't be sentimental 'bout it. I loss Cha'ston becuz of my own weakness."

"What do you mean? You lost Charleston?" I asked.

"Matt'u, he fo'ced me out an' claim it fo' his own."

"Matthew!" I closed my eyes and saw the one who had attacked me and left me for dead.

"I take you wid me an' Matt'u he be t'inking dat you be dead. You stay wid me, gadder strengt' an' den do what you see fit."

"Elijah, are you telling me that the only reason you gave me this life was for your revenge upon this Matthew?"

He looked hurt again, and the expression was ghostly upon his shrunken face.

"Ole Lijah save you becauz you be an Ainjul an' you come to Lijah fo' saving. Ef you want revenge, den you have it, but it be yo' fight wid Matt'u, not my own."

"Why did you let him take Charleston?" I asked.

Elijah shook his head slowly and reached for the radio. I watched as he turned up the volume, and knew he was not yet ready to tell me.

The news blared from the speakers. A tornado had killed six people in Mississippi. Donald Regan was clearing his

34

things out of his office in Washington. NASA had a successful launch and Gorbachev was ready to disarm Europe. The expected highs tomorrow would be in the low seventies. Around me life continued its endless struggle. Within me, I wandered back in time.

What kind of life had Elijah lived? Did he have family? Who made him a vampire? My immediate thoughts were that Elijah had been a slave. His use of what I thought to be the Gullah language drew pictures in my mind of early days working the rice fields upon the great plantations of the low country. But I felt that these thoughts and questions were, for the time, too personal, and the noise issuing from the radio and Elijah's empty stare made me aware that he was tuning me out anyway. I could only guess that his hunger was gnawing within like an open wound, and I knew he needed to feed.

Except for the country songs wailing from the radio, the next few miles passed in silence. The rain had become an annoying mist; Elijah had to continually stop and start the wipers. A blanket of fog rose from the wet road, swirling aside as we sped through.

The glare of the headlights caught the shimmering reflection of a road sign ahead. Beaufort, ten miles. I could read it even at this distance. In some manner the sign gave Elijah a new sense of urgency because we climbed up to a droning 85 mph.

I clung desperately to the armrest, wishing that Elijah would slow down.

We reached the sign, and it flew by in a flash of green. I could now see what had spurred Elijah on, the lone outline of a man with his arm outstretched and his thumb up. What superior vision Elijah must have, or perhaps it was another sense prevalent within the starving vampire that allowed him to seek such distant prey, I did not know.

My stomach fluttered with butterflies in anticipation of what was to come.

Our car slowed, passed the man, and pulled over to the curb. I did not turn around, but instead slid over closer to

35

Elijah and watched in the rearview mirror as the man ran to us.

I thought Elijah would take him quickly, but again Elijah surprised me by not making a move. I wondered if I had not been here, would Elijah have taken him immediately or toyed with him before the kill?

The hitchhiker climbed in next to me. He mumbled something about Beaufort to Elijah, but I was not listening to his words. The contact of his firm, warm thigh against mine caused a current of excitement to fill me with such a rush that I had to move away.

Elijah put his hand on my arm, soothing my racing heart for only a second.

I wanted to touch the hitchhiker. I wanted to bathe in the warmth his living flesh was radiating. The closeness of him was causing me physical discomfort and my body quivered. I was no longer human, no longer a mere mortal, but this creature right next to me was, and a new desire began to flourish inside me. A sharp pain caught me by surprise, and I think I gasped out loud because the man turned to look into my eyes and I found that with very little effort I was able to hold him in my gaze and his very will became an object for me to play with.

This must've been the sign Elijah waited for. With a quick swerve to the left we ran onto a dirt road and into the thick cover of the woods. The car bounced and lurched over the ruts that pulled at the tires. I had the man in a paralytic trance of some kind and was damned if I knew how I was doing it.

With cunningly blind speed, Elijah was over me and on top of the poor hitchhiker. The man never knew what was happening. Elijah had him in a death embrace and was drinking with such fervor that each pull was forcing the man's spine to turn rigid and bend into the again-powerful arms of Elijah.

My own heart was pounding and I could not help but move toward Elijah. He never looked up as he pushed me away. His gray head was tucked neatly against the short-cropped military cut of the man, and he rocked lovingly

36

with each drag, slowing as the blood slowed, his sucking noises becoming less and less audible to me.

Unable to tolerate the teeming excitement within me, I opened the car door and got out. I left Elijah to finish his feast and walked away from the car, away from the noises and smells that were tormenting me.

The pain I had felt a minute ago centralized in my lower jaw and throbbed there tolerably. I didn't have time to dwell on it because Elijah was soon beside me. Like a creator who knows what his creation was experiencing he smiled at me, rolled up his sleeve, and offered me his bared arm.

I looked to him for an explanation.

"Ainjul, I sorry I tease you like dat, but I did it fo' to show you de power dat you be gadderin'." He shoved his arm closer to my face. "Take my own arm."

Did he want me to bite him?

I took hold of his flesh, now firm and ripe from the blood. I looked to him and he nodded his approval, then I bent down and brushed my cold lips across the expanding warmth that pulsed under the skin. As I opened my mouth to clamp down upon the black flesh, a wonderful thing happened. From the floor of my mouth I felt the tiny fangs burst forth. A small amount of my own blood mixed with my saliva and brought with it the overwhelming desire to feed the thirst that burned through my very core.

With an awkward motion, I bit upward with my lower jaw. The tiny teeth were so sensitive I could feel the very texture of the tissues they passed through. When I had to rip the skin to the left in order to hit the vein, I felt Elijah steady himself from the sharp attack, but he did not pull away.

The vein was rubbery and slid beneath my tongue, but the blood came in a small, steady trickle. I was aware that my fangs retracted into my jaw as I began to suck up the warm fluid.

Elijah did not let me linger long, and only an unfulfilling taste slid down my throat before he pulled his arm away.

Since I did not really hunger, I also withdrew, fascinated by the new teeth in my mouth.

37

I tried to figure out how they sprang forward and retracted. I opened my mouth slowly as if to bite and they were there, two lethal scalpels. When I rounded my lips and relaxed my tongue they slid back into my jaw. I did this over and over, flexing the teeth like a cat would flex its claws.

Elijah watched me with interest and at last spoke.

"You have in yo' mout' de weapons of survival." He pulled my lower jaw down with his thumb and peered into my mouth. "Can't tell why dey be on de bottom. Maybe becuz you a woman," he said, and released my jaw.

Did I detect a bit of male chauvinism in his speech? It didn't matter, I rather liked the fact that mine were different, that I was a vampire with individuality. I reached for his mouth, wanting to compare, and he allowed me to watch as he pulled his tongue back and opened his mouth widely. His fangs sprang forward from the roof of his mouth. They looked large and cumbersome, but nonetheless evil. As his tongue relaxed, the fangs retracted into the soft tissue of his gum, disappearing altogether.

We did this several times, studying and comparing each other, and finally we began to laugh. Our gleeful sounds penetrated the wet forest around us as we returned to the car.

I glimpsed the body in the back seat and was thankful that Elijah had moved it. It did not bother me that the lifeless corpse was in the car, just as long as I didn't have to touch it. I slid onto the bench seat with the laughing enthusiasm of a child, and immediately turned the mirror toward myself to watch my teeth spring up as I opened my mouth to strike. They were pearly white and delicate. They fit neatly behind my normal teeth and were located more toward the center of my mouth than directly behind my canines where I had expected them to be. As badly as I wanted to touch them with the tip of my tongue, I could not, for they sunk out of the way when my tongue fell to the floor of my mouth. I thought this a rather unique safeguard to keep me from biting my own tongue.

"We have to hurry befo' daybreak come," Elijah said.

He patiently coaxed 'Melia back through the ruts of the road and onto the highway once more.

We traveled briefly along Route 21, and then Elijah made a right-hand turn onto another dirt road that was little more than a path beside the marsh. I was worried we might become stuck in the mire, but could tell Elijah was no stranger to these back roads. Before long we reached a river, and I waited in the car while Elijah deposited the body.

With that grisly task done, we headed back onto the open road, and I began to wonder how I would ever be able to get rid of a dead body. I decided the best thing to do would be not bring death, but I was too young and naive to know the real consequences either way. I would learn from Elijah, take from him all the lessons he could offer, and digest them for my own use.

The road had become another pounding dirt path, and I watched the woods grow thicker around us. Spanish moss hung in thick clumps from the giant live oaks, and the road twisted and turned, snaking deeper into the haunting depths of the trees. I was able to make out a ramshackle cabin nestled below the dense canopy of the forest. We pulled up to the weathered structure. It was no bigger than a one-car garage, and it leaned in two different directions. The roof was bowed in, reminding me of an old, swaybacked horse.

I followed Elijah up to the warped front door.

"You live here?" The amazement was not concealed by my tone.

"I have odder homes, but dis is secluded an' a good place fo' to hide you 'til you gadder strengt'. I tell you, Ainjul, trus' me fo' sho', out of every ten newbawn vampires only one lives past de first year."

"But I thought I was immortal, that I could not die now," I said.

"We can die. Except fo' de sunlight or de fire, what else I dunno becuz I have never come in contact wid any vampire deat' befo'. But dis I tell you, dat 'speshly de women die. A woman vampire, an old woman vampire, is rare an' beautiful. I do know of one. I t'ink you be one of dese

39

survivors. You very powerful dis soon, t'ink what you become.''

I really hadn't thought of myself as powerful, but again felt pride at my ability to survive.

"Ainjul, you be bawn anew, an' de young dey do 'dapt. Dis is what kills de old vampires, 'speshly European vampires. Dey can't 'dapt. De one education I give you for all time is to stay on top de world 'round you. Don't live in de past. Dat would be yo' destruction as it is my own.''

He took my hand and led me into the crooked little shack. The small, one-room interior was just what I imagined it would be. A worn rag rug, a rocking chair, and a table were arranged near the crumbling brick fireplace. Ashes from long-ago fires spilled out onto the floor. The glass of the only window was cracked and fogged with dirt. A tattered curtain hung over the frame and was thickly coated with dusty black cobwebs and scattered groups of spider eggs.

Elijah walked to the corner of the room nearest to the ruined fireplace. He pulled up three warped floorboards. A damp stench filled the room, and I walked over to gaze into the hole.

It could not be called a basement or even a root cellar, for such things are practically nonexistent in the lowcountry of South Carolina. It was a hole, reinforced with rotting timbers and moss-covered stone.

Elijah lowered himself into it, dropping out of sight with a splash.

"Come, Ainjul, sleep here today," he called.

I edged over to the opening and sat with my legs dangling into the darkness below. Before I could protest, and I was about to do just that, Elijah had a firm grip on my calves and was pulling me into the pit.

The air was heavy with moisture and the ground writhed beneath me, sucking my feet down into the cold muck of the floor. A coffin stood on top of four concrete blocks near the bracing timbers. The bronze handles were heavy and ornamental. The wood was polished to a bright sheen, and the little drops of moisture that formed on it beaded up and rolled away.

40

I was not ready for this, getting into a coffin for the day. Confronting the truth of what I had become was still sinking in, and the cold hard fact was, I was terrified of sleeping in there.

"Elijah, I am not powerful. I am not a survivor. I cannot do this," I pleaded. I pointed to the coffin, and the tears began to spill over.

He leaned forward and wiped them away with his finger.

"Yaas, Ainjul, you can."

He gently took my hand and pulled me close to him. He walked with me through the muck of the floor and stopped beside the casket. With one arm still holding me to him, he used his other to raise the lid.

I knew at once that he had bought this especially for me. The pink satin that lined the interior was padded, and a ruffled pink coverlet was pulled back to show the fine lacy edges of a matching pillow. Upon the pillow was a single white rose, still fresh in the coldness of this hidden antechamber.

"Dis jis' be wood an' metal. Dis jis' be a box, a bed. Don't be afraid of it, don't t'ink it is an object of deat'. It is yo' place to sleep."

"But do I *have* to sleep in a coffin?"

"It is de safest place. Come, jis' touch it."

He guided my hand along the polished wood and onto the cool satin. He went over every inch of it with me, until I no longer recoiled but grew familiar with it. A deep weariness fell upon me and I knew the sun would rise soon. Elijah remained fully alert and I wanted to question him why I had become so tired and he had not.

My tiredness was druglike, and I could not resist the oncoming sleep. I fell against Elijah. He picked me up and gently lifted me over the edge of the casket, setting me ever so slowly upon the thick padding of satin.

I fought to keep my eyes open, listening as Elijah pulled the floorboards back into place above. I didn't know if he had left me, and I managed to call out his name.

His broad face appeared and he reached into the casket,

41

arranging my hair so it fanned out around my head, spilling across the delicate little pillow.

I was terrified that he was about to close the lid and seal me alone in the darkness.

"Lijah, please don't leave me," I said.

"E-Lijah not leave Ainjul dis night," he said.

I was no longer able to keep my eyes open, but had not succumbed to the sleep yet. I felt him climb on top of me, his weight a protective shield over me. The lid shut, and the only sounds I could hear were our hearts beating together in the dark.

CHAPTER THREE

Twilight aroused me from a deep, undisturbed slumber. Unlike the pleasant stages of awakening from mortal sleep, where the real world mingles with dreams until the brain relinquishes fantasy and focuses upon surrounding material existence, I simply became aware. And my awareness became disoriented fear. Elijah was no longer with me, only the darkness greeted me, muted, suffocating, and complete.

The sides of the coffin closed in around me and the lid loomed closer, bringing a siege of claustrophobia upon me. I pushed against the lid; it did not budge.

A cold sweat broke out across my upper lip and my armpits began to itch.

I pushed again, a little more frantically, still nothing. My fingers began a fumbling search along the rim of smooth satin. Was there a hook or latch of some kind? Had I been nailed inside or buried alive?

My mind began to scream for release but soft whimpers escaped through my trembling lips and I knew *it* was happening, the uncontrolled regression that would leave me paralyzed and shrinking within myself. I knew it would happen because my bouts of claustrophobia followed me from childhood where they started when my big brother taped me inside a cardboard shipping box. Just like now, the complete darkness then had pressed upon me and the necessary reaction to escape it was jammed by unwarranted stimuli that left me helpless.

Strain pulled at my eyes as I rapidly searched for a light source, perhaps a crack or a hole, anything to prove the blackness was not solid. But there was no light and the pressure upon my unseeing eyes brought an eerie gold glow which I refer to as "cat's eyes" staring back at me. I closed my lids to snuff out the strange apparition and quietly began to whine.

"Let me out. Oh God, please let me out. Let me out. Let me out."

I could not pound on the sides or kick the lid with my legs. The fear controlled me completely and it showed no mercy, leaving me cowering against the cool, slippery satin.

I was regressing back, back to the first episode inside the shipping box, curling into a fetal position with my eyes closed, no longer able to struggle against the stiff corrugated structure around me. I could only murmur and cry and wait.

The silence of my tomb was finally interrupted by a distant squeak of floorboards above me. It was something to focus on and it was enough to displace the fear.

"Elijah?"

At first I strained to hear, but soon realized this was unnecessary because everything was pure and clear to my vampire ears, and even from my position, sealed inside the coffin, I knew it was Elijah pacing the floor above me. If I could hear him then certainly he should be able to hear me.

"Elijah, come and help me," I shouted.

The footsteps above stopped briefly as if to listen, then hurried across the floor.

I could more than hear him now, I could feel his very presence as he lowered himself to the soggy ground and stood beside my coffin. But he did not raise the lid.

"Elijah, open this damn thing." My shout was angry.

Still, he did not open my coffin.

"Please Elijah, please open it." I began to tremble again and it was evident in my voice.

"Ainjul, what be de matter wid you. You got hands, open it yo'self."

"I tried, Elijah, I tried and I can't push the lid, it's too heavy or stuck. Please help me." I was pleading now.

"Use yo' hands an' push. Ain't heavy an' ain't stuck."

I tried again, but still the lid would not budge. I was about to let out a protesting whine.

"Ainjul, dat be de wrong side yo' pushin', push de odder

44

side. What kind of vampire you gonna be, can't git out of yo' own coffin.''

This so infuriated me I forgot about the darkness that previously had been suffocating me and gave the lid an almighty shove, sending it ripping off the hinges and slamming against the creaky floorboards overhead. I was awestruck by my new strength. I sat up, forgetting that the lid was already on its way back down. It would've knocked me senseless had Elijah not intervened and caught it before it smacked into my head.

He held it aloft while I crawled out of the casket and then he gently put it back in place. He turned to face me and a smile spread across his broad black face.

Any anger I interpreted in his earlier tone was gone. He seemed genuinely pleased to see me and reached out to embrace me. I immediately noticed something different about him, and as he pressed my face to his chest I recognized what it was. His clothes were freshly laundered; I could smell bleach and Bounce clinging to the fibers. But when and where had he changed? How come he was up before me? Had he been up all day? Was it only a delusion that vampires must sleep during the hours of sunlight?

I had never given any thought to the fact that a vampire had to do laundry. Good God, was I in for an eternal cycle of wash, spin, and dry! I chuckled softly against him and he pushed me away to study me.

Then I realized what a mess I must be. Blood was crusted into the knitted ribbing of my sweater and a dark stain spread like a half moon against my thigh. I also became aware of a vague rotten smell, like body odor but not quite the same, drifting around me. I wanted a shower and a change of clothes.

Elijah helped me up through the opening in the floor and I was relieved to see he had foreseen at least part of my needs. Propped next to the old fireplace were my suitcases.

"Elijah, how, when did you do all this?" I asked.

"Lijah rises early, but you will too in time. I wait fo' you outside. Git changed an' come. We feed togedder dis night."

The clothes in my suitcases were exactly as I had thrown them, balled up and wrinkled. The only jeans remaining were bib overalls, and I chose them over my dress slacks simply

45

because I didn't care how soiled they might become. I knew the large, half-moon bloodstain presently on my Levi's would not come out.

I pulled the dirty sweater over my head. Even in the darkness I saw where blood had seeped through the loose knitting and made an obscene pattern of ripples across my chest, right up to the synthetic lace edge of my bra where it soaked into the beige nylon. I unhooked the bra and let it drop to the floor.

The dark crust of dried blood was splattered against my small, bare breasts; such an ugly intrusion on my beautiful white skin. I spat upon my fingers and tried to scrub it off. This proved difficult. My saliva only reconstituted the dried liquid, and the harder I rubbed the more it spread, and the more spit I put to my fingers the more I tasted blood. A strong need to feed my ignited thirst enveloped me, and I began licking the residue from my hands, knowing that just beneath, within those tiny blue veins, was blood.

What happened next was beyond my control. I bit into my own arm and began to suck feverously at the very fluid that had given me immortal life. Each swallow roused the delirium and caused me to fall to my knees. The small vein in my arm collapsed and I slashed into the next. The amount of blood was minimal, so I held my elbow with one hand and pressed my face into the crook of my arm, severing the flesh and searching for the veins that held the most bountiful blood. A moan, more of rage than of anything else, escaped me. Only unfulfilling trickles of blood could be coaxed away from my damaged veins. I could not be sure if it was my delirious state that caused the hallucination, but I swear upon my grave that as I tore into each vessel it instantaneously sealed off, like the blood itself was alive and fighting to remain within me.

"Sweet Jesus, Ainjul, stop dis." I heard Elijah.

But I could not control the racking seizure forcing me to rip away at myself. Like my brain had short-circuited, I was drowning in the desire to devour blood.

Elijah forced my face away from my arm with such a powerful grip it felt like his thumb and little finger were boring holes into my temples. I grabbed onto his arm and shook it violently, and this time I was a match for him. He released his hold upon my head and was about to stand when I sank my fangs into his forearm.

His scream was one of surprise and fear. I knew what I was doing was wrong, very wrong, but it was out of my conscious control, and as I wallowed a moment when that first gulp of his blood swirled down my throat, he was able to throw me to the ground.

I was stunned, but not enough to give up the fight, and when he landed on top of me I kicked and clawed at him. But he had the advantage of leverage and forced my arms to the ground. My only defense was to writhe beneath him. He rearranged himself over me, straddling my hips, and now I could only shake my head wildly from side to side.

The madness within me boiled over, and I pounded my head against the dusty floorboards. My teeth sank into my lower lip as I repeatedly smashed my face from side to side.

"Ainjul, dis be 'nuff. Stop it, stop it, STOP IT!''

Elijah's fear matched my hysteria; his eyes had grown large and his lips trembled visibly.

I began to calm down, but the fierce grip that Elijah had upon me did not relinquish.

"What's wrong with me?" I whimpered.

My ability to speak, to ask an intelligent question, to know something was amiss, freed my arms from his crushing hold. He remained sitting across my middle, urgently struggling to control his own fear. At last the old look of unruffled composure surfaced upon his beautiful black face.

"Self-mutilation. It happ'n to many newbawn vampires, an' it mostly ends in deat'.''

"Will it happen again?" I asked. I could not bear to think that I would have fits of uncontrolled delirium.

"No, only one time. Yo' body is a changin' fast an' t'ings git confused. I did not t'ink it would happ'n dis soon yet. My own fault, Ainjul. Fo'give me.''

His sorrowful look changed to one of embarrassment, and I saw him shift his gaze away from my bare breasts. He rose off me and helped me to stand, always keeping his eyes cast down and away from my nakedness.

47

"You git dressed an' we gonna find somet'ing fo' to satisfy dat thirst you got now."

He started for the grayed, warped door.

"Elijah, please stay here with me," I said. I didn't trust myself and wanted him near in case that overload hit me again. The gashes in my arm were nasty and raw. Bruises had already formed around them, but only a clear cellular fluid surfaced inside them, no blood would free itself from the attack.

He kept his back to me.

"Ainjul, you be all right. I gonna git 'Melia ready." He stepped outside and gently nudged the door into place.

I did not waste time changing. I slid a turquoise-colored T-shirt on while kicking off my soggy tennis shoes. In no time I had the bib overalls on and was tying the leather laces of my last pair of shoes, J.C. Penney hiking boots. I grabbed my favorite red-and-white Ohio State sweatshirt and hurried out of the dank little shack into the shadows of the night.

The damp smell of the marsh was just a bit stronger outside than it had been within the crooked walls of the cabin. The drifting sweetness of wild jasmine filtered through the woods and I drew in a deep breath of the aroma.

'Melia's engine was idling like a kitten's purr. The headlights reflected off the front of the shack, and I saw the brilliant candy-apple red paint and flashy chrome fenders.

Elijah reached across the big bench seat and opened my door from inside. I climbed in just as the radio disc jockey said it was eleven o'clock.

It was March. I knew the sunset was sometime between six-thirty and seven. I had been asleep a long time and Elijah had been up. I was about to question him when the news caught my attention.

Mr. Jay Krull of North Charleston had been found dead in his apartment late last night. There was no evidence of forced entry or robbery. His throat had been slashed.

"Matt'u, he is gittin' sloppy," Elijah said. He leaned forward and turned down the volume. "Remember dis I tell you for all time. Ef you gonna leave dem clues dey probably find you."

The very tone of his voice sent chills down my spine. I was

48

beginning to learn that immortal life existed only for those who were agile enough not to get caught.

"Elijah, how many of us are there?" I asked. It suddenly seemed to me we were many, but I needed to hear it from him.

"Ainjul, in de past hundred years I seen our kind become like an infectious swawm. It is mostly becuz of de new ones. Dey can't understan' what it means to go on fo'ever. Dey t'ink dat it is one great pahty. Dey be careless of who receives de seeds of immo'tality. By givin' one 'nudder E.L. dey make dey own enemies. Dey become savage an' cruel an' dey kill one 'nudder. Trus' me Gawd, ain't nutt'n like dese young ones. Ef you mus' seek our kind, seek de ole ones fo' mostly you can trus' dem, 'less you give dem reason to t'ink odderwise.

"E.L. ?"

"Everlastin' life."

"And just how old are the old ones?" I asked. I imagined wrinkled, wizened creatures that somehow had grown to look like Yoda. Elijah must've understood what I was thinking.

"Oh, dey look young as you, but dey have walked de nights fo' centuries. Matt'u, how ole you t'ink he be?"

"I don't know, my age, I guess."

"An' how old you be?"

"Twenty-three."

Den Matt'u was jis' a year younger den you when he entered E.L. He was born in 1651."

A quick calculation in my head told me Matthew was 336 years old! If he had been mortal for twenty-two of those years, that left 314 years of E.L., as Elijah referred to our existence. How could I ever hope of competing with a creature of his knowledge, let alone destroy him? Elijah's voice droned on, but my thoughts turned to Matthew, and I pictured the millions of lifeless corpses he must've fed upon. A mass grave of nameless victims stared at me with dead eyes. I was not going to kill. I would drink their blood, but I would not kill them.

I shuddered.

"What be wrong, Ainjul?"

"Nothing. Somebody just walked over my grave, that's all."

49

The old expression I used brought a fit of laughter from Elijah. I was not in the same frame of mind he was in, and I gave him a disgusted look. He saw my mood and quieted.

"Dis is de t'ing you mus' do now. You gonna have to let go yo' mo'tal existence an' be dead to yo' family. De sooner you do dis, de easier it be on dem. Let me call de policeman 'bout yo' cah."

I understood completely. The police should find my car, and my belongings, and assume I had been dragged away in the swift currents of the river. Dead.

It was a good scenario. Better than planning one like I had tried to do in the motel room. Mom and Dad would have tangible evidence. I would indeed be gone. But my body would never be found.

"I will tell de policeman dat I saw a car go into de river. Den dey can begin to investigate an' notify yo' kin."

Investigate. I knew immediately it wouldn't work.

"Elijah, someone knows that I wasn't dead. Someone knows that my car was stolen." I thought about the petite black maid and grew sick with the knowledge that she would have to be eliminated. I no longer felt like a vampire, but more like a mafia hit man. Evidence had to be concealed.

"Dis not be a good t'ing."

"I can't just kill her," I said.

Elijah did not respond. Like a wolf that had smelled the prey, Elijah swerved off the highway and entered another tire-gripping dirt road.

We bottomed out several times and the large steering wheel jerked against Elijah's grasp, but he maintained control and came to a stop under a lone loblolly pine. The cloud of dust chasing us caught up with our car and showered the windshield with fine particles of gray dirt.

A dog was barking. The sound was not fierce but playful, like the dog was amusing itself. Elijah got out of the car and headed toward the sound, and for a moment I was afraid he was going to kill the dog. I would not permit it. My love of animals had always been more than my love of people. After all, people can take care of themselves and people abuse animals. I would not stand by and let Elijah kill a defenseless dog.

50

I stayed glued to him, weaving among the shadows and underbrush. I breathed a sigh of relief when I realized the dog was now off to our right and we continued straight ahead.

Soft singing reached my ears, a woman's voice. The melody was slow and sad, but the voice was clear and sweet. Another sound joined the singing—rap, thud, rap, thud. Ahead, the thicket cleared and Elijah held me back.

A quick survey of the place showed a woman seated on the front stoop of a shanty shack watching a man split logs and throw them onto a small wood pile. I wondered why they were doing this in the middle of the night. They were black and obviously poor. The firewood must've been needed for the night. I wanted to feed, and the hunger bloomed inside me. Their scent made me lose control.

I bolted across the clearing and had the woman in my arms just as she finished her solemn song. I clenched her so tightly that her large breasts completely flattened mine. She screamed, and the shrillness damn near made me deaf in my left ear. I found the curve of her neck, nestled my mouth against the smooth black skin, and glanced up just in time to see the man swing his axe in my direction. But Elijah stepped between me and the flying weapon, catching it with a swift lunge and breaking the thick handle with one hand like it was a toothpick.

The man was no longer brave. He turned tail to run, and I chuckled softly as my fangs pierced the throbbing flesh. I did not hit the artery on the first try, or the second. I closed my eyes and let the magic work my fangs into the rubbery vessel.

She was fighting me, kicking my shins and squirming to unpin her arms from my embrace. The moment I opened the fountain of her life she went limp. Her blood filled me and I was caught up in the rapture of receiving her essence.

Was this as beautiful for her as it was for me? I stumbled forward, aware that I had lifted her completely off the ground and was squeezing her body to the beat of our hearts. She let out little moans of ecstasy and I was glad it was a good experience for her.

I drank and drank and drank. Her body, though lithe under my powerful hold, did not do justice to the strength of her heart. It beat strong and pure, and when I thought I could tolerate the welling passion of her life no longer it began to slow.

My own heart also began to slow and I became engrossed in this. Finally, when I was so full of her blood that I feared I might pop like a tick, her heart stopped, and for a fleeting moment mine did too. This caused me to swoon, and I fell with her from the porch to the damp ground. The audible snap of a bone sickened me, and I felt her leg crumple beneath my thighs.

The lovely treasure she had just filled me with was not enough to displace my aversion of death, and I sprang away from her like I had received an electrical jolt.

"Damn," I said with a bit of pity.

I, only a few minutes ago, told myself I would not kill them, but the hunger had controlled me. She was a nameless corpse with dead eyes that stared up at me. I just placed my first victim upon the ever-growing heap of death.

The gash on her throat certainly did not look like a vampire had taken her. It was a ragged, gaping hole that a Doberman might inflict. I touched my own throat, remembering the two neat punctures Matthew had left upon me, and knew my technique was messy. I could picture Matthew laughing at my amateur status, and wondered again how I could possibly destroy the bastard.

Elijah joined me. In the white glow of the moon I saw he also had gorged to the point of bursting. His face looked swollen, and I felt my own cheeks. They were puffy and hot with fresh blood. The skin had the texture of an overripe tomato.

"Take her to de cah," Elijah ordered.

"I'm not going to touch her," I said with a lilt to my voice that marked the words as a statement and a question at the same time.

He made a guttural muttering sound and bent over to pick up the lifeless body.

"I only do dis becuz yo' still young, but I won't dispose of yo' victims fo'ever."

"Fine. That's just fine, Elijah. I didn't ask you to." The bitchy tone of my voice caused some more muttering.

52

"You leave dead cawpses all over de place an' dey will hunt you widout mercy. Lijah won't protect you den."

He turned and walked away from me, and I started to go after him but stubbornness held me back. I knew he was right and it angered me even more. Next time I would not kill my victim. I would not touch death. Never.

The moon was directly over the clearing and it spilled an eerie glow across the scene of our crime. I no longer heard the barking dog. In fact, the silence was so complete it gave me the heebie-jeebies and I hurried back to the safe sanctuary of 'Melia.

When Elijah finally climbed into the car the smell of fresh dirt was clinging to him. I figured he buried them somewhere in the woods, but did not ask.

He started 'Melia and we rode off in silence. He even turned off the radio so the silence would be heavy and punishing.

My sense of direction had always been acute and I knew we were heading back to Charleston. Perhaps he was going to hand me over to Matthew. But I really didn't think so. Actually, I knew Elijah was crazy about me. Even his silence could not mask the pride that had surfaced after he witnessed my first kill. I knew he thought of me as his daughter, and in a manner of speaking, I was.

I was the one to break the silence.

"Elijah, did you have a family?"

"Lijah have fo' beautiful daughters." His face was glowing with pride but quickly clouded. "But I lost dem all."

"Did they die?" I asked.

"No. Dey not die. Not right 'way. Dey be taken an' sold at de slave mahket."

"Did they know about you. Did they know what you had become, what had happened to you?"

"Good Lawd in heaven, co'se not. Ole Lijah was ready to meet Jesus very soon anyway. Dey t'ink dat de river took me to meet my Lawd."

I was beginning to understand Elijah. He was an old man and had been prepared to die. He was ready to go to heaven. It suddenly became a very cruel joke that his chance to be with

Jesus was snatched away from him, and I guessed before I asked him who it was that had made him a vampire.

"Matthew did this to you, didn't he?"

"Yaas. Matt'u gave me E.L. Matt'u stole my own spirit from de Lawd. Matt'u, he should burn in hell."

The last thing he said was with more vengeance than I had ever heard from him.

"Ainjul, it not be so bad a t'ing. I see my children have children an' dey children have children. I see my family rise 'bove de struggles after dey be set free. I have a great-great grandson dat is a doctor in Columbia."

His pride had returned and he started to ramble on about his family, who begot who, and so on. I nodded and smiled at the appropriate places but was only thinking of my family. Matthew had robbed Elijah of heaven. Matthew had robbed me of my own children. I would not see any sons or daughters grow up and become something as meaningful as a doctor. Bitterness clenched my heart, and without warning silent tears spilled from my eyes. I was crying.

Elijah stopped his chatter and reached for me. I accepted his invitation of comfort and slid beside him. He wrapped his arm around my shoulder and drew me close. I buried my face into his side and felt the wetness of my tears soak into his jacket.

"Elijah, I could not do this without you," I sobbed.

"This be a tender time fo' you. Dis is why so many new-bawn vampires die. Dey have no one to lean on, no one to guide dem t'rough dis transition. Dey sink in remorse an' lie outside fo' de sun to burn dem up an' deliver dem from dere sorrow. I won't let dis happ'n to you."

"I didn't want to die, Elijah, but I didn't want this either."

"Nobody as young an' full of life as you want to die. I promise, in t'ree months you be over dis an' be in control. I promise you."

"I thought it would be different. I thought I would be changed overnight."

Elijah sighed wearily.

"You hear too many tales 'bout vampires, Ainjul. I tell you

from my own change dat it takes t'ree months fo' you to be done changin'.''

I started to pull away from him but he pulled me closer. He needed to hold onto me as much as I needed to have him hold me. I closed my eyes and tried to imagine how long forever was. The hum of the tires guided me into a sleep that was not quite like sleeping, and I immersed myself into the relaxing darkness.

It wasn't until the car slowed that I came out of my strange slumber. I sat up and yawned.

"You feelin' stronger every time you sleep?" Elijah asked. "Dat is de way it is fo' newbawns. Sleep an' mo' sleep 'til yo' change is done."

Indeed, I did feel stronger, but I had felt just as strong when I held that struggling woman to me. How strong was I going to become? As strong as Superman perhaps? I remembered the way Elijah snapped the axe handle in two with just one hand. So this was why I slept much later than Elijah and why I napped, I was newborn and growing stronger.

The empty scenery along Highway 17 gradually became dense and commercial. We were back in Charleston, or more precisely, in the West Ashley area of Charleston. The golden arches of a McDonald's glowed against the sky to the left. A Ford dealership to the right provided enough lights in the sales lot to re-create twilight.

There was not much traffic, but we managed to hit every red light at every block and our progress to the Best Western motel was slowed. Elijah used his turn signal and pulled 'Melia into the center strip. He waited for a station wagon to pass before making the left-hand turn across traffic and into the motel's entrance. The road made an unforeseen dip before we got over the birm and the front bumper ground against the macadam. I saw Elijah wince painfully as if he could feel 'Melia's suffering.

After the car's engine died, Elijah slipped the keys into his pocket and turned to face me.

"Do you remember what dis maid looked like?" he asked.

"Well, she was black and very petite."

"Yaas, but her face, what did she *look* like?"

"She was black and, well, she looked like a black girl." I was embarrassed. I didn't want to tell my old black vampire friend they all looked alike to me.

"You maybe see her name tag?"

"Yes. Oh yes, I did see it. Very clearly. Her name was Elaine." I again pictured the Best Western logo and the neatly printed name.

"Dis be what we do. Remember how you held de hitchhiker in yo' gaze?"

I had forgotten about that, and Elijah's mention of it made me wonder how I did it and if I could do it again. I nodded.

"You jis' hold de desk clerk like dis 'til I can pull de employee list on de computer. We find her dis way. Understan'?"

Before I could answer, he was out of the car and I found myself scrambling behind him.

The lobby of the motel looked exactly as it had the day I checked in. A young, good-looking man was stooped over the counter writing, and I saw him look past Elijah to me. He started to form a word upon his thin lips, but it was left unspoken. I looked into those crisp blue eyes and locked myself to him, aware of doing it but not aware of how.

I glanced away once as Elijah rounded the corner of the desk and immediately realized my mistake.

The desk clerk turned to confront Elijah. I had to do something. The urge to leap across the desk and physically quiet him surfaced, but I knew we had to do this as secretly as possible.

"Excuse me," I said.

That was enough to regain his stare, and I locked upon those eyes and thought of nothing else. The black pupils were dilated even though the lobby was well lit with fluorescent bulbs. I concentrated harder while walking closer to the desk. The blue in his iris ranged from a pale blue to white and the outside of these striated hues was encompassed by a gray circle. As I grew even closer, tiny flecks of gold shone through and I imagined the very light of the sun had been captured within this man's eyes.

I heard Elijah's soft tapping on the electronic keyboard and the bell-like tone of the response from the CRT, but didn't dare look away from those eyes. My old black friend surprised me with his computer know-how.

"I found it, Ainjul. She lives on Johns Island."

I felt Elijah rush by me, but still did not release my lock upon those blue orbs. I backed slowly across the lobby. I didn't know if I actually had him hypnotized, or if I could make him forget, but gave it a try.

I silently told him nothing had happened and took him back with my images to the point before we had entered the lobby. Then I glanced away, letting the heavily tinted door close. My curiosity held me motionless. I watched him. He was bent over the counter, writing something, exactly the way he had been when we walked in. This elated me, knowing that I could control a human mind. Even if the degree of control was unknown it was, to me, a fantastic adventure.

"Shouldn't I check out of the motel?" I asked while pulling the car door shut.

Elijah started the engine and shook his head no.

Of course he was right. If I was to be dead then I could not possibly check out of the motel. The bill would be left unpaid. I guessed that my mom or dad would settle it.

The drive to Johns Island was not far, but to me it seemed a cross-country trek. All I could think of was the poor unfortunate girl we were about to kill.

Elijah told me to look for Brownswood Road and I saw the sign just as we sailed by. We made a U-turn in the intersection.

A single wide trailer was propped precariously upon piers of concrete blocks. The property was fenced with rusty, bent chain link. The yard was littered with old car parts. A battered pickup with one flat tire was parked next to a newer Toyota Celica. No lights were visible from within the trailer.

Elijah pulled up to the fence and turned off the headlights. He opened the car door but left the engine running.

"I do dis quickly," he said, and was gone.

And he was gone too long. I stared anxiously at the metal structure. There were no sounds, no lights, no signs of movement. I couldn't wait any longer. I leaned over and removed

57

the keys from the ignition. As if protesting my touch, 'Melia coughed and sputtered before her engine stopped.

I moved carefully across the yard, staying clear of the assorted junk, following the sandy path that led around to the backyard. A lopsided, rotted wood deck jutted out from the rear door, and as I climbed onto it, it bounced and wriggled under my weight. The door was ajar. I peered inside to the small kitchen. Beer cans littered the countertops and a bottle of Jim Beam was spilled across the little white Formica table, dripping its contents in a copper puddle on the floor.

The images were profound to me, and I refused to believe the little maid was such a lush. A sound, a gasping gurgling moan, drew me into the living room. I stopped and listened. It came from the hallway and I followed it though I really didn't know why. My stomach turned sour as I spied the scene in the bedroom. Elijah was bent over the girl pressing a pillow down upon her face. She was not struggling.

Then I heard that sound again, more pitiful than before. It came from the corner of the room, and when I saw what was making it I nearly threw up. A man clung to the headboard, trying to hold himself in a sitting position against the wall. His neck was obviously broken. His final attempt to right himself ended in a strangled groan, and his fingers released their death grip upon the bed. He slid slowly to the floor.

Elijah was satisfied the girl was dead and removed the pillow from her face. With disbelief I watched as Elijah began to ransack the room.

"Ainjul, help to do dis. Make it look like a robbery," he ordered.

I obeyed him this time simply because I needed to do something to vent my frustration of this incident. After we were finished tearing the place apart we had discovered an amazing amount of drug paraphernalia and a small amount of marijuana.

"This be good, this makes it look like a drug-related death," Elijah said. He did not hesitate to take the small amount of pocket money from the dresser, and then he emptied the girl's purse, picking up the crumbled bills and stuffing them into his jacket.

We systematically went through each room. By the time we were finished we had collected a handful of cash. I was not only a murderer, but now could add breaking and entering and petty theft to my list of crimes. Becoming a vampire was beginning to be more and more unappealing.

Once we were back inside the car and headed away from the scene of our crime, Elijah handed me his wad of bills and I began to smooth and arrange them in order of denomination. We had netted $235.57.

"You take de money, Ainjul."

"Is this how we derive an income, Elijah, by stealing from the dead?" I asked bitterly.

"What you want, a night job with a big business firm?" he laughed. "A joke, Ainjul, jis' a joke."

"Why didn't you drink their blood? Why did you make it such a violent death?" I was angry with him for causing such suffering.

"Ainjul, I tell you befo' dat dis be Matt'u territory. An' you can't feed in 'nudder vampires territory widout his permission."

"But how would he know?" I demanded.

"Trus' me fo' sho', Matt'u, he would know."

CHAPTER FOUR

Our trip back to Beaufort was made in haste. 'Melia's engine roared as we barreled along the highway. I was praying that no cops would be cruising at this hour, but I knew that Elijah would have no trouble dealing with them if they stopped us. We were racing the sunrise and though no hint of dawn showed in the eastern sky, I could feel that special tiredness beginning to wash over me.

I welcomed this weariness, using it to escape from my first night of vampiric meanderings. I wondered if the first night was such a vivid experience for all newborn. I doubted that even forever could erase the memory of mine.

'Melia suddenly bounced and lurched over the rugged dirt path; her headlights pushed back the darkness of the woods. Our little shack appeared in the distance, silhouetted in the high beams. Instead of pulling up to the front of the shack, Elijah stopped about a hundred yards away and craned his head forward, searching the surrounding trees.

Something was wrong. Something did not feel right. I followed Elijah's gaze and could see dark objects hanging from the branches of the live oaks that stood beside the shack.

He inched 'Melia forward. The car's headlights illuminated a wider area as we cautiously approached. The objects swung in the southerly breeze, twirling and dancing to life.

Dolls. They were dolls. Hanging by pieces of baling twine and yarn. We grew closer, and the detailing upon the little faces grew clearer.

60

Some dolls were crude, made of corn cobs and sticks. Some were store bought, Barbie and Ken dolls. Each one had either been painted black or brilliant white.

I didn't understand what had happened here but could sense Elijah's fear rising. He pulled 'Melia right up to the front door while his gaze shifted from one dark shadow to the other.

"Ainjul, it not be safe here. Ef you want yo' clothes, hurry an' git dem."

"But where are we going to sleep?" I asked. The need to rest was swallowing my energy.

"Jis' git dem, hurry."

He was edgy, and I was surprised at how quickly I was out of the car.

The squeak of the old, weathered door was not heard above the steady hum of 'Melia's engine, but I could feel the vibration of the rusty hinges as my hands pushed the warped door inward. As the light of the high beams spread across the bare wood floor I saw movement within the cabin. Before I could react, they pounced upon me from all directions.

I could not think. Bodies encircled me. The smell of their blood and the warmth of their skin flooded me. How had we fallen into such a trap? Perhaps in my weary state I would not be as perceptive, but Elijah, he should've foreseen the danger.

They were sweeping me farther into the one-room shack, away from the door and the light. I wanted to cry out, but they were chanting in a slow murmur that rose and fell and reminded me of the sea. I felt them touching me, stroking my hair, petting my skin. They were awakening my senses, working their magic on me, and I didn't care any longer. They were not going to harm me; I could tell this by the look of admiration in their eyes.

A tall one among them lifted his arms toward the ceiling and the others bowed down around me. His dark eyes met mine and I could see his longing.

"Leave her be, she'll not give you de power."

It was Elijah's voice.

He stepped boldly into the room; the edginess was gone from his actions.

The dark bodies surrounding me moved back when Elijah approached. But the tall one stayed planted, holding his ground.

Surely the sun would come soon. I felt weakened by the heaviness that began to usher me again toward sleep.

Elijah circled the tall one, inspecting him.

The tall one moved with slow caution. His black hand carefully unbuttoned his shirt and he pushed the collar down, baring the black skin of his neck for Elijah.

"If she will not give me the power, then you do it," he said.

Elijah chuckled softly, but I heard uncertainty in his laugh.

"You don't know what it is you ask," Elijah said.

Seeking a way to end this confrontation, I watched them both. They seemed to be stalemated. Why was Elijah letting a mortal get away with this? Why didn't he strike him down swiftly?

"I have been prepared to serve Satan," the tall one said.

A low moaning issued from the others in the room.

"We don't serve de devil," Elijah said.

The moaning stopped.

"Then I am prepared to kill you." The tall one moved very fast, for a mortal.

Elijah was swifter. He caught the tall one up in his arms and sent him flying across the room with such force that his hurtling body shattered the dry wood wall and disappeared into the darkness outside.

Those surrounding me rocked and screamed but remained upon their hands and knees, never looking up at the two of us. They started a new, wilder chant, undulating and writhing around the floor below me.

"Ainjul, run," Elijah yelled.

I jumped over their bodies and bolted for the door. Without missing a stride, I leapt outside into the light of the high beams. The brightness was painful and blinding, and I staggered a moment, reaching out to block the glare.

The tall one hit me like a battering ram, and we went down together. The punch of impact hid the purpose behind it, and I screamed as his sharp weapon tore into my chest, piercing my heart.

He grunted and rolled off me, the last movement he would ever make.

Elijah squashed him like a bug and ground the pulpy mass that was his face into the sand.

"Ainjul, oh my beautiful Ainjul," Elijah whispered.

The pain paralyzed me and I held onto the crude wooden stake that the tall one had used on me. Blood, warm and alive, spread across my bib overalls. Darkness seeped in as my blood poured out.

"Elijah, am I going to die?" I asked.

I never heard his answer.

I have little recollection of what happened during the next two weeks. What I do remember is the constant care that Elijah gave me.

Every evening he would lift me from my coffin and make me comfortable upon a large antique four-poster bed in his house. He made sure my senses were constantly stimulated. Even if I dozed, the chatter of the radio or flicker of the television screen kept my mind focused away from the blackness.

Since I could not feed myself, every night he nursed me by offering me his blood. Often he would sit on the edge of my bed and talk to me, telling me tales of old Charleston while I drank from him, and though I hadn't the strength to add to his conversations, I was a good listener.

During this time I often had visions of Matthew, especially after I had feasted, but these visions became less prominent as I healed.

On the fourth night of April I had gained back enough strength so that I was able to rise from my sickbed. The house was dark and quiet, Elijah had gone out to feed.

I smelled death and decay and upon further examination realized that my own body was the source of this putrid odor. Though still weak, I wanted a shower, I wanted to scrub the offensive odor off me. I began to search the house for a bathroom.

Each room I entered was dark and I turned on the lights as I went, wanting to soak up the warmth of the yellow glow. The decor of Elijah's house did not surprise me. It was filled with antiques, originals to boot, and each room was pleasant and inviting.

I stopped a moment to peer out the large bay window in the living room, wondering if Elijah had surrounded his house with elaborate security measures such as guard dogs, electric fencing, or infrared detectors. To my surprise, Elijah's house was in a normal subdivision and only a decorative lattice fence lined the walkway up to the front door.

The house directly across the street was a large, two-story colonial, and on either side of it were two equally large contemporary dwellings. From all three houses lights shone, giving the appearance of activity within.

I could tell by the tiny shrubbery and sparse-looking lawns that this was a newer development. It lacked the character and charm that only time gives a neighborhood.

My body rot drifted around me, and again I headed back the hallway where the bedrooms and baths should be.

Everything was so normal, I could've forgotten what I had become. The house was a human dwelling, and every human convenience was there.

I found the bathroom. The walls were papered with a pale-yellow flowered print and the shower curtain matched. Towels had been set out beside a little dish of scented soaps that were shaped like seashells.

The large mirror hanging over the vanity was illuminated by a row of lights, reminding me of a movie star's dressing room. The bare bulbs were gaudy and not in conformance with the decorative taste of the rest of the house. It was obvious that they were here before Elijah moved in.

I turned on the water and closed the bathroom door, locking it.

The white gown that Elijah had seen fit to clothe me in was beautifully old-fashioned. The high collar was edged with lace, and the long, puffy sleeves were gathered at the

64

cuffs and hand-embroidered with tiny violets. A row of small buttons closed the neck. With utmost care I began to open the delicate placket.

As I slipped the gown over my head I noticed brown stains running down the inside of my thighs. The odor grew stronger, this was the source. Something foul was slowly leaking out of my body. I did not touch it. I looked into the mirror to be sure I hadn't turned into a creature from *Dawn of the Dead*.

My skin was pure white. My face, though slightly withdrawn, was still beautiful and my eyes had that new spark of vampiric fire emblazoned within them. I looked normal enough, and I felt all right, but the stuff continued to ooze out of me.

A sudden feeling of pressure squeezed my heart. I saw the scar to the right of my left breast. It looked like plastic, or a better description would be cellophane, stretched across the area where the stake had penetrated. It was quite large, about the circumference of a tennis ball, and the edges were ragged. The scar had just the slightest hint of pink to it. I felt the pressure in my heart again. I wondered how I had survived such a mortal wound.

"Ainjul, you be all right in dere?"

Elijah's voice startled me and I glanced at the closed door.

"Yes, I'm just getting cleaned up," I answered.

"I leave some clothes here fo' you, an' I feed you when you be ready." Elijah's voice was muffled over the sound of running water.

I stepped into the shower. Using one of the pretty, scented soaps, I washed the brown stuff from between my legs.

In spite of my physical weakness, which was making me dizzy, I felt more powerful than I had ever felt before in my life.

I thoroughly rinsed myself and turned the shower off. After wrapping up in a big bath towel, I opened the door and found the neatly folded selection of clothing waiting for me on the hall table across from the bathroom.

The clothes were new; I could smell the sizing in them. The tags in the shirt and pants revealed that they had come from the Banana Republic. I knew of such a store in Charleston, but didn't know if there was one in the Beaufort area. I wasn't really sure if I was in the Beaufort area, but knew Elijah wouldn't own a house in Charleston—Matthew's territory.

The long-sleeved safari shirt was all cotton and a muted gold tone. The pants were also all cotton safari-style, but they were tan. A bulky seam ran around the thighs of the pants where they could be unzipped and worn as shorts. Beneath these garments were a new bra and a pair of panties. Beside the table, on the floor, were a dazzling white pair of Nikes and sports socks.

I grabbed the clothing from the table and saw something fall to the carpet. When I reached down to pick it up, I became embarrassed; it was a Kotex pad. Elijah knew what was happening to me.

After I finished dressing I met Elijah in the den. The room was large, sunken into the ground two steps below the kitchen. The cathedral ceiling was interrupted by exposed beams, and the walls were paneled in pine. A large brick fireplace was centered in the far wall, flanked on either side by heavy bookcases that were overflowing with a wide variety of novels. I spied Faulkner and Hemingway next to Bradbury and King. A Judith Krantz novel leaned against a medical terminology dictionary.

Elijah was bent over the hearth, just lighting the fire. When he was sure it was going to burn he stood up and turned to face me.

The overabundance of papers crumpled beneath the black andiron caught fire quickly and in the light of the blaze Elijah's gray hair sparkled.

He did not say anything but stood from afar, admiring me with the loving expression that I remembered from my feverish nights in the sickbed.

He joined me on the couch. We sat together. No words that I could say would be enough to thank him for all he had done. So, instead of spoiling the moment, I said nothing and accepted his outstretched wrist. As had become our private little joke, he offered it vein side up, and I flipped it over to accommodate my lower jaw fangs. I clamped onto the same sinewy vein of his arm as I had done for so many nights, and let his nourishment fill me.

I had learned to control my thirst and I drank slowly, letting every drop of blood linger in my mouth before swallowing. The burning desire to suck up his very life force was no longer there, and I knew that pulling hard upon his blood only caused him pain. I was gentle. My heart began to beat a little faster, and I immediately knew why I had learned control, my torn but mending heart could not take the strain of vigorous feeding.

The crackle of the fire and the warmth flooding into my veins soothed me.

It took nearly a half hour before my hunger was satisfied. I released my hold upon his arm and leaned contentedly against the pillows of the couch.

Elijah showed me the two tiny, neat puncture wounds I had left in his wrist. My technique was greatly improved from the first throat ripping job I'd done. He pressed the wound with his thumb, stopping the flow of blood.

Elijah got up and crossed the room. He turned on the large console television and placed a cassette into the video recorder. The picture appeared. A recording of the local news began.

"Good evening, I'm Debra Kasson," the pretty brunette anchorwoman said.

"And I'm Gary Daniels. It's Friday, March twentieth, and here is what's making headlines in the news.

"Rescue personnel recovered the wreckage of a car from the Ashley River early this morning. An anonymous tip to Crime Stoppers led officials to the scene of the late-night accident. The car apparently slid into the water from a private boat ramp where it was caught in the strong currents and swept to the middle of the river. At this time no body has been recovered and rescue personnel will continue to search the area. Local authorities suspect foul play and will investigate further. Personal belongings found inside the car trace the owner to a photojournalist from Ohio. The name of the missing victim is being withheld until the family can be notified.''

As his words resounded through the room, a footage of film ran on the screen showing a tow truck dragging my car out of the murky water. The missing door on the driver's side, the one I had kicked off with my preternatural strength, was propped against the rear of the tow truck.

Elijah stopped the recording and walked over to the fireplace. He reached up and removed a small white envelope from the mantel and crossed the room, handing it to me.

My hands were shaking as I reached for the envelope. The flap had not been sealed, but instead was tucked neatly into the inside. I drew in a deep breath as I pulled the triangular flap out. I saw my name on the newspaper clipping. It was my obituary.

ANGELA M. TRENTON

PITTSBURGH—Angela Trenton, 23, an employee of the Akron *Beacon Journal*, died Thursday in Charleston, S.C.

A memorial service will be held Sunday, March 29 at 2 P.M. in St. Stephens Lutheran Church.

Ms. Trenton was born in Hamilton County, Ohio, and was a graduate of the University of Ohio.

Surviving are her parents Clifton A. and Marie L. Trenton; a brother, Clifton A. Trenton Jr., of Tampa Florida; and a sister, Elizabeth A. Rabon of Cleveland, Ohio.

I looked up from the obituary. I felt a deep sense of relief that it was over. The arrangements had been taken care of and the worst of the shock to my family was probably dimmed.

''I did dis fo' you becuz you was in no shape to do it yo'self. It had to be done.'' Elijah had the most sorrowful expression on his face as he spoke. He avoided eye contact with me. "I hope you ain't mad at ole Lijah fo' doin' dis."

"Of course I'm not mad at you. How could I be mad? I'm in your debt, Elijah."

"No, Ainjul, you never be in my debt. I do dese t'ings fo' you becuz I love you, you be my own Ainjul an' I feel de sadness in my own heart fo' yo' loss."

"What have I lost, Elijah? I'm still here, my family is still there. The only thing I have lost is my mortal, human self."

"Don't ever be a sayin' dat. You don't lose being human. You may t'ink you become a monster, but you never lose being a human, it is a human world, an' to survive in it you better well hold on to yo' human soul."

Of course my old friend spoke truth. In my mind I had to reason what I had become. Yes, my needs had changed. Somehow my physiology had changed, but I still felt like me. My soul, if defined as my innermost passions, was still the same.

"Did you mean it when you told that man who wounded me that we did not serve the devil?"

Elijah pondered this question a moment, then sat down next to me on the couch and gazed into the fire.

"I been a vampire fo' a hundred fifty-seven years an' I have never seen de devil or any of hell's demons. My own beliefs tell me dat I do not serve de Lawd, but I believe dat de good Lawd maybe could take pity on us."

"Blasphemy," I said.

"No, Ainjul, is not. De Lawd created all life, did He not?"

"Yes, I believe that God created all life. But you can't make me believe that he created beings like us who must feed upon the life of others. We are evil."

"Ef you t'ink dat you be evil, den evil you will be."

"Elijah, what am I?" I demanded.

"Dat is de question we all ask of ourselves. Jis' as a mo'tal asks what is my own purpose? Why am I here? Our kind seeks answers to dese questions as well. I can't answer yo' question, you must seek yo' own reasons."

My mind was spinning with deep questions of life. Was I some kind of alien? Were there planets out in space populated with our kind? Animals in the wild killed to feed. Was I reduced to being an animal? Did God create something that went haywire and produced vampires? Those people in the cabin had thought we were instruments of the devil, who were they?

"Elijah, who were those people in the shack?" I asked.

"Dey be crazy Satan wo'shipers. Dey be perhaps de closest t'ing to de devil dat I have encountered."

"But those dolls in the tree, isn't that voodoo stuff, witchcraft?"

"Yaas, de dolls be voodoo, but voodoo ain't nutt'n like de wo'ship of de devil. De dolls in de tree were a warnin' to me. De people who practice voodoo mean me no hawm, but dey do keep an eye on me."

"Why?"

"Becuz I be black, I t'ink. Dey don't mess wid Matt'u, but dey do follow me."

I thought then that these voodoo practitioners were the same seven people we had run from in Charles Towne Landing on the night Elijah gave me E.L. and I asked him.

"They chased us that first night. Why? What did they want?"

"Dey want to see you. But I keep you from dere sight becuz you still be so young. Dey can find you after you be a changin' no mo'. I guess dey jis' be curious 'bout what I be up to. Dey ain't to be feared, jis' a problem."

"I thought voodoo was evil, black magic stuff."

"Voodoo can be evil, or can be good. Dese few people have never been evil. Dey do cures an' work hexes to protect dem from de likes of dese odder, devil folk."

"Do they know what you are?" I asked.

"Dey know dat I be somet'ing unlike dem. Dey know dat I not be bad like Matt'u is bad. Dey hope dat I will protect dem from him."

"Then they know what he is?" I gasped.

"No. Dey only know dat he is evil. Dey t'ink he leads de devil group."

"Elijah, do you think I will be able to destroy Matthew?"

"I t'ink you be very, very strong. Odderwise you would be dead. A young vampire dat is still changin' would not have survived such a wound. Though you still be sufferin', I can . . ."

"Why? Elijah, why am I so strong?"

"I give dis some t'ought while you been recoverin'. You been feedin' primarily on my own blood an' I be an ole vampire, my own blood be strong. But stronger den my blood is Matt'u. I do t'ink dat he knows 'bout you."

Elijah rose from the couch. For a minute I thought he was going to get something from the bookshelves. He ran his long fingers over a row of titles, searching. He shook his head as if what he sought alluded him.

I did not want to believe that Matthew knew of me, of my survival and change. I hoped that the element of surprise would be on my side when I finally confronted him.

"Everything comes back to Matthew," I said.

"He be very powerful," Elijah whispered, still far off in thought.

I studied my black vampire friend. The wrinkles upon his face etched out a hard life. I always found such mystery in old faces and I often thought of those wrinkles as road maps of human history. But how could I hope to read identity into the ageless face of Matthew?

"Tell me, Elijah, if we are immortal how can I destroy him, how will I kill him?"

"Drink him dry," Elijah said.

His voice was so positive, so calculating and cold I wondered if he had killed a vampire in this manner.

"But to do dis you will be at de disadvantage. You will have to be stahved fo' blood, so stahved dat you can take him quickly."

It was very evident that Elijah wanted Matthew dead. I remembered one of our earliest conversations when I had asked Elijah if he had saved me from death only to seek revenge. He had told me then that any quarrel I had with Matthew was my own, but now he was telling me differently. Had my old friend lied?

"You *do* have a quarrel with Matthew. You want him dead as much as I do," I said.

Elijah looked into my eyes. There was something like grief or remorse in his stare.

"No, Ainjul. Matt'u wants Matt'u dead."

"Then why doesn't he just kill himse—"

" 'Nuff of dis talk," Elijah cut me off. "I need to feed. You should be restin'. I be back soon."

A clock began to chime. I counted along. It was ten o'clock. I had been rising earlier every night. There was plenty of time left until dawn would come and force me to rest.

I leapt off the couch and, like a child, tugged on the sleeve of Elijah's shirt.

"Take me with you. I need the fresh air."

"Yo' heart needs to heal. You oughta be takin' it easy."

"Please," I begged.

His look softened.

"Okay. But no mo' talk 'bout Matt'u."

"No more talk about Matthew," I agreed. I couldn't promise not to think about him.

We went out into the double garage where 'Melia waited, polished and ready. Elijah lifted the large garage door and while he fussed over his car, I walked out into the night air.

Spring had arrived while I had been recovering. Daffodils were already on the tattered side of their short life, but the azaleas lining Elijah's driveway were bursting with blooms.

It saddened me that the colors all appeared as shades of gray in the darkness. I wished that the tiny flowers could be seen as brilliantly as daylight allowed. I closed my eyes and tried to imagine vivid reds, purples, and pinks nestled among the deep green leaves, but it wasn't the same.

A delicious smell swirled around me as the breeze flowed through my hair. I opened my eyes and spied the funny-looking tree that was giving off the scent. It was funny looking because there was not a single leaf on it, but the branches held large, wonderful blossoms.

"Dat be a tulip tree," Elijah said.

I stepped closer to the small tree. It wasn't what we

northerners called a tulip tree. It was, to me, a magnolia tree. But when I said something to this effect, Elijah rebuffed me with a "damnyankee" look.

He, of course, was only teasing, and that wide Elijah grin surfaced. He turned back into the garage.

I waited for him to back 'Melia out, then I pulled the garage door down and climbed into the roomy old Chevy. I felt at home inside the old car.

Elijah continued to carefully back 'Melia onto the narrow residential street. From the road I saw that Elijah's house was a large, rambling ranch. The lawn, even in the darkness, had a manicured look. He drove slowly down the block, pointing out the neighbors' houses. The Timmons lived next door and Elijah talked about their young son, Greg.

Greg had just received a scholarship to Clemson. Greg was a straight A student. Greg had a keen interest in science, botany in particular. Greg kept up Elijah's lawn and Elijah paid him forty dollars a week.

I didn't give a hang about Greg. Greg wasn't a vampire.

Elijah exhausted the subject of Greg and out of the blue said, "I miss de birds de most."

I stared blankly at him.

"Don't git to see birds at night. Dey be sleepin'. I always loved de swallows in de stable an' de egrets in de mahsh."

I thought a moment about birds. Would I never see the brilliant red of a cardinal, or the orange breast of a spring robin?

"I think I will miss colors most of all," I said to Elijah. "Night is a time of black and white, except of course for the neon signs, but that isn't the same as nature."

"Dat be true," Elijah said.

He flipped on his turn signal, the green arrow flashed against the black dashboard.

We were out of the subdivision and on open highway again. I didn't know Beaufort any better than I knew Moscow. But Elijah had an uncanny sense of the back roads and we soon turned onto a one-lane path that zigzagged through the wetlands.

We came upon a group of ill-kept cabins in a small clearing. People were still up and about. A group of young, bedraggled-looking children were playing in the middle of the dirt road. Elijah stopped in front of them and cut the engine.

Certainly he was not going to feed here. There were too many witnesses.

The children looked away from their play, and a squeal of delight rang out in the darkness.

"Uncle Lijah is here. Uncle Lijah is here," they called.

They ran for the car, reaching to help Elijah disembark. The little dresses were tattered and the little faces were dirty, but the smiles upon their small black faces melted even my heart.

Elijah motioned with one hand for me to stay put and then he closed the car door. I watched him scoop up two of the children and carry them. Their laughter had aroused the adults in the community and suddenly the front porches were teeming with people.

I felt the trunk open and turned in my seat to see Elijah distributing candy and toys to the children. When the last of the little vagabonds was pacified, he removed some boxes and bags and began to deliver an assortment of grocery items to each house.

He was greeted kindly at each front door. Like Santa Claus he had something for everybody. When he finished with the seven cabins on the left, he started back along the five cabins to the right.

I was growing bored with his goodness and was not aware at first of what was taking place at the last house.

There on the front porch, in plain view of all those people, Elijah had gathered up the young, willowy girl, and was drinking from her. Not a head turned his way, and I knew they were oblivious to his actions, but I was keenly aware of it.

I was sitting bolt upright, my hands clasping the hard padding of the dashboard. She seemed to swoon against his embrace. Maybe to the others it looked like an innocent hug. Had he done this to more than one of them? I had seen him hug most of the women, the young mothers, and the old mothers. I watched as he released her and saw her thank him and wave goodbye.

The children had dispersed to their own cabins, showing off the gifts that Elijah had bestowed upon them.

He walked down the middle of the dirt road and waved a final goodbye before climbing back into the car.

His smug expression almost made me laugh. He had fed well. His color had deepened and his body was radiating with the warmth of fresh blood.

"Ainjul, sometime I make like a big black mosquito," he said, and laughed.

I could not hold it back, and my laughter joined his as 'Melia roared to life.

We had just pulled out onto the paved highway when a car flew around us. I saw movement from the edge of the woods and then heard the squeal of rubber on the blacktop. Something flew into the air. The vehicle in front of us regained control and sped away.

My first thought was that a deer had leapt onto the road, but as we approached I could clearly see that it was a dog, and it was still moving, still alive.

"Elijah, stop the car," I said.

"Ainjul, ain't nutt'n you can do."

"Please, stop the car," I pleaded.

"Let it go. Dawgs don't take to us," he said.

I could not let the animal lie there and suffer. I had no idea what I would do, but knew I had to help it any way I could. Since Elijah was not stopping, I opened the door and leapt from the moving car.

My agility surprised me. I rolled down the embankment but was up and running back toward the dog before Elijah had stopped 'Melia.

I slowed as I approached the dog and began to speak softly to it. It did not move, but I could hear the weak wimpering sounds, and tears flooded my eyes.

It was dying, I could feel it. A dark pool of blood was spreading into the gravel beneath its nose.

I knelt beside it. Even though it was dying it sensed what

I was and the hairs on the back of its neck raised visibly. A deep, throaty growl issued from it but was cut short by a wheezing cough.

I had to put it out of its misery. The only way I could do this was to drink its blood, and though I had never wanted to drink the blood of an animal, I could not stand by and watch it suffer.

"Such a beautiful animal," I whispered. I placed a hand on its belly and began to feel for any pulsing to indicate a vein or an artery.

The dog was a he, and he tried to growl again. I found a weak pulse on the inside of his thigh. I looked at his failing body for a minute, working up the courage to end his life.

His coat was short and smooth. And he was a big dog, big boned. His feet were damn near as big as my hands. He looked, in the darkness, like a Great Dane, but not like a Great Dane.

Oh, how my heart ached for him, and the tears spilled from my eyes as I leaned into the soft fur of his leg. As soon as his blood began to flow into me, he quieted. But he was not dead. His heart was beating irregularly and my own wounded heart tried to match his. I wanted it to be over quickly for him, but could not drink fast enough. Pain began to spread through my chest, forcing me to slow my pace.

The dog had lost a considerable amount of blood and I drank steadily, waiting for his heart to slow. It didn't. I began to drink deeply, fighting off my own pain to end his. But his heart would not slow.

With sudden horror I felt the irregular heart become regular. It began to beat stronger, pulling upon my own weakened heart. I could not let go, and I could not stop the pull on my heart. I felt nothing but the pressure within my veins. I was pulling frantically against his blood, sucking deeply, wondering why he was not dying.

A hand grabbed me from behind, wrenching me away from the dog.

"What de hell have you done?"

It was Elijah. I looked up at him, wiping the blood away from my mouth.

The dog raised his head and I heard the smacking sound of his jowls.

Blood was smeared across his muzzle and hung in stringy strands from his salivating mouth. While I had been concentrating on putting the dog out of his misery I had not been aware that he had bitten my leg and was partaking of my blood.

He was still lapping the wound on my leg when Elijah reached down to push him away.

The dog growled and clamped down on the torn flesh of my calf. Jesus, it hurt, but I was too scared to move.

"For Christ sake, leave him alone, Elijah. He'll tear off my damn leg."

The minute Elijah backed off, the dog released his hold on me and I instinctively pulled my legs away.

CHAPTER FIVE

"You gonna have to destroy it," Elijah said.

I couldn't, and I wouldn't let Elijah do it either.

The dog was still wounded, but already the vampire blood was healing him. He had a new light in his eyes and an alert expression about him that was almost comical.

"It ain't gonna live," Elijah stated.

"How do you know that?" I demanded.

"It will linger a couple of days like you did an' den it will die," Elijah said.

I remembered the hell I had gone through for three days, the sickness I had endured alone in the motel room. I would not abandon the dog to the mercy of the grim reaper. It had already gone beyond that. The only course of action now was to feed the dog enough of my blood to sustain his life. I slid closer to him, petting him reassuringly.

He whimpered softly, and gave me a feeble wag of his tail.

"Ainjul, I can't let you do dis," Elijah said. He stared down at me and then at the dog.

"Go away then, Elijah, go wait in the car," I said. I might as well have physically struck him. My words stung and Elijah's expression went blank. He realized that he could not control my actions. For the first time since I had met him, I was asserting myself and he was baffled. He turned away, hesitated, and then walked slowly back to 'Melia.

The wound in my leg was already healing, the blood had stopped.

I rearranged myself next to the dog and cradled his big head upon my lap. He rolled his eyes up, expectantly, and whimpered again as I bit into my own wrist.

The blood began to flow into my mouth. Afraid that I would freak out and begin that awful self-mutilation thing again, I spat the blood onto the ground and offered my wrist to the dog.

Immediately he began to lick the wound, pulling the life-giving fluid into his mouth. He could not suck the fluid, but did very well just nudging the vein to keep the blood flowing.

I felt a slight burning sensation in my veins but it was not unpleasant. The area around my wrist tingled as the dog continued to feast.

I stroked his head and scratched behind his ears, keeping rhythm with his gentle lapping.

"Such a dumb dog. What did you think you were doing, running in front of that car? You get bonged like that again and you'll be dead for sure."

The dog raised his eyes in my direction, but continued to lick up my blood.

"Bong," I said, hitting him lightly on top of his head.

He whimpered and wagged his tail back and forth in the gravel beside the road.

"Bong. Bong." I hit him again, and he responded with more licking, whimpering, and tail wagging.

"Think I'll call you Bong. How about that for a name, boy?"

He squirmed against me, pleased with his new name. His eyes were growing heavy, and when he peered up at me again he had a dopey look to him that made the name fit even more.

I hadn't thought of the word bong since my high school days when Friday night football games went hand in hand with a wild party and some pot shared between friends as we passed around the old water pipe. Bong.

He struggled against me, attempted to rise, and made it to a sitting position.

"Think you've had enough, Bong?" I withdrew my wrist, and pressed it tightly with my hand to stop the bleeding.

Bong did not try to fight me on the issue. He licked his chops

79

and picked up a large paw, cleaned the blood from it, and finally hoisted himself off his haunches to a standing position.

Good God but he was a big dog! He was basically white, and in the darkness I couldn't be sure if the large shadowy patches were his markings or splotches of blood. He stared down at me, pushed his cold nose into my face, and whined.

I stood up beside him. He came to my hip, that's how tall he was, and I don't mean his head, his back was that high! I imagined that if he stood up on his hind legs he would tower over me, and I was five feet seven.

And he was a beautiful animal. Definitely a Great Dane. He was not filled out yet, and I estimated that he was perhaps a year old, give or take a month. He still had that awkward ungainly, puppy look about him, all the more suited for his new name.

There was no collar around his neck. No way to know where he had come from or who his owner might be. It didn't really matter anyway, he was now my dog. I certainly could not give back a vampire puppy.

"Come on, Bong, let's go home," I said. I slapped my hand against my leg and he limped obediently beside me.

Elijah had 'Melia's engine running. I approached the car and opened the back door for Bong. But he cowered away, backing down the embankment.

"Let him go," Elijah said.

"I will not, he won't live," I said.

"He ain't gonna live anyhow," Elijah said.

I was so pissed off that I was ready to scream at the old black vampire. I was not going to let the dog go. How would the dog know that daylight would kill him? How was the dog to know anything of his new existence?

I crept down the embankment and slowly coaxed Bong back to the car. He was still frightened, and I could appreciate that. After all, a few minutes ago one of these metallic beasts had slammed into him. Before he could slip into reverse again I grabbed the loose skin on the nape of his neck and literally pulled him into the back seat with me.

Once inside the car, he seemed to quiet down. I pulled the car door shut and cracked the windows on either side.

Bong would not let me climb into the front seat with Elijah, so I sat with him lying across my legs.

Elijah and I said nothing for a long time. Once in a while we would catch each other's gaze in the rearview mirror, and we both saw disappointment in each other.

Bong wanted to be constantly cooed over. Each time I would stop talking or petting him, he would burrow his cold nose into my side until I would start fussing with him again.

"Dat demon dawg is yo' responsibility," Elijah said, breaking the silence. "I don't want nutt'n to do with it."

Silence again.

Bong stretched and yawned. He curled his legs under his big body and fell promptly asleep with his head upon my stomach.

"He ain't gonna survive," Elijah said.

I looked up from the closed eyes of Bong and returned Elijah's stare in the rearview mirror.

"How do you know he won't survive?" I said defiantly.

"I ain't never seen or never heard of a demon dawg."

"That just proves you don't know everything, do you, Elijah?"

"I never said I did. But I do know dat I ain't real proud of what you have done."

"All right, Elijah. The deed is done. It cannot be changed. I will take care of the dog. If the dog lives or if the dog dies, I will take care of it." I had tears in my eyes. I could not bear to think my mistake would mean the end of my friendship with Elijah. I didn't want to lose him, but I felt a deep responsibility to Bong.

'Melia slowed and I looked up, surprised to see we had already returned to Elijah's lavish home.

Bong remained asleep, sleeping the sleep of the dead. The slight rise and fall of his sides reassured me that he was not dead, but I could not rouse him.

After Elijah had closed the big garage door, I stepped from the car and gently lifted Bong into my arms. He was an easy hundred pounds, but with my ever-increasing vampire strength I had no trouble carrying him into the house.

Elijah held the door, but kept his gaze turned away from

me and my dog. As the light of the den surrounded us, I could see Bong was a beautiful harlequin Great Dane.

"What you gonna do wid it now?" Elijah asked.

I turned to face him.

"It is a him, and his name is Bong." My words were cruel. "He will sleep in my coffin. Since it is quite obvious your disapproval is causing this dissension between us, I'm going to settle Bong for the night and remain there with him." I turned away and headed for the hallway.

"Good night, Ainjul." Elijah's voice was unsteady and I knew I had hurt him.

My own eyes flooded with tears, but I did not look back and did not return Elijah's good-night wish. I climbed the ladder into the attic where our coffins were discreetly hidden.

It was stuffy up here, but I welcomed the heat. The days of April were gradually growing warmer, but the nights still held a chill. Elijah had previously told me that in the summer the attic was unbearable, we couldn't sleep up here due to the heat, and he would move our coffins into the small, secret room on the other side of the large bookcases in the den. But tonight the heat helped to wash away my cold bitterness.

I opened my coffin. This one was lined with white silk. We had had to leave the pretty pink one in the shack and Elijah just happened to have this one waiting for me. I picked up the long-stemmed red rose from my pillow, a habit Elijah continued to bestow upon me.

I gently lifted Bong into the coffin. He took up a good third of it. I was going to have to sleep with my knees curled to my chest but it would have to do for now.

It wouldn't be dawn for at least another three hours, and though I didn't want to spend all that time inside the claustrophobic confines of my coffin, I couldn't bring myself to go back down to Elijah. I was that damn stubborn.

I looked around the unfinished attic, hoping to find something to keep me occupied. There was nothing up here except our two coffins, and a few rolls of pink fiberglass insulation. I didn't feel like rolling out insulation, so I climbed into the coffin and settled myself around the dog. I left the lid open and began to think about what I had done.

I had never heard of a vampire dog either, but I couldn't think of one reason why there could not be one. After all, what is a vampire? I had begun to think of a vampire as blood. Ancient blood that needed to be stored within a receptacle. Alien blood that needed to be tended and cared for. In return, the parasitic blood gave its host everlasting life, the ability to survive most anything. Was it not logical that if such blood was put into an animal it would react and treat that host the same?

I did not believe that Bong would become any more demonic or diabolical than I had become upon receiving E.L. But in the back of my mind I wondered if I could be wrong. What if the dog woke up while I was still sleeping and drank me dry? I shuddered to think of it.

Bong was snoring and his paws were twitching as he dreamed.

Funny thing was, I had not been able to recall a single dream since I had become a vampire, but Bong was obviously dreaming.

His face twitched and he whimpered. His tail thudded against the silk padding. Then he became quiet and peaceful again.

Eventually I fell into a semiconscious state. Still, I had the vague awareness of Elijah when he peered in at us before closing the lid of my coffin.

When I awoke I was cramped and sore. I tried to stretch, forgetting that my vampire puppy was tucked beneath my feet. I kicked him a little too hard and heard the breath rush out of his lungs. He stayed sound asleep. At least I knew he was still alive.

I pushed the lid of my coffin up and was greeted by the anxious look of my black friend.

"Is he still alive?" Elijah asked.

A note of curiosity was evident in his voice, and he leaned over and placed a hand on Bong's head.

"I didn't think you would really care?" The words slipped out without control, and I was immediately sorry I said them. I did not want to continue this feud with Elijah.

"Ainjul, I be very sorry 'bout last night. I know it was an

83

accident an' you didn't mean fo' it to happ'n,'' he said. He gave me a hand as I climbed out of my casket and pulled me close in a big, forgive me hug.

"It just happened," I said.

"I sometimes fo'git dat you still be young an' dat you will be makin' mistakes. But dis is some mistake." He tilted his head to the side and glanced at Bong. The malice of his voice last night was gone, replaced by a sense of awe. I felt like we were involved in an experiment and could do nothing but wait and see if it would be a successful one.

"But come, I bought you a gift to show how very sorry I be."

"Elijah, your apology is enough," I said.

He shook his head no and led me away from my sleeping dog.

I followed him down the ladder that extended from the hallway ceiling. He waited while I pushed it back into place. The three sections folded neatly within each other and disappeared into the plaster above.

He grabbed hold of my arm and hurried me through the downstairs. He stopped in the den and made me close my eyes, and then he opened the door into the garage.

"Okay, Ainjul, you can open yo' eyes."

Parked next to 'Melia was a brand-new, customized Chevy van.

Elijah pressed the keys into my hand and squeezed my fingers around them.

"I was gonna git you a lil' sports cah, but I jis' can't see dat big ole dawg in a lil' ole cah," he smiled.

I was in shock. Nobody had ever done anything like this for me, ever.

"Elijah that had to cost at least twenty thousand dollars. I can't accept such a gift."

"Please, Ainjul, it is a gift from me to you."

"Oh, all right," I said. My grin spread from ear to ear, and I could not help but to lift him off the ground and twirl him around in my embrace.

"Take a look inside," he said when I put him down. He ushered me over to the van and slid the door open.

84

It was wall-to-wall beauty. Every conceivable accessory adorned the interior. It was gray with black trim, inside and out. Even the windows had tiny Levolor blinds over them. Two captain's chairs swiveled around a table in the midsection, and a small television was strategically placed on a movable stand above the refrigerated bar.

The big bucket seats in the front looked so comfortable I could not resist climbing into them. The console was loaded with fancy, digital display columns. I was about to turn the key in the ignition and bring the vehicle to life when an unearthly howl pierced the night.

I looked to Elijah. His mouth was hanging open and he had turned pale.

I could almost imagine his thoughts. What would the neighbors say!

We ran back into the house where the howling was louder. We could hear the dog pawing above us, the pitiful howling stopped as we approached the hallway ladder.

I reached up and pulled the string to release it. It came down fast, and Bong came right with it, falling on top of me and Elijah.

Bong scrambled to his paws and climbed over me, licking my face and nudging me with his big head. His overwhelming greeting knocked the wind from me and I could do nothing but endure his slobbery hello.

He planted a foot on my lower abdomen and a sharp, stabbing pain cut into my side, causing me to gasp.

Elijah sensed my pain and quickly pulled Bong away. I saw that Bong didn't appreciate being held by Elijah one bit, but he succumbed to the older vampire's wishes.

I managed to sit up and the pain in my side eased. Something inside me had been torn loose. I could feel it move, and when I stood up it was sliding down my vagina like a big clot.

I had forgotten about the dripping rot from last night. But again the smell drifted around me. Elijah and the dog must've noticed it too. But Elijah was too polite to say anything.

"How long am I going to smell like this?" I asked.

" 'Til it be over."

"I think it is totally gross. Why didn't you tell me about this before you made me a vampire?"

"Mus' have slipped my own mind." Elijah shrugged his shoulders sheepishly.

I had to see what in the hell was falling out of my body and wash myself.

"I'll be right back," I said.

I started for the bathroom and heard Elijah call behind me, "Dere be mo' of dem pads in de vanity."

I raised the lid of the toilet and pulled my pants down. The smell was overpowering and something vile slid from me and plopped into the water of the commode.

I stood up, ran hot water in the basin, and lathered up a washcloth with some more of the scented soaps. As I washed myself I examined the thing in the toilet.

It was brown and mottled looking, about the size of my fist. What was it? My uterus, part of my liver or spleen? I didn't know what body parts a vampire did without so could only guess what it was. Maybe it was my bladder. I did know that we vampires did not go to the bathroom anymore.

I rinsed out the washcloth and wiped the suds from between my legs. Whatever it was, it was foul, and I flushed the toilet and watched it swirl down the hole.

I found the box of Kotex pads and replaced the soiled one in my underpants with a fresh one. I pulled my pants back on and realized that Bong had left a big bloody hole in the leg of my new Banana Republics. I definitely needed a bigger wardrobe. Vampiring was tough on clothes.

The smell, though not completely gone, was a bit more tolerable and I hurried to join Elijah and Bong.

I found them in the garage checking out my new wheels. Bong was extremely impressed and found the passenger seat to his liking.

"Let's show Bong how we hunt," I said. I climbed into the driver's seat and waited for Elijah to climb in the back. But he did not.

He circled around behind my van and lifted the big garage door. Then he came up to my window and motioned for me to roll it down.

I had to play with the row of buttons before I figured out which one controlled the driver's side. At last the window went down.

Elijah leaned on the edge of the door.

"I ain't gonna be goin' wid you dis night. You an' de dawg can start to learn yo' own way 'round," he said.

"Elijah, I . . ."

"Git going. You can't be dependent on me fo'ever." He smiled and reached in to brush the hair from my eyes. "Be careful, Ainjul. Come back to me." He handed me another set of keys and hurried back into the house.

They must've been keys to his house and I slipped them into one of the many pockets of my safari clothes. There was something else in the pocket, a piece of paper. I didn't remember it being there before, and when I withdrew it I saw that it was a fifty-dollar bill. I smiled and searched the other pockets. Tens, twenties, and even a few more fifties had been stuffed into my clothing. Elijah had seen to it that I was not going out poor.

I started my van. The gas gauge showed both of the tanks were full.

"Elijah thinks of everything, doesn't he, Bong?" I looked over to my dog.

Bong had slobbered all over the windshield in front of him and was now sniffing the vent control. I flipped the fan on high and his saliva splatted back against his jowls. He pulled away in surprise and cocked his head to me as if to say, what the hell did you do that for?

The van was automatic and handled like a boat. I was not sure of its size yet and backed slowly out of the garage, hoping the mirror on the passenger side would clear the doorframe.

We made it into the driveway and from there entered the street. I felt tall up in the driver's seat. The ability to look down on the cars parked along the curb was exciting. The van gave me a new kind of power. Freedom.

"Well, Bong, it's just you and me, kid. I gotta show you what to do."

Bong yawned and whined at the same time.

I noticed the white flash of his teeth. His large canines still looked like dog teeth. Would a vampire dog grow extra fangs? I had no idea.

The night was still on the left side of midnight, and we had plenty of time to cruise. I was nervous. I had no idea where I was going, when I would find a likely victim, or what reaction this vampire puppy would display upon his first kill.

I tried to keep to back roads but found that many of them simply ended in the woods. Bong began to grow restless, and his whining became more frequent. If I didn't know better, I would have thought he needed to go to the bathroom.

When we headed back on yet another sandy dirt road, Bong's whines turned into that awful howling and he began to scratch at the door.

"Bong. No," I said. But he paid no attention and continued to scratch at the upholstered armrest. I stopped the van. I was afraid that he was going to go crazy on me and I didn't want him tearing up my new van. I leaned across his wriggling body and opened the door.

He leapt from the van and vanished.

"Bong, wait," I screamed.

I was out after him, but he was nowhere in sight. I listened for any sign of movement but could hear nothing. My heart was racing and the pain of the damaged organ spread beneath my ribs. I had to find Bong. I had to calm down.

I took a deep breath and decided, despite the urge not to, to wait at the van. If I headed into the woods I might never find him. But he knew where the van was and might come back if I called.

"Bong. Come here, Bong," I called.

I could hear nothing.

"Bong. Bong. Come here, boy," I called again.

To my left I heard the rustling of underbrush. My heart began to pound again and I had to wrestle with my fears. Though my vision was keen and my hearing acute, I could not tell what was out there.

"Bong?" I said.

Even when his big body appeared from the thicket I could not relax. He looked transformed, and for a moment I thought that he might turn on me.

He approached the van and I stayed poised, ready to leap inside and close the door if he threatened me.

I had not turned off the headlights and they caught Bong's reflective eyes, making me fear him more.

He padded softly over the sandy ground and stopped a few feet away from me. He cocked his head and looked at me with such a whimsical expression that my fears dissolved.

"Bong, don't be running off like that."

The mention of his name brought him bounding for me, and I held my arms up to protect myself from his slobbery kisses.

Blood.

The scent was all over him.

"What did you catch?" I asked him.

I swear that he could understand me. He gently clamped his mouth over my hand and pulled me away from the van.

"You want to show me something?" I asked.

He pulled me again, and I followed him into the thicket. Once he became aware that I was going to come with him, he released his hold on me and trotted ahead, stopping every few strides to look back at me as if to say, hurry up.

Then I saw his kill. It was a deer, a small doe to be precise. It was dead. I saw the odd angle of its head and knew Bong had broken its neck. I did not want to go any closer, but Bong was adamant I inspect his prize. He pulled upon my hand again, and when I would not budge he walked behind me and pushed me with such force I either had to take a step forward or fall down.

As soon as my foot moved, Bong ran in front of me and stood proudly beside his kill. He wagged his tail and whined. He looked at me and then at the deer. I saw the wound on the animal's neck. Bong placed his big front paws on the deer's shoulder and began to lick the blood away from the wound.

"Bong, no." I ran beside him and pulled him away from the dead deer.

Bong cocked his head and peered up at me. The blood was smeared all over his muzzle and he licked it away with two clean sweeps of his large, pink tongue.

Never drink from de dead. I remembered Elijah's warning.

How could I tell a dog this? I could not control what the dog did. If the dog drank from a dead animal, what would happen? I wished Elijah were here to tell me the answer.

Bong pulled away from my grasp and settled again on top of the deer's shoulder. I studied him as he lapped up the dark fluid. There was no indication he was suffering from drinking from a dead animal. In fact, he seemed to be quite content and feasted leisurely, occasionally looking my way with an inviting expression upon his broad, furry face.

"Forget it, Bong, I don't want to share it with you," I said.

I waited patiently for Bong to finish. His noisy lapping was the only sound in the dark forest. I watched him with interest. His body had expanded visibly but I made no attempt to pull him away from the deer again. He would know when to stop. I knew his was pure instinct. He did not share an emotional viewpoint of what he had become. That was our curse, but the dog's blessing.

From the corner of my eye I saw the deer's hind leg jerk, and I jumped. Bong jumped too, a startled growl issued from his throat. He sniffed the carcass and walked around it once. When he was satisfied that it was dead, he went back for a few more licks before returning to my side.

We spent the rest of the night cruising around Beaufort. I had no desire to feed. Witnessing Bong's kill had left me empty inside. It was the first night of my vampire existence that I did not hunger. I hoped nothing was wrong with me.

Bong had taken so much blood he had that swollen look about him. Somehow the feeding had rejuvenated him too, because he looked more puppyish than I had previously remembered.

He was leaning wearily against the cushioned seat of the van, wanting to curl up on the seat but unable to do so because of his large body size.

He settled for a half-sitting, half-lying position, and his head lolled around the edge of the seat.

I reached a stretch in the road that was heavily populated with commercial enterprises. The only stores showing any signs of life were a Shoney's restaurant and a Pantry store. I wanted to see if I could excite my appetite by mingling with humans.

I pulled into the parking lot of the Pantry and told Bong to stay put.

I locked the door of my van and headed into the fluorescent glow of the store. A black woman was behind the counter. She was reading a pocket romance novel and only glanced over at me for a second before turning the page of her book.

Outside, a car pulled up to the gas pumps and an electronic chime sounded from behind the counter.

I wandered along the aisles, thinking I should buy something to make my visit look legit. In the farthest corner of the store was a pet display, and I walked over to it.

There wasn't much of a selection but I was able to buy a blue nylon collar and a matching leash. I picked up the items and smiled, thinking Bong would look much better in a black collar with two-inch spikes around it. *Demon dawg.* I recalled Elijah's words.

I approached the counter and the store clerk grudgingly put her book down to ring up my order. She stared at me and then spoke.

"You feeling all right? You look like death warmed over."

"Touch of the flu," I said.

"Honey, looks more like new-monia to me."

I decided to take advantage of her talkativeness.

"I found a dog. A big, harlequin Great Dane. You know anybody who lost one?"

"Honey, there are so many dogs running loose in this state, they oughta declare hunting season on them. No, I ain't seen anyone looking for a Great Dane."

I was shocked to hear her comment about hunting dogs and I pressed her further.

"Why are there so many dogs roaming here?"

She counted out my change and deposited it into my outstretched hand. I made sure she didn't touch me.

"Military bases," she said.

"What?"

"People move in and out and just leave their pets behind. The dogs wait outside for a couple of days and when their owners don't show up to feed them, they wander off to fend for themselves."

She looked into my eyes.

"Got a pair of those newfangled contacts? Yours are the greenest damn eyes I've ever seen," she commented.

"No. Yes," I said. "How do you know this, about the dogs?"

"My man is in the Marines. I've lived on bases for three years and in three different states. It's always the same."

"You'd think they would do something about it," I said.

"You'd think," she agreed.

She picked up the novel again, but I wasn't done with her yet. I was still trying to entice the hunger.

"Aren't you scared, working here by yourself all night?"

"Scared of what? Honey, look at this face. Do I look very pretty to you? Do I look like the kind of person that someone is going to rape? If someone comes in here and wants money they can have all I've got. But they ain't gonna look twice at me. Besides, I gotta work. I got a baby girl at home and one on the way." She patted her stomach.

She wasn't showing, but I did agree that she was ugly, in every sense of the word she was ugly. But I liked her ability to laugh at herself, and I gave her a smile as I picked up my package from the counter.

"Honey, you're the one who oughta be scared. Even looking as sick as you do you are a beauty. You a model or something?"

"No," I said, and turned to leave.

"Well, you be careful out there. There is evil in the night." She laughed as she gave me the warning.

"The joke's on you," I mumbled.

Bong had changed seats and sat behind the steering wheel. All he needed was a driving cap to make him look like my chauffeur. I opened the door and pushed him out of the way. He grudgingly climbed into the back of the van and settled on the floor under the stationary table between the swiveling chairs.

I leaned between the seats and removed the new collar from my bag for Bong's inspection. He sniffed it and nudged my hand with his icy nose. I slipped it around his neck and found that it was just big enough. The buckle slipped into the last hole and the fit was perfect.

During our drive back to Elijah's house, Bong dozed restlessly on the floor. I was worried. Worried about both Bong and what he was going to be, and about my inability to feed, or even work up a hunger. I had been feeding regularly since the first night, but had no idea what was "normal." I wondered if a vampire had to take blood every night.

Elijah's car was parked in the driveway and I pulled my van alongside it. The garage door was up and I could see Elijah putting the cap back on a can of Turtle Wax. He took better care of 'Melia than I had ever given to a car. I had been brought up with the sixty thousand mile trade-in system. My father had always been a stickler about oil changes, servicing, and immediate repairs when needed, but also always got a new car when the odometer climbed over sixty thousand. That worked out to be a new car approximately every three years.

If it breaks, get a new one, was the philosophy I had always followed. I could still hear my grandmother lecture about the Great Depression and how wasteful society had become. Well, Grams, I wasn't around during the Depression and I never had a need to be frugal, with anything. I had a job to make money so that I could spend money.

But now I had no job. It suddenly dawned on me that not only was I worried about my lack of hunger, I was growing depressed.

I waited for Bong to crawl out of the van, then followed him quietly past Elijah and into the house.

Bong sniffed the furniture in the den, explored the kitchen, and then circled three times before lying down on the cold slate hearth of the fireplace. I sat next to him with my legs folded beneath me, elbows resting on my knees. I propped my chin in my hands and stared at Bong.

Dobermans will stare back at you until you have to glance away. Great Dane Bong looked into my eyes for only a second before becoming intent upon cleaning his paws.

I heard a car engine start and felt the vibration of the engine as Elijah pulled his baby into the garage for the day. After the engine died down, I caught a whiff of exhaust, knowing that when I was a mortal I would not have smelled it at all. I was aware too of my own smell, but decided morbidly that since I was a dead creature my body might as well smell like death and decay.

I was still staring at Bong when Elijah came into the room. I heard the rattle of keys and the slam of the door. Then the van came to life and again a whiff of exhaust followed the groan of metal as the big garage door came down.

The door between the garage and den opened; more rattling of keys. This time I looked up. Elijah, frozen in time to be an old man of seventy odd years, looked well fed, almost saturated. I could see the swollen artery in his neck pulse with life. The area around his eyes looked puffy. Even the gray Brillo pad of hair upon his head had a lively sheen to it.

I was dull. I didn't need to look at myself to know it. I felt dull, listless, limp.

"De neighbors t'ink dat I be a senile nut a waxin' my own cah in de middle of de night. Dey leave me be, tho'," Elijah said.

I didn't say it, but I thought the same. Well, maybe not senile, but certainly eccentric.

"Elijah, I have no hunger. I can't pinpoint what I'm feeling, but it's not the hunger. Do you think the dog's blood did something to me last night?"

He didn't answer me right away.

I began to make handprints in the plush tan carpet. I'd press my hand firmly against the thick fibers, wiggle it a little, and lift it away. The impression of my hand remained in the rug.

I looked up to see why he wasn't answering me. He was standing against the kitchen counter, actually a bar area separating the kitchen from the den but not used as anything, reading the newspaper.

He hadn't heard me. I felt nonexistent, immaterial. I had had days like this, especially before my period would start. Days when I was the ugliest-looking grub on the face of the earth. I dubbed them "bag days." Days when I would just like to put a paper bag over my head so nobody could see me.

I thought a moment and calculated it was close to that time.

"Elijah, vampires don't menstruate, do they?" I asked.

94

"I sorry, Ainjul, de dawg blood would not make you feel dis way. Dawg blood is jis' as good as any odder."

He didn't hear me again. He didn't even look up from his damn paper.

"ELIJAH!"

I got his attention.

"Will I still menstruate?"

An embarrassed look surfaced upon his face and he quickly hid behind the curtain of newsprint.

"What you t'ink is comin' out of you now?" he asked.

"You mean this rotten stink is blood?" I asked. Could it be that in place of normal human excretory functions, a vampire shed waste products in this manner?

"No, co'se not. It is de pahts of you dat ain't needed no mo'. Yo' womanly pahts be some of dem. Odder t'ings come out too. T'ree months 'til it all be done."

"Well, why do I feel this way? Why is my hunger gone?" I thought of the night I had fed on the black woman in the woods. Her very presence had ignited such a thirst in me that I could not control the desire to consume her. Yet, the woman in the store had no such effect.

"Jis' happ'n sometimes. When you be ready to feed you will feed. I have gone days widout feedin'."

Bong finished licking the dirt from between his toe pads. He rolled away from me, and I momentarily lost my balance when his large back was no longer supporting mine. He got up and padded across the kitchen floor, his nails clicked on the no-wax linoleum. I watched him head back the hallway and out of my view.

"De dawg fed well," Elijah commented.

"Elijah, he drank from a dead animal. You told me to never drink from the dead. He killed a deer and drank from death."

I watched Elijah's dark, wispy eyebrows raise together. The black skin of his forehead wrinkled in three distinct lines, ending where the gray hair joined his scalp.

"Dis be a curious t'ing."

"Why can he drink from death? You told me to never drink from the dead," I repeated.

"I only pass on what was told me. I never have drunk from

95

de dead. Never gave much t'ought 'bout why. You do too much t'inkin' in dat pretty lil' head of . . .'' He stopped, listened.

I strained to hear what he was hearing. Was the look on his face puzzlement or danger? When he walked into the kitchen, I stood. I was concentrating on the sounds outside. Nothing seemed unusual. He motioned for me to follow him.

We crept soundlessly through the kitchen and back the hall. I could hear the sound now. Water. Splashing water. It came from the bathroom.

Elijah pushed the door open and there was Bong, head in the toilet bowl, slurping up huge amounts of water.

"Well, I have never . . ." Elijah stopped short.

"Does this mean we can drink wa—" I started but Elijah cut me off.

"Dis dawg jis' might be a learnin' us some new t'ings," he said. He reached down and patted Bong on the shoulder.

Bong pulled his head up and turned to look at us. Water dripped from his lips, and he seemed to smile as he licked it away from his loose jowls.

CHAPTER SIX

Maybe I was pushing my luck, but in the weeks that followed I continued to work my way north on Highway 17, expanding my hunting ground, knowingly encroaching on Matthew's territory.

Bong always accompanied me. My hunger had returned, though it was sporadic. Bong hungered only for animals, for which I was thankful. His kills were always swift and clean; he always drank from the dead.

I had not killed since the night Elijah and I had taken the poor black couple in the woods. My heart was completely repaired and could've easily handled the excitement of a kill, but my learned control allowed me to stop drinking before my victims would be in any danger of death.

Of course, this meant that most of my evenings were spent completely on hunting. A pint here, a pint there, until my thirst was satisfied. Bong would often grow impatient with me, and I'm sure he wondered why I didn't just kill one and be done with it. My new life revolved around death, and still I let it repulse me.

Bong played a big role in my new hunting technique. What caring person could resist the subtle charms Bong worked? He could sense the people who would submit to me. Throughout my many victims I found one, common, human characteristic. Compared to my will, they were weak and easily controlled. Upon making contact with them I could bend them so they wanted, or actually yearned, for me to drink from them.

By Bong's example, I found water would often drown the

burning need to feed. I could not be completely sustained on it, but could cut the amount of blood I required almost in half.

Elijah too began to drink water. Often upon returning from our separate nightly excursions (Elijah never hunted with me anymore) we would sit in the den and sip water from fine crystal wineglasses. Such a frivolous thing, but oh so delightful!

It was a tossup as to which one of us smelled worse, me or poor Bong. I don't know if I was getting used to the rotten odor, but I could ignore it. Bong was driven nearly mad by it. He would constantly be licking and cleaning himself. His privates were raw and I tried everything, baby oil, Vaseline, doggy deodorants, to help relieve him, but he promptly licked those off too.

In fact, had I been a little more observant I would have noticed that Bong was changing.

One night in particular showed me that Bong was depressed.

We had driven north to the town of Ravenel. Actually, there is no "town." The area of Ravenel is loosely connected. A house here, a trailer there, lots of woodland and plenty of dirt roads to hide on.

I made a left-hand turn onto Highway 165 and then took the first dirt road to the right. I could see the outline of a building straight ahead and thought for a minute I should turn around. But the building was a barn, and it was new construction, nobody lived out here.

Bong saw the horses in the field the same time I did. He began that awful howling, but before I would let him out of the van I hooked the leash to his collar, the first time I had ever restrained him as such, and told him harshly to settle down.

Just like a big dog can out-muscle a human master, my vampire puppy was no match for me and I knew that this would be a test of his obedience. I would not allow him to feed upon horses. Wild animals were one thing, but domesticated pets were another.

I opened the door and made Bong wait until I was out of

the van. Then I allowed him to jump down. He immediately yanked my arm and lunged toward the pasture fence.

Two horses stood alert in the shafts of light that came from my van's headlights. Both of them began to prance nervously in a tight circle, tails erect and nostrils flared. The smaller one snorted in our direction.

I pulled up on the leash, and forgetting my own strength, realized that I had Bong off the ground.

His legs flailed beneath him, and he gagged. I set him down and told him again to settle.

I could sense the horses' fear of us, but could also sense their underlying curiosity. They wanted to examine us closer. The large one in particular wanted to check us out and trotted a few paces in our direction, then stopped. The smaller horse was running around the larger one, trying to turn it back. The quickness of those legs amazed me. That little horse was agile. Sliding stops, rollbacks, spins, all performed with a natural cadence that led me to believe this little horse must've been used for cutting or reining competition.

Despite the energetic efforts of the little horse, the larger one moved closer. A breeze suddenly blew against our backs and I knew that once the horses smelled the decaying odor of death we both emitted they would turn tail and run. And I was correct.

The very ground shook under the impact of their thundering hooves. Bong went crazy, and before I was able to pull him back, he was gone, over the fence and after the horses.

His posture was that of the kill. He ran low to the ground, like a great cat on the prowl. His speed and agility were no match for the horses. I had seen him take his prey time and time again, but this time I was going to interfere.

I was running through the field with my own blinding speed. I hardly crumpled the dried, winter grass, let alone the new shoots of spring grass, my feet glided over the ground. I knew that I could not catch Bong before he sprang for the kill so my only hope was the horses, if I could just make them turn and face him, fight him. I was no stranger to horses and I understood their "fright-flight" instinct, but now I used my power to make them stand their ground.

Miraculously, it worked. The little horse wheeled around just as Bong was upon its heels and reared, striking out at him with a quick flash of a sharp hoof.

I heard the impact.

Bong howled in surprised pain. He jumped to the side, away from the little horse, and turned to run back to me.

I quit sending commands to the horses and they again turned, widening the distance between us as they galloped to the far end of the field.

When Bong ran by me I dived for the trailing leash, catching hold of the end. I curled my fingers into the flat nylon, but Bong was running so fast the force bent back my long fingernails and I had to let go.

He didn't miss a stride as he sailed over the wire fence and came to an abrupt stop beside my van.

When I reached him I saw blood dripping from his mouth. He was quiet, but in obvious pain. His lower jaw was visibly broken.

No matter how hard I coaxed him, he would not get into the van or let me examine him. The way he looked at me made me feel that he knew I was responsible for his failure. Did he distrust me?

A rustling in the nearby brush sent him off at a dead run. In the ensuing chase Bong failed again. I saw the possum run up a nearby tree and Bong, try as he might, could not jump high enough to catch it.

This time he returned to me with such a look of despair about him that sorrow welled in my heart. It was his awful smell that gave him away when he stalked his prey, and no matter what I did to help him, he was growing more and more depressed.

Then I had a brainstorm. I knew where Bong could hunt successfully and not be smelled. With a little coaxing, and one great push, I had him loaded into the back of my van and we headed for the beach.

Beachwalker Park was not open and I had to park the van in front of the padlocked wooden gates of the parking lot. Bong showed little excitement as we walked across the dark blacktop.

The breeze blew off the yet unseen ocean, and carried with it the heavy smell of salt. Bong followed reluctantly, dragging himself behind me with his tail hanging limply. I led him onto the boardwalk that allowed us to cross over the precious sand dunes.

The storms of winter and the unusual high tides had caused considerable beach erosion. Even in the darkness the dunes were ragged looking. In some places they looked like they had been sliced down the middle with a knife.

Bong perked up at the gentle sound of the waves. The tide was low and the beach wide. We climbed down the steps of the crossover and stepped onto the sand.

Though the wind had a nip to it, and the night air was damp, I bent down and untied my hiking boots. I balled up my socks, stuffed them inside the shoes, and set them on the last stair. Bong had run ahead and was sniffing curiously at the foaming water. His reactions told me this was the first time he had ever seen the ocean, and he was a pure joy to watch.

Despite what I had made Bong, he was first and foremost a dog. And this night he behaved like one. He romped alongside me. I would pick up pieces of driftwood and throw them into the surf. Bong would splash awkwardly into the cold water to retrieve them.

Once he realized the water was not going to hurt him, he began to hunt. At first he would bring up small fish, but soon grew bold and swam out deeper. He actually dived beneath the surface and would be gone for periods of time that left me breathless with worry. But he would reappear and swim back to me, offering me a share of his catch. He had some difficulty carrying the larger fish, but already his jaw was mending.

He continued to hunt and his confidence grew. I walked along the edge of the water, letting the icy numbness wash over my cold white toes. Each time Bong returned from his watery excursion he would drop a fish at my feet. Finally his urgings, or perhaps my own growing hunger, allowed me to try fish blood.

The next fish he deposited at my feet was a big one. I don't know a thing about fish so didn't even try to guess what kind it was. It flopped and wriggled in the sand, trying to struggle back into the water. To prevent its escape, Bong promptly put his big wet paw on its tail and held it fast while I reached to pick it up.

It squirmed in my hands and I dropped it. Bong was a bit dismayed by this and pounced upon it, holding it for me. I grabbed for it again. It fought wildly, flipping and bending its body in my hands. When I at last had a good grip on it I began to laugh. Its gaping mouth and black eyes were grotesque, and I didn't think I would be able to bite it. But Bong's insistent look urged me on.

I wasn't about to bite it in the head, or the tail, so I chose a spot in the middle that looked the least scaly. I was still laughing, but each time I brought it close enough to my lips, repulsion pulled me away.

Bong whined loudly, and in his doggy way said, get on with it.

"All right, Bong, here goes," I said. I closed my eyes and held my breath and let my mouth close over the belly of the fish. My fangs pierced the scaly, wet skin and a trickle of blood ran into my mouth. The fish flopped against my face and I had to pull it away, but the blood was already working its magic in me and I could not stop drinking. I held the fish aloft and squeezed it like an orange, letting the juice of life flow into my open mouth.

The fish blood was cold and the reeking taste of the sea mingled with it, but it was fulfilling. Before I was finished with my first fish, Bong had caught me another one. After five subsequent catches I was satisfied and let Bong take the sixth one as his own.

The smell of the ocean and fish was all over us, and for the first time since I had received E.L. I could not smell the decay that permeated us.

We walked all the way to the end of the island. From the point I was able to see the next island, Seabrook. A distant

102

twinkle of lights glittered in the night breeze, and at this distance it was hard to tell if the lights came from a house on shore or a boat off shore. I stood a moment and watched the lights. They were definitely moving away. Must be a boat.

I turned around and began the trek back. Bong ran ahead, searching for sticks I could throw for him. His mood was elevated, and I felt happy for him. I jogged alongside him, imagining it was daylight and the sun was high in the sky. The gulls would be squawking over the dead fish we had left on the sandy beach.

I was searching along the dark outline of the dunes for the stairway we had crossed, when movement caught my eye. Someone else was on the beach.

Bong let out a deep, throaty growl and stopped behind me. I watched the dark figure. It stood still, staring down the beach at us. The wind was in my favor, and though I tried, I could not detect the human scent. Bong growled, and I looked down to him. His lips were peeled away from his large teeth, his nose wrinkled so severely it made him sneeze.

A second or two, that was all the time that passed as I glanced in Bong's direction, but when I looked up again the figure on the beach was now standing in full view on top of the wooden crossover of the dunes.

"Matthew," I whispered. I grabbed Bong by the collar and held him to my side. He did not pull away. He was still growling, but shaking also, and I felt his fear.

My joyful little escapades into Matthew's territory had been discovered.

The tall figure on the dune did not move, but stood, watching. I'd say about five minutes ticked by as we stared at each other.

I was not ready for this confrontation. I needed more time. I knew my encroachment into his territory had its purpose, I hoped to taunt him with my telltale marks of feeding, but I had not expected to encounter him.

There were two choices. Walk right up to him, or walk away.

103

He turned slightly, and I saw the luminous glow of his skin in the darkness. He leaned against the railing, studying me while I studied him.

Finally I turned my back on him, half expecting he would rush me, but nothing happened. With a few words of encouragement I led Bong away and took his mind off Matthew by picking up a stick and tossing it into the waves.

Bong splashed after the stick, retrieved it, and came loping back to me. When I looked back to the dunes, the figure was gone. Goose pimples raised across my bare arms and I sensed he was nearby, still watching us. Bong dropped the stick at my feet and whined impatiently. I picked up the wet stick and threw it again, directly at the stairway. If Bong went to retrieve it, it would be safe.

Bong didn't hesitate. He was soon on his return trip, the stick and his tongue hanging out of his mouth. I continued to throw the stick in this manner, and each time Bong brought it back we gained ground in the direction of the van.

The rocks on the blacktop parking lot hurt my feet, so I stopped a minute to put my shoes and socks on. I couldn't get all the wet sand from my feet and was undecided as to which hurt more, the rocks or the abrasive little grains that rubbed between my toes.

I tossed the stick a final time for Bong, but he stopped halfway between me and the van, growled, and backed away.

Matthew was inside my van. He was going to force me into a meeting. I felt my pocket, the keys were still there. He couldn't steal it and leave me stranded.

I swallowed and boldly stepped toward my van. *Drink him dry.* I recalled Elijah's words. I certainly could not take him, I was filled with fish blood. But I wasn't going to let him take me either.

Bong was with me. His growls long and deep.

The sliding door of my van closed with a bang and Bong was off in pursuit before I even saw the tall dark figure glide into the woods. I ran after them, afraid for Bong, and of what Matthew might do to him.

An unearthly screech rang out against the silent night, stopping me in my tracks.

"Bong? Bong, come here, here, Bong," I called quietly.

I heard a whimper and the rustling of brush.

Bong came trotting from the woods with the look of victory all over him. He walked over to me and pushed his head into my hands. He had a piece of dark-blue cloth in his mouth and dropped it into my palm.

"Good boy, Bongers. Good boy." I patted his head and felt the fine wool cloth. "That should make him think twice about us, take a bite out of his style," I laughed. "Come on, Bong, let's go home, sunrise is coming soon." I opened the door for Bong and carefully folded the piece of fabric, tucking it neatly into my shirt pocket. I couldn't wait to get home and tell Elijah what had happened.

Knowing that Matthew was nearby made me nervous. As I drove away from Beachwalker Park I kept scanning the dark roadside, expecting to see his tall figure appear from the marsh.

Bong was no longer concerned. He sat, quietly composed, in the passenger seat looking forward through the windshield. His coat was dripping and sand clung in patches to the wet fur, giving his harlequin coat an added shading of gray.

The fishy smell on both of us was overpowering, even stronger than a freshly opened can of cat food. I wondered if the interior of my van would ever be rid of the odor.

Once off Kiawah we were on Johns Island. The narrow, two-lane road twisted and turned. Heavy live oaks stood solemn guard along the way, many so close to the road that reflective discs had been placed directly on the protruding trunks.

Matthew could not possibly be following our progress now.

From out of nowhere high beams gathered speed behind us. I gripped the padded steering wheel.

"My God, Bong, he has a car," I said. Bong looked my way at the mention of his name, and then turned back to enjoy the view.

"Relax, you're just paranoid," I said. But I wasn't fooling myself. I was spooked.

I maintained my speed and kept one eye glued to the outside mirror. Two square headlights on the left side of the car remained in the small rectangle of my mirror.

When I was sure the car was following me, I made a wild break for it, flooring the gas pedal. But my van was not built for sudden power bursts and reacted sluggishly, shifting through each gear until it pushed into automatic overdrive.

The little car behind us had no problems staying on our rear bumper.

The lights in my outside mirror shifted and I realized he was going to overtake us. There was nothing I could do. It was too dangerous to maintain my present speed. I feared smashing into an oak tree and bursting into flame—certain death for us undead—more than I feared Matthew. I slowed down.

The car pulled alongside, and when I glanced down into it I saw two people, mortals.

The one in the passenger side made a motion for me to pull over. I ignored this, but they were persistent, and when I looked over again the passenger was leaning out of the car window, screaming at me and motioning for me to roll my window down.

This so amused me I complied. With my window down I heard a masculine voice coming from the androgynous-looking being, and his plea was to have a word with me.

I might've been flattered. Whatever their intentions, they had to be no good. I wanted to teach these punks a lesson. They obviously thought I was a lone female. They had no idea what I really was. I pulled over.

I waited in the van. In the mirror I saw both of them approach.

Bong stood up and stepped over so that his big front paws were standing on my thigh. He remained alert, staring at the two strangers.

"We know you are a friend of Elijah's," the androgynous-looking one spoke.

They were both black. I could not take my eyes off the one who did the talking. He was pretty and strangely handsome at the same time.

"Please, give Elijah this," he said. He reluctantly handed me a small envelope and I sensed his wonder of me. "It is an invitation to our spring festival. You are invited as well."

Bong whined.

"And of course the dog too," he added.

I nodded but did not say a word to him. When my eyes met those of his short companion I held him a moment in my gaze, enough to let him know what power I possessed. The short man let out a long sigh as I released him.

They both backed away from my van.

"Please come," the androgynous-looking one said.

They turned and refrained from running back to the false security of their car. I overheard the short one exclaim, "She touched me with the power," in such an exalting tone I was momentarily lifted into a status with the gods.

Bong crawled back into his seat.

I waited until they had pulled away before starting my van. When the red glow of their taillights disappeared into the night, I ventured out onto the blacktop.

The small envelope was sealed. I slid it into the pocket with the fabric from Matthew's pants.

"Elijah," I called. I opened the door to the den wider so Bong could squeeze through.

"I be in here," Elijah answered.

I walked over to the kitchen table where Elijah sat amid his newspapers. I leaned over his shoulder to see what he was reading. A small headline in the middle of the grocery store ads read: HOSTAGE'S WIFE PLEADS FOR HUSBAND'S RETURN.

My excitement was boiling inside me and I could not contain it. Elijah must've felt it too because he closed the paper and looked at me.

"You two been a fishin'? By de way you smell must've caught some of dem too."

"Elijah, we dined on fish blood, but that isn't the whole story. I saw Matthew. He was right there on the beach. He

107

was watching us. God, I was so scared. I couldn't take him, I was so full of fish blo—"

"Hold on dere, missis. Catch yo' breat' befo' you ramble on like dat," Elijah said.

I drew in a deep breath and continued.

"Look what Bong did." I pulled the piece of fabric from my pocket. "Bit it right off of Matthew's pants."

Elijah took the fabric and examined it. He handed it back to me and looked into my eyes. The disheartening look upon his face smoldered my excitement.

"You be real careful now. Matt'u, he knows dat you ain't dead. Won't be long 'til he possesses you," he said.

"Matthew is never going to possess me. It won't be long until I have revenge on him. I'm telling you, Elijah, he was scared of Bong. I have a weapon against him now."

"Ainjul, I tell you dis but one time, you tread slow where Matt'u is concerned. He have a way 'bout him dat makes t'ings happ'n jis' de way he wants dem to happ'n. You be t'inkin' all along dat yo' plans be workin' den he strikes you down."

The no-nonsense tone in his voice shut me up for a minute. I was getting a bit cocky. Had I forgotten so quickly how scared I had been when I thought he was going to overtake me in the car?

"I met some of your friends tonight," I said, closing the subject of Matthew for now.

"What friends might dese be?" Elijah asked. His brow raised and the dark eyebrows closed together in a single line above his eyes.

"We have been invited to a spring festival," I said as I handed Elijah the envelope.

"Well, we ain't gonna go," he said, handing the envelope back to me.

"But, Elijah, they seemed sincere about it. Why don't we go. Aren't vampires allowed a night out on the town?" I chided.

"Dese be de voodoo group dat I have trubble wid. Ef you want to go den you can go, dey mean you no hawm."

"I can't go by myself," I pleaded.

108

"Dey won't hawm you," Elijah repeated.

"It's not that I fear them. It's just, well, they are all black and I would feel funny."

"I be black, you don't feel funny here wid me?"

"Elijah, that's not the same. You are like me, and you are only one man. They are a group. I couldn't go by myself, even though I'm a vampire. I would feel funny. Please go with me." I laid the charm on the last plea.

He didn't respond, but shifted uncomfortably in his chair, a visible clue he probably would go if I insisted.

I opened the envelope. The little festival was tomorrow night precisely at midnight out on Johns Island. I showed the plain white card to Elijah.

"Please, for me," I said.

He sighed and nodded. "But you ain't gonna like it."

"And will you hunt with me and Bong tomorrow? Let me show you the things he has taught me."

"We talk 'bout dat tomorrow," he said.

I didn't understand why he would no longer hunt with me. Since the night I made Bong a vampire dog Elijah had stopped hunting with me. At first it was fun to be out on my own, but now I truly missed his companionship.

"Okay." I agreed. Hopefully he would really consider my invitation and join me and Bong. "I'm taking Bong with me for a shower and then we are going to sleep."

"Good night den, Ainjul," he said.

I slung my arms around his neck and leaned forward, kissing him lightly on the cheek. "Pleasant dreams, Elijah."

As I left him I heard the rustle of the newspaper and the scratching of pencil lead. The old vampire was becoming too interested in world affairs for my liking. Every night when I would return home he would be engrossed in his papers. And it wasn't just the local paper, he collected them from all around the country.

Bong did not take to the water in the shower as he did to the ocean. I had to bodily place him in the tub with me. I ignored his woeful howls and lathered us both, then rinsed and repeated the procedure until the fishy smell was gone.

109

When I scooted Bong to the rear of the tub so that I was able to stand under the shower his howl dropped to a whimper and he lifted one paw, then the other, like the water was too hot.

"It's not like I'm burning you, you dumb dog," I said. And Bong's whimper rose an octave to a whine. "How come you never bark?" I asked. I finished rinsing the shampoo out of my hair and turned off the shower.

Bong had a wide range of vocal expression: Growls, whimpers, whines, howls, even moans. I had never heard him actually let out a woof. I squeezed the water out of my long hair and pulled the shower curtain back so Bong could get out of the water.

Immediately he shook himself, sending water flying in all directions. Before I would open the bathroom door and let him loose, I used three bath towels on him. But I suppose to a dog that wasn't quite dry enough. As I freed him from the confines of the steamy room, he ran down the hallway, propelling himself with his haunches as his head and shoulders were pressed against the carpet. The way he carried on made me think he would end up with rug burns. Just as I pulled the X-large Mickey Mouse shirt over my head he came back in my direction and I had to jump aside to avoid a collision.

He careened wildly into the hall table and it fell with a loud crash. Elijah no longer came running at our noise. Bong's destructiveness had become part of our not-so-normal household.

Sunrise was less than an hour away. My body succumbed to the weariness that gathered before I slept. I had grown lopsided in my sleeping and awakening. I still did not rise until after nine in the evening, but the mornings were long and when my eyes finally closed I'm sure the light of dawn was upon the eastern sky.

Bong shared this pattern with me, but he had recently begun to rise before me, and during the past several nights I had awakened with the crushing weight of the dog upon my chest and the wet kisses of his cold tongue.

I steadied the ladder for Bong and helped push him up

into the attic. He ran to my coffin and waited as I propped the lid open so he could crawl in. A fresh yellow rose was resting on my pillow. I picked it up and smelled the fragrance of its bouquet while waiting for Bong to quit his customary three circles. He settled down at the foot of the coffin, yawned, and rested his head upon his feet.

Sleeping with a Great Dane in a coffin is no easy trick, but I had found that the best position was on my side with my legs curled up in a fetal position. I held onto the rose and let my mind clear. I didn't pull the lid down, Elijah had grown accustomed to checking on us before he went to sleep, at which time he would close my coffin. I was grateful for this, I could fall asleep without suffering the suffocating closeness of being entombed.

Something was wrong. I knew it before I was fully awake. As my awareness sharpened I rolled over onto my back and stretched my legs. Bong was gone.

I pushed the lid of my coffin up and searched the dark attic for him. He was not there. Worry gripped me and I flew down the ladder and into the main section of Elijah's house. Bong was nowhere to be seen. I began a systematic search of each room, each closet, but the dog was gone.

When I reached the den, Elijah was there, pondering over his newspapers.

"Elijah, have you seen Bong?" I asked.

"Ain't he wid you?"

The paper folded down away from his face and I could see that he had already fed. He was plump with blood and his black skin shone with renewed freshness.

"No, he isn't with me, he's got to be here. He can't get out of the house by himself, can he?"

"Dat dawg be very clever animal, he jis' might be able to let himself out ef he want to." Elijah turned back to his newsprint. "He be all right, don't be worrin' over him."

"Don't worry! How can you say that? What if he kills someone, what if someone kills him?" I had a gut-wrenching feeling Bong had crept out on his own to kill a horse. I hurt his pride last night and knew Bong would be out there proving to himself he could master his prey, any prey.

"Ef you want to git to dat festival we better be leavin' soon," Elijah said.

If my hunch was right, Bong might be back in Ravenel, hunting those very horses we had encountered last night. I didn't want to miss the festival, my curiosity demanded I go, but I felt obligated to search for Bong. I gave Elijah an indecisive look and he smiled at me.

"Ainjul, dat dawg can take care of himself. Git dressed an' we'll go to de festival."

Of course Elijah was probably right, but why wasn't I able to shake the feeling that Bong was going to get hurt, or even killed. I studied my old black friend. He had on a beautiful gray sweater that accented his hair. His slacks were neatly creased down the center and a gray tweed blazer was slung over the arm of the couch. The only thing ruining his "Sunday best" appearance were the white Adidases on his feet.

"What does one wear to a voodoo festival?" I asked.

"I got you a real pretty outfit," he said. The smile on his face beamed with pleasure.

"I thought you might've," I said. Elijah had insistently bought clothing for me. I couldn't complain. I had never been a shopper as a mortal and to be pampered by him was nice. Some things he chose were not me, but I wore them anyway, just to please him.

One outfit in particular comes to mind. It was a pair of baggy man's slacks with suspenders, a large man's shirt with a tie, and a bulky man's coat with a fedora. I was the vampire version of Annie Hall in that one. Luckily, the first time I wore it I fed sloppily and ruined it with large, strategically placed bloodstains.

I hurried back to my bedroom. I did everything in here but sleep. The double-wide closet was beginning to grow crowded with clothing. The outfit Elijah mentioned was not in the closet, but instead was hanging from the canopy of the large antique bed.

He had outdone himself this time. The black, one-piece jumpsuit was more than beautiful, it was sensual. I slipped into it. It was cut low enough in front to be seductive without disclosing the fact that I was not overabundantly endowed. The crepe satin fabric clung against my every curve and when I examined myself in the mirror I looked much older than my twenty-three years. My beauty scared me. I tried to keep my eyes only on my hair as I brushed it. I experimented, and drew my long auburn curls up on top of my head, but this made me look even older and was too far away from "my look." So I let my hair hang loose and flowing and I slid my feet into the black satin sandals.

I dared one more glance in the mirror. The edge of the scar on my chest was visible and I self-consciously pulled the fabric over it.

"Maybe I look so old because I haven't fed yet," I whispered. But the image in the mirror was something from fantasy, like my fairy godmother had zapped me into this exquisitely bewitching woman.

Somehow I did not feel complete, something was missing from my ensemble. I glanced at the few pieces of jewelry on the dresser. I picked up the small diamond necklace, choosing it over the other two pieces because it was delicate, not overpowering and gaudy.

Even with the diamond around my neck I did not feel complete, and realized that it was because I had no makeup on. To be this dressed up and have no makeup was against all my principles. And it wasn't because I didn't have the makeup, I did, but one night I had decided to put it on and I looked garish. The subtle pink blush might as well have been dayglo red against my pure white skin. The moss-green eye shadow I had always worn to accent my eyes gave me the appearance of death. I had scrubbed my face raw that night with experimentation.

When I met Elijah in the garage he didn't even comment. I had learned to accept this as neither compliment nor complaint. He once told me that I was beautiful to him no matter what I wore. I was his unearthly Ainjul and I loved him for it.

We climbed into 'Melia and began our journey into Matthew's territory, into the realm of voodoo rituals. I admitted to myself that I was nervous. My stomach was churning with tension. I worried about Bong, I worried about Matthew, and I was excited about this festival.

I had an hour and a half to worry before I remembered that the flashing yellow lights ahead marked the turn where Bong and I had encountered the horses.

"Elijah, turn left at the lights," I said.

He glanced at me and shrugged.

"Just turn," I said, and waved my hand in the direction he should go.

I had him turn again down the dirt road to the right. The headlights caught the reflection of the two horses in the pasture. They looked up. I looked around. Bong had not been here. I allowed a part of myself to relax.

"What you be lookin' fo' out here?" Elijah asked. He slowed 'Melia and turned around beside the fence.

"Bong and I hunted here last night. I thought he might've come back," I said.

"You can't be tellin' me dat you an' de demon dawg fed on hosses," Elijah said.

"No, but Bong tried. I stopped him and I just thought he might've tried it on his own tonight. I upset him by not allowing him to take a horse," I said.

"Ainjul, you got to let dat dawg be what he is," Elijah said. He sighed an "I told you so" sigh. "De Dawg don't know a possum from a cat, a deer from a hoss, he only know de blood."

"I know you're right," I said, but then added, "But why doesn't he ever take humans?"

"Maybe cuz dawg is man's best friend," Elijah said. He was not being sarcastic.

I thought about that. I hoped it was true. Bong didn't deserve to be a killer. He drank from the dead, always killed his prey before taking the blood. If he suddenly took man, they would hunt him until they found him. I could not bear that fate for my mistake.

"De dawg ain't here, we best be gittin' on," Elijah said.

It was another fifteen-minute drive until we crossed the Limehouse Bridge that linked Johns Island to the rest of Charleston. Elijah drove as though he knew where he was going. I looked for a street sign and saw that we were on Main. I felt 'Melia slow.

"Look fo' Back Pen Road, it be on yo' right," Elijah said.

Even the acute vision my vampire nature supplemented me with was not enough for me to read the small sign in the darkness until we sailed by.

Elijah threw the car into reverse and backed the hundred yards we had overshot it.

I was surprised. The road was paved. We traveled for approximately five city blocks, and the road turned to dirt and changed names to Jimmy Mitchell Lane. Elijah followed the curve to the right. Three small houses were situated around the corner. They weren't shacks, but weren't middle-class dwellings either. None of them looked like the setting for a voodoo ritual.

However, I was not to be disappointed. Elijah stopped the car in front of the last building on the right. In the light of the headlamps I could see that it was a rusty red shack and the walls were wrinkled. How in the hell could the walls be wrinkled? I studied the structure for a moment. My guess was that it was constructed of aluminum or tin.

There was no sign of anyone, no cars were parked outside.

"Are you sure this is the place?" I asked.

"Co'se I am sho'," Elijah said.

"But it looks like a Kotex box house," I exclaimed.

"A what?"

"Oh, never mind," I said. What was the point of explaining that once when I was a kid I had been looking through a *National Geographic* magazine and had seen crude houses in some desolate place like Chile or somewhere. The little houses had been made from cardboard shipping boxes. The word Kotex was printed all over them. Thus they became in my mind, Kotex box houses.

"You ain't gonna like dis," Elijah said as he opened the car door for me. "Jis' try an' keep yo'self from doin' any-t'ing rash," he said.

"Why? What do they do in there?"

Elijah did not answer me but took hold of my arm, and like a date escorting me to a dance, led me to the side door of the shack.

The door had once been painted white, but now the paint had peeled away from the splintering plywood beneath it. The door had once had a frame, but now only two crossed pieces of rotted wood braced it in place.

It opened inwardly as we approached.

CHAPTER SEVEN

The heavy scent of incense billowed from the dark interior. Spices: cinnamon, clove, and nutmeg. The smell was so thick it worked its way to the very back of my sinuses and coated my tongue. I had to fight the urge to spit.

Inside, the Kotex box house was no larger than fourteen by fourteen at the most. The two windows, one on the south side of the shack and the other on the east, had been covered over with a coat of white paint. The floor was dirt, and I felt the dampness through my satin sandals. As the door shut behind us the walls closed in around me and I had to control my claustrophobic fear.

Six men and one woman were seated on the floor before a large iron cauldron. The androgynous-looking young man, the same who had given me the invitation last night, came over to greet us. I was surprised he should be the leader of this motley group. Two older men, at least old enough so their black hair was graying, sat among the group, and it would have been my guess one of them was the leader.

The androgynous man led us to a matched set of new metal folding chairs. After Elijah and I had been seated, he took his place up front and stirred the simmering cauldron with what appeared to be an elaborately carved wooden stick.

My gaze shifted from him to the others. As I had anticipated, all the members of the group were black. The two older men sat on either side of the lineup. They were dressed in simple black cloaks and each held a burning candle. I could only see the backs of their heads from my position, and since they had not turned around to look our way, which I guessed must have been forbidden, I tried to imagine what they looked like. The only image I could stir up was the same as my old vampire companion, Elijah, and I smiled to myself, not really believing they looked like him.

Between them sat three men. By the thickness and dark color of their hair and the condition of the skin on the back of their necks they appeared to be much younger. Each of them was cloaked in the same black dress, but instead of holding a candle they held different objects. The one closest to me had a rather worn-looking book resting upon his knee. The man next to him was playing with the drawstrings of a cloth bag, the material reminded me of cheesecloth. The third man was holding something cupped in his palms, but from my position I could not tell what it was.

The woman, perhaps yet a girl, was seated in front of the row of men. Upon her lap was a black cat, black as tar pitch. Unlike the men, her cloak was white. She had a small cap over her head, very similar in design to the caps the Amish women wear. Even her hands, as they stroked the cat, were adorned with white gloves. I wondered if she was a virgin, an integral part of the festival.

I wondered what in the hell they were going to do.

Steam was rising from the heavy cast-iron pot, and the tripod it hung from looked unsteady. As the androgynous man continued to stir, the pot began to swing back and forth. In the light of the fire blazing beneath it, I could see the clawed iron foot of the tripod nearest to the girl lift off the ground with each rocking motion. I had the urge to get up and pull her away, afraid the pot might spill.

The smoke from the fire spiraled upward to a vented shaft in the sagging ceiling. I watched Mr. Androgynous like a hawk, taking notice of his every movement as he tended to the steaming brew. He reached into his pocket, and with a bit of theatrics threw something into the water. Steam shot up and the water foamed over the rim. A strong cloud of spice aroma rolled across the room and my eyes began to water.

I looked over to see what Elijah's reaction to all this was. He had his eyes closed. His face was flushed from his early-evening feeding, and the soft skin beneath his eyes was still a

118

little swollen. I thought for a moment his lips moved as if in prayer, but decided he was sleeping. I nudged him with my hand. He blinked and looked over to me with bleary eyes.

"What are they going to do?" I whispered.

Elijah put his finger to his lips and motioned for me to keep quiet.

I could barely stand it. None of them moved or even said a word. And frankly, I had better things to do than to sit and watch Mr. Androgynous stir a boiling pot of water and play magic hocus pocus. I had not yet fed and the closeness of these humans was irritating my hunger. I squirmed in my seat and it squeaked loudly.

The girl looked in my direction. Disgrace was written all over her pretty black face.

"Well, why don't you get on with it. You invited us here. This is the boringest damn . . ." I started to say.

"The time must be right," Mr. Androgynous interrupted.

"For what? What are you going to do?" I asked.

Elijah placed his hand on my thigh. His skin, still warm from his feast, sent a surging desire through me to feed and be filled. I must have given him a wild look because he shot me his "calm down" glance and patted my thigh.

"Elijah, this is nuts," I said, pushing his hand away.

My interruption of their little quiet party had caused the old man near me and the young man in the center to turn their heads and look my way. I immediately recognized the younger one as Mr. Androgynous's companion from our encounter the evening before, and I caught his gaze and held him there.

He moaned under my power, and I heard another gasp issue from the man to his right.

I don't know what I was trying to prove, possibly nothing except to show them who had the power here. I was bored with their silly charade and I was beginning to burn with the thirst. I should've fed before I came here, perhaps that was why I was so uneasy.

Another burst of steam drew me away from my contact with the man. As I released him I could not help but laugh as he bent forward, touching his head to the damp earth in prayer.

"Elijah hasn't explained our festival to you?" Mr. Androgynous asked. Though the question was directed to me, he was looking at Elijah, and I saw Elijah shake his head no. "If I may be permitted," Mr. Androgynous said.

"Please," I replied.

Another shot of spices hit the water, and a cloud of steam hid him from my view as he began to speak.

"Every spring we must replenish our power. We seek to find the source of that power." He removed the long carved stick from the water. "A sacrifice must be made so the power can again shield us from harm." He motioned, and the girl in white stood. "And we must hear the words of wisdom." He took the cat from the girl and held it close, stroking it.

My eyes darted from him to the girl. Who was the sacrifice? What was the source of power they sought? And from which of us would the words of wisdom come?

"When the black cat talks like a man we shall hear wisdom," he said. He lifted the cat and kissed it upon the head.

I needed to see no more. His arms stretched out in slow motion, and the cat was already falling for the boiling water.

My movement was unseen to them, yet I caught the cat by the scruff of the neck and returned to my seat before Mr. Androgynous had withdrawn his open hands.

The girl screamed, obviously thinking the cat had dematerialized before ever hitting the water.

"And just how will this cat talk like a man?" My voice boomed with demand.

Even Elijah was caught off guard by my interference. All eyes in the room were upon me. I remained seated, and they all stood, mouths open and eyes wide. Elijah too was on his feet.

"I told you dat you won't be likin' dis," he said, shaking his head.

The others in the room backed away from him as he stepped in front of me.

"Ainjul, you jis' let dem do dis festival," he said.

"Why?" I demanded. The cat was purring against me. I imagined it screeching as it hit the scalding water. The sounds it would make might be misconstrued as a man talking, or more likely, a man screaming.

Elijah turned and asked the others in the room to give us a moment. When they had gone and the door was closed, he came back and sat beside me.

"Ainjul, ef you don't let dem have dere way dey will give you no peace. Dey will 'spect you to keep Matt'u from hawmin' dem, an' dis you can't do," he said.

"Elijah, they are going to kill this cat. Matthew isn't going to bother with them or he would have done so already. I can't let them do this."

Elijah took hold of the cat and started to pull it away from me, but I held on. He did not give up and the poor animal was caught in a stronghold between us. I sensed Elijah would just as well tear the animal in half, and when it yowled in pain I had to let it go.

"Damn you, Elijah."

"I very sorry, Ainjul, but you want to come here, not me," he said.

"You knew what they were going to do!" I said. The hatred in my tone was as hot as my burning need to feed.

"Dis is but one cat, Ainjul. An' it is jis' one time a year. Let dem have dere magic, we know it ain't real."

He was trying to convince himself their magic was not real, but I knew he believed.

"All right, have your little murder," I said, and started for the door. "But I won't take part in it."

The cold night air rushed in as I pulled the door open. Clear, crisp air. I breathed long and deep, hoping to cool off the fire inside me. The members of the group scattered as I hurried by. I felt a fiendish desire to see how many of them I could strike down. I thought of the cat. I thought of Bong.

I walked alone under the blanket of a starry sky, searching the night for something to quench my burning thirst. Life was all around me, yet I was unable to find it. I had been relying too much on Bong for my hunting. His senses had grown keen and swift while mine had grown stale. At last I spied the scurry of movement in the dried grass. A field mouse ran swiftly across the dirt road, but not swiftly enough.

I heard the demonic wails of the boiling cat the same moment my fangs pierced the warm belly of the tiny, squealing

121

mouse. The blood flowed into my mouth. Two gulps, that was all there was and then the life subsided. I threw the dying mouse to the ground. Was I any better than those mortals playing with their voodoo magic? Could my survival justify my killing?

The taste of blood maddened me. I had to have more. I must be filled and fulfilled.

The lust for blood was more powerful than I had ever experienced, and I thought for a moment it was my anger that stirred the fire inside my veins. But I knew anger had nothing to do with it. I wanted, I needed human blood. I was meant to feast on the life force of mankind. Mice and fish would sustain me, but these things were not what I craved. I was more than a host to the alien parasite that flowed through me, I *was* the alien parasite. And this knowledge that I had kept stifled and repressed had suddenly been freed.

Every sense had awakened, and I caught my prey's scent on the night breeze. Quickly I followed, winding my way through the tall dead grass of winter, instinctively seeking my victim.

The musty smell of decomposition and the increasing wetness of the ground ushered me into the marsh. The stiff bullrushes snagged the fine material of my jumpsuit and mud seeped around my sandals and between my bare toes. The human smell grew stronger.

The bullrushes gave way to soft, yielding stalks of sweetgrass and I reached the bank of the creek edge. The water was high, spilling across the flat wasteland of the marsh. I saw the fisherman, alone in his small boat, and before I had a chance to think of how I would lure him I was swimming soundlessly beneath the water.

My vision was as keen in the murky depths as it was in the night air. I saw his line and swam by, giving it a tug like he had snagged a big one. The boat dipped in the water; he was alert. As he began to reel in his catch, I went under his boat and came up on his blind side. My swiftness hardly brought a splash to the water. I was over the edge of the boat and locked to him.

He was a big man. Despite my strong armlock around his

122

shoulders, he turned and his big beer gut slammed into me. But I had already gone rigid, ready to feed, and it was he who let out a moan of pain, not me. I bit upward into his neck, my fangs alive, feeling for the pulsing cord of his jugular. When the warm metallic fluid filled my mouth, I drank deep and strong.

He went limp in my arms, and though I lost my balance I stayed attached to his neck like a leech. We plunged into the water. I wrapped my legs around his body, holding him fast to me as we sank slowly to the bottom of the creek.

I drank quickly, his heart was slowing already and I heard the water begin to fill his lungs. The beating of his heart became a slow murmur and I had to let him go. I would not touch his death. When my legs uncoiled from around his waist the current caught him, and as I released his shoulders from my embrace I viciously tore the wound in his neck again with my fangs so his death would be ruled an accidental boating mishap.

He floated away downstream, and I broke the surface with his life blood warm and alive inside me.

I swam for the shore and crawled onto the muddy bank. I had never felt this way. Something had changed me, some unexplained physiological occurrence had transformed me. I pulled my hair back and wrung the water from it, then let it loose and combed through it with my fingers.

The journey back to the voodoo shack gave me time to think about what had happened. I walked slowly, frequently stopping to mentally search myself for the metamorphosis that had occurred. Since receiving E.L. I had never been so taken by blood lust. When I first received Elijah's blood, I had burned for it. When I mutilated myself, I had burned for it. When I had taken the poor black woman in the woods I had been consumed with the desire. But this time it was different. It was like I had graduated from a gawky student to a learned scholar.

I had lost something but had gained more. And suddenly I knew what it was. The smell was gone. The putrid slime that had been oozing out of me for three months had stopped. I was no longer a newborn. Every fiber of my being was awakened. I was a full-fledged vampire.

123

A new thrill coursed through me and I started to run for the rusty-red Kotex box house. I wanted Elijah with me, I wanted to share my graduation with him.

The door of the shack was open, and when I burst inside, they were gone. The fire had been extinguished and the pot was leaning against the far wall, cleaned out and empty.

I rushed back into the cool night air. 'Melia was still parked out front. I made myself listen, they must be nearby. My hearing was acute. Every scampering, scurrying night creature added to the background noise and had to be tuned out so I could focus on the sound of human footsteps.

They were approximately five hundred yards away, and on the move. I sprinted along the path of bent grasses they had left in their passage. It did not take me long to join them and I bolted around the mortals, seeking my immortal companion.

"Elijah, do you notice anything?" I said, leaping in front of him and walking backward so I could see his expression clearly.

"I see you been swimmin'," he said.

"Come on, take a good look," I said.

He kept walking and studied me briefly. "You fed well," he whispered.

"Besides that. Can't you sense the change in me? The smell, it's gone. My three months have ended. I've changed, Elijah, I've changed." I was laughing as I flung myself around his neck. My joyful outburst startled the mortals but they realized it was a good sign and I let them believe their magic was going to be more powerful than ever before.

Elijah carried me for several yards, allowing me to share my elation with him, but his kisses and hugs were not enough to hide his underlying sorrow. I let him put me down and walked beside him.

"What's wrong, Elijah? Aren't you happy for me?"

"Yaas, Ainjul, I be very happy for you. But now you will spread yo' wings an' fly away from me fo'ever."

"No, Elijah, I won't. I won't ever leave you."

"Yaas, Ainjul, you will. Fo'ever is a long time an' you will be needin' to find yo' own way in our world of darkness."

I thought I saw a tear spill over onto his cheek, but he hid

124

himself away from me and I released my hold on his hand as he walked ahead. The motley group of humans passed me, and I watched them follow him like a litter of pups would trail their mother through the stiff bullrushes and into the heart of the marsh.

Since the cat was already dead and I was filled, I tagged along, curious as to what they were going to do now. My clothes were beginning to dry, and though the night air was chilled I was warm with the fresh blood.

"Dis be de place," I heard Elijah say. They stood in a half circle near the edge of the tidal creek.

I walked around them and stood next to Elijah, watching with interest.

The man with the cheesecloth bag shook the contents and banged it against his thigh. He knelt down beside the flooded pool of water. The others dug in the mud with their bare hands, forming a small dam along the creek edge so the pool was cut off from the currents of the creek. The man placed the bag into the water and swished it around until no more air bubbles escaped. Then he pulled the bag out of the water and the others crowded around him, switching on flashlights to illuminate the murky puddle.

"What are they doing?" I whispered.

"Dey look fo' de magic bone," Elijah explained.

I could see the pile of bones on the muddy bottom.

"Which one is magic?" I asked.

"De one dat floats to de top," Elijah answered.

"But bones don't float, do they?" I watched with disbelief as a long bone gently bobbed to the surface. The man with the cheesecloth bag quickly bent to retrieve it, but Mr. Androgynous stopped him. Another, smaller bone floated to the surface.

The group let out a moan of surprise. I guessed two magic bones were better than one.

This time Mr. Androgynous stooped down and scooped up the bones with his hand. He held his hands out toward Elijah and bowed his head. Elijah stepped forward, bowed his head, and touched each bone. Mr. Androgynous stepped in front of me.

125

"Jis' touch dem," Elijah said.

I obliged, lightly placing my index finger upon each wet bone.

Mr. Androgynous closed his hand over the magic bones, shielding them from everyone. He looked up into my eyes and smiled a smile that literally beamed with his pleasure.

"Our power is renewed," he said.

The rest of the group now fell to their knees in the mud beside the puddle. Their dark arms thrust into the water and they retrieved the other bones, placing each with care into the cheesecloth bag.

"Why do they keep these other bones? There is no magic in them, is there?"

Elijah was handed the dripping bag and he ceremoniously tied the drawstrings in a bow. "Every paht of de cat is used, no paht of de sacrifice is t'rown away."

Was I supposed to feel glad about this?

Mr. Androgynous bowed his head solemnly and the others followed suit. They started back through the marsh, slowly snaking their way amid the tall bullrushes. They reminded me of a group of monks.

Elijah held me back, waiting until they became a speck of dark movement in the night, then he turned to face me and I knew what was coming.

"Ainjul, I tell you befo' dat you ain't to be feedin' in Matt'u territory," he said.

"What difference does it make? He hasn't done anything to stop me," I said.

"Dis not be de point."

"Well, what is the point, Elijah? Explain to me the rules of territory."

"Dey ain't rules, mo' like eddykit. You can only feed in 'nudder vampire's territory wid his permission. You know dis an' you choose to ignore it. Ef you aim to take over Matt'u range, you must challenge him fo' it. An' you will lose," he said.

"Like you lost it?" I asked. My question opened an old wound in Elijah, and his broad face seethed with controlled rage.

"Yaas, damn it, like I lost it." He looked like he wanted to strike out at something, vent his anger. "You remind me to much of . . ."

"Who? Who do I remind you of? Sometimes, Elijah, I know you aren't telling me everything. You hold back on me. Why?"

He moved away, walking quickly along the muddy path the others had taken. I watched him go, his white Adidas were stained with mud and the hem of his slacks dragged against the water that oozed beneath his steps.

It dawned on me that he was a frustrated old vampire. A vampire that had never gotten his way. Perhaps he thought by taking me under his wing he could dominate me. But mine was an indomitable spirit. His need to be the lead figure, and his inability to achieve it, were flaws in his immortal character. I could not help but smile as I followed him. I loved him so much, these flaws only made me love him more.

But he must have, at one time, challenged another vampire and won his territory. I wondered who that vampire was and what the challenge involved. Was it like a duel? Stand back to back, pace off ten steps and turn and fire? Was it a battle to the death?

"Elijah, wait, please." I caught him by the arm. He slowed but did not stop. "Tell me, what is the challenge. What do I have to do?"

"You ain't strong 'nuff yet to go an' challenge de likes of Matt'u."

"What do you mean I'm not strong enough. All along you've been telling me how strong I am. You have even wondered why I am so strong. You told me once that I was strong because I fed from your blood for so long. Now you change the story and say I am not strong? What are you keeping from me, Elijah?"

"Ef you want to take Cha'ston den make yo' challenge known to Matt'u. He decides what dat will be," he said.

I was hoping Elijah would tell me more, but he remained silent until we reached 'Melia.

My clothes were still damp and Elijah removed his coat, spread it across the bench seat, and motioned I sit on it. God forbid that my marshy, wet clothes should stain his dear beloved 'Melia.

"Make sho' you want Cha'ston. De challenge ain't nutt'n to be made a joke of," he said, and started the engine.

The radio played softly. I was thankful Elijah had not turned it off. I wanted so badly to know what his challenge had been that my questions were eating away inside me, but Elijah's reaction made it very clear I might never know.

We were back inside the Beaufort area before Elijah spoke again.

"De festival went well. I ain't never seen two bones rise wid de magic. Dey be very pleased."

"Elijah, tell me what Matthew challenged you with, I really must know." There, I had said it, it was out and I waited for Elijah's reply.

He sighed. A good sign that he would tell me.

"I guess you mus' ef you be takin' yo' revenge on him. I do want you to win. He been needin' to be shaken from his almighty pedestal a long time now."

"Well, what was your challenge?" I asked.

"I tell you first why I failed," he began. "I did not want it badly 'nuff. Ef I really want it, I would have it. You mus' want it so bad dat it burns worse in you den de desire fo' blood. When de want be dat bad, nutt'n will stop you from gittin' it."

I didn't want Charleston that bad. And I didn't know if I would ever want it that bad. But I did want to topple Matthew's little empire, just to be able to tilt him on that pedestal would give me satisfaction.

"Matt'u, he know what scares you," Elijah said. "He know what scares every one, not jis' mo'tals, immo'tals as well. He be very clever at dis game. He have over three hundred years to play. Matt'u challenge fo' me was simple 'nuff. He told me to go out an' make a vampire. He knew I could not do it."

Elijah's voice dropped in shame, and I could tell revealing this knowledge to me was hurting him.

"But, Elijah, you made me," I said.

"I give you de blood of E.L. but I did not take yo' life away.

128

And it took me a hundred and twenty-six years to do it. I was tired of all de . . ." He stopped again.

"Elijah, don't. Tell me what you're hiding from me."

"I can't. But dis much I can say. He will know what it is dat you fear and he will know yo' weakness."

"Like you knew I would release the cat before I would let you tear it in two?"

"Yaas."

Death.

Matthew would use death against me in his challenge. I was destined to fail.

When we pulled into the driveway, I knew something was wrong. And when 'Melia's engine stopped, my fears were verified. A pitiful howl came from inside the house.

Elijah and I looked at each other, both thinking we had mistakenly gone off and locked Bong in the house. The poor dog would be starved for blood, and sunrise was less than an hour away.

I rushed into the den. Bong was sitting on the edge of the hearth, staring into the fireplace. Dried blood coated the top of his head and neck.

"Bong, what have you been up to? What did you do?" I asked as I slowly approached him.

His tail swished once, sending a pile of newspapers across the carpet.

He continued to stare into the fireplace.

"What do you have in there?" I said. I craned my head to look up the chimney thinking he had something trapped inside, but I could see nothing. "There's nothing in here, boy."

Bong whimpered.

I turned around in time to see him get up and stagger like a drunk before falling down on his side.

He moaned painfully as the air rushed out of his lungs.

"Elijah, he's hurt," I said. My hands searched along the joints and tendons of his legs, but I could find nothing wrong.

Elijah bent down near his head and gently began to stroke him.

Bong let out another whimper and Elijah bent even closer to examine the bloody area behind Bong's left ear.

"Looks like he been shot," Elijah said.

"What?"

"You can feel right here, I t'ink it is a bullet hole. See fo' yo'self," he said as he stood up.

I thought the blood was from his kill. Bong was very neat, always licking up any blood that he got on himself, but he wouldn't be able to reach behind his head.

Sure enough, my fingers felt the hole in his skull just behind his ear. The wound was raw but the blood had sealed itself off. I checked the rest of his head, thinking that the bullet had to come out somewhere, but I could not find an exit hole.

"Will he be all right?" I looked over to Elijah.

"Well, ef he ain't dead from it by now, I t'ink he will be fine."

I gently caught Bong up in my arms. He moaned but managed to lick my arm, letting me know it was okay to move him.

"I'm going to take him up with me," I said. But Elijah was already engrossed in his evening paper so I carried Bong back down the hall and into the attic.

I held Bong tight and used my foot to nudge the coffin lid up. After settling Bong at the foot of the coffin I picked up the long-stemmed pink rose from my pillow.

The rose smelled good, and I let it linger against my nose as I waited for Bong to fall asleep. His smell was terrible. Now that I had graduated, I couldn't tolerate the decaying stench.

Death.

If I were to ever challenge Matthew for the territory of Charleston he would surely make me do something gross like sleep with a corpse. I shuddered. I didn't want Charleston. I wanted Matthew to pay for what he had done to me.

I closed my eyes and saw his blood-covered mouth smile at me, but then I saw his tall dark figure standing alone on the dunes at Kiawah, watching me.

The special tiredness washed over me and I didn't even have time to get out of the soiled jumpsuit. There is one thing to be said about this tiredness, it masks everything else and I was able to climb in my coffin with Bong's horrendous smell and let the darkness of sleep swallow my senses.

When I awoke Bong was gone, again. I could only hope his wounds had healed enough so he wasn't staggering around and in pain.

The house was empty, Elijah was not back from his hunt. I hoped Bong was with him, but I knew better. Elijah didn't want to hunt with me, and I knew he sure as hell didn't want to hunt with the *demon dawg*.

The reeking smell of decay lingered in my coffin and I decided until Bong was over his rot, which hopefully would be soon, I would have to find someplace else to sleep.

After a quick shower and a change of clothes I found myself sitting with the yellow pages upon my lap, searching for a place to get a new coffin.

Under the listing for caskets it said see Pet Cemeteries. Maybe I could get Bong his own, doggy-sized coffin, but when I looked under pets, nothing like that was listed.

I looked up Mortuary, but there was no listing. Where, I thought, would one look for a coffin?

Funerals! I found several listings under Funeral. Each one said something like, Consideration for the living, and reverence for the dead; or Dedicated to the principles of sympathetic and conscientious service; but better still was, Dignified services within the means of all.

I liked the "within the means of all" part. I didn't have the foggiest idea how much a coffin would cost. I wondered if it was proper to just buy a coffin and not the complete burial package. I picked up the phone from the kitchen counter and dialed the number of the funeral home. It rang over ten times and I hung up. I realized that even the dead had to stick by the nine-to-five workday schedule of the modern world.

Could I ask Elijah where and when he had purchased my coffins? Since he had already furnished me with two, would it be asking too much for a third?

Then I knew what I could do. I could get in my van and find the shack where I had spent my first night. The coffin would still be there and I could bring it home. Yes, that's what I would do.

I grabbed the keys from the fireplace mantel and hurried

from the house. I wanted to get it and be back in time to have it in the attic before Elijah returned.

Finding the place was not as hard as I thought. The dirt road was wet in spots where the marsh crept right up to the edge. The tide was high. I wondered if they had found the body of the fisherman.

My remembrance of him ignited my hunger, and though I tried to think of other things I could not suppress the burning passion within my veins. Too bad a cold shower can't smother a vampire's passion, there would be a lot less victims in the world.

I slowed the van when the shack came into view. The voodoo dolls had been removed from the tree, but the hole remained in the front wall where the leader of the Satan group had been thrown out by Elijah. I looked at the spot where I had been mortally wounded by his crude wooden stake. His body was gone, no doubt his fellow devil worshipers had removed it. I studied the shack, stalling for time. I did not want to get out of the van, and only when I confronted the fact that I was scared of this place, of what had happened to me here, was I able to take hold of myself and make myself do it.

"No mortal can hurt you now," I said to myself. "You are a full-fledged vampire and the power burns in your veins," I convinced myself.

I left the engine running and climbed out. I opened the sliding door and judged if there was room for a coffin in back. There would have to be. I certainly wasn't going to tie it to the luggage rack!

The shack was empty. I found the three floorboards and pulled them up. The acrid smell of decaying earth hit me in one cold, cloying wave. I held my breath as I lowered myself into the dark hole.

The floor was wetter than I remembered and the muck came above my ankles. I should've taken off my shoes but it was too late now, they would be ruined.

The coffin was resting on top of the cement blocks, exactly as it had been. I walked over to it and grabbed both handles on my side.

It wasn't heavy, but the bulk made it awkward to maneuver

132

up through the floor. I hoisted it up and got my shoulder under the end of it. With one mighty shove I had it resting on its side on the floor above.

I was so intent on accomplishing this task, and so consumed by the burning thirst for blood, I had closed off my other senses. But now the unmistakable smell of a human hit me as I crawled through the hole in the floor.

I was not going to be tricked again. Using all my vampire strength, I shoved the coffin across the room toward the door.

I saw the body of a man go down when my missile hit him, and I was upon him before he had a chance to get up.

He struggled beneath me, trying to push his face from the sandy dirt. Something about him was familiar, and I loosened my grip on him enough to turn him over so I could see his face. It was Mr. Androgynous.

The gash on his black forehead was bleeding freely and the blood ran down across his right eye and off toward his ear. The smell almost caused me to attack but I swallowed and forced my fangs back into the gum before I spoke.

"What do you want here?"

"I've waited for you to return. I knew you would," he said. His voice had a yearning to it that I could not help but translate into "take me." I looked away from him, scanning the shadows for his voodoo companions.

"Where are your friends?" I asked, holding him tighter.

"I am alone," he answered.

I was able to discern truth in his facial movement and I let him go, standing up away from him and wondering what I should do with him. He knew what I was, there was no doubt. But if I killed him his friends would know and Elijah and I might both be in danger.

"I want your power," he said.

And I thought about his boldness before I laughed at him.

"There was another that wanted my power and he died right on this very spot," I said. I kicked the dirt beneath my feet. "Who told you that I could give you power?"

He stood up and faced me.

"Matthew."

133

His face was as innocent as a child and his truthfulness sent a chill through me like the hand of death had touched my soul.

"So, you're a traitor. You lead a group that fears Matthew, and yet behind their backs you are in cahoots with him." I tried to hide the shock in my voice.

"Matthew came to me. I did not seek him. He knew what I wanted. He knew my every hidden wish and desire, and yet he never said a word to me. He gave me images and he gave me an image of you."

Matthew has been playing this game for over three hundred years. I heard Elijah's words. Was I already involved in his game? Had the time come when I *must* confront him. He obviously knew about me, there would be no surprise attack. The time had come to stalk him, and though I began to tremble I wasn't sure if I trembled with excitement or fear.

I had to decide what to do with Mr. Androgynous.

"What would you do to earn this power?" I asked him.

Before he had time to answer me, I pulled the shirt away from his neck. There were no marks upon his tender black skin. I pushed his sleeves up; no marks were visible on his arms. Matthew had not taken any blood from him. Was he a gift to me?

Mr. Androgynous endured my touch, but the coldness of my skin scared him.

"Is this what you want to be?" I asked, closing my hands around his warm wrists with such crushing power that most mortal men would have screamed.

He only moaned quietly, ready to endure whatever I was going to do to him.

His closeness was driving my hunger crazy, but I was still able to control it. He was so beautiful. Both feminine and masculine. What a fine vampire he would be. And his boldness, well, perhaps he could even be a match for Matthew. What does one look for in making a vampire? And why was I even thinking of it? I wasn't going to do it, not now.

I let him go.

He staggered away from me but kept his beautiful brown eyes on mine. His long lashes fluttered and his innocent face showed patience and trust.

134

"I will let you think about it," I said, and quickly loaded my coffin into the van. I shut the door and stood beside him. "Do not tell anyone about us, Matthew, Elijah or me. I will know if you have, I will be able to read it in your face, and then there will be no power, only death. Do you understand?"

"Yes, I understand," he replied.

Why had I defended Matthew? Why had I included him in my little group? Did I really care what happened to him, or if others found out he was a vampire?

These questions bothered me and I climbed into my van knowing that I had to confront Matthew, tonight.

Mr. Androgynous stood quietly, watching me turn the van around. Before I left I lowered my window and called out to him.

"Don't seek me again. I shall find you."

He nodded and I kept an eye on him as I pulled away into the night.

CHAPTER EIGHT

My van rocked precariously, I didn't even look when I pulled onto the highway. The force of the turn knocked the coffin from its perch upon the swiveling chair and the broken lid flew off as it tipped to its side.

The delicate pillow and satin lace coverlet fell beneath the centered table along with the dried petals of the white rose Elijah had left that first night.

My mind was spinning with thoughts. I was scarcely breathing, and when I realized this I gasped for air like a person who had downed a big glass of water and needed a breath. But my burning hunger had dulled and it was not unlike ignoring the rumblings of an empty stomach. All I could think of was Matthew and I drove like the very demons of hell were chasing me.

Clouds had been gathering all evening, and now the stars were completely obscured. The air was heavy with rain, but none fell. I remembered a saying I had heard about Charleston, something to the effect that the air is so humid your clothes rot right off your back. And though the humidity did not bother me (but it had when I was mortal) my clothes were damp against my cold skin.

I slowed down when the road merged into a four-lane bridge that crossed the Ashley River and brought me onto the heart of peninsular Charleston. I had no idea where to look for him, but had no doubt that I would find him.

There was an unusual amount of traffic, and each red light gave me the opportunity to glance at the mortals who lived and played in Charleston. Many of the cars were going the opposite direction from me and I saw that the occupants were dressed up for the evening's entertainment. It wasn't until I came closer to the Galliard Auditorium that I learned there had been a ballet tonight.

The silent talking and laughter I observed through the windshield only stirred my anger. All these smiling, warm-blooded creatures were free to live in the realm of light and gaiety. They were capable of love, of being loved. They would grow old and die happily with the promise of ever-lasting life in heaven.

And what was my promise? An everlasting life of dark-ness, loneliness, all revolving around the passions of feeding upon life. There had to be more.

Before I was caught in the tangle of traffic leaving the auditorium parking lot, I made a right-hand turn the wrong way on a one-way street. My sense of direction led me into the historic district of stately renovated homes. I drove slowly, scanning the dark shadows for the tall figure of Mat-thew. I had a score to settle with him and I wanted answers.

I made my way to the Battery and was about to turn back on King Street when I saw him. He could've been anyone standing there in the park but I knew instantly that he was one of my kind. He was talking with a human woman and they stood close to the very spot where he had attacked me in my car. The woman's posture and attitude told me what she was, a cheap slut.

I simply reacted. My van sped around the point and came to a screeching stop only a few feet in front of them. With a vampiric illusion of speed, I was out of the van and stand-ing before him, and the human slut gasped in shocked amazement.

The words I had planned to say would not come. The curses I wanted to swear at him vanished. I was reduced to the newborn vampire and my look of awe brought a smile to his boyishly handsome face.

Our eyes met briefly. The cool, coppery-brown color of his eyes was unnatural and I glanced away, but enough contact had been made for him to send my mind wheeling with a kaleidoscope of images. I staggered backward but composed myself before the human woman had time to notice.

"So you've come back to me, luv," he said. His accent was British with a slur of good old southern over it.

"Come back to you," I said, and there was an animal hiss to my voice that drove the woman closer to him.

"Who is she, Matthew?" the human demanded.

"She's the one with the broken heart," he said.

My eyes wildly searched his expressionless face; the double meaning of his words caused a panic to rise inside me. I watched as he pulled the human woman to his side and pressed his face into the stiffly moussed bleached blond hair. He looked over to me, teasingly.

"Even time will not mend the torn flesh of her wounded heart," he said.

He was confusing me. He knew about me, about my mortal wound, but he was playing out a lover's quarrel before this human slut. How should I react? What role did I play?

"What in the hell do you want from me?" I asked. It came out with more of a whine than I intended.

"I want you to come home, luv," he said, pulling his nose up from the short moussed hair.

"Stop calling me that, damn you."

"But it's true, luv," he said, and reached out to touch me.

I moved with speed that made his outstretched arm appear frozen, as if caught in a strobe light. He nodded, and smiled at me with approval.

"Matthew, you told me you had no involvements," the human whined.

"Don't worry, bitch, I'm not involved with him," I said.

"Who is she, Matthew?" she demanded again.

"You owe me," I said to him.

Silence.

The human's thoughts were easy to perceive. She thought I was an ex, maybe there was child support involved or a property settlement.

Matthew was unreadable. His smooth face was that of a

138

boy, but the heavy jawline and the sharp, chiseled nose were that of a man. He had become a vampire in the transition of his adulthood and he used it to his advantage. He could be appealingly innocent or hideously malevolent. I had seen this face when he had drunk me dry and left me for dead.

His hair was dark, cut squarely at the collar and feathered around his face. The curls were natural, wavy wisps of tousled movement, and where my highlights were red, his were golden, which gave him more of a supernatural appearance. But the most noticeable feature was his skin. I had seen the white glimmer of it that night on the beach, I'm sure of it. But now it was tanned, and I stood there a long time trying to figure out how he managed to do that.

His long, tanned fingers slid beneath the woman's chin and he tilted her head back so the light of the streetlamp played over the beautiful, baby-pink softness of her throat. He lowered his head and looked into the woman's eyes. Dark shadows crossed his face and accented the cleft in his chin.

"Oh my sweet lovely Laura, can't you see who she is?" he said with such tenderness I could've gagged.

But then he changed, and his expression turned into the monster that I remembered on that night. He pinched her face so tightly the heavy makeup smeared beneath his fingers and he pushed her in my direction.

"Look at the lovely white skin. Look at the fire that burns in her eyes. She is the goddess of death, a creature of the night," he whispered.

The human's eyes widened, but with disbelief, not fear.

"Those were just stories," she said. "Let go of me, you're hurting me."

He pushed her closer to me, and in my strange fascination with his little game I did not back away.

"And she has come for you, she is starving for your blood right now."

His words spoke truth. The burning passion again enveloped me. I glanced around the park. There were no other mortals around. I looked at him. Was he offering her to me?

"You're hurting . . ."

"But I won't let her take you," he said, and pulled her close to himself, so close his body seemed to physically consume hers.

She was still looking at me when his mouth opened and his fangs sprang forward.

He forced her to look up at him, allowing her to glimpse the weapons of death in his mouth. But just as quickly he closed his mouth and watched as horror flooded her eyes.

"Do you know why I won't let her take you?" he asked, and the mask of innocence flooded his face briefly.

She opened her mouth to say something, but no words would come and she shook her head.

"Because she is trespassing in my territory and only I have the right to take you."

I could see her trembling and I could feel her fear. The very scent of her had changed.

"Please, please let me go," she begged. A tear spilled over and ran in a black mascara smudge down her red-blushed cheek.

"I shall kiss you like no man has ever kissed you," he said, but he smiled at me. "I shall take you to the heights of ecstasy. Wouldn't you like that, luv?"

She was sobbing against him now.

He was talking to her but looking at me, teasing me, making my hunger pitch inside like an angry black serpent. And the look in his eyes was pure pleasure. He was feeding more off her fear than anything else. He was smugly enjoying this game.

"Would you like to share her?" he asked.

The woman moaned in anguish.

"You disgust me," I said.

"Very well," he said. His shoulders shrugged as he bent into her neck but all he did was kiss her. Then he let her go.

She was terrified, so terrified that she could not move away from him.

"I was only playing with you, luv," he said gently.

140

And I wondered which of us the comment was directed to.

"But your teeth look . . ."

"It was only a game," he said, and from his closed hand produced a pair of plastic five and dime vampire fangs.

Oh, he was clever and I couldn't help but find him remotely interesting.

"Look, no fangs," he said. He opened his mouth and showed her. Of course they were hidden beneath his gum, even I could do that. "Here, you can have them."

He placed the plastic fangs in her hand but she dropped them to the ground.

"The human brain is such a gullible organ," he laughed. And I knew he said this to both of us.

I turned to leave.

"Going so soon, I was just starting to have fun," he said.

"Yes, I'm going," I said.

"Good," the human slut said.

"Oh, she'll be back, luv," Matthew said.

"Over my dead body," the woman replied.

As I climbed into the van I saw her clinging protectively to Matthew's arm and his laughter echoed in my ears as I shut the van door.

What I did next was perhaps the most foolish thing of my vampire existence.

I could not take my mind off Matthew's tanned skin. If the sun would destroy us, how was it that he looked like some surfer boy tourist? Yielding to my sometimes failing logic, I stopped at a local tanning salon for an experiment.

The place was deserted. The windows were covered with decorative, Charleston-style iron security bars and the door was locked. But this is no problem to a vampire and I don't know how it is accomplished other than simply willing a lock open. I was inside the salon in seconds and the door was locked again behind me.

I found the tiny tanning booth and peered inside. The timing mechanism was on the outside, as were the controls. Instead of risking my entire body, I waited outside while

141

the room filled with a bright glow and then I stuck my hand in.

The pain was instant. Reflex pulled my hand away, but the damage had already been done. My white skin began to wither away and my fingers were frozen in place, outstretched and stiff. The blood boiled inside my veins and my stomach heaved. Had I fed earlier I'm sure I would have vomited.

I grabbed my burnt hand and squeezed hard around the wrist, afraid the boiling pain would flare up my arm and eventually consume me. But the pain did not crawl up my arm, it stayed only on the exposed skin. The back of my hand was shrunken, like a mummy's hand might be, but the palm side was still plump and firm. I watched, horrified, as the nails of my index and middle finger peeled away and fell to the floor.

All I wanted was to stop the burning but the thought of running cold water over my scorched hand scared me. What if the skin actually peeled off like the nails did? Would it ever grow back?

I blew on it. It had the consistency of a ripe, puffed marshmallow and I decided it would be best not to touch it. Cradling it against my chest I hurried back outside. It wasn't until I pulled the van onto the highway that I felt tears begin to spill from my eyes.

"Oh God, what have I done?" The pain was intense, still burning, boiling.

I was steering with my left hand, and the air from the vents blew across my damaged right hand causing such agony that I was sure the flesh had blackened and fallen away from the bones. My mind's eye produced macabre pictures of the skeletal claw that would be attached to my otherwise perfect arm. Like a pirate's hook, the death ray from those old B-rated sci-fi movies had zapped my hand into nothing. I refused to look at it.

Laughter filled my mind, Matthew's laughter. Mocking my stupidity. And all I wanted was Elijah to comfort me and tell me that it would be better. Elijah would never laugh at me.

The skies opened and the rain that had been threatening all night released itself in a torrential cacophony. I welcomed the noise of the big, splattering drops and the thick smell of wetness that drifted in from the air vents. The suddenness of the spring storm jarred my senses away from the searing self-inflicted pain.

A jagged bolt of lightning split the night horizon in two. The thunder followed exactly as I said three-one-thousand and the sudden forceful crack scared me so badly that I began to laugh.

I was driving wildly, racing into the storm with a frenzied fervor that I didn't care to understand. It was beautiful. The elements of nature unleashed in all the raw splendor that the universe can offer. I felt electric with the energy expending from the black sky. The empty highway was a long dark tunnel and at the end the sky ahead sparked with brilliant whites, muted pinks, and sulfuric yellows. Lightning played among the big black bulkheads of clouds.

All too quickly the winds carried the storm off to my right. I was nearing the outskirts of Beaufort. My flooded senses calmed; the pain grew into an intolerable itch, but I dared not touch the wounded flesh, fearing that I would tear it away if I did. The emptiness of my veins was now causing light-headedness.

I began to think about feeding. Matthew certainly had dined on his human slut by now, of that I had no doubt. Elijah too would be sated and satisfied, probably deep in thought with his newspapers right now. Blood would heal me, it was blood that I craved.

As if taunting me, the darkness ahead swirled into a throbbing red glow. I slowed down, puzzled by this manifestation of the night. The timber line gave way as I approached and I saw the fire engines and ambulance whose strobe lights cut into the blackness. Thick smoke rolled above them and a few persistent flames licked evil orange tendrils against the sky.

When I drew nearer I saw where a car had run off the road and was burning down in the ditch.

My heart stopped. It was unmistakably 'Melia.

Dark soot covered most of her gleaming red paint and the door of the passenger side was smoldering near the pavement. The hood was up and twisted into a grotesque black thing that reminded me immediately of my own hand.

I pulled over and leapt from the van. A fireman came running hollering for me to move out of the way.

The insaneness of this night was driving me mad. I ran down the embankment. More flames shot out of 'Melia's ragged hull and I wildly thought the car was actually spitting the flame at me.

I froze with horror.

"Elijah." My voice was a mere whisper.

Everything around me grew dark. The smoke and the thick smell of burning rubber brought me to my knees in the tall wet grass. I cradled my burnt hand and rocked back upon my legs. Was my accident a premonition to this catastrophe? Had my wild frenzied drive through the storm been psychically forced because Elijah needed me?

A soul-wrenching moan escaped my lips and I was vaguely aware of the fireman kneeling beside me.

"Was there a body, was he in there?" I asked.

"Miss, do you know who was driving?" he asked. His voice was soft and kind.

"Is there a body?" I turned to look into his eyes.

The gray-blue irises filled with concern and I locked onto him with desperation, trying to pull the knowledge of what he had seen out of his mind. His hands went up to his head and I knew I had pulled too hard in my need.

I glanced away, releasing him. He fell against me and one of his partners saw what was happening and called out, "Joe, are you okay?"

"Yes, just the smoke." He stood up.

I followed him.

A paramedic rushed over and helped him to the back of the big white ambulance. He took a drag of oxygen and I looked beyond him, into the brightly lit interior of the meat wagon.

The curves and bumps of a body were visible beneath the blue cover that draped it. I had to know. I stepped into the

144

ambulance and was about to draw back the sheet when the paramedic climbed in behind me.

"Lady, you don't want to do that," he said.

"But I have to see, I have to see if it's him," I said.

"The body under there isn't recognizable. Only dental records are going to be able to identify it, if even that is possible. This was a hell of an explosion."

"But he is my friend. I know that is the car," I said, and pointed with my good hand hiding the other from his sight.

"Listen, you go home and see if your friend is there. If he is missing, you can call and make the identification. It's dark and the car is badly damaged. Your friend is probably okay."

I think I nodded. A policeman came over and wanted my name and telephone number. I mumbled the first name that came to mind, that of a co-worker at the Akron *Beacon Journal,* and made up a phone number.

"Looks like you've had a nasty shock. I think the medics should take a look at you," he said.

"No. I'm fine, I'll be fine," I refused, and rushed back to my van.

Another fireman started hollering and the car rocked as a small explosion burst into the night. Everyone was scrambling and I drove away quickly, praying that Elijah was not in the wreck, praying that no one had taken down my license number.

I began to convince myself that it was impossible. Elijah was not that burnt body in the back of the ambulance. He was an old vampire, a fire like that would have reduced him to a pile of ashes. Look what a little bit of filtered sunlight had done to my hand. But what if it was him and he was still alive? What if he needed me?

I felt pain everywhere. The thick smoke had stung my sensitive eyes and the heat of the blazing car had made my body prickle with hot flashes. My hand hurt again and my empty veins seemed to be collapsing within me as my heart beat furiously for a new quota of blood to pump.

I pulled into the driveway of Elijah's house and turned off the engine. I sat and stared at nothing for a long while and then made myself face whatever the situation might hold. Either Elijah was in the den with his papers, or he had been horribly burnt, perhaps dead, perhaps needing me to come bring his body back home to heal. I would have to do it before sunrise. If he were somehow alive, in that condition, and the daylight came, he would be lost forever.

The very night spelled doom, and when I slipped my key into the locked door I was certain Elijah had met a terrible end. The den was dark.

"Elijah, are you here?" I called softly into the gloomy interior. No answer.

Worn out with worry and sick with pain I fell exhausted onto the couch. What should I do? What could I do? There was less than two hours before sleep, and sunrise would force me into my deathly slumber.

I must've dozed momentarily, for I awoke with a start, aroused by the metallic blood smell.

I sat up, my head was swimming, and scanned the dark room. Movement in the hallway, then the familiar lapping of water from the toilet bowl, greeted me.

"Bong," I called.

I heard him whimper and slowly stood, waiting a moment for the dizziness to cease. But it did not cease and I had to grope my way along the wall as I walked back the hallway to see Bong.

I switched on the bathroom light. The brightness hurt my eyes and I squinted. Bong had dried blood on top of his head.

"Oh, Bongers, not again," I said.

He pulled his big head out from the toilet and turned to look my way. His left eye was covered with blood and very swollen. I bent down, more to relieve my dizziness than anything else, but Bong took it as an invitation and came over to nudge me with his cold nose.

His eye looked bad. I gently felt around the swollen lids with my good hand, probing for a cut or, God forbid, another bullet hole. I pried the lids apart and gagged. His eye was gone. A cold stream of pus and blood ran over my thumb.

146

"Bong, what am I going to do with you?" I asked.

He moaned feebly and wagged his tail. Though he looked terrible, he was, in fact, in better shape than he had been last night. At least he wasn't staggering around.

I felt the bullet hole. The skin had healed completely, but there was a definite depression in his skull where the bullet had entered.

"Is immortality worth this, Bong?"

His head dropped to the floor and he peered up at me with his good eye. If I was reading him right he didn't think immortality was worth this.

The air pressure in the house changed. The door of the den opened.

"Elijah!" My yell must have had a tint of wild panic to it, because in the blink of an eye my old black vampire friend was standing in the doorway of the bathroom looking at us with great concern.

"Sweet Jesus Ainjul, what has happ'ned to both of you?"

I flung my arms around him and hugged him tightly. He had a distant, bewildered feeling to his return embrace, but as I clung harder to him, reaffirming that he was not that awful burnt thing in the back of the ambulance, he began to hold me tightly.

He pushed me away finally, and carefully pulled my injured hand toward his lowered gaze.

"Ainjul, how did dis happ'n?"

"Oh, Elijah, 'Melia was . . . I though you were . . . Matthew knew . . ."

"Jis' calm down," he said, and he pulled me close again and slowly stroked my hair.

I leaned against him, aware that I was trembling terribly.

"Ainjul, dere is somet'ing I have to tell you, somet'ing dat is hard fo' me but my own mind is made up."

He held me tighter, and in his embrace I knew that he was letting go.

"Elijah, please . . ."

"No, Ainjul, jis' let me finish." He gently nudged the long pieces of my hair away from my face and smiled. "You

147

will always be a paht of me. We be bound togetter by de blood of everlastin' life.''

He stopped a moment and searched my eyes with his. His lips quivered slightly. He released his hold on me and stepped back.

"I be leavin' tomorrow night," he said. His words were abrupt, final.

I was shocked, so shocked that I became numb. I thought he might eventually ask me and Bong to leave. He valued his privacy, he was a definite loner. But for him to go, I could not bear the thought.

"Elijah, if it's anything that I've done, please let . . .''

"It ain't got nutt'n to do wid you or dat crazy animal you have created. I been plannin' to do dis since befo' I ever made you.''

"But where are you going?" I asked.

"To de Middle East.''

And I knew he wasn't talking about New Jersey or New York.

"But why? Elijah, you promised me that you wouldn't leave until my first year was up.''

"No. Dat not be de promise I made you," he said.

"You can't leave me here with Matthew. He is an evil, awful person . . . being. He plays games with his victims. Elijah, he feeds off of their fear. Don't leave me, take me with you. I won't be a plaything for Matthew.''

"My own plans be made," he said, and turned away from me. "You have overcome everyt'ing dat you have so fah encountered. You will overcome Matt'u.''

"Elijah, please, don't go. You're all I've got. You are my family. I can't exist alone," I said. Begging was beneath me, but I was more than desperate; I didn't want to be alone.

He turned again to face me.

"Ainjul, you will be jis' fine. I leave everyt'ing fo' you. You have de house an' all of my own money. You will learn yo' own way in our dark world. Everyt'ing I have I give to you, 'cept of co'se 'Melia. I destroyed her becuz she was somet'ing special to me," he said.

148

"But you always tell me I'm special to you. Are you destroying me, Elijah? If you go I will certainly die, Matthew will *kill* me."

"Matt'u ain't gonna kill you," he said.

There it was again. That tone, he knew things that he would not tell me. He was holding back information.

"Elijah, you better tell me what it is you know. You can't run off with knowledge I need. What are you hiding from me?"

"I can't tell you," he said. Again his words were final.

"All right, then will you please tell me why you are going to the Middle East. What are you searching for?"

"I owe you dat much, yaas," he said, and motioned for me to follow him upstairs into our attic sanctuary.

After Bong and I had climbed through the attic floor, Elijah pulled the ladder up and secured it. I watched him in the darkness. His gray head bobbed slightly as he walked over to his coffin. He opened the lid, climbed in, and arranged himself in a sitting position so that he could still see me.

I opened my coffin and waited for Bong to climb in and settle down. Then I hooked the leash to his collar and tied the opposite end securely to the handle. There was enough slack that I would still be able to close the coffin lid.

I picked up the rose from my pillow and turned to face Elijah. I leaned against the edge of my coffin and waited for him to begin his explanation.

"Ainjul, maybe I jis' be a funny ole man," he began.

Old man, this was the first time I had ever heard him refer to himself as a *man*.

"I truly b'lieve dat Gawd will pardon my own existence ef I am able to bring good out of my new life."

He stopped, waited for a reaction from me, but I remained quiet, thinking to myself that I had turned my back on God. I did not think of Him as my maker, not anymore.

"You see, Ainjul, I never asked to be a vampire. I never wanted everlastin' life, not really. In my own mind I knows dat my Gawd can fo'give me. But I mus' prove myself wort'y of His fo'givness. Only den can I go home to Him wid a free soul."

I grew worried. My old friend was talking crazy stuff. He was telling me that one good deed and he was ready to die.

"Elijah, you're not going to commit suic—"

"No, Ainjul. I not be ready to lay an' wait fo' de sun to burn me up. My own b'liefs don't hold wid dat. I have an opportunity to be helpin' odder folk an' I have turned away from it fo' years an' years. Now is de time dat I mus' do it. I can help an' I will help."

"What are you planning to do, kill the Ayatollah or Kadafy?"

"No. I know you been wonderin' 'bout all de newspapers. I have a plan to git hostages back. I have already contacted some of de families. I have given my own word dat ef dere loved ones be alive, I will bring dem back."

"Elijah, this is crazy. You've been seeing too much Rambo stuff. What are you going to do. Contact the CIA and tell them that nothing can destroy you so you will go in and get those people out?"

I heard him sigh.

"No, I ain't gonna go to de CIA. But t'ink what a weapon I am."

And it was true. Even with all their high-powered technology, mortals were slow and languid when matched to us. If Elijah was determined, then Elijah was unstoppable. No human could better him.

"Elijah, this is truly a worthy thing. If your God will forgive you then this is the thing to do."

"Ainjul, I need you to help me," he said.

I didn't say anything. He didn't even need to ask me. He was the one who had given me back my life, changed though it was. I had gone to him and that night he had taken away all my torment and pain. Anything I could do for him, anything at all, I would do.

"You have to deliver me in my own casket to de airport an' be sho' I git on de plane safely."

I walked over to him and leaned against the cool, burnished edge of his coffin.

"We must say our goodbyes now, before the sun rises," I said.

"My own heart is already achin'," Elijah said.

"I will worry about you."

"An' I will t'ink of you always."

My eyes clouded with tears and I squeezed them shut, fighting back my sorrow.

Bong made his little whimpering dream sounds and I turned away from Elijah, thankful for the interruption. I walked over to my coffin and petted Bong as he dreamed. His paws twitched and his body jerked with spastic, running movements. What did he dream of?

"Ainjul, sleep wid me today. I want our last moments togetter to be as long as we can make dem."

Yes, I wanted that too. To share with him every last moment, even our deathly slumber.

I closed my coffin lid, sealing Bong inside.

Elijah was holding the rose that I had left on the edge of his casket. He handed it to me. Was it my last rose?

He stretched himself out upon the dark velvet that lined his casket. He looked so small in there, so frail.

The only way his coffin would accommodate the both of us was for me to lie on top of him, and I climbed in carefully, slowly letting my weight sink upon him. His powerful arms encircled me, pulling me tighter to his breast.

"Elijah."

"Yaas, Ainjul."

"Don't close the lid until I'm asleep," I said.

He hugged me even tighter and chuckled softly. His breath was warm and smelled of blood.

"Now you tell me what happ'n to yo' hand," he said.

I started to explain about Matthew, about how he had been tan and how my experiment burnt my skin nearly off the bone. My body began to go limp and the special sleep slipped into my conversation.

But before I was taken by sleep Elijah cut his forearm, to accommodate my position, and pressed the warm stream of life to my lips. I sucked up the blood like a baby, nursing until the only sound was our hearts beating in loud rhythm

151

and my swallows growing weaker as I floated into the dark abyss of nothing.

The day had passed too quickly. I awoke alone. Elijah was gone. I pushed the lid of his casket up and found a note taped on the edge.

Ainjul,

I went to feed. I have Bong with me. Be back soon. Please load my casket into the car in the garage.

Elijah.

I read the note twice before I realized what was wrong with it. Elijah didn't write like he talked. His gullah accents and pronunciations were missing. He was a stranger already.

The car in the garage was a hearse. We were playing out this scenario to the hilt. I slid the casket in and secured it with a strap through each handle. I was just stepping out of the car when I heard Bong's howling greeting.

What a picture they were. Bong was so swollen from overfeeding that he looked like I could pop him with a pin. And Elijah too was near the bursting point.

Elijah was dressed in a dark suit, complete with a tie and a hat. Again the only thing that spoiled his "Sunday best" appearance were another spanking new pair of Day-Glo white Adidases.

"We must hurry," he said. He climbed in the back of the hearse, handed me the keys, and opened the lid of the coffin. "Go to de Cha'ston airport. It is a private flight, dey will be lookin' fo' you, dey will tell you what to do," he said.

He was very excited. More excited than I had ever seen him. This mood helped to keep the edge off mine, but the minute we hugged each other a final time and he closed the lid of his coffin my mood dropped. I was alone. My friend was truly leaving me.

Bong settled next to the coffin, and I hurried to the driver's seat. I concentrated on driving, trying to block out the concerns and worry that were surfacing.

Elijah had taken nothing with him. No guns, no money, no clothing, nothing. What if the plane crashed and burned? What if someone opened the coffin and the light of day destroyed him? He was taking a big risk, bigger than I ever dared to think about. Where would he find shelter? What if he ran into other vampires over there who meant him harm?

I was driving myself crazy. Elijah knew the risks and had taken them. It was important to him; I should abide by that. But God, I was going to miss him.

I never made it to the airport proper. A car pulled alongside me and the man inside motioned that I follow him. We cut behind the small terminal buildings and headed for a cargo hangar.

The man stopped his car and got out. He was small and dark-complexioned, but not a black. He looked Arabic or Iranian. Elijah had indeed made contact.

He moved quickly to the back of the hearse and another man ran from the building to help him unload Elijah's coffin. They slid it gently on to a rolling cart. Bong followed them, staying beside Elijah's coffin.

When they reached the side of the hangar they stopped and gently lifted the coffin on to a disassembled crate. With quiet speed they nailed the sides of the shipping crate around the coffin and spray-painted a big "this side up" arrow on each side.

It bothered me that my friend was in there. I knew he could get out, but it still bothered me.

I approached the small man.

"Please, take care of him," I said.

He said nothing, but nodded to me and handed me the set of keys, making a motion with his other hand around the edge of the hangar.

I looked closer at the keys. They were my van keys. How had Elijah managed all this? With whom had he made contact, and did they know he was a vampire?

No. He wouldn't put himself in that kind of jeopardy.

153

My van was parked along the grass strip separating the hangar bay from the runway. The men had already wheeled Elijah's crate over to a cargo plane and were loading it into the huge, swollen belly of the aircraft.

I climbed into the van, pulling Bong in with me.

The cargo plane began taxiing down the tarmac. I watched the red lights blink on the tail of the aircraft. Elijah had been whisked away so quickly. I didn't even know where he was going. Libya? Iran? Syria? The Middle East could mean anywhere over there.

A light-colored sports car sped around the hangar in a flash of dangerous speed. It raced wildly across the grass strip and onto the paved runway. It almost seemed alive, rushing after the plane with great urgency. But the plane was already turned around and gathering speed for the take-off.

The car was on a certain collision course with the huge, winged structure. Just before sudden impact the giant bird roared into the heavens and the lone occupant of the car leapt onto the dark, empty runway.

I gasped when I saw the luminous white hand wave skyward.

Matthew!

CHAPTER NINE

He stood there a long time, his head tilted back and his gaze directed upward into the dark heavens. There was no light to illuminate his face, but I could see the whiteness of his skin against the dark background. What was he feeling? Why had he come?

The cargo plane was gone, swallowed by the expanse of black sky. Another plane was coming in for a landing, and the roar of jets vibrated endlessly into my empty thoughts. The tiny, square windows were all lighted and I could clearly see the passengers inside. They all belonged somewhere, to someone, and all I could think was that I was alone. The world was a human world, the time of myth and legend was gone. How could I continue without my friend? Is there a place for me among my undead kindred?

Matthew got back into his car and slowly drove in my direction. I held my breath, hoped that he hadn't seen me, but knew he already had. His car inched along the grass strip and then pulled beside my van. He did not stop, but slowed and I could see his face clearly. We held each other's gaze for just a moment, but the moment was enough to share a common, deep-rooted feeling. Sadness.

There was more between Matthew and Elijah than I had ever dared dream. Despite my deep loathing of him, I had to know. I pulled out and followed him, hoping to be discreet, hoping to just watch him and perhaps find out where he slept each day.

His silver-metallic Ferrari was easy to tail. At first I stayed a few cars back but then grew bold and pulled right up behind him. His license plates were South Carolina and personalized with EARL IV.

Was I to believe that he was from the British aristocracy? Could be. After all, he was born in the seventeenth century when England was ruled by kings.

Knowledge. My need for it had never been so great.

I slammed on the brakes and sent Bong flying into the dashboard. Matthew's car had gone through the light and was making a right-hand turn farther up the road.

"I'm going to lose him, Bong," I said, gripping the steering wheel and willing the light to change.

Bong let out a whimper and arranged himself back onto the passenger seat where he could hang his head out the window and let the breeze flap his big, loose jowls.

At last the light turned green and I switched lanes so I could make the same right turn and hopefully find him. Traffic was still pretty heavy, and I tried to remember what night this was. Time was somewhat irrelevant to me. Since eternity stretched farther than my mind could comprehend, the days and weeks no longer meant anything. But by the amount of traffic I guessed it must be Friday or Saturday night.

There was no sign of the silver Ferrari, and I was crammed along with the other vehicles at the neck of the bridge that merged into two lanes from a four-lane access. I peered along the tops of the cars in line in front of me. The bridge rose into a small hill, the only hills that the low country of South Carolina can offer, and I could not see beyond the ridge. But as we crested the manmade concrete and steel slope, the traffic dipped below me and I saw his car again in the distance.

I weaved into the left-hand lane to a blare of a horn and the squeal of brakes, and then I weaved back into the right lane, again trying in vain to close the widening gap between us.

The bridge ended and the road opened up into four lanes, two curved off to the left and the other two to the right. Matthew went right and I stayed with him.

We were not in a good section of Charleston. The houses,

156

though large enough, were in a state of decay. I had never before ventured this far north on the peninsula and found it hard to believe that this was still Charleston. It could have been any city, the romantic old-world charm of historic downtown was not here among these dilapidated buildings.

He made another turn onto Spruill Avenue, hooker haven. The ladies of the night were out in full force this evening, and it didn't take Matthew long to find a victim. His car swung alongside the curb. A buxom redhead leaned against the car, nodded casually, and climbed in.

I stayed far enough behind to not look suspicious, but I'm sure Matthew knew I was there. At the very next red light I saw the redhead lean over toward him and witnessed the unmistakable posture of a feeding vampire. She rocked against him while the opposing traffic light went from green to yellow, and before it changed to red, and our light to green, the victim was out of his car, staggering along the sidewalk in a dazed, bewildered state.

Another block, another victim. Again Matthew drank in the quiet solitude of a traffic light and again left his victim staggering alongside the curb.

My own hunger was rising but not to the point of doing what Matthew was doing. I could not believe he was being so blatantly open with his feeding. And to leave his victims right out on the curb, this was not only foolish, but reckless as well.

He pulled over again, his third victim chosen. She was a petite black girl wearing a skintight, dark leather skirt that was slit so high along the thigh it was obvious she had no underwear on. She glanced back over her shoulder before she climbed into Matthew's car and I saw the tall, slender black man who must have been her pimp. His eyes met mine, and before I realized it I had contact with him and was bringing him closer to my van. I wanted to know how he could exploit these girls, how he could lower them to accept his false morals.

The light changed, and the flow of traffic made me release him. He stumbled forward a moment and reached out toward my van. The look on his face told me that he knew I

157

was somehow different, that I had reached into his mind and touched him with my power. He smiled and I caught the reflection of a gold tooth in the side mirror.

What did he think I was? What did any of the mortals with whom I made this special contact think? I did not lead them to believe anything. I never force-fed images to them. In fact, all I did was empty their minds and make them accept that emptiness as peace. And after I had my fill of their blood, they were left with empty peace and the fleeting memory of goodness, that was always my goal.

What was Matthew leaving them with? He pulled up to the next light and this time I was right on his bumper. He caught my glance in his rearview mirror and stared back at me while he pulled number three closer to him. I maintained contact with him, noticing the difference in his look. The mischievous fire did not spark when he drew in his victim. His eyes were empty, souless, dead.

His gaze fell upon his intended, and he went visibly rigid as he sucked upon her life. She arched against him, and I could see her small mouth making unheard moans.

When the green arrow lit up for the left-hand turn across traffic, he pushed her away and leaned across her body to open the car door. She stumbled out and walked away, teetering upon the high spiked heels that she wore.

Victim four was picked up three blocks farther down the street. She was an anorexic-looking waif. Her long dark hair was hanging limply against her bare shoulders, and her eyes held a faraway, forlorn look. But she eagerly accepted Matthew's invitation and climbed into the Ferrari.

How many was he going to take? How long was he going to continue? He had already fed enough for four vampires and the very thought of all that blood was nauseating even in my state of hunger.

This time he did not take her at the traffic light. He turned right and sped away, trying to put distance between himself and me. He was zigzagging back into the historic section of Charleston with his young victim, and he was toying with me. Just when I thought I had lost him he would reappear, beckoning me to follow. I grew angry with his game, but still continued to play. I needed to learn his rules, Elijah was gone and Matthew was now the only one of my kind that I knew. He had me at a great disadvantage.

He drove with care, making sure he was far enough away from me but not losing me. He made a left-hand turn on Legare Street and I lost sight of him when the narrow road jogged abruptly before heading south again. I slowed down, he had to be around somewhere.

The almost silent sound of a closing car door brought me to a stop. Bong pricked his ears forward and tilted his head out the window, listening. Laughter. Matthew's laughter.

I pulled my van beside the curb and peered past the iron bars that fenced off the property. He was leading his young victim along the brick path that wound through his lovely little courtyard, up to the great piazza of his fine old Charleston home.

Bong began to whine. I hooked the leash to his collar and made him wait until I was out of the van. He jumped down and immediately began to sniff the old mounting block that was green with moss and cracked with age. I stood upon it to get a better glimpse of Matthew's house. I didn't care whether or not he saw me as it was very clear he didn't care that I was and had been following him.

Yellow roses were in bloom and hung heavily against the iron fence that topped the brick wall separating his yard from the tourist-traveled sidewalk. The flower beds were full of pansies and impatiens; meticulously pruned low shrubs made neat borders along the walkway. The tiny area of grass was circular in shape, and in the center of the miniature lawn was a small marble statue of a little girl with a fawn. A soft yellow spotlight illuminated the artwork and I was struck with the poignant beauty of this singular piece.

A light came on in the interior of the house, but it was hard to tell which room they were in as the house sat sideways upon the lot, like so many homes in Charleston do. I was gazing at the double piazzas and thinking how easy it would be to enter his house from these great porches. Bong pulled against the leash, begging to move on.

I stepped down from the mounting block and walked with

159

Bong along the length of Matthew's brick-and-iron wall. We reached the narrow double gate of iron that closed off his driveway. The Ferrari was parked just inside the gate, the engine pinged with heat against the cool night air.

The gate was an elaborate mosaic of curls and interlocking circular designs. Large brick gateposts towered above the gate, and more ironwork rose up from the tops of these pillars to form a twisted semicircle of black above the driveway. Wisteria had entwined itself along the cold iron, and the purple grapelike flowers dropped in a quiet shower as the breeze swayed them toward the yard.

Medieval-looking lamps hung on either side of the overhanging iron semicircle and twentieth-century lightbulbs burned brightly inside. The light illuminated a shiny brass plate that was set into the brick gatepost. My fingers traced the cold carved number of his home. Twenty-eight.

My hunger was fast becoming a driving passion and I didn't linger near Matthew's home very long before taking Bong for his walk, and me for a hunt.

Since being shot in the head, Bong had acquired a habit of walking right up against my leg and he constantly veered to the left. His back pushed against my hip and I had to push him back to the right so that we were navigating in a fairly straight line down the sidewalk. Besides this tendency to walk toward the left, his accident had left him with no other scars. The bullet hole was completely healed.

His second accident, however, left him without a left eyeball. Maybe this contributed to his veering left, I would never know for sure. One thing I did know was that his eyeball did not reappear after the swelling and cuts had healed. His eyelid was closed and droopy and gave him a forlorn look that demanded sympathy. All the better for attracting victims to me.

We pushed each other left and right like a couple of drunken sailors until we ended up in White Point Gardens, the place where I had confronted Matthew and his bleached blond slut, and the same place where I had been fatally drained by him. I walked Bong to the center of the park and climbed the stairs into the gazebo.

Usually just sitting and waiting brought a victim my way, and I never minded that most of my victims really meant me harm, in one way or the other. After all, a pretty girl sitting alone in the middle of a dark night was only inviting trouble, wasn't she? Often Bong would scare away victims and I would force him to hide somewhere nearby, a game he had learned to enjoy. Tonight the hunting looked grim. I could see no lone victim, only couples or groups. But I decided to wait and arranged myself on the steps of the gazebo that faced out to the water and just sat there, watching people in the darkness.

Bong did what he usually does after feeding to the bursting point, he fell asleep behind me on the wood floor of the gazebo. Soon I heard his soft, doggy whimpers and the swish, thud of his tail as he was swept away in his doggy dreams. Why did I never dream? Even a nightmare would be fun in place of my deathly slumber. Perhaps *I* was the nightmare, and nightmares are for other people's dreams.

I sat there a long time, thinking. Elijah was probably over the middle of the Atlantic Ocean by now. I hoped to one day be with him again, but my inner voice told me that I never would, he was gone and like so many things in life would become a good but fading memory.

A breeze picked up and blew in from the point. The sea was calm tonight. The sound of water gently lapping against the stone sea wall that surrounded and made up the Battery lulled me into a peacefully dull state of mind. When I finally cleared my thoughts and sharpened my senses, I found that the night had grown late and the park had grown empty. I pulled at Bong's leash, and he stirred awake with a woeful moan. We both stood together and stretched. My hunger, unsatisfied, had dulled but was not forgotten. Bong's swollen, overfed look had subsided a great deal during his nap.

"No sense in waiting around here any longer, Bong, let's go home," I said.

Bong shook himself, and his paws flew out from beneath him, momentarily knocking him off balance. He quickly recovered and followed me down the stairs.

When we got back to Matthew's house the iron gates

were open, and as I approached I saw that the Ferrari was gone. I *had* to take a look inside his house. It was as simple as that. I had to see how he lived.

Bong was hesitant, he wanted to get in the van and go home. But I tugged at his leash and he obeyed, walking beside me with his great back banging into my hip.

The brick drive led to a brick walkway and up to the side door of the lower piazza. The door was painted black, the house and the great pillars of the piazzas were white. I turned the old brass door handle and stepped onto the wooden deck of the great porch.

From the long piazza Matthew's narrow side yard and rear yard were visible. Like the front, the place was a virtual garden spot. He no doubt had a gardener, and a very good one by the neatly groomed appearance of his yard. I crept quickly by the first large window and glimpsed into the darkness beyond the open drapes. The house appeared empty.

I reached the front door, which for all intents and purposes was situated on the side of the house, and stopped. The curved brass handle was cool against my cold skin. I tested the lock, the door swung inward inviting me into the dark, cavernous interior.

I did not go inside immediately but took a moment to study the fine old woodwork and the carved detail that comprised the doorframe. It was a grand entrance, a southern style that reflected a simpler, more elegant time.

Two large weeping fig trees graced the entrance, and the white marble containers they were planted in added warmth and charm to the place. I turned and faced the yard. A semicircular marble stairway led down onto the manicured lawn. More statuary pieces were arranged among the flowerbeds, and large azalea bushes graced the fenceline of the property. Though the yard was small, it held a grand statement of elegance. I loved it as much as I loathed its owner.

Bong pulled me back to the front door, his own curiosity led him across the threshold and into the foyer. I followed cautiously, tuning my senses to any sign of movement. There was none.

I pushed the front door closed and scanned the dark interior of Matthew's home. How I wished I could dare to turn on the lights. Even in the darkness the place appeared to be a stately mansion, like those I had drooled over in *Connoisseur* magazine. The heavy scent of antiquity sent chills through me. A thief would have great fun in this house of treasures. Why no security?

A muffled noise drew my attentions away from the Oriental, hand-painted crackled wine jar and other curios that adorned the top of a beautiful lacquered sheet iron commode.

Bong was halfway up the grand circular stairway before I hit the first step. My hand stayed on the smooth, dark wood of the banister and my feet landed quietly upon the thick wool runner that covered the stairs. The runner was dark, but I saw a floral, or perhaps paisley design of yellow or gold. At the top of the stairway the runner became a carpet that ran the length of the long hall.

Bong was sitting patiently outside a closed door. His head was cocked to one side, listening. I stopped and listened too. The sound was sad and human. Matthew was not in there. I turned the marble doorknob and pushed the door gently inward. A flow of light seeped out into the dark hall and I stepped quickly into its glow and shut the door before my intrusion might be known.

It was a bedroom, decorated in soft shades of peach, pink, and mauve. My immediate attention was drawn to the center of the room, where a large four-poster, carved-and-gilt walnut bed stood. The anorexic waif that Matthew had brought to his home was lying upon pink satin sheets. A wide piece of white adhesive tape covered her mouth; her arms and legs were spread outward and tied securely to each bedpost. Except for a fine cover of sweat that bathed her pink skin, she was naked.

Bong approached the bed. She had not seen us yet and was busy trying to wrench her arm free from the crude cotton rope bindings.

Bong poked her in the side with his cold nose and she screamed a wild, muffled scream of complete terror. Her head turned my way and her brown eyes opened wider with fear. If she knew what Matthew was, then the brightly lit interior of this room told her what I was. My white skin absorbed the light and reflected it back with a preternatural glow that was unmistakably alien.

I stepped beside the large bed. She was completely mad with fear and began to pull away from me as far as the rope bindings would permit. Her long brown hair was stuck to the sweat around her brow and the edges of the adhesive tape had peeled back a little to show the red, irritated skin beneath.

"I'm not going to hurt you," I told her. I wanted to touch her and reassure her but knew that my death-cold skin would only frighten her more. I looked for a tissue, but could not see any, so I used the edge of the fine satin sheet to mop the sweat from her face. Holding the sheet between my fingers and her skin, I started to tear the adhesive tape away. "I'll get you out of here," I promised.

Her eyes narrowed into a more normal appearance, but they were frightfully bloodshot and glazed. She was obviously on some kind of drug and from the wild outbursts of eye movement and the visible trembling, she was in the stages of a withdrawal.

I pulled slowly on the tape and she winced with pain. I had just decided to yank it quickly when a door banged shut somewhere downstairs.

Bong growled and started for the door. The girl's eyes grew wide again, and fear blazoned in the muddy brown irises.

"Damn," I said. I pulled the sheet from under her body and swiftly draped it over her nakedness. Her muffled screams started again, with more urgency than before. I turned away from her, grabbed hold of Bong, and looked for a place to hide.

Matthew was already on the stairway. I knew it was him because there was no human scent, no human sounds. There was also no place to hide that was big enough for me and a Great Dane.

I looked back to the girl, and she made a frantic motion

with her eyes and head toward the door on the far side of the room. I swept Bong up into my arms and flew across the bedroom into the darkness beyond the doorway that I hoped would be an alternative exit. It was not. It was a bathroom. There wasn't even a window from which I might attempt to crawl out. I pulled the door shut but left a small crack from which I could watch. Then I forced Bong to the floor and clamped my hand around his big muzzle until he quieted and remained that way.

Matthew entered the room. My heart was pounding so hard that I clutched vainly at my chest to silence the internal cacophony. He definitely looked directly at the bathroom door before turning his back and his attention to the young girl.

"Well, my dear, I hope that your moments of solitude have calmed you," Matthew said, and he reached toward the bed and pulled the sheet away. "I paid good money for you and I want you to be lucid when I take you."

He moved around the bed, and I could see his face clearly from my hidden position. He studied the girl's naked body a long while but from a distance. She began to cry. Her tears slid along her temple and dripped onto the sheets, making big dark spots that grew larger as the salty flow nourished them.

Suddenly he stepped closer, towering over the bed. She shrank away from him but still he did not touch her. He held her in his gaze, and his hand went to the pocket of his navy-blue blazer. With no emotion whatsoever, he dropped something onto her bare chest and I saw that it was a cockroach.

It crawled over her left nipple and down the underside of her small breast. She writhed wildly, trying to knock it off, but the ropes held her too tightly and she was unable to turn far enough on her side to dislodge it.

I looked away from the bug to Matthew. His gaze had not left her face. He did not follow the path of the cockroach as I did but stared intently into her eyes, drinking up her wild terror.

The cockroach ran down the flat surface of her belly and

became ensnarled in the thick tuft of pubic hair. She began to bounce her hips forward in a provocatively sexual movement, but the roach would not be shaken.

"What's wrong, Carol, do you think there are bugs crawling on you?" Matthew asked.

She made a pathetic gurgling sound.

"It's only the DT's, darling. You'll be over them soon enough," he said, and dropped another roach upon her chest.

I watched the bug while it crawled along the shallow curve of her throat and disappeared into the hair at the nape of her neck. She picked her head up and slammed it back against the pillows and then frantically looked in the direction of the bathroom where I was concealed.

What was he gaining from all this? I tried to see the look upon his face, but his head was bent forward and shadows covered his face like a mask of evil.

His hand went again to his pocket and I could suffer no longer with the poor girl. The third roach was falling. I moved in a blinding burst of speed, caught the bug between my thumb and finger, and squeezed it dead.

"That's enough," I said. My voice was a dark, angry hiss.

Matthew looked across the bed at me. A slight smile twitched on the edge of his small, perfect lips but he repressed it and twisted it into an angry leer.

"Are you going to stop me?" he asked.

Our gaze was locked and I felt the power, the ancient power that he commanded. The very color of his turquoise-blue eyes was unsettling, especially since I'm sure that the last time I had seen him his eyes had been a light coppery brown. But I tried not to dwell on this and repositioned myself so that I could assert myself over him.

"Yes, I *am* going to stop you," I said.

"And how might you attempt this?" he asked. I detected a note of wonder in his speech.

"Bong, here," I called.

With one flying leap Bong landed beside me. I grabbed hold of his collar and had to restrain him from flying over

166

the bed at Matthew. His dark lips were curled back and an unearthly, guttural snarl rose from deep inside his wide chest. Only my final command was needed to send him in a vicious attack against Matthew.

"I see the demon Dane has survived, though he is starting to look a tad ragged," Matthew said.

He was trying to make light of the situation but his fatal mistake was a half step backward and I knew his fear of Bong was complete.

"That damned Dane has made you a legend before your time. The stories of your vampire dog have spread among our kind up and down the eastern coast," he said.

The mention of "vampire dog" and "our kind" sent the girl into another struggling bout of frenzied terror.

"Am I supposed to be impressed?" I asked him.

He only shrugged his shoulders.

Silence.

I really had no idea what I would do to stop him. He sensed this and reclaimed his half step toward the bed.

"How *are* you going to stop me?" he asked again.

My own eyes narrowed with hatred. "I'm going to kill you. I'm going to drink you dry until your veins are left hollow and collapsing inside you," I said.

The girl, overcome by our otherworldly conversation, had lapsed into a catatonic stare. She was still conscious and I saw her chin, all pinched up like a peach pit, trembling out of the corner of my eye.

"By the starved look of you I have no doubt you could do it, but do you really think it would destroy me?"

Bong lunged forward and almost broke free of my grasp. His big paws landed on top of the girl's bare stomach, and as I pulled him back his nails dug into her skin and left angry red welts.

Matthew backed away, uncertain if I could control my dog. I was again at the advantage but still did not know what to do. I wanted answers to so many questions. If I turned Bong loose on him and killed him I would never gain the knowledge I sought.

I remembered Elijah saying that Matthew would know

what I feared but now I sensed that Matthew knew what I wanted. He looked from the girl to Bong to me.

"At least give a condemned creature a last wish," he said.

"What did you have in mind? A last meal perhaps?" I nodded my head toward the girl. Her eyes stared straight up at the ceiling. If she was hearing us she made no attempt to acknowledge our words.

"I want to show you something," he said, and he started to turn for the door.

"Bong," I yelled.

Matthew wheeled around expecting an attack from my dog. The fear in his face was serious. I almost laughed. I had not called out for Bong to attack, only to stop his pulls upon me. I wondered why Matthew was so afraid of the dog. If I could hold Bong back in mid-lunge, surely Matthew could defend himself.

"I give you my word this is not a trick," Matthew said.

I nodded and pulled Bong around the edge of the four-poster bed. His hip butted against mine and forced me to bang into the heavy footboard. We followed, somewhat clumsily, as Matthew led us back down the beautiful, sweeping stairway.

We wound through the darkness to the rear of his house, and came to a large double doorway. I waited while Matthew pulled the heavy ornate doors open. He entered the room first and turned on the lights.

I gasped when I saw my unexpected reflection in the heavy gilted Chippendale mirror that hung on the far wall. It was centered above an antique serpentine Hepplewhite server and graced on either side by lovely dried floral arrangements.

This room was as masculine as the bedroom upstairs had been feminine. The floor was inlaid marble, but the pattern of the black-and-white tiles was hidden beneath a thick Oriental rug. The wool of the rug was gold and black; the pattern an interesting floral motif.

I counted four Louis XVI salon chairs that appeared to still be covered with the original silk brocade. A Pepys-style bookstand towered against the wall and was filled to capacity. Next to the bookstand stood a Queen Anne walnut-and-inlaid sideboard. Curios of pewter, silver, bronze, marble, and crystal were scattered about the room. The wall covering was dark paneling, mahogany. And the oil paintings had to be from the Old Masters.

A lovely serpentine couch with clawed feet was strategically centered in front of the huge fireplace. Matthew had moved over to the mantel, and I watched as he reached up to pull the protective brown cover from the large painting that adorned the fieldstone wall of the interior chimney.

"Before you destroy me, I want you to know about Maria," he said, and with a grand sweeping movement unveiled the portrait.

I was physically stunned. It was an old painting, a beautiful painting. But it was a painting of me.

"What kind of trick is this?" I demanded.

"You recognize the similarities," he said.

I moved across the room, dragging Bong with me. The painting appeared to be old, but it could have been stained to look that way.

"When did you have this done, and why?" I asked. The oils were crackled along the canvas, but that could have been reproduced also.

Matthew stepped away from the fireplace and positioned himself between the couch and me, keeping his attention alert to Bong. But Bong was no longer hostile, my own fear had been replaced by curiosity and this was picked up by my canine companion.

"The painting was commissioned in 1673. It was a wedding gift for my sister. She was to be married in September of that year. I paid a hefty sum of 28 pounds 10 shillings for it. But it was well worth it, certainly captured her spirit, wouldn't you say?" he said.

The portrait was done from the waist up. The emerald gown was cut low and white lace spilled over the bodice giving the appearance of more cleavage than the girl actually had. The overall look, though demure, showed an almost intense boldness or rebelliousness that was very unlike

169

portraits of ladies of that time. The long auburn hair hung in loose curls about her bare shoulders. Her face was finely chiseled with high cheekbones, narrow nose, and delicately small lips. Even the green eyes were my eyes.

Her jewelry was large, expensive, and befitting her stature. The tiara of emeralds and diamonds matched the choker around her neck. Her hands were visible, neatly folded one on top of the other upon a chair back. Instead of an emerald ring a large sapphire adorned her ring finger, and I peered closer at the painting wondering if this could be the same ring Lady Diana had chosen from the tray to be her engagement ring.

"This is Maria," I said.

"Maria Abigail Anne, my beloved sister," he said, and I heard a longing for the past echo in his voice.

"Is this why you wanted me to die. I reminded you too much of your long-dead sister?"

"I never intended for you to die," he said, and there was a bewildered tone of shock in his voice. "I had to be sure you were strong enough to survive."

"You left me to die," I said, and turned to face him.

He smiled a sly slow smile. "I saw to it that you had enough of my blood to sustain you."

I wanted to be angry with him, but the inevitable happened. The sun was soon rising and my body began to grow weak, my senses dull and groggy. I glanced at Bong. He had already succumbed to the sleep and was curled up at my feet upon the fine Oriental rug.

"I was sicker than a dog for three days. You never came to me. Elijah saved me."

"I came to you every night, only you didn't know it. I sent Elijah to you."

"But why?" I asked again, and my voice cracked with tired emotion.

"Because you are more than a reminder of my sister, you are family."

I covered my hands over my ears, not wanting to hear any more. This monster standing before me, this torturer of young girls was not and never would be family. The

170

Trenton line that I came from had no skeletons, no vampires, in the closet.

The room began to swirl, and the sleep began to ascend upon me. I reached down and gathered Bong into my arms and started to walk away.

Matthew stepped in front of me and reached out to put his hands on my shoulders but I sluggishly pushed him aside.

"You can't make it back to Beaufort. Stay here. You haven't fed, come upstairs and take the girl," he said.

I was too tired, too shocked, and too afraid to stay with him.

"You'll die if the sun lights upon your skin," he warned, and he looked at my scarred hand.

"Then I'll die," I said. I staggered by him and hurried awkwardly for the door. Bong was dead weight in my arms, and my own weakness was draining my energies.

Matthew followed me to the front door but did not attempt to cross the threshold. The eastern sky was already growing light. This was the latest I had ever been awake, and as the barely perceivable light of dawn fell across my skin the tingling sensation began.

I remembered the day at the motel when the tingling grew into a hot itchy pain, and I began to run for my van. I heard Matthew slam the door of his house. He was not going to follow, his own destruction would also be found in the light of day.

I had to set Bong down upon the sidewalk to slide the van door open. I quickly righted my coffin, it was still turned topsy-turvy from the other night, closed the Levolor blinds on the van windows, and lifted Bong inside. The coffin was wedged tightly against the back of the van and the swiveling captain's chair, but it fit. I pushed Bong to the foot of the satin interior, locked the van doors, and crawled in with only enough strength left for me to pull the coffin lid closed.

CHAPTER TEN

The lid of my coffin was raised and the yellow flicker of a fire burning softly nearby greeted me as I awoke from my slumber. I stretched against the cool, slippery surface of satin and rolled over onto my back. Bong was already gone.

I studied the high, lofty ceiling. It was plastered in such a way that the concentric circles gave the effect of a pebble that had been thrown into a still pond. Of course, Matthew had moved me into his house, the smell of antiquity surrounded me and calmed me.

I didn't want to get up. I stared at the ceiling for a long time, watching the way the firelight danced along the bumps and puddles of plaster. As surely as I know when the sun is setting, I knew Matthew was in the room, but still I was content to just rest quietly in my private oasis of solitude.

Maria Abigail Anne. She was my double, my twin. But centuries had separated us. Now we were brought together by Matthew and for what?

Family. His family was my family. I remembered my grandmother telling family stories about Uncle so and so, Crazy Cousin Someone, and Poor Aunty Can't Think Of Her Name. My family was a big one to be sure, but not a close one. Except for my mother, father, brother, and sister I had met the others on rare occasions only and was so young I didn't care anyway.

And now I was thrust into immortality with a crazy perverted sadist who called himself family. My family. I did not believe Matthew was lying. The portrait was too much evidence.

172

Matthew neared my open coffin, but I still made no attempt to rise. His closeness was like a draft and I wondered if I was felt by him in this way. His face appeared over the coffin edge. The dark curls of his hair did not stay in place as he lowered his head closer to mine. His eyes were a noxious green color this night, but I found myself drawn to the gentle look in his gaze.

He bent closer still, and his cold lips touched softly upon my forehead.

I thought of grabbing him in a headlock and wrenching his neck. I thought of spitting into his face. But I just remained motionless and held his gaze again as he righted himself above me.

"You are a late riser, I could fix that if you like," he said, and his smile was affectionate.

He expected an answer, but I didn't give him one.

My lack of response frustrated him, and I watched as his fingers went to his hair and he began to twirl a small brown lock around his index finger. It struck me as a prissy thing to do and I had to hold back the laughter that rang silently in my mind.

He kept twirling that piece of hair and looking at me with a bewildered expression. Finally his finger stopped and he pulled the lock of hair straight, but once set free it bounced into a defensive little curl above his ear.

"Your dog left earlier," he said.

No kidding, I thought. But then I had another thought that perhaps he had done something to Bong. Maybe even killed him.

"I didn't try to stop him," he said. And the words were almost an apology.

His frustration was beginning to turn into a malevolent rage and I could feel it seething within him. But his anger was not directed to me, it was turned inward.

"Damn it, girl, why don't you rise up from there?" he said.

He was no more than a child having a temper tantrum, and I was doing something he could not control. A vampire just doesn't raise up another vampire from the coffin, it's, well . . . it's unethical.

And I don't know why I didn't rise up. The only reason I can clearly see now is that it is a personal thing, rising up from one's coffin and his standing there was preventing me from doing it. To put it on a more human level, it's like having to urinate very badly but not being able to because someone is standing in the bathroom watching.

His hands were resting on the polished wood edge of my coffin. His long fingers with meticulously square-cut nails curled tighter and tighter until the delicate white skin over his joints and under his nails began to flood with pink. His grip released and he flung his open hands up in an exasperated motion and walked away.

My moment had come. I leapt out of the coffin and slammed the lid down with a bang. With my arms outstretched I grabbed both brass handles and lifted it like a giant briefcase.

Matthew followed me to the big double doors, but when I had to drop the coffin to push the doors open he did not offer to help. I juggled the doors and slid my coffin across the smooth marble floor and into the hallway. When he realized I was firm with my intentions of leaving he spoke.

"Ainjul, I thought maybe we could talk," he said, and when he spoke my name it sounded French.

I didn't want him to call me Ainjul. That was the name Elijah had given me. But then again, I didn't want to be called Angela because I wasn't her anymore either.

He started to say something else, but the doorbell rang and he frantically shoved my coffin back through the double doors and closed them to conceal it. For a brief moment I thought he might shove me behind the doors too. He glanced at his watch, a gold-and-diamond Rolex.

"Expecting someone for dinner?" I asked.

He laughed, and his face became the handsome tall stranger. He dug his hand into the pockets of his white slacks and pulled out a wad of money. He peeled back two fives and a couple of ones and put the wad back.

I followed him to the front door.

The door was open only a crack, and the human scent was overpowering. I was drained and needed badly to be fulfilled. The last blood I had taken was Elijah's two nights ago. And the hunger I had repressed twice last night gnawed inside me with a self-survival vengeance. I had denied myself too long.

I pushed past Matthew and stopped in front of the pizza delivery boy. His blond hair was plastered against his brow with sweat and his face was spattered with small freckles. Such an innocent-looking boy. Probably got good grades in school.

Matthew paid him and waited until the boy unzipped the black thermal bag. Pizza smell flooded the air and I gagged. It was totally revolting. Maybe it wouldn't have been such a vulgar smell had I not been so hungry myself.

The boy handed Matthew the pizza and Matthew handed the boy a tip.

I waited until the boy was off the porch and out of the courtyard before I removed my hand from my mouth and nose.

"You're not going to eat that, are you?" I had to cover my face again, the smell was overpowering.

"Carol ordered it. I do suppose it's her last meal," he said, and he winked.

I turned away from him and started down the lovely marble steps that sparkled under the porch light.

"Where are you going?" he asked.

"Home. Back to Beaufort," I answered. I had forgotten the van keys and again faced him with my hand outstretched. "If you will please give me the keys to my van I'll be on my way."

"Carol is for you, come back inside and take her," he motioned with a shrug toward the door.

I thought about the poor girl tied to the bed upstairs.

"I can hunt very adequately. Please, give me the keys."

He edged back into the house, disappeared from my view, then came back out and tossed the keys to me.

"You can't stay in Beaufort," he said. His smooth white face clouded over and his handsome smile faded. His finger

175

went to the lock of hair and he began twisting it round and round and round.

"Elijah gave me his house and I am going to stay there."

His finger stopped. He pulled the curl straight and I watched it bounce back into position above his ear.

"It was not Elijah's house to give. Elijah owned nothing. Even that old Chevy was mine. That damned nigger never cared about anything but himself. If it weren't for me, he would have lived in the old shack where he took you your first night."

"Don't you ever call him that again," I said.

"What? A nigger? He was a nigger when I met him and a nigger when I left him. It's all you Yankees that have a problem . . ."

"Why are you making me hate you more?" I asked.

"Well, well, well. I struck a nerve. You loved him, didn't you?"

I turned away. Matthew didn't deserve an answer. Matthew didn't deserve anything.

"And I want the van back before morning. It's mine too, you can check the registration papers in the glove compartment if you don't believe me."

I walked away from him and he was shouting after me.

"If you don't bring it back I will come and take it."

I heard the front door slam.

I climbed into the van, but before starting the engine I opened the glove compartment. The owner's manual and registration papers were neatly contained in a clear vinyl envelope. I turned on the overhead map light and slid the papers out. The small circle of light fell on his signature, C. Matthew F. Trenton.

Was it really possible that even the family name had remained unchanged down through the centuries? My mother's maiden name was Schafer, but Dad was from the Trenton family. I could not see the slightest resemblance between my father and Matthew. Dad was fair-skinned, red-haired, and built like a linebacker. And all the Trenton's bore these characteristics. I took after the Schafer side of the family, the only hint of Trenton was the red, auburn, high-lights in my hair and the fat little Trenton toes.

And why had Elijah lied to me? Why had he claimed to own the house and 'Melia.

"Elijah, damn it, why didn't you tell me," I said aloud to no one.

Driving away from Charleston and Matthew gave me time to think.

It grew obvious in my mind that Matthew had taken care of Elijah's needs, and in turn Elijah's needs had become my needs. But something eluded me, what was the reason Elijah stayed? He had told me enough to lead me to believe he and Matthew were enemies. And why his sudden departure? Was it because he feared I was on the brink of discovering his secrets and his lies?

More than anything in the world I wished to talk to Elijah.

The two-hour drive south sped by and soon I was back on familiar roads. Elijah's neighborhood was quiet tonight. Out of habit I put my turn signal on and pulled into the driveway of the large ranch house were we had spent so many lovely evenings together.

The garage door was up. A small sports car was parked inside. If Matthew truly did own this house, and I had no reason to believe otherwise, then he must've rented it out. I was undecided about going in. Finally I cut the engine and stepped from the cool climate-controlled interior of the van into the humid warmth of the Carolina night.

Some of my things were inside. I say some because it was clearly Matthew who had been supplying me with the necessities. I never could picture Elijah out shopping for my clothes, and now since meeting Matthew I was sure of it. Nonetheless, I wanted the few items of clothing that were mine.

I entered the garage and knocked on the door that led into the den.

There was no answer.

I knocked again.

Still no answer.

177

My hand went to the doorknob. It was not locked. Cautiously, I opened the door.

The hall light was on and gave enough illumination for me to see a figure of a person on the couch, asleep.

I crept silently closer.

Music, soft, muted, and static was playing. The heavy bulk of headphones were visible along the pillow edge.

I drew closer still.

What a wonderful victim this was! My hunger rushed over me, commanding me to strike, but as my victim's face came clearly into view I pulled away.

Mr. Androgynous!

Matthew had set this up.

His beautiful black face was at peace. His eyes moved back and forth as he dreamed, the long, innocent lashes fluttered gently against his smooth skin.

I stood silently watching him, silently fighting the consuming flames that burned inside my empty veins. I stood on that threshold of desire for longer than even I could tolerate. The passion was a rushing sound of wind that whirled up from the depths of my being.

Wake up before I kill you, my mind shrieked but no words broke the silence.

His eyes stopped their rapid little movements and his body twitched. Had he heard me?

I began to bend over him.

He drew in a long, slow breath, and his eyes began to open.

My fangs thrust from my lower jaw and the trickle of blood from my own gums spurred the hunger.

He became electric and jolted with sudden energy back against the pillows. His eyes widened and he screamed.

With movement he never saw I ripped the headphones from his ears and pulled him up into a sitting position. But then I let him go and backed away.

"I told you not to seek me," I said.

He leaned back against the couch, obviously shaken.

"Matthew told me to come. He told me to take care of things here for a while," he said.

178

My guess was correct. But did Matthew really send him to watch the house or did he send him so that I would take him?

"Have you given serious thought to the everlasting life I can give you?" I asked.

"Yes." His answer was a soft but firm yes.

My need for blood was severe. If I took him could I give the blood back and make him a vampire without depleting myself? All I remembered was how drained Elijah had been after I had received his blood. When I made Bong I lost very little blood, but Bong was not human and did not clamp onto me with the same fervor which I had sucked up Elijah's blood.

I looked at Mr. Androgynous. He was subtly handsome, strangely beautiful. His smooth skin was more tan than black, and I wondered if after his transformation his color would darken to the polished effect that Elijah bore.

"What is your name?" I asked. Funny that I was contemplating making him immortal and I didn't even know his name.

"Chris," he answered, and slowly rose from the couch anticipating what was to come.

"Chris, there is no turning back. If you've made your decision I will oblige you. But be warned, once the deed is done it cannot be changed.

He nodded.

The hunger within me swelled.

"Let me explain what I'm about to do," I said, and I moved toward him.

His eyes, deep pools of earthy brown, showed patience. The expression upon his lovely face was intense.

"I will take your blood and then give it back to you."

Moving closer still I circled him slowly and came round to face him. He was just a bit shorter than I was and his head tilted back as he looked up into my eyes.

"You will be near death. When I give the blood to you, you must drink it or you will die. At first the blood will repulse you but very quickly the passion will take hold and you will devour the gift of my everlasting life," I explained.

His facial features softened as he mentally prepared himself.

"Your actual death will take several months. During this time you will be vulnerable to the perils all new vampires face, but I will explain these things to you as they occur."

Oh how calm, how serenely innocent he looked. If I had been approached this way I would be asking a million questions, but he remained silent, apparently his mind was made up. Every inconspicuous gesture he made showed an unfailing trust in me.

I reached out and unbuttoned his shirt, pushing the collar away from his neck.

He shuddered involuntarily when my icy hand touched his skin. He drew in a slow, deep breath.

"Tell me now if you are sure."

"Yes, I am sure," he said, and his eyes closed.

Gently I embraced him. This was how I would have wanted it to happen, slowly, with feeling.

He gave himself to me completely. The tender frailness of his human body pressed against mine. My lips went to the supple skin of his neck and sensed the throbbing vein buried there. Quickly, I bit upward.

The blood was hot against my cold tongue. I let it fill my mouth slowly, swallowed, and shivered with delight as the warm coppery taste slid down my throat. I began to drink steadily.

His arms encircled me, and as I sucked he tried to pull me closer, hugging me in rhythm to my pulls against his heart.

I prolonged our pleasures by pacing myself, but even this could not mask the death that approached. His heart began to slow, his arms grew weak and fell to his sides.

"Not yet," I whispered. My lips never left his skin.

I slowed my drinking, waiting for the moment when his heart would flutter. Every sense was tuned on him. Coldness crept into him, his breathing grew shallower. When his legs gave out I held him closer, supporting him against my increasing strength.

I concentrated on the heart sounds, Lub-dub, lub-dub.

A faint ringing sounded in my ears but his heart continued to beat.

Lub-dub, lub-dub, lub-dub, ring. ring.

My attentions shifted to the harsh jangle.

Ring, ring. Lub-dub, lub-dub. Ring, ring.

His heart was giving two beats between the rings and I almost missed the moment when the lub sound stopped and only little dub, dub, dubs fluttered inside his chest.

I withdrew, and eased him to the floor.

Ring, ring. Ring, ring.

The telephone!

Elijah! Who else would be calling here?

"Hold on, Chris, think only of the blood, think only of life."

His eyes were open and he blinked rapidly, trying to clear the glaze of death away.

I put my wrist to my mouth, ready to open my veins and give him his first taste of immortality.

Ring, ring. Ring, ring.

I looked down on Chris and then over to the white phone on the kitchen counter. I moved toward it, and Chris reached out for me.

RING. RING.

The sound was almost desperate now.

One quick leap and I had the receiver in my hand.

"Hello?"

"Ainjul, don't give him your blood."

The accent was British, softened by a slur of Old South.

Uncanny, damn uncanny that Matthew always knew things about me.

"But he's going to die," I said.

"Don't do it. Let him die," Matthew said.

I glanced over to Chris. He was still, too still. Maybe death had already begun to claim him.

"He's dying right now, I have to go to him." My voice was anxious. I started to put the receiver down.

"AINJUL," Matthew screamed over the line and I was overcome by confusion. "Please, don't give him the blood. Go up to the attic. Leave him."

The voice on the line took a new accent, one of deep melancholy, one of sadness and reserved desperation.

"Matthew, you don't understand. He's dying. I can't leave him here in the house and I can't touch him once he's . . ."

"Yes, I do understand. I will take care of it. Please. Leave him and go to you coffin. Sleep. Tomorrow he will be gone, I promise you."

"But . . ."

"Ainjul, listen. You will spoil a very precious thing if you give him your blood. Besides, it's too late now anyway."

The receiver dropped against my neck and I cradled it there as I looked at the death that slept upon the floor. It *was* too late. I heard Matthew's voice again, something about Bong. But I hung up and turned away from the shame I had left in the den.

As Matthew instructed, I climbed into the attic and found solace in my coffin. I rested against the smooth silk and was flooded with deep sadness. I had made a promise and had broken it. Chris had trusted me and I had killed him. His blood had given me new life, replenished my drying veins, lubricated my body with freshness and warmth.

To punish myself I pulled the lid down and let the suffocating darkness take me.

The remorse was still with me when I awoke. I only hoped Matthew had taken care of the body. Even before pushing up the coffin lid I heard voices below, and as I focused upon them I realized it was the television. I felt Matthew's presence in the house. It was like a cold, dark part of me. Never had I felt Elijah's presence in this manner. I wondered if it had anything to do with our family ties.

I took my time going downstairs. I wasn't in the mood for Matthew and his childish games. He had toyed with me long enough, and I wanted answers.

When I walked into the den only the flicker of the television lit the deep shadows of night. Ted Koppel was on, talking about a hostage who had been freed in Syria. Matthew was sitting on the edge of the couch, watching intently. I walked deliberately in front of him and turned it off. In the ensuing darkness I thought I saw Chris's body upon the floor.

"What did you do that for?" Matthew asked.

I turned, saw the whiteness of his face, and said, "I want some answers."

"This is important," he said.

For a brief moment I thought he was being sarcastic and my anger flared.

He brushed by me and turned the television back on.

"Damn it, I want some answers and I want them now," I shouted, and grabbed hold of his arm, pulling him toward me.

"Would you look at that. There he is," he said.

I glanced at the television. Behind a crowd of people pressing upon one another with cameras and microphones was the beaming black face of my old vampire friend.

The camera swung away from the crowd and zoomed in on a haggard-looking gentleman. Then the large face of Ted Koppel appeared.

"After four hundred fifty-seven days of captivity Mr. David Morgan is on his way home," Ted said.

"The old nigger really pulled it off, he really did it," Matthew said, and hugged me in an elated burst of joy, lifting me completely off the ground.

The image of Elijah's face stayed burned into my mind, and when Matthew released me I moved closer to the television, reaching out to touch the spot where I had seen his face among the crowd. Instead of Elijah, a team of Clydesdales trotted by and the announcer proclaimed, "This Bud's for you."

"What went on between you two?" I asked. My voice was barely a whisper, and I was asking Elijah but hoping Matthew would tell me.

"Isn't it about time you changed those clothes?" Matthew asked.

Either he hadn't heard me or he was ignoring me. I turned away from the television and faced him.

"I guess what I'm asking is, will you go out with me tonight?" he said.

I couldn't help but laugh. A hurt expression surfaced upon his face, and for the first time I saw that he was indeed vulnerable.

"You mean like a date?" I asked.

He shrugged. The vulnerable expression became shyness, and I was flattered but somewhat stunned that someone centuries old still held on to the age of chivalry.

His own dress was semiformal. His gray sport coat was tailored for an exact fit and the white turtle neck gave him a crisp, neat appearance. The crease in his black slacks was sharp. Only the shoes did not match his ensemble, a pair of high-top Reeboks. The little British flag emblazoned on them seemed appropriate.

"Are you copying Elijah's style or was he copying yours?" I asked, pointing down to his feet.

"When you've walked as many years upon this earth as I have, you'll learn to appreciate comfort."

He smiled again, but there as a faint look of sadness there and I knew the years had been lonely ones.

"Will you go?" he asked.

"No."

A cloud of anger and deep resentment flooded his startling blue eyes.

"Then at least come back to Charleston and collect your dog." The tone of his voice made it a command, and I was tired of being ordered by him.

"What do you want from me?" I asked.

He turned away. I heard the jangle of keys as he pulled them from his coat pocket. I felt the rejection that wavered inside him.

"Matthew, I am not your sister. And I'm not some stupid little girl who you can control. Immortality might bind us, but that is all."

"No, you are very wrong, Ainjul. That is not all," he said, and turned to face me.

"From my viewpoint it is," I said.

We studied each other for a silent moment that stretched into eternity. At last he spoke.

"What can I say to change your mind? What must I do?"

"I want answers. I want the truth," I said.

"Then ask and I shall tell you," he said.

This was the moment I had yearned for. To me he was a book of knowledge, and I wanted badly to open the pages and read the story that was hidden there.

"Why did you leave me to die? Why didn't you just come to me and explain? What was the point of making me suffer so?"

"I suffered with you," he said.

"Answer me!"

"If I had come to you and offered you everlasting life explaining to you the consequences it held, what would your answer have been?"

I had to think. I had to remember life, human life and the pains and pleasures that humans struggle with every day of their lives.

"I would have said no."

"And I could not bear that rejection," he said.

This was an answer I was not prepared for. I wanted to sit and think about it but he continued.

"When your mother married your father I felt a sense of completeness. It was as if time had come full circle. The Trenton name at last surfaced again in my family. The first time I saw you I knew it was more than fate. Even as a child you were so much like her. Your boundless spirit and carefree energy was her rekindled. I lost her, but I could not lose you."

The realization that he had known me, watched me since childhood was unsettling. And knowing that he had planned my destiny and taken control of my life angered me.

"Just how long did you watch me?"

He smiled as he recalled my past. The private moments of my life that should have been mine alone, not shared with him.

"I was there the night you told your little sister there was no Santa Claus," he said.

My mind wheeled back to that wintery night in Iowa.

My little sister was sitting in front of the living-room window, peering hopefully into the night sky. I was only in the second grade at that time, and I had found out there was no Santa Claus and hated her for still believing. She refused to believe me when I told her, so I took her into Mommy and Daddy's bedroom and showed her where all the toys were hidden. Boy, had I caught hell for that.

"And I was there the following night when you explained to her there was a Santa Claus but he couldn't possibly get to everybody's house in one night so he delivered presents earlier to the mommies and daddies to be sure everyone got their toys on Christmas morning. You were a precocious child."

"I was a brat," I said, and returned his smile.

"Remember your ballet recital? You played the part of a tree."

"Because I was a klutz," I explained, and laughed.

"But you were an elegant tree. You stood so straight and so still. I have a picture of you as a tree."

A deep longing to recapture those years filled me, and I was suddenly wishing that I could go home and see my family again.

"How come you didn't believe in Santa Claus but you held so much faith in the tooth fairy? I saw, on three occasions, the way you wrapped your lost baby teeth in a Kleenex and carefully tucked them under your pillow."

"The tooth fairy left money. And each tooth was worth more than the last. I wished I had a million teeth so I would be rich," I said.

"That explains it then," he said, and smiled. "Your prom gown was beautiful, but you were too tall in your high heels and your young escort was mad about that all night. What was his name? Michael?"

"Mike," I said.

"You could have done better than him. He was a real twit."

"Excuse me?"

"Doesn't really matter now. I was in the audience the

186

night of your graduation. Where did you go when the row in front of you stood up to accept their diplomas?''

God, I had forgotten that. I had to go to the bathroom so bad that I couldn't squirm any longer. The superintendent had talked forever, the principal talked forever, and the valedictorian rambled on so long my bladder was ready to burst. I had disappeared discreetly, even my parents hadn't noticed I was gone. But Matthew had.

"Shall I go on?" he asked.

"No," I said, though it was fun remembering all these moments again. "Why did you watch me?"

"Because I had to make sure nothing happened to you."

"You mean that if something . . . fatal had happened you would have saved me?"

He thought a moment. "Yes, I probably would have."

"You were my guardian angel, so to speak."

"You needed one. The games you played were dangerous. Hang gliding, rappeling off of rocky cliffs, hot air ballooning, I'm glad your boyfriend wouldn't go parachuting with you. I don't think even my blood could have revived you if you would have splatted on the ground from such a height."

"What about Elijah?" I asked. His knowledge of my past was beginning to get creepy. I didn't want to hear about all the nights he had watched me. I didn't want to hear how he violated my privacy.

"What about Elijah?" he asked.

"Why did you make him a vampire. He told me he never asked to receive E.L."

Matthew laughed. "E.L., is he still using that term?"

My look of disapproval cut his laughter short.

"Eber lastin' libe," he said with a mock gullah accent. "I didn't make him a vampire. I found him one night, cold, wet, and tired. He had tried to drown himself in the river, but of course he couldn't die that way. He had already received the blood, but it wasn't from me."

"But he told me . . ."

"He lied. Elijah's one flaw was his pathological lying. You know what I'm talking about. You've had three friends

187

who were pathological liars. They live in their own fantasies.''

Unfortunately I did, and I knew how they lied to get out of lying until even I couldn't separate the untruths. Nonetheless, I still loved Elijah and would welcome him back despite what Matthew was telling me.

''I did everything I could for Elijah. Perhaps his age is what kept confusing him. I will never understand him,'' he said softly.

''Then you didn't make him a vam—''

''I have never made another vampire, until I made you.''

''But you didn't make me. Elijah . . .''

''Yes, I did. When you bit into my palm I knew you had enough of my blood to sustain you. Elijah was only a receptacle for me. It was my blood he fed you that night on the boat. And it was my blood he continued to feed you after you were mortally wounded.''

''But why? Why did you do it that way?''

''Ainjul, I told you before, I could not bear to be rejected by you. I waited too long.''

Everything he was telling me was true. I could sense it as clearly as I could see the resemblance between myself and Maria Abigail Anne.

''Will you come with me?'' he asked again.

There was only one answer. I had opened the book and glimpsed at a few pages. I wanted to know more.

''Yes. I will come,'' I said.

CHAPTER ELEVEN

Before we left the house Matthew made a thorough check of all the windows and doors. I followed him, taking time to have a final look around. He didn't need to tell me; I knew once we drove out of Beaufort we would never return.

Matthew entered the bedroom that I had used. He turned on the light and crossed the room. I heard him slide the latch on the window and jiggle the frame to be sure it was locked, but my gaze fell upon the bed.

A lovely orchid skirt was draped across the spread. Around the hem was a delicate lace eyelet that accented the tiny white flower print. Next to the skirt was a beautiful knit white cotton sweater. And next to the sweater was a single white rose.

"Elijah," I said softly, and picked up the rose. Why did even this have to be a lie?

I buried my nose against the velvety softness of the still-unfolding petals and looked over to Matthew.

"I'm a hopeless romantic at heart," he said. "I hope you've enjoyed the clothes I've purchased. Please wear this tonight." He pointed to the outfit on the bed. "Maria looked so beautiful in orchid and white."

That longing, needing tone was in his voice, and I nodded.

He turned away from me, and as he walked out of the room he closed the door gently behind him.

I undressed quickly and put the outfit on. The skirt was full, and I twirled around feeling it swirl about my calves.

The sweater had a deep V front, and I tugged the loose yarn over my scar.

I found Matthew sitting at the large dining room table in the darkness. He was so still and so perfectly white that he appeared more of an apparition than a vampire. He could not see me but I heard him say, "You look so very beautiful this evening."

I hung back in the doorway, watching him. His expression was focused inward. He smiled slightly and nodded his head, his hand reached out for something that was not there and he pulled whatever the object was closer to him.

"There can never be another," he whispered.

Whatever role he was reliving, whatever scene was being replayed from his past did not include me, and suddenly I felt deeply embarrassed for having witnessed this private little act.

His hand, holding fast to the invisible object, rose into the air and his face turned upward. Though I was unable to see his vision, I imagined someone else there. Someone who was now leaving him.

"Never will there be another." His voice was riddled with yearning and anguish.

His hand, letting go of the object, fell in slow motion to the polished tabletop.

Another what? Another vampire?

I was so caught up in his actions I didn't realize I had stopped breathing. My first gulp of air was a loud, wheezing hiss.

Matthew leapt from the chair, wheeled in my direction, and nearly attacked.

I stepped away quickly but banged into the corner of the kitchen counter and fell flat back onto the smooth linoleum floor.

He peered down at me, his face became very animated as if searching for the right expression to put on. Finally he smiled, and the cleft in his chin began to grow shallow. He reached out his hand to help me up.

"You startled me," he said.

I took hold of his hand. It was cooler than mine, and the

skin had a rubbery feel to it. When I stood up I held his hand closer to inspect it.

The skin was different than mine. It was smooth. There was no trace of the ridges and waves making up fingerprints. All the extra little skin lines were gone. The only creases remaining were exactly where the hand folded and the fingers bent.

I let go of his hand and held my own hand up for comparison. My skin still held the familiar pattern of little triangles all over it.

"It is rather bizarre," he said.

I was shocked, horrified. He wasn't like me at all. He was something old and ancient, something so alien and removed from the human world that he suddenly terrified me.

I looked into his chlorine-colored eyes.

"Let me see your eyes," I said, and it was a demand.

His hand went to his face. His thumb and middle finger held the lids apart and his index finger pulled the contact away.

White, pure white eyes, broken only by the blackness of his pupil. I stepped away from him.

"When does this happen?" I asked.

He placed the contact on his finger and pressed it back onto his eye.

"Sometime around three hundred years. I don't know exactly when it happened. It happened gradually and I refused at first to believe it was happening. Then one day the last trace of my blue eyes all but dissolved and I was left with nothing."

He was telling me in a factual manner, it was to be expected, it was a change like the other changes my body had already been through.

"I should have realized it would happen. The vampire that made me had eyes like mine are now. Originally I got a pair of blue, hard contact lenses, but every time I blinked they rode up in my eyes and the color shifted. The night I saw these advertised on the television I went out and stole several pairs."

"Tell me about the vampire that made you," I said.

"No, not tonight. When I tell you I want you to hear the complete story and there isn't time tonight. I want to get back to Charleston."

He took my arm and led me out of the house.

The van was parked where I had left it in the driveway. The little sports car that was Mr. Androgynous, Chris's, was gone.

"What did you do with him?" I asked as I climbed into the van.

Matthew hesitated before closing my door and said, "I got rid of him."

While Matthew pulled down the big double garage door and locked it I realized there was no other car here. If he hadn't driven down how did he arrive? For all I knew he could materialize at will.

Once we got out to Highway 17 Matthew floored the accelerator and the van bucked roughly through its gears before settling into overdrive. Our speed continued to increase and the body of the van began to vibrate. I pressed my hands against the seat and curled my fingers into the upholstery. The needle on the speedometer was flat down on eighty-five. God only knows what that meant, it was the last number on the dial.

"Do you have to drive so fast," I yelled over the rushing wind that roared in his window.

"I love speed," he yelled back. His hair was all in motion from the blast of air and his eyes were wild with delight. "Best time I ever had was riding on Space Mountain."

Picturing him on Space Mountain made me laugh. And he began to laugh with me.

The vibration grew stronger and a grating noise, metal upon metal, peeled out into the night. Matthew slowed, a little.

"This is a mighty sluggish machine," he yelled.

"You keep abusing it like this and it will fall apart," I said. I remembered my dad telling me that once the needle fell on the end of the speedometer the car would fall apart because they didn't build them like they used to.

After about fifteen minutes the speed, noise, and vibration became normal and I relaxed.

"What if a cop stops you?" I asked.

"I just make him forget," he answered, and glanced at me. "Surely you've discovered that ability, haven't you?"

I nodded, and he smiled a pleased smile.

"It's almost too easy, isn't it?" he asked.

And I didn't know what he was talking about.

"To play with them, to capture their minds and bend them any way you want to bend them."

The malevolent Matthew had surfaced again. I looked away from his sly sneer and focused my attention out the window. Though the dark outline of trees and bright reflection of mileage markers whizzed by, I only saw the poor wretched girl tied to his bed.

I leaned back against the seat and closed my eyes. I cleared my mind, or tried to. Just when the great black void would surface I would see the portrait of Maria Abigail Anne, the portrait that linked me to this crazy vampire driving at breakneck speed through the Carolina night.

The van slowed. I heard the blinking of the turn signal and opened my eyes. We were already in Ravenel, I could tell by the flashing yellow lights strung across the intersection of the highway. Matthew turned left onto Highway 165 and I thought he must be going somewhere to hunt. My own hunger was slowly rising but I wasn't desperate, yet.

But he didn't stop anywhere and he made another turn, right, onto Highway 61.

The darkness of the night grew denser once we entered the forest of live oaks that straddled the two-lane road. This was the very route I had walked on the night Matthew had drained me and dumped me in the river. I saw the entrance to Middleton Place, and then farther up the road Magnolia Gardens and Drayton Hall. In my mind I was retracing my trail back to the sanctuary of my motel room.

Matthew was recalling something too, and for a brief instant when he caught my gaze I felt fear coming from his mind.

"You were afraid, that's why you dumped me in the river." It was an astonishing realization.

He quickly looked away.

"You were afraid of losing me too."

"Yes," he said, and it was barely a whisper in the wind. "Sometimes wanting is so much better than having. I simply panicked." He looked at me again. "And I'm still afraid."

There was something so powerful about his love that it seemed unreal. After all, can love survive centuries? Was the vampire mind so acute that memories of long ago remained as fresh and vivid as the body remained alive? My memories of being human had grown clouded, yet every experience I encountered as a vampire was indeed remarkably preserved in the most splendid detail that it was like a video tape. No, it was more than a tape, because all the senses were encapsulated within my mind, not just pictures.

The van was turning again. Matthew pulled beside an unleaded pump at the Sav-A-Ton gas station off Highway 61. He climbed out of the van and disappeared around the back of it. But soon I saw him in the side mirror, his white skin reflecting the bluish cast of the abundant overhead fluorescent lights.

The smell of gasoline was just as pleasant to me as ever and I took in a deep breath noticing in the mirror that Matthew had his hand covered over his nose. Perhaps if I had originated from the seventeenth century, gasoline would smell foreign and foul to me also.

He replaced the nozzle and the pump shut off. I watched him walk across the pavement island and enter the store.

The walls of the store were glass and I could see him wandering along the narrow aisleways. He made his way to the rear where the cold boxes were and walked back and forth, studying the contents of the shelves.

Not counting the attendant, there were two other men in the store and I began to wonder if he was waiting to take one of them. But then I saw him open the cold box door and remove something from the shelf.

He walked up to the counter and paid for the purchases,

took a small brown bag from the attendant, and hurried back to the van.

He handed me the bag and reached to pull his door closed.

I opened it. One small container of Yoplait custard-style yogurt, lemon flavor, was all the bag contained. I folded the bag closed and held it on my lap.

"Did Carol order this too?" I asked.

"Carol is no longer with me," he said.

"Then what did you buy the yogurt for?"

"Because mine is past the expiration date," he said matter-of-factly.

I didn't even want to know. This was a lunatic beside me and every moment I spent with him grew stranger.

We pulled back onto the road and I reached for the radio.

"Please. No music. I'm not in the mood for music," he said, and held my hand away from the controls.

"All right," I said, withdrawing.

The rest of the journey into downtown Charleston was made in silence.

The iron gates of his driveway were open and we pulled right up to the great piazza of his home. His little Ferrari was parked on the grass next to the azalea bushes.

"How *did* you get to Beaufort?" I asked.

"Steven dropped me off," he said.

"Is Steven a vampire?"

"No. He's my gardener. I gave him a few days off. He went down to Savannah."

"He knows about you?"

"Of course." His answer was short.

It made sense. If Steven was trustworthy he could serve Matthew well. But I wondered just how Matthew held his trust. There must be a threat riding over poor Steven's head.

"Wait here a moment," Matthew said. He took the package from me, got out of the van, and hurried to my door. He opened it and helped me out. "Welcome to Twenty-eight Legare, my home," he said.

I had said Legare as in hair, but he said Legree and I made a mental note of the pronunciation.

He escorted me up the fine marble steps to the porch. I

waited while he unlocked the front door and pushed it open. He motioned for me to enter. The door closed and we were sealed in darkness.

His hand closed around my arm and he led me through the entry and deeper into his house. At last he stopped, and I heard the light switch a split second before brightness flooded my eyes.

We were in the kitchen. Despite the darkness hanging outside the windows the room was bright and cheery. I imagined the morning sun filtering past the yellow sheers.

Matthew went to the refrigerator. He opened the door. The shelves were full of a variety of foods. He reached in and found his expired yogurt, then carefully replaced it with the new container.

I stepped closer and saw him turn the container so that the label faced front.

It was something to behold, this vampire's refrigerator. A package of Twinkies, some Fruit Roll Ups, a small tub of margarine, cream cheese, an assortment of candy bars, Cracker Jacks, snack-size Fritos, a jar of Tang, one can of 7-Up, one each of Coke, Pepsi, Budweiser, Dr Pepper, a package of Uncle Ben's rice, small foil-wrapped cheese wedges, the list was endless.

"What is all this for?" I asked, overcome by the display.

"I collect it," he said.

"You collect food?" I was surprised.

"I started a few years back. Before that I never paid it much mind. But look at these," he pulled out a package of Jiffy Pop popcorn and shoved it at me. "Such clever things and such remarkable packaging. I'd love to go back to the court of King Charles and present these foods to him."

I laughed, and his excited expression turned sour.

"I'm not laughing at you," I said. "I just never thought of junk food as remarkable or cleverly packaged."

"Yes, I suppose it is nothing new to you. But often I wish I could explore the tastes and experience the textures of these," he said and again shoved the Jiffy Pop at me.

"If you think this is exciting, you should watch it pop," I said as seriously as I could.

This time he laughed. He put the Jiffy Pop back on the shelf and opened the freezer saying, "Want to see something really exciting, check out my Frusen Glädjé."

Now he was teasing me, and suddenly he came across as someone exotically fun.

"Matthew, did you ever try to eat it?" I asked.

He closed the freezer door.

"Yes. But it had no taste," he said.

"Well, what happened? Did you get sick?"

"I wish I would have. It would've been better than that smell."

"Smell?"

"Remember your first three months?" he asked.

My nose wrinkled up in disgust. "God, you don't mean . . ."

"The food went to wherever it goes and slowly decayed inside me. I learned a hard lesson."

"What if you just chewed it up and spit it out?" I asked.

"What would be the point. It had no taste. Only the blood can . . ." His voice trailed off and he reached out, gingerly touching my chest. "I'm so very sorry about this," he said.

My cellophanelike scar was partially visible, and I tugged the sweater over it.

"If your body had been completely changed it wouldn't be there. You'll carry that scar for . . . ever."

He was genuinely upset.

"It's all right," I said.

"No. It is not all right. I nearly killed that nigger for allowing this to happen to you."

I winced visibly when he used that word and he muttered an apology.

"If you didn't make Elijah do your dirty work it would've never happened in the first place," I said.

Shame pushed the anger from his eyes.

"I nearly died myself when Elijah brought you to me. Three long nights of fever and delirious pain threatened to take you from me. I had to force my blood into you."

"But I don't remember you . . ."

197

"Of course you don't."

I tried very hard to remember but it was all a gray, misty memory. I did remember Elijah sitting with me and I did remember him giving me his blood.

"Every time I took Elijah's blood it was your blood?" I asked. It seemed impossible. What was Elijah, some kind of walking thermos?

"Yes. Except your final night together. But you succumbed to the sleep and only took a small amount from him."

"How do you know all this?" I asked. Dawn had nearly been upon Elijah and me that night and I could see no explanation as to how Matthew might've watched us. He was not in our attic.

"It's my blood in your veins. I've harbored it and nurtured it for three hundred and fourteen years. I know it intimately. I know when it's been contaminated."

I shuddered.

"What about the human blood I've taken? Has that contaminated it as well?"

"Human blood, even fish blood, is utilized quickly. Nothing can corrupt our blood," he said.

"Well, that certainly explains why you don't mind feeding off those hookers," I said.

He smiled knowingly. "Ainjul, even AIDS won't affect us. We are immortal."

A mosquito buzzed in front of me and I instinctively smacked it between my hands. I released my hands slowly, picked the squashed body of the bug off my palm, and without thinking licked the small smear of blood away.

"Why won't AIDS affect us?" I asked.

"I don't know the medical reason why. The blood is replenished and renewed. No diseases affect us. Even bacteria cannot survive on our bodies."

I wasn't totally dumb. I had noticed that even when my body perspired there was no odor. Bacteria causes the most putrid odors upon human flesh, but neither Elijah, Matthew, nor myself ever had a smell, unless we had just fed and were fragrant with the blood smell.

"Don't you ever want to know more about it, from a medical point of view?" I asked.

"No," he said. "I don't care. It has sustained and improved me for centuries. To be perfectly honest with you, I cannot remember the slightest human sensation. As far as I'm concerned, I've always been a vampire."

I walked over to the sink and turned the spigot on. The dead mosquito swirled down into the garbage disposal.

"Can mosquitoes transfer our blood to others?" I asked.

"Have you been bitten?" His question was tainted with surprise.

"I don't think so. I was just wondering."

"If a mosquito were to penetrate our skin, which I doubt can be done, I think our blood would kill it. In any case, the world is not swarming with vampires. The act must be planned and carried out. Even then, the majority of new vampires do not survive, or do not choose to survive long. I am the oldest vampire that I know," he said.

He was not bragging, instead his voice was lost in a long, lonely past.

"Please. My home is your home. You are welcome to come and go as you will. What is mine is yours," he said, and smiled as he gestured around the room.

"Then I'm going out for a while," I said, and took the keys from the kitchen counter.

"If you are going to hunt there is no need. I've acquired a victim for you upstairs."

"So you are to be my provider," I said, and it came out a bit snotty.

"It's the least I can do for you," he said.

The least indeed, I thought.

"I'm going out to look for Bong," I said.

"He had a small accident last night. I tried to tell you on the phone but you hung up."

"What? What happened to him? He's not dead . . ."

"No, he's not dead. He came in early and a large chunk of his ear was missing. If only he would bring the missing parts home with him, they would heal back onto his body."

"You mean that if I would lose an arm or leg it would reunite with my body?" I asked morbidly.

"Most certainly," he said.

"Well, I hope that never happens because I sure as hell couldn't carry it on home with me," I said with evident disgust.

He laughed softly. "Then I hope it never happens also."

With the van keys in my hand I started to walk out of the kitchen but Matthew stopped me.

"Ainjul, you never did say if you would go out with me," he said.

"I'm here, aren't I?"

He took my hand and pressed something into it. I looked down and saw two tickets to the Dock Street Theater.

"Spoleto begins this weekend. I'd like to take you to the plays, operas, and ballets, if you would want to go with me."

"All right," I said. It would be fun, doing normal things, enjoying the nights with other activities instead of hunting mortals. "But promise me, no stalking victims in the crowds, just fun evenings out."

"We'll feed before we go," he said matter-of-factly. "I don't think you could sit surrounded by them with the hunger kindling inside you."

"And you could?" I asked.

"That is one compensation for being as old as I've grown to be. I no longer need to drink as often, or as much."

"But the other night, all those girls you took," I said.

His finger went to his hair and began to twist that little curl above his left ear as he sought out the appropriate response.

"I was upset that evening. When I'm upset I need to possess and I need to exert power."

He let the lock of hair go.

I handed the tickets back to him and he put them in his inside coat pocket.

"The evening grows late, don't be gone too long. I have a few phone calls to make so I'll let you be on your way."

Imagining him doing something as mundane as making

a few phone calls struck me oddly, but he was not only a product of the seventeenth century, he was obviously wealthy and no doubt had business ventures to maintain his lifestyle.

Again I started for the kitchen door.

"Ainjul, one more thing," he said.

"Do you mind, I'd like to go find my dog," I said.

"Spoleto also marks the yearly get-together of our kind. A convention, if you like. I loathe it, but we will be going. If we don't show up, they will begin to seek you out."

"Imagine that. A vampire convention. What do you do there, sip Bloody Marys and talk about ways to have fun with victims?"

"They don't boil black cats, that much I can tell you. The point is, you must show up," he said.

"Why would they want to seek me?"

"Because I made you," he said, and again started to play with the tired-looking lock of hair.

"Can I go now?" I asked. It was the hunger that was putting me on edge. He sensed it too and nodded.

Urgency consumed me and I knew something was horribly wrong but could not pinpoint the feeling exactly. I trailed back through the dark house, remembering perfectly the direction which Matthew had led me. When I reached the double hallway it led left into the room where Maria Abigail Anne's portrait hung or right to the grand foyer and the front door. I hesitated. The portrait beckoned me. I had to gaze upon it again and reaffirm my past connection with Matthew and his family, our family. I turned left and walked down the hallway.

The room was lit by only a small light mounted directly over her portrait. The soft white light gave her face a surreal appearance, but her face was still my face. I walked closer to the fireplace, keeping my gaze tilted up to the old painting. Her eyes were painted so no matter where I stood in the room her gaze appeared to follow me. The lifelike quality in the dried oils had captured her spirit, and I was overwhelmed with the feeling that at any moment she would come to life and speak to me. Words appeared formed and ready upon her small, perfect lips, only time had kept those words forever unknown to me.

"Matthew loved you dearly, didn't he?" I asked her.

The portrait seemed to become dimensional.

"Why didn't he make you a vampire, like himself?"

I moved closer, stretching up on my toes to reach out and touch the hands, her hands, that were resting on the edge of a chair back like a delicate butterfly waiting to fly and reveal motion.

The canvas gave inward. The rough texture was cold and hard. I wondered if he had made her a vampire and she had not survived and I asked her, "How did you die?"

The expression upon her lovely face seemed to change, but I knew it was only my imagination. I could stare at objects so long and hard they would appear to change before my very eyes, but it was only tired illusion from my mind's eye that produced the wavering effect like heat shimmering from a hot surface in the bright sunlight.

I stepped away from the hearth and fought to control the flood of questions spilling into my mind. What had she been like? Whom had she married? How many children did she have? What things did she enjoy? What had she done to put such a powerful hold upon Matthew? Did she allow him to drink from her? Did she know he was a vampire? Did she have a happy life?

The fiery tendrils of hunger spread out within me, forcing me to abandon my preoccupation with the past and focus on the immediate need to feed. Though on several occasions I had fought the hunger until it dulled back to a nearly forgotten sensation, I didn't fight it now. I let it begin to consume me, for I knew the actual feeding would be more pleasurable and more fulfilling if I was utterly controlled by it. I wanted to feel that pleasure, I wanted to feel it now.

I hurried to the front door and pulled it open. The smell of rancid blood and rotten flesh poured in from the open night and Bong fell over onto my feet.

He was conscious, and managed to wag his tail. His left ear was ripped in half as Matthew had told me and his eye was still missing. These old wounds, pathetic looking as they were, didn't worry me. The gaping hole in his side and his front leg, dangling only by a flap of skin on the shoulder, caused me to panic.

I screamed out Matthew's name and then I screamed it again, and I screamed it until it became a long, moaning plea.

My sudden panic started Bong into a frenzied howl that only made me scream again, for I was sure he was dying and I was sure I couldn't go any nearer to him. He tried to rise up from the floor, but his howl turned into a painful yelp and he sank back down and the air rushed from his lungs.

I began to cry. Tears of desperation slid down my cheeks because I was frozen in place, unable to comfort my vampire dog, unable to do what had to be done, and now unable to even look at him.

"What a bloody mess," Matthew said. It was purely an exclamation, there was no blood.

He hung back from Bong and Bong growled a deep, menacing, throaty growl, and I knew Matthew would not help him either.

But I was wrong.

Matthew moved in closer, slowly, trying his best to pretend he wasn't afraid, but I sensed his fear as surely as Bong did, and when Bong snapped at him and those wicked canines missed by only a fraction of an inch I wasn't surprised to see Matthew leap gracefully into the air like he was prepared to do it all along.

"Ainjul, you have to help me. He doesn't like me," Matthew said.

My sobs came up from my soul in a harder deluge than before.

"He's not going to die, if we can just get him inside, in your coffin, he will be fine," Matthew said.

"You're lying. He's dying. Elijah said he wouldn't survive and he's dying and we can't stop him from dying," I said, controlling my sobs the best that I could.

Matthew looked away from me. This subtle gesture confirmed my knowledge of Bong's condition.

Bong began to whimper softly.

Matthew circled around him and came over to me. He slid his arm around my shoulder and drew me close, pushing my hair away from my face.

"We can make him comfortable. Ainjul, you must help me," he said.

"Can you end it? Can you destroy him and end his suffering?" I asked, wiping the spent tears away from my cheeks.

"After tomorrow he will be whole again. He heals quickly, you know that he does. We'll let him sleep and he will recover on his own."

Bong's whimpers grew softer and I felt his suffering. Sleep would heal him. Dark, peaceful sleep.

"Yes, we'll make him comfortable," I said at last and knelt beside the torn body of my disastrous procreation.

"Gently," Matthew said as I gathered Bong into my arms.

"You just watch his leg and make sure it doesn't fall off," I ordered him. I could feel it dangling against my side.

Matthew moved to support it but Bong's lips curled back and he became rigid in my arms. A low, rumbling growl started deep inside him like a tremor but I cooed to him reassuringly and he allowed Matthew to touch him.

We moved Bong slowly, carefully, through the house. I followed Matthew's lead.

At the end of the long hallway was a door, and Matthew nudged it open with his back, being watchful of Bong's injuries.

We entered a small sitting room. A large built-in bookcase graced the entire wall behind the door. There was a single wingback chair beside a reading table. Behind the chair was a tall, narrow window, heavily draped in a deep burgundy floral fabric that accented the Persian rug on the floor. I barely had enough room to turn around with Bong in my arms as Matthew closed the door.

"I thought we were putting him in my coffin." I said.

"We are," Matthew said, and the bookcase groaned and shifted back to reveal another room behind its false facade.

"I should've known," I said, and smiled. Elijah's house had the same hidden room, behind the fireplace in the den, but I had never slept there.

I stepped behind the giant bookcase and listened to it groan again as it slid back into place. Now I knew why the sitting room was so tiny. This room was a master suite, so to speak. The moving bookcase had neatly partitioned what might've been a walk-in closet.

Soft yellow track lighting lit every square inch of the hidden antechamber. But the light was not overpowering or harsh, instead it reminded me so much of sunlight that a feeling of rapture spread through me.

My coffin had been moved in, next to his, and I hurried toward it when Bong began to moan again in my arms. Matthew raised the lid. I gently set Bong upon the white satin coverlet, allowing him as much room as he needed. Once he was settled, Matthew motioned for me to move away from him.

"Let him drift off into the sleep. I will arrange his torn leg then so that it will heal properly," he whispered.

I stood back, glancing once again upon my dog. Already his eye had half closed and his head fell lopsided against the little pillow. A single pink rose poked out from under his muzzle. I left it there for him. Perhaps he would dream dreams of bright sunny days and fresh fields of flowers.

The faint hum of something electronic forced my attentions away from Bong. I glanced across the room.

Matthew was bent over a computer keyboard and I watched as his long fingers flew over the keys. The humming was from the processor located in the far corner of the room. A modem sat on top of it, red lights blinked frantically as data was being received from somewhere, or perhaps it was being sent somewhere. The muffled clacking of a printer joined the electronic orchestration and Matthew moved in front of the printer. He shoved his hands deep into his pants pockets while watching the paper jerk up over the back of the machine.

As I joined him I realized now how Elijah learned to work a computer. The printout continued to feed out of the plastic slot. I read the lines as they appeared. It was clearly the results of the night's horse racing from Penn National near Harrisburg, Pennsylvania.

"Do you bet?" I asked.

The printer stopped and Matthew ripped the paper from the machine and folded it along the tiny perforations.

"No I don't. I had three horses running tonight. Just checking the results," he said.

"You own race horses?" I was amazed.

"Our existence doesn't have to revolve around death. I've owned race horses since the time of my father's death. He was a dog man and also a falconer. Within days of his passing I had the mews burned down and the kennels dismantled. I imported a fine German stallion and bought six good broodmares. Two years later my colts were racing for the pleasure of the court."

His attention turned back to the printout and he picked up a red pen from the desk and began to make notations on the paper.

"Did they win?" I asked, glancing over his shoulder.

"They did pretty well," he said. He drew a line under Sometimes A Prince. "This colt has only been started four times. He placed third out of a field of eleven. And this colt also placed third, his second start," he said, circling the name Can't Miss By Much. "Now this little filly should've been entered in the Derby. Look at that time, she blew the field away." His pen boldly underlined the name Fanta Sea Gold.

"How do you manage all this?" I asked.

"Anyone can own race horses. All it takes is an investment. Once you obtain a good trainer you can step aside and reap the glory of winning, if you're lucky enough. But I do miss the hands-on experience with them. I was a good horseman. I would like very much to take you to see my hunters."

"You own hunters too?" I was growing more and more amazed.

"I have a stable near Philadelphia. In fact, I've got a beautiful stallion, he traces all the way back to my first German stallion, and he will most likely be going to the Olympics. He's as black as pitch and so powerful, yet graceful, that I am humbled by his prowess."

"Is there anything you don't do?" I asked.

"Well, I'm not into Quarter Horse racing yet. I've been waiting to make sure it wasn't a passing fad, but the number of quarter tracks is growing. Now, they're something to watch, nose to nose finishes almost every race. Shall I buy you a race horse?"

He had to do it, he had to work in the Quarter Horse. I owned and showed a quarter mare for ten years. If he knew everything about my past, then he knew I competed on the circuit, and was pretty good too.

"I don't know much about racing," I said.

"That's right. You showed those pampered fat halter horses," he said.

"And was damn good at it," I said angrily.

"I'm not knocking you, the breed was at fault, but they've come a long way since then," he said.

Bong began to make his little dream sounds and I walked over to the coffin to check him.

He was sound asleep. His paws were twitching as he ran off somewhere in his dreams. Even the torn leg had movement, and it was ghastly, lying there twitching and not attached to much.

I motioned for Matthew.

"Is he sleeping?" Matthew asked, but I didn't answer him because he walked over and saw for himself that Bong was in the throes of a good dream.

Matthew reached in and grabbed hold of Bong's leg. He gently eased the flap of skin back away from the shoulder so the torn joint was exposed. There was no blood, only raw-looking meat. His hands gently manipulated the leg into the joint and I heard bone against bone and looked away.

"He'll be in one piece tomorrow night," Matthew said, and he closed my coffin lid over Bong.

"I'm going out now," I said, aware that the hunger was still with me, though not as intense as before.

"There isn't time. Go upstairs and take the victim I've left for you," Matthew said.

I walked over to the wall and tried to figure out how it swung open. There was no visible control, and when I stepped closer it automatically began to move.

"Show me how this thing works so I can get back in," I said, still searching for the secret to its movement.

"It's controlled by temperature. Nothing over sixty-eight degrees can open it."

"Are we that cold?" I asked, surprised.

"After a full feeding we are that warm," he said. "Please, take the victim upstairs. It is too late for you to go out." His voice was anxious, almost pleading.

I wondered what was so special about this victim upstairs. All I could picture was the naked girl and the roaches, and I didn't want to take such a helpless victim.

"Not if you've left it naked and tied to the bed," I said.

"I wouldn't offer you something so easy. Where would the pleasure come from if you weren't able to seduce your own victim?"

"All right. But don't come with me," I said. I didn't want him to watch me feed. Not yet.

"I'll be waiting here. But do be quick about it," he said.

The bookcase slid shut and I was alone in the sitting room, ready to fulfill that which must be fulfilled.

CHAPTER TWELVE

I took the stairs two at a time, propelled by the hunger and rushed by the approaching dawn.

The middle of the darkened hallway was cut in half by a bright shaft of yellow light. The light came from the same bedroom where Bong and I had found the naked girl, Carol.

Instead of rushing blindly to my feast, I stopped outside the open door and cautiously peeked around the frame.

Butterflies fluttered inside me and I knew I was nervous because this was a victim Matthew had chosen for me. And what a victim she was! She easily weighed three hundred pounds. It was hard not to use the cliché, such a pretty girl, because she was extremely attractive.

Her dark hair was cut short and feathered stylishly away from her face. Her makeup was perfect. Despite her weight problem she appeared proud of herself.

I stepped into the bedroom. She looked at me, smiled, and said hello very softly. She had been reading, but she carefully marked her place and set the leather-bound volume on the bed beside her.

Every indication led me to believe that she was expecting me. She was not restrained in any manner, even the bedroom door had been left open. Did she know why I had come?

"You are very beautiful, just as Matthew said you would be," she said.

My hunger pitched inside me, forcing me to move closer. She stood up.

The old bed creaked and groaned, almost in relief of losing her enormous weight.

"Please, drink from me and satisfy the thirst that brings you here," she said.

Yes. Damn it, she knew. And I wanted to know why but the hunger blossomed. My fangs burst forth and I was no longer in control. I took her. The fat folds of skin upon her neck were soft and downy against my lips. She had on perfume, honeysuckle, and when my fangs pierced the skin, but before the blood flowed into my mouth, I tasted the sweetness of her scent. Her blood, warm and fragrant with its own distinctive flavor, filled me. She was no longer an obese woman, but a seductress that sent me swooning with abundant pleasure.

I drank slowly, and as I suckled upon her life force she talked softly to me as a mother might coo to a young infant at her breast. I could not understand her words, as a feeding vampire is only aware of the rapture of drinking, but her hands gently caressed me and I allowed her to hold me close and nurture her needs as I was nurturing mine.

I was not near to the point of being full when she gently began to push me away. Why I let her do this is something I am unable to explain. For the very first time my victim was in command of me, and as she held me away I realized we were both silently weeping. Such was her power upon me.

Matthew appeared in the doorway and I was overcome by embarrassment that he should see me weeping like this. He said nothing as he approached us.

She was still clinging to me, and I to her, but the special bond between us was already dimming. Matthew gently separated us.

"Let me show you something," Matthew said, and he pulled me closer to him. "Extend your fangs."

Still somewhat dazed by my experience I did what he asked. The sharp little teeth erupted through my lower jaw and the tiny spray of my own blood ran along my gums.

"Pull them back," he instructed.

I did and he held my mouth open and put his finger right

on the gum spots where my fangs rested. He withdrew and showed me the tiny amount of blood mixed with my saliva. Then he turned to the fat woman and gently, but deliberately, placed the blood-saliva mixture on the puncture wounds in her neck.

Instantly, the blood still oozing from her wounds stopped and as I watched, dumbfounded, the wounds began to seal off. My vampire blood was healing her. Within minutes, only a red mark, like a hickey, remained on her neck.

"Delores is very special, aren't you, dear," he said, and kissed her lightly upon the forehead.

Dawn was upon us and my body was heavy and thick with the oncoming sleep. It was unfair. I wanted to know about this woman, Delores, and her gift. But Matthew took me by the arm and led me away.

As we walked down the stairway together I managed, with a groggy voice, to ask one final question before the sleep took me.

"Is she going to become one of us?"

I was thinking about the small amount of my blood that had mingled with hers and had miraculously restored the punctures.

"No, Ainjul. Maybe one day, but not now, not just yet." I heard him say.

The sleep paralyzed me and Matthew swept me up in his arms. I was vaguely aware of being carried. Sleep melded me into the deep folds of darkness.

When I awoke I was surprised and somewhat overcome with the feeling of being defiled. My clothing had been changed and I was dressed in a black cocktail dress, simple in design but flattering nonetheless. The satin crepe bodice was strapless and accented with tiny, sparkling beads. The waistline was dropped to my hip and a large, ruffled bow hung delicately against my left side. The floor-length skirt was slit from the bow to the hem allowing most of my leg to be seen if I was inclined to flaunt it.

A lovely diamond-and-emerald bracelet hugged my wrist and I could feel a choker around my neck and imagined it matched.

211

I was propped up against several pillows in a near sitting position. The coffin lid was open and I saw Matthew sitting across the room, waiting most impatiently for me to rise.

"We have fifteen minutes to get to the theater," he said. He brushed a bit of lint from the sleeve of his tuxedo and turned away from me. I carefully climbed from my coffin, anxiously looking about the room for Bong.

"Is Bong healed?" I asked.

"Yes, yes. He is well, and unlike you a very early riser." He hurried toward me and started fussing like a matron with my dress. "Putting this thing on you was like dressing a Barbie doll," he said, and finished straightening the bow.

"I am capable of dressing myself," I said.

"Well, of course you are. But there wasn't time."

He rushed away from me and removed something from the small hot plate that sat upon his desk beside the computer terminal. The smell was intoxicating, but when he handed me the large mug I could only stare in disbelief. It was filled with blood, still warm but beginning to congeal on top.

"You don't expect me to . . ."

"Yes I do. Come on, Ainjul, don't be squeamish. Drink up so we can get going. It will be most unseemly to arrive after the opera has started."

"Matthew, really, I can't . . ."

He stepped closer and pushed the mug to my lips.

"Blood is blood. Bottoms up," he said.

The first swallow had the lumpy texture of tapioca pudding, but as he said, blood is blood, and the warm liquid rushed into me with the same enlightening experience as any other feeling.

Before I had a chance to let the last drop slide into my mouth he was leading me out of the hidden antechamber and down the hallway.

"If that wasn't enough to satisfy you I've packed a thermos in the car," he said.

How very thoughtful, I thought. We hurried outside where the Ferrari was idling, ready to depart.

It hadn't been enough to satisfy me, and after Matthew

closed the car door for me I reached for the thermos and began to drink straight from the bottle.

In no time we were winding recklessly through the narrow streets of Charleston, heading uptown to the Dock Street Theater.

Needless to say, we arrived in time, and before Matthew opened the door of the theater he quickly took a handkerchief from his pocked and dabbed the blood from the corner of my mouth.

Our seats were in the front row of the balcony. An excellent vantage point to see the stage and all the people below us. The orchestra was busily tuning up for the performance. The shrill burst from a flute and the sweet hum of a violin filtered into the muffled talk and coughs of mortals all around us.

I was filled and content and excited. This was the first time I had ever been to an opera, and the charm and gaiety of those around me infected my senses.

The lights in the theater dimmed and the audience became hushed. The orchestra, poised and ready, struck up all at once and the vibrations of sound coursed through me like delightful currents of energy.

"Matthew, what exactly is this?" I asked, quietly leaning closer to him so as not to disturb the others around us.

"This is a French opera, *Platee,* by Jean-Philippe Rameau. It's a parody of the French Baroque style, about the god Jupiter and goddess Juno. You don't speak French, do you?"

"I didn't know it was a prerequisite," I said.

"Well, I'm sure not many here do. But you'll be able to follow it. It's a fun opera, you'll enjoy it."

And as the stage filled with characters I knew I would. The costumes were simply dazzling and the set designs fantastic. I watched those players perform, ignorant of the language but held entranced with every movement. I laughed in most of the right places and even oooed and ahhhed when Jupiter appeared in the cloud machine.

Never before could I remember two and a half hours flying by so quickly. When the final act came to a close I found myself nearly exhausted with the surging enthusiasm that held me on a high for the duration of the performance.

When the players lined up on the stage for a final bow, and the audience began to applaud in great waves of noise, Matthew hurried from his seat dragging me hastily behind him.

I didn't understand his urgency and I pulled back.

He had no choice but to stop. The rows of people were already emptying into the aisleway and we became ensnarled in a human traffic jam.

"Ainjul, quickly," he said, pulling me and pushing through the crowd.

"What is it, what's the problem?"

"There is someone here I don't want to run into."

It could only be one of us, another vampire, and I began to scan the wavering sea of people looking for the telltale white face. But I saw no one.

Suddenly the crowd of humans around me became suffocating and I stayed close to Matthew as he rudely forced a path toward the exit.

I stumbled over the metal doorframe and fell against a young man but Matthew pulled me back toward him and I heard the young mortal mutter an apology.

The cool humid air was a refreshing escape from the closeness of the theater. I was glad to be leaving the crowd of mortals, and glad to be back in my own element of darkness.

Before I had a chance to regain my composure Matthew was dragging me through the groups of people that were milling about and on down the sidewalk. I again tried to pull away from him, but his grip on my wrist was bone-crushing.

"I can't run in these shoes," I said. My black pumps were awkward enough to walk in let alone jog down an uneven walk.

"Well, take them off," he said, still dragging me.

"Damn it, do you want me to make a scene. Slow down!"

We turned the corner and Matthew stopped. In a vampiric blur of movement he dodged back behind the old brick building and flattened himself to the wall.

"It's too late, he's already seen you," I said. From where I was standing, in the middle of the sidewalk and in full view of the parked Ferrari, I saw the vampire Matthew didn't want to run into, and I saw another vampire standing solemnly beside him.

"Oh, shit," he said.

His remark made me chuckle. He had been cornered.

Unlike Matthew, I was anxious to meet these other creatures like myself and I strode purposefully toward the parked car.

"Wasn't that Matthew I just saw?" the taller vampire called as I approached.

I glanced behind me, but Matthew wasn't there. I couldn't imagine him hiding back there forever so I made up an excuse.

"He just stopped to tie his shoe."

The tall vampire took a step toward me with his arms outstretched as if to embrace me, but suddenly Matthew was between us and the tall vampire was embracing him instead of me.

"Matthew, my dear dear friend. Charles Matthew Francis Trenton, how long has it been? I do look forward to these get-togethers," he said, all the while hugging and kissing Matthew upon the cheeks like the Europeans often do.

Matthew endured it.

I leaned back against the Ferrari and watched the exchange. It was obviously one sided and I wondered why Matthew didn't like this tall one, he seemed very pleasant.

Of course, he almost had to be pleasant. He was easily six feet five and even his face was tall. When he smiled, which he did often, he looked gawky. His hair was dark, greased back from his high forehead. His eyes were also dark but sparkled with mischief. He was older than Matthew, in human years, that is. I guessed his mortal age to have been around forty. I could not help but notice his hands. Expecting a man his size to have big hands, and seeing the small, almost feminine, hands around Matthew's

215

back was unsettling. For a moment I imagined he was pieced together like Frankenstein.

When he was finished with his greeting he stepped away and turned to examine me.

"Ahh. Such sexy curves, elegant lines, and sensuous . . ."

"That's quite enough, Frederick," Matthew interrupted.

"I was referring to your car, although your friend here is some looker too. Allow me to introduce myself. I am Frederick Holmes. Lived in Detroit, died in Wichita, residing undead in Jacksonville."

"Hello," I said. What could I say. With an intro like that how could I not like him?

"Well, Matthew, you've outdone yourself. Debra won't be the belle of the ball this year. You are coming, aren't you?"

"Yes, we're coming," Matthew said.

"Don't sound so excited about it. Oh, but I forgot how much you loathe us. Not one of us is in your league, Matthew. But you should be very proud of this beautiful creature. I would want to show her off to everyone. Look what I have to present," he said, and pointed to the other vampire hiding in the shadows behind him.

His young vampire friend was no more than a boy. I guessed nineteen at most. He was short, stocky, and still wore his high school jacket with a varsity letter emblazoned on the side. He sported a tousle of thick blond hair which was most unbecoming against his white complexion. His hands were large, with fingers so thick that as he twisted the opera program in them they looked as if they pained him.

I wanted to see his eyes but he kept his gaze on the sidewalk, and even when I willed him to look up at me, he would not. His very essence was sullen, lethargic.

"Do the others bring their newest creations to show off?" I asked.

"Oh, I do like her, Matthew. What a sense of humor," Frederick said.

"Well shucky darn, do they?" I said, mocking him. Suddenly his effervescent attitude was annoying.

"And spunky too," he laughed, oblivious to my changing

216

tone. "Ainjul, we come together to show off our progeny, yes. And no one will top you."

"How the hell did you know my name?"

"Any vampire who wouldn't know you by name by now is ready for a bath in the sunlight. In our hierarchy Matthew is king. We've been waiting a long time to see what he'd catch. When he finally decided to go fishing, he sure caught a trophy."

"So what are you gonna do? Mount me on a slab of wood and hang me in your den?" I said.

His laugh was shrill in the night air.

"You're a real killer," he said.

"Aren't we all? I said, playing right into his hands.

His laughter came in great, gleeful gasps and I could tolerate it no longer. I opened the car door and climbed in. Unfortunately, I could not seal out his merriment. The little sports car was a convertible.

"Come on, Ken," he said to his young companion. "We'll see you two tomorrow night at the Omni."

I watched them depart. Ken, the short stocky blond, followed obediently. Never once did his gaze lift from the ground. Something was not right with him and I felt sorry for him.

"Now you understand why I didn't want to see him," Matthew said. He closed his car door and started the engine.

"What's wrong with him?" I asked.

"He's a frustrated comic at heart. Always playing it up for a few laughs."

"No, Ken, the boy, something is wrong with him," I said.

"You felt it too," Matthew said. "He's not going to make it. He has no will to survive. Doesn't surprise me, though, none of Frederick's procreations have survived."

I knew I had witnessed that sullen look and felt the same dejected attitude before. Bong was like Ken.

"Bong won't live either, will he?" I asked.

"Bong is all right," Matthew said.

But in my heart I knew Bong wasn't and Matthew was

only protecting me from the inevitable. Every time he came home torn up and broken he was dying. There was no way another animal was beating him up like that, he was too strong. No matter how much I rejected the facts, Bong was trying to destroy himself.

"Did you enjoy the opera?" Matthew asked.

"Yes, very much. Thanks for taking me," I said, glad for the interruption of my deeper thoughts.

"I'm glad. Eternity is a long time to live surrounded by death. To go out and be one of the living, to partake of life and the pleasures that abound will help keep you sane."

We turned right and got caught up in a traffic jam as the other patrons were making their way home. A battered Ford station wagon pulled alongside us and the horn tooted as it inched beyond our lane. It was Frederick and his friend. They cut in front of us and I started to laugh. Hanging in the back window was one of those little yellow caution signs. The message was: VAMPIRE ON BOARD. When they pulled farther away I saw the bumper sticker. I BRAKE FOR VAMPIRES.

"He's crazy," Matthew said, shaking his head.

We followed them another two blocks. When we came to the stop sign they went straight ahead and we turned right. I wondered where they were staying? How had they managed to travel? Did they bring their coffins along? How might they get them into the hotel, if that was where they were lodging for the days?

"How many of us are there?" I asked.

"I have no idea," Matthew said.

"You must know how many come to the convention."

"I haven't gone for several years. I told you before I don't care very much for them. The last time I went there were twenty seven."

"That many," I said. I was surprised. I thought perhaps five or six.

"Only the southern coastal vampires attend. And who knows how many they've created or how many of their creations have survived and created their own."

The iron gates of Matthew's small driveway were open

and we pulled into the yard. Delores was sitting in a rocking chair on the front piazza accompanied by Bong and another man. When Bong saw me he jumped down the marble steps and ran to my side. Nothing was wrong with him. His leg looked fine. Only his old wounds remained to tell of his misadventures.

Matthew and I ascended the steps and the man got out of his chair and motioned that I take it.

"Steven, will you get the gate?" Matthew asked.

The man nodded and hobbled down the steps. The strange swing of his jolting walk made me aware that his leg was not his own. Though I could not see the prosthesis, I saw the stiffness of his ankle and foot.

"Did you enjoy the show?" Delores asked.

Her rocking chair squeaked on the wooden planks of the porch and I turned to see which of us the question was directed to.

She was looking at me.

"Yes. It was excellent," I answered.

"And did you enjoy it, Matthew?" she asked again.

"It certainly took me back a few years," he said. "Did you take care of the entries in the ledger today?"

"They are awaiting your approval," she said.

Bong padded quietly over to her and rested his head upon her large lap. He looked up at her with an expression of adoration, and I immediately felt betrayed by him. But then I remember how she had affected me. Was she affecting Bong in the same manner? What was it about her that made her so different?

Matthew had entered the house and Delores and I were alone on the porch. We stared at each other for a few silent moments. I wanted to know about her but she was the one who spoke first.

"Ainjul, sit down and tell me about yourself," she said.

Her voice was soft, soothing, and I was ready to spill out my life's story for her. But it seemed wrong, and suddenly I was unnerved by her presence and made an excuse to get away from her.

"I'm going to change out of these clothes," I said.

"But you look so beautiful," she said, and she sighed with such longing that I wondered if she wanted me in a sexual way.

"I'd hate to ruin them," I said, and hurried away from her.

I ran down the hallway and into the small sitting room. The bookcase opened as I approached, but the hidden room was dark and empty.

More than a change of clothes, I wanted to talk to Matthew. It took me several minutes to find him but at last I did. He was upstairs in a small room that served as an office.

"Who is she?" I asked as I approached the big oak desk.

He didn't even look away from his ledger when he answered me.

"If you are referring to Delores, she is my accountant."

"That's not what I mean," I said.

He held up his hand to silence me. I waited for what seemed an intolerable amount of time before he closed the large black book and gave me his attention.

"Ainjul, I can't explain her to you. She came to me a few years ago. Like so many other mortals have done, she sought me. As you found out last night, she has a certain gift. Call it psychic or supernatural, it is beyond explanation as we are beyond explanation. It seems that by sharing her gift we are fulfilled and she is fulfilled," he said.

"But how is she able to control us like that?"

"I honestly don't know." He stood up and took off his black coat. "Why don't we get changed and go outside and talk to her. I'd like you to meet Steven also."

For the life of me I was at a loss to understand these people with whom Matthew shared his life.

"How do you maintain their trust?" I asked him.

"Trust and loyalties are easily established when the mortals come to you. They want what only we can give them and they are prepared to do anything to obtain it," he said.

"So you use them with the hopeful promise that they might achieve immortality."

"That's a hard way to look at it," he said.

"They are slaves, bound to you by a . . ."

"I won't stand for your criticism."

Though his voice remained quiet his words stung, and I turned away from him. In my mind I saw the goon Frederick and his complacent young companion. Was I any different? Was Matthew?

I felt him move behind me. His hands lighted upon my bare shoulders and he gently turned me around so we faced each other.

"Ainjul, I'm sorry. Please understand. Hundreds of years have made me what I am. If I'm not what you expect me to be, or if I am, I ask only that you accept it as I will accept you."

"What if I told you I loathed you and what you have done to me. What if I told you I wanted you dead," I said bitterly.

"Then I would say you are lying to yourself because what might've been true the first night I took you is true no longer."

"I think you're wicked."

This time he walked away from me.

"I think it's wicked the way you play with your victims. It's wicked the way you've deceived me and the way you pretend I'm your long-dead sister. What's worse is the way you've been deceiving yourself all these years thinking she would somehow come back. And I hate you for doing this to me."

I didn't understand where and why this sudden anger had surfaced. Perhaps it was because what he said was true. He was not the evil creature that Elijah had led me to believe in. Any evil in him was in all of us.

I watched as he walked out of the room. Part of me wanted to go after him, part of me was too riled up to make the effort. The emotional upheaval within me weakened me physically and I wanted to sit down and unwind but instead I remained standing and began to try to understand myself.

At last I knew what it was that was upsetting me. It was the other vampires. It was the convention. Frederick had said that Matthew was king in their world. I was a product of Matthew. But more than that I was, in reality, related to him and what affected him affected me. And damn the rest of them anyway. My life and Matthew's life were ours. I knew now why he hated them. They were no more than busybodies and gossips. I hadn't even met the rest of them but knew they only wanted to see me to glimpse Matthew's personal life. We were on display and there was nothing I could do about it.

Laughter from outside reached my ears. Either I could stay by myself and let my thoughts drive me crazy or I could share myself among Matthew and his mortal companions. The choice was mine. But before I wandered downstairs I made my way farther along the hallway where I sensed Matthew.

Dim white light filtered into the hallway from a door left ajar. I pushed it open and was immediately embarrassed.

Matthew's tuxedo was strewn carelessly across the footboard of a beautiful brass bed. He was just stepping into a pair of tweed slacks. Before his right leg was fully encased in fabric I saw a horrible scar behind and above his knee.

He hadn't seen me yet and I watched him smooth his shirttail into his slacks and ease the zipper closed. He pulled the end of his belt through the buckle and then glanced up and saw me.

"Matthew, I'm sorry for what I said. I've ruined a perfect evening," I apologized.

He pulled a sweater vest over his head. This created static electricity and the hair around his face danced wildly for a moment before he ran his hand through it.

"Ainjul, I want you to understand that I know you are not my sister. Each day I remain on earth makes me aware of . . ."

"I don't need you to explain yourself," I interrupted.

"But I need to explain. What you said to me was very, very true. I have been deceiving myself. Maria is dead and nothing can change that fact. But I love her still. Can you imagine how the years, long and empty years, have reinforced my love?"

No. I couldn't understand. What kind of woman was she to have such a hold upon him?

"I don't want you dead," I said, letting him know that he had also told me some truths. He was no longer the creature I yearned to destroy.

He smiled.

"What happened to your leg?" I asked.

"It's an old scar and a long story."

"I have an eternity to listen. Tell me," I said.

He sighed, preparing himself to recall his ancient past. Then he began with a soft voice and slow speech that made his accent more British.

"When I saw a small boy my father thought I should learn responsibility. He gave me charge of the kennels and every day I cleaned up after his dogs, fed his dogs, and brought water from the stream for his dogs. One morning his prize bitch whelped and I hadn't noticed as I entered her cage. Though she knew me she was an extremely nervous animal and this, being her first litter, only added to her anxious attitude.

"When I saw the pups I did what any young boy would do. I was thrilled and delighted and I rushed over to her box to see them. She attacked me."

He stopped, and I saw him shudder with remembrance.

"Bear in mind that I was only seven years old then and not a big child. All I could do was roll over onto my stomach and pray that the dirt beneath me would swallow me up so I could be shielded from her vicious attack. I had enough sense to cover my head with my arms, and I cried and screamed for help but the kennels were far from the house and nobody came.

"She was all over me, growling and biting, and my pitiful little sobs only aggravated her more. She settled down on top of me and began gnawing on my leg. My panic and my pain caused me to faint. Father said that was what saved my life," he said.

I remembered the night Bong had my leg in his powerful jaws. I was absolutely helpless to stop him. But I was a vampire then, not a seven-year-old child. Now I understood his fear of Bong.

"Father killed her and drowned all her pups. I have never trusted dogs since then. It is not such a big deal as dogs don't like our kind anyway, but when I was a young mortal man it caused me terrific problems. Whenever I was asked to go on a hunt I'd always panic when the hounds began baying around me. Such terrific noise they would make."

"I'm so sorry," I said.

"There is no reason for you to be sorry. I survived, but unfortunately the physical and emotional scars remain."

Stepping into his past brought forth all kinds of questions that I wanted to ask. I especially wondered what kind of man my great-great-great (how many greats?) grandfather was. Did he treat his son cruelly or was he kind?

"If you want to change you'll find the bureau and the closet in the bedroom across the hall filled with clothes. Choose what you like and then please come join us on the porch," he said.

Matthew was not a stranger to my tastes. I found, as he had said, many clothes to choose from and I finally chose a pair of painters pants with lots of pockets and little loops to hang tools from. To complement my ensemble I slipped on a Mickey Mouse T-shirt, wondering if he purchased it the same night he had ridden Space Mountain. For shoes I selected a brand-new pair of high-top Adidases from the rows of shoes, all in my size. Apparently Matthew was prepared in advance for my arrival.

I joined the others outside on the front piazza. Delores was still seated in her rocking chair but now was munching contentedly from a box of assorted chocolates. Bong stood attentively beside her, and if I didn't know better I'd have thought he was begging.

Matthew had taken a chair from the house and was sitting near his gardener, Steven. He was watching Steven's quick hands work a pocket knife around a bar of soap. In less than a minute Steven had carved the effigy of Bong and he stood up and presented it to me.

"It's so nice to see someone with casual character," he

said, and he lowered his voice so only I could hear, "Matthew is never casual."

I glanced at Matthew. It was true. I had never seen him in jeans or a T-shirt but it only added to his character. He leaned back in his chair and propped his feet against the nearest great pillar that supported the porch. His attitude certainly reflected casualness at the moment.

"Perhaps not in dress, but in manner surely," I said.

Steven smiled.

"Where did you learn to do this?" I asked as I studied the small sculpture of Bong.

"In 'Nam," he said.

His words answered my questions about his leg, and I imagined a mine or some other explosion had torn his leg away. Too bad he hadn't been a vampire, he could've carried it on home with him and let the magic of sleep heal it back to his body. It was a terrible thing, losing his leg, I shouldn't think otherwise, but becoming undead was just as terrible to me. Actually, it wasn't so terrible anymore. I had adjusted to almost everything, except of course death. Death still revolted me.

"So why do you hang around here?" I asked.

"The pay is good and I enjoy the work," Steven answered.

I was expecting a different answer, a clue to his search for immortality, but he revealed none.

"Please, take my seat. I'll get another from the house," he said, pointing to the empty chair next to Matthew.

"No, you sit. I prefer the floor anyway," I said. The truth was that when he moved, his leg pained me and I didn't want to trouble him. I crossed in front of Delores, who didn't look up while she selected another chocolate, and settled beside Bong. I leaned back against another great white column and stretched my legs out on the porch in front of me.

For a long time no one said a word. Even Bong kept a quiet vigil beside the hulking frame of Delores. I felt alienated from the rest of them. What was I supposed to do? Keep up come idle chitchat with these mortals whom I re-

225

ally didn't trust? What were the rules? Could I talk about vampires and blood-sucking gore in front of them? Might I be that bold? I stared at Matthew a while but he was lost in thoughts. Finally I broke the silence.

"What are you thinking about?"

All three of them looked at me.

"Oh, nothing." Their answer was in unison and they all started to laugh.

"Actually, I was thinking about you," Delores said first. She popped another chocolate into her mouth and I felt her pleasure as she slowly chewed it. The scent reached me. It was caramel.

She swallowed.

"I was thinking how remarkably extraordinary it is that you resemble the portrait in the den."

"Do you think I am her?" I asked.

"Yes and no," she said. I watched as she again rummaged in the box of chocolates. "Matthew, you've been perfectly rude. You haven't introduced her to Steven," she said, putting another candy in her mouth.

"So I haven't. Ainjul, this is Steven Berger, my gardener," Matthew said.

I returned Steven's nod. He was a nice-looking man. Except for his leg the ravages of war had not scarred him physically.

His hair was reddish brown, cut close to his head in military fashion. He was shorter than Matthew, but had the same slight muscular build. His skin was deeply tanned, a trademark of his profession.

"And what are you thinking about, Steven?" I asked again.

"I was thinking that I should fertilize the lawn tomorrow. It's supposed to rain," he answered flatly.

Either he was lying or his mind worked very simply. How could he sit here among vampires and think of something so mundane as fertilizer?

"What are you thinking?" Delores asked.

"That you are both a bit weird. Don't you know what we are?"

226

"Of course we know what you are but that doesn't mean we sit around thinking about it," Delores said, and closed her candy box.

"Why are you *really* here?" I asked. I was determined to hear them admit they wanted to become like us. Neither of them answered me.

I began to fidget under their scrutinizing stares. Maybe I was the crazy one. Did what they want really matter?

"So, whose blood was it that I drank from the thermos tonight? I don't think it was yours, Delores, or you would be dead. Was it your blood, Steven?"

"It was probably the frozen reconstituted stuff that Matthew buys by the gross," he said.

I nearly gagged but then I saw the twinkle in his large blue eyes and knew he was toying with me.

"I came to Matthew shortly after the war. I faced death every day for three years and I didn't like it. Immortality is every man's desire and I am no exception," he said.

"Then you've been with Matthew for sixteen or seventeen years. Don't you wonder when he is going to grant your wish. How long will you wait?"

"At first it mattered to me very much. Now it is enough to know him and to know you and to know that it does exist but maybe not for everyone," he said.

"And you, Delores? What about you?"

"Well, dear, I've given it some hard thought and like everything else in life immortality appears to reach those who don't seek it. If I should be the exception to that, then so be it. I'm in no hurry. I'd like to be thin and beautiful like you before facing eternity." She stood up from her rocking chair and smoothed her long skirt. "If you'll excuse me now, I'm going to go to bed."

Steven pressed the side of his watch and I saw a momentary flash of blue light upon his wrist.

"It's nearly two o'clock. I'd better be going too. It's been a pleasure to finally meet you, Ainjul," he said.

I remained seated on the wooden floor of the porch and watched them both enter the house. Bong followed her as

227

far as the front door, but then he turned around and came back to me.

"Aren't you going to ask me what I'm thinking?" Matthew asked.

I looked over toward him. For a minute I feared I was going to get a lecture.

"I don't think I want to know," I said.

"Well, I'm going to tell you anyway. I think you are the most refreshing creature I've ever known."

"You don't think I was rude or callous to them?"

"No. I think you were honest," he said.

"You may be right. But what I really am is confused. I don't trust them and I can't explain why. They've done nothing to me, but I can't let down my defenses and trust them the way you do."

"In time you will learn. What you feel is part of our nature. They are, after all, our prey. You have become a hunter, and even as mighty and powerful as you grow there are always the vulnerable times, during the day, when the hunted might seek to hunt you. I assure you neither Delores nor Steven will."

"Did you want this?" I asked him.

He wasn't thinking along the same lines as I was and he looked at me for clarification.

"Immortality. Delores said it seeks those who don't seek it. Did you seek it?"

"No. It was passed along to me as I passed it along to you," he said.

"Who gave it to you?"

"Of course you have a right to know because his blood is within you also, but try to understand, Ainjul, I can't dredge up all those memories until the time comes when I no longer fear losing you."

His blood is in me also, I thought. Another man had made Matthew a vampire. Was it a friend or maybe a relative?

"When is the time going to come?" I asked.

"We will both know."

228

I wondered what that meant. The time was obviously not now because I didn't know.

Matthew began telling me a story about the old house next door to him. How it had once been a girl's school and how the girls would sneak out at night to see their beaux. He rambled on and on, and I heard some mention of the unique sword gates that sealed the property shut.

I pretended to listen but my mind was thinking about him, the one who took Matthew. Was he still around? How old must he be?

"Ainjul, you're not listening," Matthew interrupted my thought.

"Pardon me?" I said.

"I asked if you would like to go home."

"Home as in to see my family? How could I? They all believe that I am dead."

"I thought you might like to look in on them and satisfy yourself that they are all right."

"I don't know Matthew. I just . . ."

"I think you should," he said.

"Let me think about it."

He was quiet for a moment but then resumed telling me the history of Charleston. I was intrigued. Almost every old house had its own story, and many had ghosts. The longer he talked the more I felt at home in the old charm that surrounded me. We spent the entire evening together on the porch. His storytelling was masterful, and the stories endless. I was truly sorry when dawn forced us way from each other, but I went to my coffin content and enchanted. I wished for dreams of our evening together, but only the black void of nothingness surrounded me.

CHAPTER THIRTEEN

Evening arrived. Again Matthew had taken the liberty to dress me before I awoke. My outfit was a black tuxedo complemented by a white silk shirt complete with ruffles, cummerbund, and bow tie. My Adidases were still on my feet but he added a cute pair of lacy anklets. I smiled to myself, thinking tonight when he wanted me to run away from the others with him I'd have no excuse.

I rose from my coffin the same instant the wall slid open. Bong came trotting in to greet me. He was all dressed up in a child's tux, minus the pants of course. The long tails of his jacket had been pinned together so they wouldn't drag on the floor. The white ruffles of his shirt spilled across his broad chest and the little clip-on bow tie hung at an odd angle beneath his jaw.

"My, my, aren't you a handsome boy," I exclaimed, and reached out to pet him.

"Why thank you," Matthew said upon entering our room. His tuxedo was like ours, we were a matching trio.

"Cute, very cute, Matthew. How did you manage to dress Bong?" I asked.

"Delores did it. It was her idea."

"Well, I guess this means it is time to go," I said.

"Unfortunately," Matthew said.

"Aren't you going to wear your contacts? You look positively alien," I said. His white upon white eyes disturbed me.

"I almost decided upon a blue one and a brown one, just to shake things up a bit. But I like it this way. They will all wonder about it and they won't be able to discern any expression in my eyes."

"True," I said. His eyes were great white emotionless orbs.

"Besides," he added, "I can think of no other way to get Bong into the Omni. This way I look blind and he can lead me in."

"Why couldn't we just bend the mortals' minds a bit and make them not see him?"

"You'd be positively exhausted doing that," he answered.

"Does Bong have to go?" I really didn't want the others to see him. After all, he was my creation and the way he looked now proved me to be a terrible creator.

"Ainjul. I don't want them coming here. If we don't take him they would make it a point to come take a look at him."

"All right," I agreed.

He led me out of our secret chamber and down the hallway toward the front door.

We were just stepping onto the front porch when Delores, out of breath and hurrying, rushed up behind us.

"Wait just one minute," she said. She pulled an instant camera from her big blousy dress pocket. "Just a few pictures before you go. You are all so sweet looking."

"Do we show up on film?" I asked Matthew.

He laughed a short, soft laugh and then posed just before the flash illuminated the darkness.

I felt like I was being taken to the prom as Delores took shot after shot. It was hard to forget, though, that we were three sweet vampires ready for a night on the town.

When the last picture came sliding out of the body of the little black camera she let us go.

Matthew handed me Bong's leash.

"We are walking, if you don't mind," he said.

And I knew immediately why. Prolonging the inevitable, shall we say.

"Have fun and save the food for me," Delores called.

Bong insisted upon walking between us, and his great hip banged against Matthew instead of me.

"What did she mean by that?" I asked.

"This is a legitimate convention. There will be plenty of food, which is shared among our mortal friends after midnight."

I wondered who was footing the bill. Keeping the employees of the Omni Hotel working for a convention that served its meal after midnight must've taken a few bribes.

"Ainjul, there are two things I'd like to ask of you tonight. The first is, don't tell anyone about healing the puncture wounds with your blood. The second . . ."

"They don't know how?" I asked.

"Maybe, maybe not. I think not. I discovered it by accident several years back."

"By accident?"

"Yes, quite by accident. Which reminds me. You do understand that fire will kill you?"

"I suppose . . ."

"Fire comes in many forms. Flame, of course, the light of the sun, lightning, electricity, and also radiation."

"Radiation?" I didn't understand.

"Amazing, isn't it. We are so superior to humans in every way but we share an ultimate fate with them."

"Nuclear annihilation."

"Yes. The final Armageddon, so to speak," he said.

"But what does this have to do with healing the puncture wounds upon their necks?" I asked.

"My accident involved a certain young seaman. He had just returned from a long vigil in the Mediterranean when he sought me out. I had no way of knowing he had been exposed to a serious amount of radiation. All I know is that when I took him his blood was different, undeniably different. The first drops entered my mouth and were automatically expelled through no action I am physically aware of. Anyway, after I had spit the blood back upon his neck I saw that the wounds healed. I've used this technique ever since. Use it. In time you'll become as good with it as I and you will do it automatically when you withdraw."

"What if I drank contaminated blood. Would I die?" I

asked, aware of another peril that made immortality not so immortal.

"From my experience I don't think you can drink it. The blood in you will repel it," he said.

"And the second thing?" I asked.

"The second thing I ask of you is please, do not tell anyone your last name."

"They don't know?" I remembered Frederick saying every vampire knew who I was.

"They know you only as Ainjul," Matthew said, and his voice lingered on my name with a French intonation.

"Then that is all they will know me by," I said.

We walked a long time until I became aware Matthew was not taking a direct route to the Omni. I mentioned this to him and he somberly admitted it and steered us back to King Street.

A fountain, centered in the brick courtyard in front of the hotel, was lighted and bubbling in the night air. Mortals mingled outside, peering into the shop windows. Most of them looked like tourists, probably here in Charleston to take advantage of the Spoleto Festival. Everyone noticed Bong. How often does one see a Great Dane dressed in a tuxedo?

Matthew took the leash from my hand and started his blind-man act. It worked. I heard exclamations from those around us. One in particular struck me as funny. An older woman exclaimed to her husband how awful it was to see a blind man being led by a dog with only one eye.

Bong played his role beautifully. Within minutes we were inside the building and walking slowly up the grand circular staircase.

I had been in the Omni before, and its attempt at luxury still gave me the impression of a casino in Atlantic City. Tacky is the word that comes to mind, not elegant.

A sign at the top of the stairs read: Southern Society for Historical Preservation Convention, Dogwood Ballroom. The little white arrow beneath the block letters pointed to the left and we went in that direction.

"What a relief," I said.

"I told you, it's a legitimate convention," Matthew said.

A brass plaque mounted on the wall indicated the Dogwood Ballroom to be on our right and we walked slowly down the hallway toward our destination.

A round of applause greeted us when we entered the room. Matthew seemed to be angered, I was more embarrassed, Bong was simply beside himself.

The cold wave of curiosity hit me just before they began advancing upon us. Everyone, it seemed, was infatuated with my dog. Questions came all at once and I could not separate the wavering cloud of voices.

Bong was my first concern. I wasn't sure how he would react to the others. But when I glanced down at him he was all wiggles and wags, pushing his nose against the white hands that reached out to pet him.

Unlike Bong, I didn't enjoy being gawked at and I turned to Matthew for help but he was no longer beside me. They continued to close in and my claustrophobia forced me to search for a way out. A gap opened up between the group in front of me, and I saw Matthew across the room with another vampire. I tried to drag Bong away from the others, but their bodies were an impenetrable wall, so I reached down and unhooked his leash. Freed of him, I managed to squeeze by the crowd. My heart was slamming inside my chest. I was overwhelmed by them.

I was halfway across the room when *she* intercepted me. Like a great swooping bird of prey she cut off my escape route.

"You must be Debra," I said. Frederick had mentioned her name and she was the only female vampire in the crowd.

"I've been waiting to meet you. I don't know any other vampires like us. There is so much we have in common," she said.

"Like us?" I questioned.

"Of the fairer sex, my dear. We aren't exactly like them or are you too young yet to have learned that?"

I studied her. She was much shorter than I, only coming up to my shoulders. Her hair was piled upon her head, carelessly, and the mousy brown color gave the appearance of being dirty. Her face, though not unattractive, was made up and looked garish. She had used red lipstick which ultimately reminded me of blood and only overplayed her already too large mouth. Her eyes were the same mousy brown color of her hair but they were set deep in her head and gave her a sad look. However sad that look was, was not enough to make me like her.

Her dress was red, a few shades lighter than her lips. It fit like a glove but that was okay, she did have a great body. However, every move she made was one of allure, and every curve threatened to gape apart the near-bursting seams of her attire.

"I'm afraid I don't follow you," I said, trying to get away from her and closer to Matthew.

"Oh you innocent young thing. I'm talking about their penises."

"Excuse me," I said, not sure I really heard what it was that I had heard.

"Well, I'll tell you right now. They practically shrivel up and fall off. That they do. While we still remain round and full," she explained, punctuating it by thrusting her chest forward. "They envy us for that, you know," she said.

I'm sure she saw my embarrassment but thankfully another vampire interrupted us.

"Debra, leave her alone. You'll destroy any virtue the young woman has," he said.

Debra laughed a shrill, piercing laugh and then wrapped herself around him and kissed him passionately. He pushed her away. A pouty look claimed her large red lips but then they smiled and she walked away toward her next target, Matthew.

"She's something of a vamp, no pun intended," he said as he wiped away a smear of lipstick from his mouth. "I'm Terrance Gillian. Like you, I have brought a new member of our race tonight, not as unique as yours, he's the one with the fair hair and the navy-blue sports coat." He pointed across the room where the young man stood alone with his back against the mirrored wall. "He'd like to talk with you.

235

His name is Eric, Eric Boyerton, and he's still quite young. Will you speak with him?"

Even from this distance I knew how young he was, the smell was still with him. The others were avoiding him.

A group of vampires still held Bong captive in their circle but he was receiving them quite graciously. He no longer smelled and I found myself trying to recall when his transformation had become complete. In the hectic pace I'd kept step with lately it simply eluded me.

I made my way across the ballroom.

"Hello," I said. "Your friend said you wanted to talk to me."

"Do you love the Master?" he asked.

His straightforwardness caught me off guard.

"The Master?" I questioned.

"The old one that made you," he said.

"Oh, you mean Matthew," I said, and turned around to see him on the other side of the room. Debra was already making her advances upon him and something close to jealously aroused my senses.

"I haven't really known him long enough to love him. Why do you ask?"

"I was wondering if I was strange in my feelings toward the one who made me. I'm not, wasn't, a homosexual in my mortal life but I honestly love Terrance and can't understand it."

I understood his feelings. I had loved Elijah.

"Has Terrance been kind and caring while nurturing you through the transformation?" I asked.

Eric didn't answer me, he didn't need to.

"It's not unnatural for you to have feelings for him. After all, he's practically given birth to you, hasn't he?"

A light of understanding surfaced in his gentle blue eyes and his attitude relaxed.

"Thanks. I needed to hear it from another," he said.

Recognizable laughter floated nearby. Frederick and his young shadow, Ken, had joined the party.

"Be thankful *he* didn't make you," I said, motioning with a slight shake of my head.

236

"I've met Ken. He is pretty upset about all this. He wants to die. I understand the Master can destroy us," he said.

I remembered asking Matthew if he could destroy Bong for me. He had declined. But I also remembered Elijah's constant reminder of Matthew's power.

"Ken is going to ask the Master tonight," Eric said.

"To destroy him?" I asked.

"He is determined to die," Eric said.

"Why doesn't he take his own life? Why doesn't he just lie outside and let the sun destroy him?"

"Well, from all I've been told the blood won't allow it. It is not simple to destroy oneself. I imagine that if the body could be tied outside . . . but even then we are incredibly strong."

My gaze fell upon Bong. It did make sense. How many times had my poor dog tried, and failed?

"Do you know many of the others here?" he asked.

"No."

"Neither do I. Debra I do know. I'll warn you now about her. She's got a personal vendetta against the Master. The longer he scorns her the deeper it grows. Terrance told me it has been festering inside her for some fifty odd years now. Your arrival, or creation, has opened that wound and I've heard rumor that if she can't have him no one will."

"I'm sure Matthew can handle it. Why do you call him the Master? He is the same as the rest of us."

"I'm not too sure about that. He was born in 1651, the young Lord Charles Matthew Francis Trenton. When his father died he became the fourth Earl of Tellingham. When he actually became a vampire is unknown, but certainly he has become a Master of power."

He sounded like he was quoting from a history textbook.

"I'm sorry, I've monopolized enough of your time. Besides, I think your dog is looking for you," he said.

Bong was indeed. He was trotting from vampire to vampire in an obvious state of confusion.

"I didn't think I would like anyone here, but you're okay,

237

Eric. I've enjoyed talking with you," I said, taking my leave of his company.

Bong and I were at last reunited. He was panting heavily. The attentions flowered upon him had nearly exhausted him.

I looked around for Matthew. He had shaken loose of Debra and was standing alone beside the long row of tables now being filled with food from the hotel kitchen. Compared to the others attending the convention he had a certain air about him and I too could see why they called him the Master. His confidence was not boastful, instead he held a quiet composure while maintaining his status above them.

Absorbed in watching them, he didn't see me approach, and when I spoke I startled him.

"There are more of us here than I expected," I said.

"Twenty-five, five new ones, counting you," he said.

"You haven't included Bong. He makes it twenty-six."

"So I haven't," he said, and he sighed a dreary sigh of boredom.

"Matthew, they're not as bad as all that," I said.

"Did you like Debra?"

"Actually, I think she's rather crude," I said, remembering her remark about the teeny weenies.

"They're all the same, you're just too preoccupied to have noticed," he said.

"I don't think you're being fair. The ones I've talked with seem all right."

"Terrance Gillian is, and his young friend probably will be too. The only other one that meets my approval is Butch," he said.

"Which one is he?" I asked.

"He's the one in the pin-striped suit with the fedora. We go back a long time," Matthew said.

Butch was easy to find among the crowd. He looked like a gangster.

"Does he carry a gun in that violin case?" I asked, trying to lighten Matthew's mood. It didn't work.

"No, and he'll tell you himself, it's not a violin, it's a fiddle, and he is remarkably good with it."

238

"Matthew, are you going to be like this all evening?" I asked.

"Like what?"

"Disagreeable," I said.

"Yes." He looked into my eyes with his eerie white stare. "As long as they are around me, yes, I'm sorry."

Debra's voice rose above the cackling thrum of the others. She asked everyone to take their places around the half square of tables in front of the ballroom.

I noticed Matthew was not moving toward the others with me and I turned to him again.

"Aren't you coming?"

"No."

"Matthew, I think you're being rude. The least you can do is sit at the table."

"Ainjul, they really don't expect that, but you go ahead," he said, gently nudging me away from him.

I walked along the table, reading the place cards that marked where we were to sit. Each neatly folded card had a name written boldly in red, befitting a vampire, and beneath the name the city and state written in black. Some were from as far north as Virginia, many came from Florida.

I found my place next to Matthew. I wasn't very surprised to find Debra had seated herself on the other side of him. We were in the exact center of the tables, a place of honor no doubt.

The vampire to my right was John Heller. He introduced himself as he sat down saying something to the effect that we were neighbors. His place card marked him as being from Hilton Head, South Carolina. He began to prattle on about his career, which, fortunately, he had not had to abandon since becoming undead. He was a mortician. I wondered if he supplied coffins at a discount for his undead kindred.

Bong rested his head upon Matthew's empty chair and whined expectantly. I pulled the chair away from the table so he could sit closer to me but he took it as invitation and climbed up, arranging himself awkwardly between the arm-

239

rests. A round of laughter broke out as the others noticed him seated regally beside me.

Debra instructed everyone to introduce themselves and tell about their existance. The storytelling began at the end of the table and each vampire boastfully proclaimed how much he had invested in art, stocks, real estate, antiques, etc. What it boiled down to was a bid to outdo one another.

One by one they told how they lived and I knew sooner or later it would be my turn. What was I going to tell them? I looked across the room at Matthew, but he had decided to rearrange the food at the buffet and completely ignored the happenings around our tables.

John Heller stood up beside me and began a long tale of the benefits of tending to the dead. He was totally disgusting, and as he explained the detailed procedure of draining dead bodies I was suddenly overcome by the burning desire to feed. I tried to take my mind off it, but it roared inside me, demanding me to take action.

I watched the condensation slide down the water glass in front of my plate. Only two small pieces of ice were left afloat in the glass but I immediately reached for it. In the past, water had subdued the flames within me and I poured the cold liquid down my throat the very moment everyone's attention had fallen on me to speak.

Forgetting my strength, I slammed the water glass down on the table and it shattered against my hand.

"I know you are all expecting me to leak some secrets about my life with Matthew. But my life, our lives, are personal and private. I'm not playing your games," I said.

In the silence following my outburst I heard a voice say in astonishment, "She drank the water."

Then another voice came from the gangster, Butch, "Bravo, young lady, bravo."

Matthew was beside me in the blink of an eye.

"Ainjul, what have you done?" he asked quietly but with a tinge of bewilderment.

Blood ran down between my fingers and dripped on the white china plate in front of me. A large spearlike piece of glass was embedded in my palm.

"It appears I've cut myself," I said, and quickly pulled the sharp dagger from my hand.

Matthew said something about drinking the water and I became enraged.

"It's no big deal, for chrissake, Elijah and I drank water all the time. Bong showed us that it could be done."

But apparently it was a big deal. I had inadvertently let out one of my own little secrets.

Whispers broke out around me.

"She'll corrupt the blood . . . she'll weaken herself . . . there is water in blood. . . . Might we try . . ."

Matthew took hold of my arm and was about to lead me away but the doors of the ballroom opened and the first of the mortals arrived. He released me but not without a word of warning.

"We will talk about this later," he said.

He walked away from me quickly, taking his place to greet the humans as they filtered into the room. The very atmosphere had changed and it wasn't all due to their arrival. Matthew was pleasant, at ease among them, yet with his own kind he was barely tolerable and I still could not accept his camaraderie with mortals.

"Thanks a lot. You've spoiled everything," Debra said quietly but with such intonation to let me know she was pissed.

"Can't handle it when the attention is taken away from you, can you?" I said.

She stood up and towered over me. Words formed upon her blood-red lips but she held them to herself and walked away.

The others around the tables followed suit and I felt abandoned, an outcast. Bong jumped down from his chair and I thought he too was leaving me, but he rested his head on my lap and looked up at me with his only eye, waiting patiently for me to stroke his forehead.

Laughter and idle chatter swirled around me. I leaned back against my chair and picked at the scar tissue already forming on my injured hand while scanning the growing crowd to see if Delores or Steven had arrived. They had.

The group of mortals with them were all young, beautiful creatures in their own right. I felt the yearning in each of them and I smiled a slow twisted smile as I imagined the feast that would end the evening.

One by one they began to fill their plates from the endless supply on the buffet: filet mignon, lobster tail, shrimp stuffed with crab, caviar, pâté de foie gras, stuffed mushrooms, baby carrots, steamed cauliflower, Brussels sprouts. Dom Pérignon was brought to the tables and the chatter was joined by the clinking of silverware.

How long would it continue before the real feast began? I reached across the table for another glass of water, not caring who saw me or what was said. My hunger was blooming again.

Bong whined expectantly and I poured some water onto a plate and set it on the floor for him. He greedily slurped it up and whined for more. I obliged him and leaned down to pour the remainder of the water from my glass. As I pulled myself upright Delores was leaning across the table, a smile upon her face and a gift in her hands.

"I have something for you," she said, handing it to me.

The present was wrapped neatly, the paper decorated with multicolored balloons and ribbons.

"For me?" I said, taking it and shaking it in my hands.

"It isn't much, but I thought you would like it," she said.

I was surprised by her kindness and I looked away from her so she wouldn't see the emotion fogging my eyes. I shook the package again and began to feel around the small box.

"Go on, open it," she said.

I tore the paper and slid the box out. My hands were shaking but I'm sure it was due to my hunger rather than my excitement. With gentle caution I opened the lid. It was one of the snapshots she had taken of me, Bong, and Matthew. She had framed it in an antique silver frame, oval in shape and still a little tarnished between the delicate grooves of lacy flowers carved in the metal.

"I don't know what to say. Thank you."

242

"You like it?" she asked.

"Yes, very much."

She reached across the table and took it from me, studied it, and then handed it back.

"The three of you look so regal standing there in the glow of the porch light. If I didn't know better I'd say it was a family portrait. You look so much like Matthew I think you're related."

"We are," I said, and then cursed myself silently for letting it slip out. "I mean in a vampire sense, we are family." I tried to cover my blunder.

She smiled knowingly, and her expression made me tingle all over. I knew that she knew, but did she know before?

"Well, I'm going to get some dessert. I hope you're enjoying the party."

She turned her enormous bulk and headed toward the buffet.

I stared at the picture for a long while. Matthew looked so perfectly elegant, regal was a good word to describe him. The snapshot had caught him just beginning to smile, and he was forever frozen with the air of mystery surrounding him. I was frozen by the moment with a blissfully serene look about me and Bong had been caught with his tongue lolling out of the side of his mouth and a big toothy grin on his muzzle.

What Delores had noticed, the likeness between Matthew and me, was hard not to ignore. It was the first time I was really able to discern it, the bone structure, the same small lips, the shape and setting of the eyes. We could've easily been brother and sister and I wondered how many of the others were noticing and whispering about it.

A soft voice startled me and I turned halfway in my chair to see who was standing behind me. It was Ken, the young blond vampire that wished to die.

"It's a very nice picture," he said.

I looked at it once more and then slid it into the inside breast pocket of my tuxedo.

"May I ask a favor of you?" he questioned.

243

"That depends on what it is," I said, watching as his stiff short fingers twisted and untwisted a linen dinner napkin.

"Will you introduce me to him. I have something I need, I want him to do," he said.

I knew who *him* referred to and I knew what Ken wanted him to do.

"Is your existence so bad?" I asked. Even before he replied I felt his sorrow. He was a pitiful creature, not able to even call the one who could destroy him by name.

"Could you end my life?" he asked me, and for a brief instant a ray of hope lighted his eyes.

"If I knew how I might be able to, but no, I think you should ask him." I stood up and watched his expression turn into one of anguish and despair. "But come, I'll introduce you," I said.

This simple introduction gave me a purpose among the crowd. I felt somehow protective of Ken as I led him across the ballroom. His very destiny was in my hands because if I didn't introduce him to Matthew I knew he would never work up enough nerve to approach and ask on his own.

Matthew was seated beside Steven at a small, round table in the far corner of the room. Delores had just returned from the dessert trip and was loaded down with baked Alaska and strawberry shortcake. She sat down as we approached.

"Excuse me, Matthew," I interrupted Steven and got Matthew's attention. "This is Ken. He wants to talk with you, privately."

Matthew's smile disappeared and I could not tell what expression surfaced because of those damn white eyes of his. He stood up slowly, eyeing Ken with a distasteful grin upon his face. He made a motion for the young vampire to follow and I watched them leave the party. Once the ballroom doors were closed, Steven poured himself another glass of wine. I sat down next to him as he set the nearly empty bottle down with a bang. I realized he already had too much.

"Well, I can just about guess what that's all about," he said.

Delores swallowed a large bite of the baked Alaska,

cleared her throat, and said, "It's a real shame, he's just a young one."

If they were waiting for me to say anything, neither made it clear and I decided to keep my mouth shut and play dumb. Delores attacked her dessert again and Steven downed the wine in three great gulps. He reached for the bottle and poured the remainder of the Dom Pérignon into his glass. He only filled it halfway.

"The young ones are the worst. I'll have a grisly mess to clean up," he said.

His comment reflected no emotion, but my curiosity was aroused.

"What is that supposed to mean?" I asked.

"The younger they are the easier they die, but the clean-up is not as easy as when the old ones die. Once I only had to remove the clothes and sweep up the ashes and particles of bone that remained."

"Are you pulling my leg?" I asked. I saw Dracula become nothing but ashes when he was destroyed but never really believed it happened that way. Actually, since becoming a vampire I never really had given it much thought.

"No. I'm not pulling your leg. It's true. The old ones wither up and become practically nothing. But the young ones. Ever see the way a spider sucks the juices from the insects it catches? When the spider is done with its meal only a dried husk is left. And that is about what Ken will look like after Matthew and the sun are done with him. I've got to dispose of him, you see, and I'd rather dispose of a few ashes than a burnt, dried husk."

"Steven, do you mind, I'm eating," Delores said.

"Well, she asked," he said.

"Sure wouldn't be much left of Matthew then," I said, picturing in my mind only a scattering of centuries-old dust in the shape of his body upon the ground.

"Don't even think about it. Matthew ain't ready to die, not now that he's got you," Steven said, and downed the rest of his wine.

He reached for the bottle but then remembered it was empty and hurriedly retrieved another bottle from the next table. Before sitting down he filled his glass and offered to fill Delores's too, but she waved him off and started on her strawberry shortcake.

"Do you watch them die? I mean, do you see what the sun does to them?" I asked.

"Ainjul, it's not something I want to see, but I have to. They fight right up to the very end and I have to be sure the chains don't give."

"So you chain them down in a place where the sun will destroy them? I thought Matthew just took all their blood away."

"Oh, that he does, but not every drop can be extracted. And only one tiny drop is all that is needed to struggle for survival. Believe me, I've witnessed it at least . . ."

"Steven, please," Delores interrupted.

"Are they in pain? Do you think they suffer?" I asked again. My curiosity for the morbid reality of what I had become was getting the best of me and I had to know.

"I think I'll just finish eating somewhere else," Delores said, and rose from the table cradling her strawberry short-cake in her hands.

"Naw, I don't think they even perceive what is happening. Once Matthew drains them they're pretty much dead. It's the blood, somehow alien and seeking desperately to continue living that makes the bodies fight. But then again I really can't say for sure. At least none of them have ever spoken to me, only animal hisses and groans come from them. Did I ever tell you about the one that almost got away? No, I guess I didn't. After the body withered down to skeletal conformation he slipped right out of the bindings and was halfway across the backyard before he dropped. God, I prayed that none of the nosy tourists were gaping through the fence. Jeez, I nearly crapped in my pants that day, I'll tell you," he said, and took another hard swallow of wine.

"You chain them up right in Matthew's yard?" I found it hard to believe.

"You bet your sweet ass. Right out in the old smoke-house. The roof fell off in the great earthquake but the walls

246

are thick and sturdy and, besides, Matthew always inspects the remains before I haul them away, to be sure they're dead."

The wine was working its charm on him. The tips of his ears were red and his eyes had become glazed but his speech wasn't slurred although his tongue was loose and his entire manner out of context with the Steven I had met that night on Matthew's porch.

"Excuse me for becoming so . . . inbibed, but it's my way of handling things like this."

"When does this little party end?" I asked him, aware that the evening was growing late and my hunger was pulling back inside me in defense of being ignored for so long.

"Pretty soon now. See the way they are regrouping. It's almost time for the feasting to start."

I looked around the room and saw everyone had separated into groups of two or three humans to a vampire.

"They're all like Delores and me, friends and servants to your kind. They will allow themselves to be taken this evening. Of course none will be killed. Good help is hard to find," he said sarcastically.

Matthew had been gone too long. I stood up and excused myself as Steven poured himself another drink. I scanned the ballroom, saw Bong sitting quietly beside Delores, and gave a quick, shrill whistle. He cocked his head in my direction, and so did most of the guests, then picked his great body off the floor and trotted obediently to me.

Before I ever reached the door I heard angry voices. Debra's I recognized, but the man's voice I did not. I pushed the door open and waited for Bong to exit, then I followed, leaving the crowded ballroom behind me.

The man's voice turned out to be Frederick, the goon. He and Debra had cornered Matthew and Ken.

Frederick was arguing obstinately that Ken was his property and Debra was backing up his argument with whining tones of agreement.

Matthew glanced at me. His white-on-white eyes reflected nothing, but his subtle gesture, twisting that damn lock of hair, told me he was more than a little upset.

When I approached I heard Matthew challenge the both of them to try and stop him. They abruptly shut up and Matthew reminded them it was Ken's decision and not theirs. The lock of hair was released and Matthew lowered his hand onto Ken's shoulder.

"Come to my home at four o'clock," he said to the boy, and then turned to face me. "Are you ready to leave?"

I nodded. I had had my fill of vampires and human slaves. I wanted to go out into the night, feed, and be left alone.

Matthew handed me Bong's leash but didn't wait for me to clip it onto his collar.

As I steadied Bong I watched Matthew hurry away. My fingers fumbled with the snap closure. I gave the leash a firm tug to be sure it was secure and straightened up.

A cold, white hand closed around my arm. The brightly painted fingernails gave her away and I turned to see what she wanted.

"I'm going to take him away, if it takes forever I will do it," Debra hissed.

I pulled away from her and with a voice as cold and uncaring as I could possibly muster I said, "If you were smart enough to be observant you would see that he is not mine, I'm his."

She backed away from me, the look upon her painted face was pure evil. I remembered Eric's tale of the woman vampire scorned. She was dangerous. Indeed, Matthew had ignored her too long.

"I will take him away," she said again, and then glided back into the ballroom in a blur of white movement.

Matthew was waiting for me just beyond the bend in the hallway and I nearly ran into him as I rounded the corner.

"Debra just threatened you," I said.

He looked at me with those empty white eyes and took the leash from my hands.

"Matthew, I think she really means it. She's going to do something . . . take you away, she said."

"Ainjul, don't you think I'm old enough to take care of little insignificant creatures like her?"

I looked up into his boyishly handsome face. Again I tried

to see beneath the youthful appearance and understand the centuries that molded and shaped him.

"I think you've underestimated her," I said.

He gave no reply but resumed his blind man role and passively led Bong onward.

There was nothing I could do to persuade him of the threat of which I felt Debra was capable. Either his mind was preoccupied with the impending destruction of Ken or he was just being arrogant, I wasn't able to tell. I followed silently, reached out to support his arm in our blind role play, and slowly descended the stairway of the hotel.

The huge lobby was empty. The night had grown late and my hunger was now a constant reminder of this fact.

Matthew kept a brisk pace and stayed on King Street. When we reached Broad Street he turned right. This time he had chosen a direct route home, no more meandering through the sleepy city of Charleston.

The headlights of an oncoming car illuminated the darkness and I could see Legare Street a block away, but my attention stayed on the car, traveling much too fast for the narrow road. The metallic hood ornament glistened for a moment, it was a Mercedes, and it gathered more speed as it approached.

In a split second the car would have passed us. But in the split second, forever frozen in my mind, Bong leapt out in front of the car. A loud thud boomed in my ears and I saw his body fly up and land on top of the hood before he rolled off and remained motionless in the middle of the street. A squeal of tires and the acrid smell of burning rubber hit me the same instant a cold wave of nausea gripped my insides.

CHAPTER FOURTEEN

I ran to Bong. His little tuxedo was covered with blood, and the smell caused my hunger to flare up with great passion. The tiny bow tie had come off, and I bent down to pick it up.

Bong groaned wearily; I knew he was waiting to die. He had done it on purpose, just as surely as he had done it before, but I still refused to believe in his death wish.

"Oh my God. I'm so sorry. He just ran in front of me. I couldn't stop. I didn't even see him until . . ."

I turned around and saw the young woman who had run Bong down and I saw Matthew beside her and heard him say it wasn't her fault.

"Damn you. Damn you, Matthew, you let go of his leash," my angry words unfurled in a maniacal hiss.

"Is he alive? Can I take him to a vet? Tell me what I can do, I'm so sorry," the young woman said.

I felt the woman's anguish but my full attention was on Matthew and again I cursed him. If it were possible for him to turn a lighter shade of pale he would have done so, the shock of my words penetrated him to the point of being speechless. I turned away from his bewildered stare and quickly gathered Bong's limp body in my arms.

I ran. Bong's weight was nothing, my strength incredible in this moment of reaction. In my mind I knew Matthew wasn't responsible, it could've been me holding the leash. But I needed to blame someone. A delirious rage of anger and sorrow spurred me faster. My preternatural speed would only be a rush of cold wind in the night, and soon I was making a graceful leap onto the great piazza of Matthew's home.

The front door was locked. In my present state of delirium I could've easily blown it from the hinges, but Bong began to struggle in my arms and I stopped and gently lowered him to the floor.

I sat down beside him and cradled his big head in my lap. Blood oozed from his nostrils and I thought about the first night I had found him. Ironic that the beginning and the end should be the same, and I knew it was the end. I could not let him continue, could not let him try and fail to die forever.

Matthew was beside me. I petted Bong's head and kept my eye on his one, sad brown eye as I spoke.

"I'm going to end it now. I'll take his blood back and you can destroy his body when you destroy Ken's." My tone had become calm but robotic.

A mixture of emotions pulsed from Matthew, and had I been in control of my senses I would have realized he was communicating with me in a manner that only vampires can communicate to one another. But my attentions stayed on Bong.

I knew I could do it; drink him dry. Blood fever pounded in my veins, and I waited another minute or two for the passion to totally consume me. I concentrated only on the smell of blood until it reached near orgasmic heights and then I plunged into Bong's artery and drank and drank and drank.

Consuming this blood was different than anything I had ever done and I was swooning with the animal power it gave me. I could hear Matthew telling me things and I felt his hands on my shoulders. Then he roughly yanked me away.

"It's over, Ainjul, you can stop now." he said.

My mind was no longer my own. It had become enshrouded in an animalistic fog, and I saw things that only Bong could have seen. Images flashed in my brain. The scent of animals filled my mind and the taste of blood from the dead carcasses of deer, raccoons, possums, and snakes caused a violent repulsion to split me into two beings. The animal side of me craved these things but the human side was terrified. Our blood mingled and I could feel a fight for control.

"What's happening inside me?" I asked.

Matthew didn't answer right away, and I looked up into his crazy white eyes and shuddered. He didn't know.

The reaction between our blood became painful. The images became more vivid and sporadic. I was running through a marsh, in human form but down on all fours naked and panting, while closing in on the musky scent of an animal. I felt the sharp sting of teeth as another dog bit into me in self-defense, but then I felt a power in my jaw unlike anything human and tasted the warm blood that spurted from the steaming entrails of my prey's belly.

My stomach churned and a sharp pain punched the air from my lungs. I gasped and doubled over. Then I started to laugh, because all I could imagine was that I was becoming a dog and I waited for the rippling of my flesh to begin and pictured the way that kid in *American Werewolf in London* changed. But nothing happened.

The images were beginning to burn out. A brief glimpse of an animal carcass or the smell of an unknown prey would swell up but quickly subside as my blood fought harder to dominate Bong's blood. A heavy tiredness swept over me, and I reached out as Matthew helped me stand.

"Are you okay?" he asked.

"I don't think our blood was compatible," I said, thinking what a hellish trip it was.

My attempt at humor eased the worried look on his face, and he unlocked the door and helped me inside.

"Help me upstairs, I want to lie down," I said.

"Perhaps you should go to your coffin," he said.

My knees buckled underneath me, another fleeting sensation of running on all fours tugged in my mind.

"Damn it, I want to lie on a bed," I said, and fell against him.

He held me close and quietly led me up the stairs. He opened the door of his room and helped me over to the big antique brass bed.

I sank slowly onto the firm mattress. The dark-blue satin

spread was cool against my skin and I realized my body was burning with fever. The room spun slowly; my head landed against the pillow. I studied Matthew. His every movement was in slow motion, and he fussed over me for a minute before pulling away.

"I have to take care of Bong. You rest here, don't get up, just rest," he instructed.

My eyes closed and I thought, I'm not going anywhere in this condition.

Emptiness, bleak and uncertain as eternity, fogged my mind. No thoughts would come and time was out of my grasp. When a glitter of light broke through, my initial thought was that I was going to be sick.

I wanted to get up but found my body would not respond, and when I began to vomit I was thankful that I had become paralyzed while lying upon my side or I might have choked to death on all the blood that was bursting from me in great rocking waves.

Wretched as vomiting can be, vomiting blood is worse. My body was purging itself of the blood, and by the amount now pooling around my face and staining the beautiful satin bedspread, I knew my body was forcing it all out, not just Bong's.

I was shivering uncontrollably except for when the heaves would force some more blood from me. And each time the blood spewed from my throat my fever began to diminish. At last it ended, though my stomach contracted violently a few more times.

Steam appeared to rise from the blood, but when I blinked I knew it wasn't steam, just a misty fog from my watering eyes. I wasn't crying. I didn't have the strength to cry. My chin and neck were covered with blood, and the left side of my body, from the head to almost the hip, was soaking in the spent liquid. It took all the power left in me to move away from the blood puddles, but I did it, just an inch or so but I did it.

My long hair was thick with red wetness and I watched the strands of soaked hair paint a lovely streak across the pillow as I pulled away. I hoped Matthew wasn't particularly fond of this bedspread because even Shout wasn't going to get a stain like that one out.

The empty fog began to invade my mind again, and instead of fighting it I welcomed it as an escape. Nothingness billowed in and I winked out.

A piercing sound echoed in the fog and jarred me back to awareness.

"Matthew, get up here, hurry," I heard Delores cry out.

When I tried to open my eyes, I found that they were open already, and then Delores yelled for Matthew again and the thick empty fog released me so I was able to see her.

She was holding a bath towel, prepared to clean up the mess but afraid to come any nearer. If indeed my eyes had been open all along, I must've looked like I had really died.

"Matthew, damn it, will you hurry up." Her voice was just an octave below a screech.

Her eyes met mine briefly, and I saw deep concern bordering with outright terror. I wanted to tell her I was okay but could not speak and suddenly felt frightened myself. I had become prisoner inside a body that was locked away from the controls of my mind.

Matthew was in the room. I could feel him. Though I wanted to look over toward the door I was frozen in place and I had to wait until he came into my line of vision. He was only there an instant, I saw his thighs still clad in the black tuxedo slacks. Even my eyes were stuck, not moving in any direction, but open and watching as he again reappeared in my line of vision. He bent down, and I watched his body become hips, waist, chest, and then at last a face.

"Ainjul," he whispered, and my fear swelled because I felt his fear.

"Is she . . . dead?" Delores asked.

Matthew's hand reached out to touch my face, growing larger and clearer but then so near that my eyes couldn't focus on it anymore. I was afraid for him to touch me, afraid that I had become hard as concrete, final rigor mortis.

He touched me. Never had his cold hand felt so comforting. He tilted my head a little to the side, and inside my mind screamed for him not to do it because I was stone and I might break, but my body moved normally and when he released me my head stayed as he had placed it.

Now my angle of vision was slanted upward and I saw part of his ear and the ceiling above. When his hand drew away from my face he accidentally pushed my right eye closed and I screamed again inside, *what the hell did you do that for,* when half my line of sight went dark.

He realized what he had done, and with a gentle touch he pushed the lid back up and I could see again.

"No, she's not dead, but I've never seen anything like this." He turned and stood up. "I'll pick her up and you pull the spread off. Then clean her up the best you can, I have to take care of Ken," he said, and again his body came forward, obstructing my view.

His hands slipped under me. I was prepared to be lifted like a statue, stiff and still, but my legs dangled and my head fell back limply.

Delores was out of my sight, but I heard her gather the spread and then felt myself being settled back into place upon the sheets. My gaze was directed at the ceiling. Matthew arranged my body in what he thought to be a comfortable position, flat on my back with my legs stretched out straight, toes pointing up, and my hands gently resting across my stomach. I would have rather been on my side but I was in no condition to complain.

Why don't you lay a lily across my chest, I said to no one. I felt like a corpse laid out for the viewing.

I sensed Matthew leaving, and again my voice broke the silence inside my head.

Matthew, don't leave me.

His face loomed large above me and his eyes met mine.

"Ainjul, I'll be back just as soon as I can," he said.

Was it possible that he heard my cries? Was I communicating with him?

He held my gaze, and I tried to send him a thought.

I'm in here, Matthew. I'm scared but I'm all right. Can you understand what I'm telling you?

255

His expression changed. Was he receiving me?

"Yes, you'll be all right," he said, and clasped my hands reassuringly. Then he was gone.

His words could've been coincidental. His reply wasn't a direct reply, but it was enough to give me hope.

I was alone in the room again and the blanket of fog began to snuggle into my mind. Nothing would displace its advance and once again I was lost in the swirling depths of emptiness.

This time the solitude was broken by pain. My left ear was burning and wetness slid around my earlobe and trickled down my neck. I thought for a moment blood was coming out of my ear but then Delores' voice broke the silence and I heard her telling me how sorry she was about Bong.

Water splashed and trickled. Then the hot wetness again hit my ear, and I realized she was washing the blood from me.

By the time she was finished with my ear it was itching terribly. My brain sent a message to my hand to reach up and scratch it, but the connection was never made and I suffered an intolerable minute until my ear gave up.

"I'm afraid the tux is ruined. I'll try and get it off you," Delores said, starting to unbutton my shirt.

A memory surfaced. A memory from that night on the front porch when she had given me the impression of *wanting* me.

Well, she's got you now. You'll lie here quiet and still while she does as she pleases with you.

The shirt was open, my chest exposed, and she was guiding my arm out of both the jacket and shirt-sleeve at the same time.

Lady, I'm real sick of people dressing and undressing me, my voice proclaimed.

I endured her touch. There was nothing suggestive in her manner but still I didn't trust her. After she had me stripped from the waist up, she slid her huge arm beneath me, and it was a mountainous arm, helped me sit, held me there and slipped a long nightgown over my head.

My pants came off next, but she did it with discreet care.

She might've been a nurse taking care of an invalid, but a nurse would have remembered to remove the shoes from her patient first, and she had to stop and do that when my pants bunched up around my ankles.

Her great bulk moved, I felt it. She was leaving with my soiled clothes and the fog was moving back in. I wondered why every time I was alone the fog rolled in, but I didn't have much time to think about it before it clouded me back into timeless oblivion.

Matthew's presence pulled me from the deep. He was sitting on the edge of the bed, quiet, composed, and watching me. His face was flush with living color, his features had softened, no longer was his nose quite as sharp or his cheekbones quite as pronounced. He was vibrant and fresh, and I knew Ken was dead.

My eyes never opened, they had been open all along, and how Matthew knew I had been released from the fog I don't know. He began to speak to me, but maybe he had been speaking to me all along.

"Ainjul, I didn't let go of Bong. It just happened. He was gone that fast, I was as shocked as you were. I think you know this to be true. If you need to blame me for it, I can understand. I'm truly sorry but he was never meant to be," he said.

My vampire puppy was one big accident. *It ain't gonna live. You gonna have to destroy it. He was never meant to be.* But he was meant to be because he showed me so many things and he was a part of me. *And I'm going to miss you so much.*

"I was pretty sure Bong's blood would be rejected, make you sick, but I don't know how it is causing the state you're in now." He got off the bed and stood so he was no longer in my direct line of sight but I could see his form coming closer.

His recent feasting had risen his body temperature, and this time when he touched me his hand was warm. As he lifted me from the bed I wondered how feasting from a vampire, the blood of which isn't alive in the true sense of the word, caused such strong reactions.

"I'm taking you down to your coffin. The sun will rise

257

soon. Perhaps sleep will cure you. Perhaps tomorrow you'll be well," he said.

All those *perhapses* told me he didn't know.

Matthew, if you don't know I wish you would just admit it, I thought.

"I've never seen anything like this and I'm not sure what to do," he said.

Again I thought he was hearing me.

If you hear me, please tell me now. I sent him another thought. He remained silent.

I was entombed in a useless body. He was holding me tight against himself, my head was pressed close to his heart. The steady, strong beating was like a metronome, constant, never faltering.

My left eye had been pushed closed against his shirt, but my right was open and I saw the inside of his strong arm holding my legs and beyond that I watched the wall flow by.

Sleep was coming. It wasn't the gray fog of nothing, it was the sleep of the dead, and I was ready because I had hope too that in the evening I'd be well and strong and my old self again.

Matthew lowered me into my coffin. He started to close the lid but then hesitated and reached out to close my eyes. I laughed silently, thinking he should put pennies on them too. Then the lid shut and the humming of his computer processor was no longer heard, but felt. I began to sink into my sleep, and as the sun rose outside I imagined the bodies of Bong and Ken beginning to crisp in the bright light of day. This is the stuff nightmares are made of, but I knew there would be no dreams for me.

When I awoke I was surprised to find myself back upon the brass bed in Matthew's room. I was curled up on my side, my legs pulled close to my chest, one arm dangling over the edge of the bed, the other curled up and twisted beneath my head. My muscles ached like they needed to be stretched but I couldn't do it.

However, my eyes were moving and I could blink and I thought this was a good sign.

Delores was sitting in a chair beside my bed. She had a big bowl of popcorn upon her lap. The buttery aroma was overpowering, but not enough to displace her smell. Chanel No. 5.

The television on top of Matthew's bureau was playing and I watched the sportscaster as he blurped out the day's highlights, then the picture became replays of Wimbledon and I recognized Jimmy Connors.

Since the sports were usually toward the end of a newscast I guessed the time to be around 11:20. I had slept late and I wanted to sleep more.

A handful of popcorn rose from the bowl and my eyes followed the movement right into the open mouth of Delores. I never realized popcorn crunched so loudly, and I was strangely fascinated by the movements her jaw made while she ground the puffed kernels into putty. I saw her throat bob up and down when she swallowed and thought of my own hunger.

My body felt dry and empty. I easily visualized what I looked like, the remaining husk of a fat spider's victim.

The news ended and *Twilight Zone* came on. The black-and-white image of Rod Serling appeared. I had always been bothered by watching dead people on television and tonight was no exception. With eerie wonder I pictured Rod in another dimension of time and space, in his *Twilight Zone*. I began to think about Rod. In his own way he had achieved immortality. There he was, alive and speaking to his audience. He would never age. How many others like him had achieved this celluloid gift of eternity? I pulled names and faces from my mind. Judy Garland came alive every year as Dorothy. Clark Gable performed his yearly revival in *Gone With The Wind*. Ernest Borgnine, oops, he wasn't dead.

"Did you try to feed her?" Matthew's South-Brit accent interrupted my mind game.

"I offered her my wrist but got no response," Delores said.

My hunger pitched inside but only faintly. I must've been asleep when she offered because I think I could drink from her now.

"Cut it and put the blood right to her lips," Matthew said.

Delores set her popcorn bowl on the nightstand and wiped her hands on a paper towel that was concealed between her fat thighs.

"I'm sorry, Matthew, but I just can't cut myself," she said

Lady cut it, I said inside myself. I needed to drink, not so much because the hunger demanded it, but because I felt if I didn't drink then I really might die.

Matthew came farther into the room. He had become godlike since taking Ken. I felt puny and weak, his power snuffed mine into shadows. By his movement and manner he was avoiding me. Was I indeed drying up and dying?

"Here, let me do it," he said.

I watched as he bit into her wrist. A stifled gasp escaped her and he guided her to me.

Blood smell, fragrant and warm, filled the air. Her wrist came closer, crimson tides spread over the roadway of blue veins crisscrossing beneath her skin.

My mouth filled with the saliva-blood mixture as my fangs burst upward from their resting place beneath the soft tissue of my lower jaw. I tried to swallow. My throat wouldn't react.

A small amount of blood trickled into my mouth. I wasn't able to lock onto her wrist, nor was I able to suck the life-giving fluid from her veins. Coppery warmth coated my tongue, but my inability to swallow allowed the blood to continue its passage through my mouth where it leaked out the other side and dribbled onto my hand, still clenched and stiff beneath my face.

No magical energies came from Delores either. Our possession of each other, like the last time I had fed from her, did not surface.

"She's not taking it," Delores said, and pulled her wrist away. She pressed the greasy napkin to her wounds and moved back from the bed.

I looked up and locked eyes with Matthew. He had put contacts back in and his eyes sparkled Caribbean blue. He reached up to grab that damn piece of hair, but stopped and stepped closer to the bed.

This time when his hand began to rise, he reached for the neatly folded handkerchief that was sticking up from the breast pocket of his gray sports coat. He sat on the edge of the bed and gently began to wipe the blood away from my lips.

"Ainjul, what am I going to do with you?" he asked.

Of course he got no response from me, but I didn't have an answer to give him anyway.

"You managed to get back upstairs and into my bed. How come you are playing dead now?"

I didn't get back here on my own. I'm not playing dead. Damn it, Matthew, I can't move.

He grabbed me tightly by the wrists and wrenched me back flat upon the bed. The expression on his face was the malevolent Matthew, and I feared that he might hurt me.

"This condition is all in your mind, my dear. Bong is gone. You took his blood and it made you sick. Now you refuse to take blood. Now you are in mourning. Now you are in worse shape than those first three nights in the motel room," he said.

I knew what he was doing. He was trying to elicit some kind of response from me and he did get one. Cold tears flooded my eyes and spilled over to run down the contour of my sunken cheeks.

It is not in my head. I can't move. Go away and leave me alone. The voice in my head shook with frustration.

"Let me give you something to think about," he said, and released his hold upon my wrists. "If you want to stay in this condition and mourn for eternity, you will, Oh, the hunger might force you out of it, but you've already learned to override that. If you don't feed you'll grow weaker and weaker until you cannot feed. But you won't die. It's not that easy, my luv. So if that is your wish, forget it. I simply won't allow you to die. But I will allow you to remain like this, if it's what you choose."

My silent tears came in a stronger flood. He stood up and hesitated over me, waiting for an answer that couldn't come.

I hated him. At that moment I would've struck him but

my body was locked away and I didn't have the key to release myself.

"Matthew, that's enough." Delores came forward in my defense. The angry look on her face made me wonder if she might hit him for me, but I knew better.

"I'll give you a couple of days and then I'll force-feed you. And don't think for one minute I can't do it," he said.

His threat was real and my tears abruptly stopped. I was going to get out of this. I was not going to let him dominate me any longer than possible.

My eyes followed him as he walked out of the bedroom, but before my gaze shifted back to Delores, Steven walked in carrying two large bouquets of flowers, one in each arm.

"Ainjul, just ignore him. He gets like this after . . ." she started to say but then she saw Steven also.

"Can she hear?" Steven asked.

Delores nodded and motioned for him to come to my bedside.

"The downstairs is starting to look like a flower shop," he said, and made room on the nightstand for the bouquets. "These are from Terrance and Eric. Almost everyone knows about Bong and they send their sympathy. They all got a big kick out of him, you know," he said.

I was glad to hear the flowers were for Bong, not for me. I hoped they didn't know my condition. I hoped they would never know about it.

"I'll bring the other arrangements up here. Maybe they will help you come back to us," he smiled at me.

For the first time since meeting them, I was glad for Matthew's mortal companions. If I were alone with only Matthew I don't think I could endure this.

Steven wasn't kidding. Each successive trip brought more sprays, arrangements, bouquets, and planters. The room became filled with colors and perfume from the flowers.

After his last trip, Steven joined Delores and the three of us spent the entire night watching old movies on television. Niven Broome's Film Festival was the best. Of course we had to put up with all his carpet commercials but they were always brief and ole Niven would get us right back into the movie action. Tonight the feature was *The Creature From the Black Lagoon*.

After the movies had ended some old serial westerns came on: *Have Gun, Will Travel, Bat Masterson, The Rifleman*.

Delores was sound asleep. Her chin was nestled against her abundant chest and she snored lightly. Steven popped the top of a Dr. Pepper, took a swig, and looked my way to "check" on me as he had been doing regularly all evening.

I heard Matthew coming up the stairs. He entered the room briskly, bringing the smell of the sea with him. He must've spent the evening at the beach. His hair was wind-blown and devilish looking. I saw that his slacks had once been rolled up, the wrinkles were wet, and the beginnings of salt stains were crystallizing around the material at his calves.

He never said a word as he lifted my body from the bed and carried me downstairs to my coffin. But he held me gently with the embrace a lover would give and I knew his anger was gone, for the time being.

He settled me upon the cool satin lining, placed my hands across my waist, and closed my eyes. Before the lid came down I felt something light upon my chest. I could distinguish the sweet scent of a rose.

Several nights went by in this same manner. I would awaken on the big brass bed in Matthew's room having no idea of walking there. Though my body still would not respond, it was loosening up and my muscles were relaxed, the aching was gone. Delores or Steven, or both, would sit with me. Delores offered me her blood periodically but I couldn't take it even when the passion was eating away inside me to drink. Matthew always returned me to my coffin at dawn, but in those nights, he never came to see me and when he held me, he never once spoke.

As he promised, he only gave me a couple of days to make up my mind and take blood. My mind was made up, I wanted it very badly, but still I was unable to suckle upon Delores's offered veins.

It was the middle of the evening when I heard him coming. This night his eerily quiet movement was accompanied by a clanking sound, which reminded me of a child's wagon being pulled behind.

My eyes widened with horror when he pushed in the IV pole complete with an electronic monitor box. I didn't want to take blood that way.

He motioned for Delores to leave the room, and he closed the door after she had gone. Then he rolled the equipment next to me and hung two bags of blood from the rounded hooks above the blue monitor box.

"This isn't the most pleasant way to take blood. Some have told me it can be downright uncomfortable. I hope for your sake it isn't," he said.

His voice was callous and he tried to avoid looking at me. I realized how frightful I must look. I had shrunken and withdrawn and I didn't need a mirror to tell me what I had become.

"I want you to understand the reason I'm doing this. I can barely stand to look upon you. Your beauty is fast becoming dim. If you are going to remain lifeless, at least you will look ravishing. You can be my Sleeping Beauty," he said, and with a quick thrust inserted the needle into a vein on my arm. "See, nothing to it. I'm quite good at finding veins," he said, and allowed a brief smile to spread his thin lips apart.

He used his thumb to release the clamp on the clear plastic tubing and I watched the deep red liquid begin the journey inside me.

The instant blood passed beneath my skin my vein began to grow warm. Warmth gave way to tingle and then was joined by a sensation of itching deep under my skin. It was uncomfortable, but not intolerable, and already the blood was working toward my heart and my pulse was beginning to quicken.

Matthew glanced at his watch and made an adjustment to the monitored drip rate. The blue box beeped steadily.

"I'm sorry but this will take about two hours to complete. If I run it through any faster I assure you it would be most unpleasant. You see, your body has to absorb and metab-

264

olize the blood differently than if you had taken it by mouth.''

I was watching the little drips of blood high above me, the bag seemed to be emptying at an incredibly slow rate. Where and how he managed to obtain the blood and the equipment was up for grabs.

My body was absorbing the fluid like a sponge, and when the time came for the second bag to be hooked up I was no longer uncomfortable, but in a near euphoric state.

The only real difference between this feeding and any other was the incredible dryness in my mouth and throat. I began to swallow convulsively, aware that my throat was responding.

Matthew jumped from the chair and slowed the drip rate once again. He peered anxiously into my face and I saw his concern and compassion. Maybe this *was* just what the doctor ordered. Maybe this would bring me out of it.

The second bag emptied. I felt remarkable. The nourishment had revitalized me but not enough to change my condition.

''You look much better. I hope you feel better,'' Matthew said. He eased the IV line out of my arm and pushed the equipment away.

I do, my inner voice said. But the feast was over and my mind was drifting into a mortal-like sleep. I closed my eyes. The last thing I remembered was the sound of Dr. Matthew wheeling my dinner cart out of the room.

Five more such feedings took place. It became hard for me to know exactly how many days or weeks had gone by. My body was becoming much stronger but still would not listen to the commands I gave it.

Matthew did everything in his power to break the unseen chains holding me prisoner. More often than not, he was angry. But every time his hostile manner lashed out at me he would go out and walk the dark, empty beaches. I knew this because he always returned home to carry me to my resting place with the smell of the sea on him.

The final night of my self-inflicted entombment came to

an end, and it wasn't Matthew who ended it, not directly anyway.

He was sitting on the foot of my bed waiting for me to awaken. Once he realized I had become aware, he removed an envelope from his inside coat pocket and held it up for me to see.

I knew the handwriting. It was a letter from Elijah. The postmark was from Istanbul.

"Shall I read it to you?" he asked.

I said neither yes nor no, but watched him tear the envelope open and pull the folded page out. He smoothed it against his thigh and then began.

My Dearest Ainjul:

I hope this letter finds you well and content. I meant to write sooner than this but my time has been filled by so many new adventures.

In the course of my travels I have met others like us and my mission has been greatly aided by them. They are, for the most part, youngsters and I have been flattered by their awe of my knowledge and my age.

Though I think of you constantly, I have been too busy to be homesick. So far I've managed to reunite four men with their families. The pleasures I've gained from this cannot be expressed in words. I think God might be smiling upon me now.

My existence has new meaning and purpose. I'm only sorry now that I waited so long to walk away from the clouds of my self-doubt and misery. Finally I've learned to accept what Matthew tried so diligently to teach me. I can *not* change what I am, but I *can* exist in any manner I choose.

I'm sure by now you have been united with Matthew, which is why I mailed this to his home, I'm sure, also, that you have learned many of the things I led you to believe about him are not true.

I allowed myself to love you too deeply. It was always meant for you and him to find each other. My own selfishness prolonged your joining, and for this I must apologize.

Please tell Matthew I sincerely thank him for allowing me such indulgence.

There were so many things I knew about you and so many times I yearned to tell you. But Matthew weaved a powerfully magic web and I was ensnared by love and loyalty.

I recall his words to me the night before he took you. He said that time had come full circle. Even though I still don't understand his statement, it is undeniable that you are the very image of Maria. I guess what I'm trying to say is—find it in your heart to forgive him. He never meant for your transformation to be as it was. I witnessed a remarkable change in him over the years while he waited for you. Once the final moment came, his own insecurity let a precious beginning slip into pain.

Whatever your feelings for him, remember that once upon a time enchantment captured him and held him forever spellbound. You are the key to his past and future, you are his family.

Remember too, that I am always near. Someday time may bring us full circle. I only hope that time will always allow you to remain, My Dearest Ainjul.

Elijah

Matthew's voice ended the letter in barely a whisper and I saw for the first time what a fragile creature he was. Elijah and he shared more than either one would ever openly admit, the very tone of Elijah's letter and the flush of emotion in Matthew's eyes plainly told their story.

Yet Elijah said I was the key to his past and his future.

If this was true then it would be so very simple to shatter him. But the fact remained that I was family, and the old saying about blood being thicker than water could never have been truer.

Matthew set the open letter beside me. Had I just read such a poignant and personal letter I would have been overcome by embarrassment. But I was learning things about relationships among vampires. Rule number one is that they don't follow any "normal" mortal relationship. Men loved other men but it was far more complex and personal than a sexual love.

Matthew left me alone to ponder Elijah's words. And ponder I did. The same thought kept surfacing. Maria. Maria Abigail Anne. What was it about her? Elijah had noticed her effect on him too. *I am the key to his past and future.* Why? Because I look like her?

A longing to go home hit me from out of the blue. Not so much to see my family, that would be nice, but to rummage around the attic and dig up our family tree. My grandmother had been fanatical about keeping family things, and in my mind I could see the very boxes her old things were stored in.

The spell holding me broke, almost unnoticed. I reached out and picked up Elijah's letter from the bed and held it closer. When I realized I had finally been freed, I slowly climbed from the bed and went to find Matthew.

And I knew where he would be, downstairs staring at the lovely portrait of her. The somber look upon his face became a smile when he saw me.

"Matthew, I want to go home," I said.

CHAPTER FIFTEEN

"How do you propose to get home?" he asked. He walked toward me and his smile faded to a serious expression.

Hadn't he said that I should go home? What was he up to now?

"I can take the van and sleep in my coffin during the day," I said.

"Do you think you would be secure? What if someone broke in and curiously pried open the lid? Do you think you would survive?" he said, still coming closer.

Confusion muddled my thoughts. My body was weak, in need of at least a six-course feeding. What was the point of his line of questioning?

"Matthew, I don't know. I hoped you would go with me. If I must go alone, then I will. But I want to go home," I said, and leaned wearily against the doorframe.

He was beside me now, and he reached out for my hand. He held it between both of his, his grip firm and cold but not quite as cold as mine.

"I'm questioning you so you'll learn to make plans. This is one of the most important things we can do. If you run blindly through eternity you'll make mistake after mistake and sooner or later you'll slip up and be discovered." His voice was affectionate and the smile returned.

"Well, I wasn't going to go off half cocked, if that's what you mean. I didn't say I had to leave tonight," I said.

"Good. Very good. I'm going north anyway, so of course we'll travel together," he said.

"And how do you propose to travel?" I asked.

He let go of my hand and slid his deep into his pants pockets. Then he grinned a boyishly sly grin and shrugged.

"You weren't too far out of line. But I have an R.V. that is much more accommodating. I know your next question and the answer is, if a mortal did happen to find you during the daylight hours your autonomic defenses take over. It is more than a bit startling to wake up with a dead mortal on top of you, I can tell you that from experience."

I shuddered. It would indeed be more than startling for me. I could picture myself flying into hysterics and bursting from my coffin in wild frenzy.

"Sometimes I take Steven along, for added reassurance, but this weekend is his anniversary and Delores has planned something quiet and romantic."

"Steve and Delores, married?" I found it hard to believe. They were an unlikely couple. They never acted married, at least not that I ever noticed.

"Yes. One year now," he said.

I wondered what many wonder, about a fat girl and a nice-looking guy. What did he find attractive about her? She was pretty, but so fat! And how did they do *it?*

"Is it so hard to believe?" Matthew asked.

"Well yes and no. I guess, well, they do live here together." My stammering made him laugh.

"Come on. Let's go out and celebrate your revival. Too bad it took you so long to come out of it. Spoleto is long over and the tickets were not used. I offered them to Steven and Delores, but they wanted to remain with you." He reached out to support my arm.

"I don't think I'm up to it, Matthew. I'm tired and weak," I started to protest.

"You will be much better once you've fed. I'm taking you to the beach. You can even dine on fish, if you desire. But you need to get out. You are quite pale," he said, and then laughed at his joke.

For the moment he was the Matthew I wished he would always remain, witty, exuberant, and fun.

We went in the Ferrari. The hot humid air of a Charleston

night billowed over the windshield and my hair flew back in a jet stream of red curls.

Already the night was working a magical spell across the land. Giant trees had become hulking shadows and the green carpet of grass stretching along the roadside was a blanket of omnipresent evil—dark, dull, and waiting. Waiting to become alive with the splash of crimson red when the grisly murders spilled blood across the land. And tonight I was going to commit murder, but as I always did, I convinced myself it wasn't murder, it was survival. As man butchers cattle, so I would butcher man. No longer was it right or wrong, no longer did the moral implications tear me away from my truest desire. Nothing would stop me from the lustful, swelling passion to consume every drop of pleasure from the feast. Tonight it wouldn't be fish I dined on.

We ended up at Folly Beach, and Matthew pulled off the road into a sandy nook that had been used frequently for parking. A public access ramp was directly across from our spot and Matthew was out of the car and across the street before I managed to get the car door open.

But he waited for me on the deck of the newly constructed boardwalk that breached the small dunes. He was looking out to sea, the wind gently whipping at his open sports coat. His hair danced under the glitter of a full moon.

I could hear the waves, angry and churning tonight, violent with the unleashed passion of nature. Bold currents of water tried desperately to rape the soft curve of beach but arrived in only a spent stream of tired foam. The energy of the sea had enough force to put out the flames of need within me, had I allowed it. But I wanted to feed in the manner I had been reborn to feed and I thought only of this as I climbed the wooden stairs to join Matthew.

"Ainjul, I hadn't realized you were still dressed in a nightgown," he said.

Neither had I. The ocean breeze caught the long, flowing fabric, and I glanced down to see the swirling silvery light of the moon play between the shadows of billowing white silk.

"No matter," he said, taking hold of my hand and pointing

271

far off into the distance where the small island ended and the next one began. "Look what can be ours tonight."

Nestled up against the dunes were three mortals. No beach umbrellas, no floating toys, no sand castles and brightly colored buckets, just three mortals sitting in the sand unaware of the danger soon to befall them.

"Shall we walk arm in arm like lovers and pass by a few times, or shall we come up behind the dunes and take them by surprise?" Matthew asked.

His excitement was making me giddy. He wanted this just as badly as I did. I half expected that at any moment warning lights and sirens would break the quiet peace and give us away. We were two nocturnal creatures about to begin a death stalk. *Beware, beware,* the waves seemed to be shouting now.

"You decide," I whispered.

He slipped his cold arm around my waist and led me down the steps and onto the sandy shore. We walked slowly, casually, and each step quickened my heartbeat. Twice my fangs burst from their resting place and twice I forced them back, embarrassed by the lack of control. Matthew was swallowed in his own fever and the closer we got to our victims, the closer he pulled me to his side.

Voices. Sweet and melodic. A man's, a woman's, and a child's. The words were Spanish.

Less than one hundred yards away our catch lay in waiting. My pace was being restrained by Matthew. He was outwardly calm and collected, though inside I felt his heart hammering just as fast as my heart was hammering.

The child stood up and began running in our direction. Her long hair, tangled and matted though it was, shone under the moonlight with the golden color kiss of the sun. I reached out, wanting to touch her, but she darted by and ran to the water's edge.

Matthew stopped. We both watched the child. She stood at the edge of the water. Each wave sprayed up against her long, spindly legs then withdrew to cover her feet with wet sand until she was held captive there, buried up to her ankles. She began to giggle and pulled her feet free. The land gave her up and with a great sucking noise covered the wounds in its surface.

272

She ran farther into the water, and behind me I heard the woman, obviously her mother, shouting. The little girl dived into the gray, tormented water and the mother began running. I did not turn to see the mother but felt the rhythmic thumping upon the sand. Her crazy Spanish cries began to grow frenzied, but the little girl broke free of the watery embrace and came up laughing. A large wave, just beginning to break with a foamy frown, rolled in behind her. She prepared her lithe body and dived, riding with the water until she was deposited a few feet beyond us. She stood up and pushed the wet strands of hair away from her face.

"I'm taking her," Matthew said.

His arm slid away from me and I wondered which her he was taking. But he went for the mother and the child went back to her play.

Matthew did what Matthew does best. He began to play with Mama, and though he was leading her away from me I heard the tone in her voice and recognized it as fear.

It didn't take Papa long to spring into action. His thunderous voice boomed harsh, unrecognizable remarks and his footsteps jarred the sandy earth beneath my feet.

Matthew had let his victim go and she was running wildly up the beach, but very quickly Matthew was in front of her again and her shriek pierced the empty night air.

Papa rushed in their direction, but I was a cold wind on his heels and he looked back only once before I took him.

His blood flowed into me and my rapture escalated while he fought to break free of my embrace. I had become a rigid pillar, planted firmly and receiving renewed strength from him. His manliness diminished and he became a whimpering boy in my arms.

Matthew had freed his victim again and she was behind me, beating me with her small fists and screaming unintelligently into my ears. But such is our nature that I simply shrugged her off and continued my blissful encounter with her husband.

The end was near. Always it came too quickly, always I wanted to linger in the unspeakable pleasure I derived from feeding, and always, I wanted to get away from death before it touched me.

The rapture that had encompassed my senses was breaking up and his heart was growing faint. I was aware again of those around me. The woman had captured her daughter and knelt weeping with the girl in her arms. Matthew was next to me, forcing me farther into the surf. And I was still attached to the man, dragging him with me into the deep. The end was so very near that I didn't mind when Matthew plunged us both under the waves. The outside sounds grew muffled, as they do underwater, but my victim's heart grew louder and more steady until the rhythm was incomplete and I had to let him go.

I came out of the surf like a goddess. I imagined that if I commanded it, even the water would stop its assault upon the shore.

Matthew had taken the child into his arms and was feeding vigorously from her while the mother assaulted him with screams, kicks, punches, and bites. But the little girl was lucky. Matthew took her quickly and cleanly and she was dead in less than a minute.

I sat down upon the beach and watched Matthew play with the woman. Water cascaded around my legs and pulled at the silk fabric of my nightgown. The body of the child floated face-up in the incoming surf. Her father floated face-down beyond the breakers. I had no grief for them, and I had no hatred for Matthew while he toyed with his catch. Like a cat, he would let her go and then reclaim her until he finally tired of the game and took her.

This is what we are. Nothing, save our destruction can change it. And at this moment I want nothing but to continue for eternity.

Matthew came to me. He took off his coat and slipped out of his wet Adidases.

"I'll be back in fifteen minutes," he said, and handed me his things.

"Back from where? Where are you going?" I asked.

He looked down on me. His face was swollen and pink and he looked tired instead of refreshed. This was the first time I had ever seen him directly after feeding and the effect on him was unlike anything I'd ever witnessed in Elijah, Bong, or myself.

274

"I'm going to dispose of our spoils," he said.

Fine with me. I certainly wasn't going to do it. But I watched Matthew enter the water and gather up all three corpses. With one strong lunge he disappeared under the shimmering water and I began to worry.

Fifteen minutes became fifteen hours and then seemed to stretch into fifteen days. He was gone too long and I scanned the water for any sign of him. Could he stay under that long without breathing? Certainly he was strong enough to swim in the currents, wasn't he?

I was pacing along the water, thinking about going after him but afraid to. The fresh blood scent on us was easily distinguishable, and there were sharks out there, somewhere. Maybe a shark had attacked him already. If I had a boat, I might go out, but not alone and not unaided. Should I go get Steven?

Something bobbed up beyond the rolling mound where the waves formed and I strained to see it clearly. But it was gone just as quickly.

The incoming tide had claimed half of the beach. I forgot about Matthew's coat and shoes and soon they were being pulled into the surf and I had to go in after them.

The water was thick with silt and seaweed. Somewhere there had been a storm, out there, and now the spoils of the storm were reaching land. I grabbed for the sports coat and caught it by the sleeve. It was heavy, the fine tweed blend soggy and sand coated. A shoe bumped by and I hurried after it, deeper into the water. I reached down, missed, and saw a glint of white as the shoe traveled still farther out to sea.

I pushed my way through the water, which was now up to my hip, and held the coat tightly against me so I wouldn't lose it too. I saw the shoe again and plunged my free arm into the murky depths.

Something grabbed me.

I let out a shriek of surprised panic and pulled free, only to stumble back against the outgoing current.

Something swam by, quickly.

I began to retreat for shallower water, keeping a watchful eye on the rippling movement of the thing under the water. It swam out about a hundred feet then turned and headed back toward me, gathering such speed the surface of the ocean bubbled with its passing.

I was frozen in place. It went by me, knocking against my leg and causing me to fall. Then it was gone, and the ocean was too still. I began to crawl backward for shore, watching ever so diligently for the signs of water movement or a fin breaking the surface. Sharks circle and bump into their prey, don't they?

A hiss of water and a boiling line of foam rushed toward me. The water was shallow but the thing was still advancing. Before it was within striking range I leapt from the water, but it did too and I screamed, came down hard upon the sand, and felt the air rush from my lungs.

It turned out to be Matthew, and he stood above me dripping wet and grinning. The swollen look was gone, the pink cast to his skin was gone, the tiredness was gone.

"You little shithead, you scared me," I said, and reached up to accept his offered hand.

He pulled me up from the sand.

"I couldn't resist," he said. "I'm not too terribly sorry either."

"What did you do with them?" I asked.

The foolish grin upon his face faded and he became utterly serious and stolid.

"I swam out about five miles and buried them deep into the sea bed. There they shall remain," he said.

"You swam ten miles, buried three bodies, and did it in fifteen minutes," I said, astonished.

"I'm a strong swimmer," he said.

"I see." I shook some of the wet sand from my nightgown. "You've cased this beach and knew they would be here, didn't you?"

"Yes. I knew they wouldn't be missed. They were in this country without papers. Many migrant workers come to the South Carolina coast this time of year. The tomato harvest brings most of them here but it will soon be over and they will be moving on. If they are missed at all, it would be a fleeting thing."

He shook out his jacket and looked around for his shoes.

"Sorry, they got away," I said.

"No great loss. Amazing what a night out has done for you, you are simply ravishing," he said.

"What? Peppered with sand and plastered with salt water. You've got to be joking," I said.

"Maria was a good swimmer. In fact, she taught me. Of course, if Father had ever found out she would've been punished. But we kept our secret," he said.

"You sure have," I mumbled. I was thinking about the secret that bound them over the centuries.

"Young ladies weren't to do things like strip down and swim in the creek," he said.

"Was Maria older than you?"

"By three years, why do you ask?"

"I just thought she was older, that's all," I said.

He walked away from me and I followed him over to a spot beside the dunes. He sat down and stretched his legs out in front of him.

"I think I would have hated you, had I been her," I said.

He looked up at me and I noticed he had lost his contacts during the swim. But his white-on-white eyes didn't mask his emotion this night.

"Why should you have hated me?"

I sat next to him, crossed my legs, and folded the ends of my sodden silk nightgown over my thighs.

"I wouldn've hated you for being younger than me but being heir to the family property and title. I would've hated it that just because I was a girl, I was not entitled to what was rightfully mine. I would've hated you for it, I'm sure."

"Things were different then. Maria certainly never hated me for my position."

"Didn't she?" I asked.

He was quiet for a moment. His long fingers curled into the sand and he began digging holes beside his legs.

"Ainjul, I don't understand what you are asking," he said, and his hands stopped digging.

"I'm asking you to be honest with yourself. If she loved you she would've let you go. Her hatred must've been deep to still be eating at you all these years."

"Oh, but you are wrong. She loved me," he said, and there was an uneasy tone in his voice.

"Did you make her a vampire?" I asked.

His white eyes widened visibly.

"No. I could never do that. Not to her."

"But she wanted you to, didn't she?" I pressed him further.

"Yes."

"And you refused her immortality and she hated you for that too."

"Drop it," he said, and anger flashed across his sharp features.

"All right, all right. Don't get so uppity."

He shot me an even darker look and I remained silent. For whatever reasons, he wasn't yet ready to tell me his past. Perhaps he thought it was none of my business, but we were family and he had made me his immortal partner and whether he believed it or not, it was just as much my business as it was his.

My nightgown was beginning to dry and I stood up to shake some more sand loose.

"I'm going for a walk," I said, and turned away from him. If he wanted to sit there and brood for the duration of the evening, that was his business.

"Wait, I'll come," he said, and joined me.

We walked silently the rest of the way to the point. From the end of the island we saw Seabrook, just across the waterway. The tide was beginning to subside, and as we turned to go back the beach had already grown wide.

"Do the tides remind you of us?" Matthew asked.

"Can't say that they do," I said with a bitter tone in my voice.

"It is one of the reasons I've stayed in the Low country so long," he said.

"And the other reasons?" I asked.

"When the tide is high the marshes flood with nourishing waters. The rivers and creeks swell with renewed life. And when the tide is low the marshes dry out and the rivers shrink and some of the smaller creeks all but wither away. The cycle is never interrupted, the cycle is never-ending. This land is a parallel to our existence."

His words were an inkling into his imagination and I too could picture the sea, like a giant heart, pumping blood into the shriveled veins of the land. Just when the land would become saturated and heavy, the sea pulled back again and the entire sequence of events would repeat over and over forever.

"Tomorrow we will leave this land. I will take you home," he said.

"For real?"

"For real," he repeated. "I'll have Steven bring the RV from the storage garage and get it ready. Before you even awake we will be on the road. So don't panic when you awaken in a strange place," he said.

"Matthew," I said.

"Yes, what is it?"

"Promise me you won't drive so fast. You might enjoy it, but I don't. Promise me that."

"Fifty-five, sixty, tops," he said. "Are you ready to get back to Charleston now?"

I felt the nightgown and it was damp but not wet, and I nodded.

"We'll get a few things together for Steven to pack on board and then . . ."

"How long will we be gone?" I asked.

"As long as you want," he said.

"And what if I want to be gone for fifty years or more?"

"Then we better also say goodbye to Steven and Delores before we leave," he said, and smiled.

Packing for our trip was relatively easy. I only wanted to take two things along. The letter I had received from Elijah, and the picture Delores had given me. But to ease Matthew's mind I pulled a selection of clothing from the overstuffed closet and set them on the bed for Steven to pack in the RV in the morning.

Delores was upset with my remark about being gone for fifty years, and it took insistent reassurance from Matthew that we would return to finally ease her mind.

Dawn was not far away and the four of us were huddled over the small kitchen table mapping out the best route for our trip when the sleep began to settle upon me.

Delores insisted upon kissing me in case we were never to meet again. Steven also kissed me, but his was easier to accept. As I left the kitchen I heard Matthew instructing them both on last-minute details.

Home was fourteen hours away. Excitement and apprehension filled me as I climbed into my coffin. I was so afraid that Mom or Dad might see me, so afraid that they would learn of my new life. Before the sleep paralyzed my thoughts I repeated over and over, *They must not see me, they must not see.*

The sound of tires humming along the highway was all I heard upon awakening. I kept my eyes closed and drew upon my childhood memories of our family vacations. The sounds and scents were the same. In my memory I was jammed in the back of our old station wagon, pillows cushioning the boxes of dry goods Mom had brought along to fill the kitchen in our rented beach house, which was solely our property for two happy weeks. I heard my sister's voice, *Are we there yet?* and I heard my brother's tell her once again to shut up.

But when I opened my eyes I wasn't in our family car and my brother and sister weren't yammering back and forth. Instead, I was in a carpeted compartment measuring about six feet long and six feet wide. The ceiling was only a few inches above my face and I had to squirm across the narrow area to reach the little brass latch and let myself out.

The interior of the RV was lit by a single fluorescent bulb over the small sink in the kitchen area. Our compartment was a storage space under the big double bed at the rear of the cabin. Beyond the spacious living area and the bar I saw a curtain that separated the driver from the rest of his crew. Before I joined Matthew there I began to nose around and I'm sure he heard me rummaging through the drawers and cupboards. I wanted to know what things a vampire took along when he traveled. But there was nothing out of the ordinary, nothing to suggest that we were anything other than a normal vacationing couple.

The narrow bathroom had a shower stall, sink, and vanity.

Every incidental was in place: soap, shampoo, deodorant, even toothpaste and toothbrushes. I ran my tongue around my mouth and wondered when I had last brushed my teeth. Suddenly my mouth had a terrible taste, but I'm sure it was purely imagined because I had learned early in my transformation that no bacteria thrived on us undead critters. I wanted to brush my teeth anyway, so I did.

The small bathroom became unbearably hot and I found a few small rubber bands wrapped around the end of a hairbrush. I pulled all my hair back and twisted it tightly before attempting the rubber band. The first one broke, but the second, though threatening to snap, held my hair in a secure ponytail. I splashed some water on my face, wondering where it came from because we weren't hooked up to any water source, and then found a hand towel to dry off with. One final check in the mirror, one last tug at the collar of my khaki jumpsuit, and then I headed up front to be with Matthew.

"What have you been doing back there, you smell like mint," he said.

I sat down in the passenger seat.

"I was brushing my teeth. I thought you said nothing had a taste. I could taste the toothpaste," I said.

"You don't have to do that. Your teeth aren't going to decay."

"I just felt like doing it, okay? Maybe my personal hygiene habits are different than yours were. Old habits are hard to break. Where are we? How long have we been on the road?" I asked.

"We didn't have toothpaste in my day. When my mother was alive she was adamant that we rinse our mouths. We used water and a salt solution. Or sometimes she would pour salt onto a soft cloth and make us rub our teeth with that. It wasn't very pleasant but we did have better teeth than our peers. About three and a half hours," he said.

I was about to ask if we had left the state but a road sign loomed in the distance: Pedro says fifty three miles to South of the Border. And I laughed silently remembering the miles and miles of Pedro signs that anyone traveling I-95 was subjected to.

"Did your mother live long?" I asked. He had spoken several times of his father but this was the first mention of his mother.

"She died when I was eleven years old," he said.

"What killed her? The plague?"

"My father's property was out in the country and quite isolated. Of course the plague was a constant threat but not so dangerous as it was in the cities. No, she did not die of the plague. She died from smallpox, and three days after her death my baby sister died of it also."

"That's very sad. I'm sorry."

"Yes, it was very sad. But do you know what sticks in my memory about her death?"

I shrugged and waited for him to continue. He was slowly beginning to leak out his past, my past, and I was overcome by the feeling of opening a crack in time and peering back upon the lives of those people whose lineage created me.

"The thing that has stayed with me concerning her death was her wish to be buried in the churchyard. Father would never allow it, and he practically severed relations with her side of the family over it."

"Why wouldn't he allow her to be buried in a churchyard? Didn't he believe in God?"

Matthew glanced over to me and smiled. "Yes, he believed in God. We were raised with strict religious beliefs. We were Protestants, which was good then because Catholicism was under siege in England during those years. But the reason he didn't want her buried in the churchyard had nothing to do with religion, it was a matter of space. During those times the longest you could expect a body to rest in peace in a churchyard was twenty, thirty years at the most. There were many, many deaths in those days, and everyone of importance or class wanted to be buried in a churchyard. Sooner or later the gravediggers would dig you up and make room for the next body. Your bones would be unceremoniously stacked in the charnel or bone house and that was that. Father demanded her body be buried on our property where she would rest in peace forever."

"What a disturbing thought. I mean, being laid to rest only

to be evicted a couple of decades down the road. When I go, I want to be cremated.''

"I assure you, that is the only way you'll go now," he said.

I laughed. I had become so absorbed in his story I had completely forgotten what I was.

"Father got his wish and the family came together at last to bury the dead. By that time Mother's body was quite ripe, and the smell was so bad that I wasn't able to eat anything later in the evening when the feast began. All I could remember was the rotten smell of death. Even the fresh evergreen twigs we placed over her coffin did not mask it. And I got my own taste of the smell again when I became what I am now. As did you.''

"You buried her with evergreen twigs. Why?"

"Fresh evergreen was always laid upon the coffin lid as a sign of immortality.''

"Paganistic ritual," I said.

"Quite the contrary. I'm sure her soul has been set free somewhere.''

"Your family was a family of five, two sisters and a brother, same as mine. More than coincidental, don't you think?" I asked.

"No. I had another brother. He and my baby sister were twins. He died two years later, from the plague.''

"What were their names? Your brother and sister?" I asked.

"Russell George Edward, the elder by two minutes, and Sarah Elizabeth Grace.''

"Did your father live long?" I asked. It was very clear that back then a short life span was considered normal.

"Father died while I toured Europe with my tutor. I was seventeen then and quite angry that he should die and cut my education short. He was born in the year 1625, he died in the year 1668. That made him forty three years old. Consumption claimed him, I think what it really was would be termed tuberculosis today. Consumption covered a multitude of diseases then.''

"I don't think I would've wanted to live back then. It must have been a hard life," I said.

"It was a time of kings and queens," he said. "It was also a time of court gossip and scandal. At one time King Charles proclaimed he had fathered fifteen bastards. His queen never bore him a child, though she did England a bigger favor, she introduced tea to England. And the havoc and scandal from the tea houses springing up across the land was something to behold.''

"I seem to recall a big scandal in this country over tea," I said.

"Yes. So do I.''

"You should've been around to coach me with history. I wasn't very good in history class. The only thing I really remember was the pomposity of King Louis, the Sun King of France. I don't even remember what number he was.''

"Fourteen. He was King Charles's cousin. Bailed him out of money problems for a while.''

Another sign for South of the Border appeared. Pedro was decked out in a large sombrero and a brightly colored pancho. He proclaimed that we were only twelve miles away.

"Matthew, stop at South of the Border," I said.

"I was planning to. We need gas and I suppose you're about ready to feed.''

He was keen to my needs. But more than feeding I wanted to stretch my legs and walk around a bit.

When we at last pulled onto the exit ramp, the line of cars behind us also pulled over. The digital clock on the dashboard read 1:03, and even at this late hour other travelers were being drawn into Pedro's villa of bright lights, hotels, specialty shops, restrooms, and carnival rides.

Matthew eased the RV next to a row of gasoline pumps and turned off the engine. Then he reached into his coat pocket, pulled out a crisp twenty-dollar bill, and handed it to me.

"Do you want more than this?" he asked.

I took the money though I hadn't intended buying anything, then shook my head no.

"Ainjul, don't kill and use the technique I showed you to heal the wounds. Meet me back here when you are finished, and don't be all night about it, we still have a long way to travel.''

I climbed down from the RV and entered Pedro's glittery world of gaudy souvenirs and tired travelers. Victims would

284

be easy prey here and I didn't waste time once I began to hunt. I took three, two young teenage boys and an older businessman. I only drank a little from each and made sure the wounds closed up before I left them, slightly dazed but none the worse for their gift of life.

While walking back to the gas pumps I came across a bookshop and entered with hopes of finding a magazine or two to read during our drive. I picked up the latest copy of *Connoisseur* and *Newsweek*. As I walked up to the cashier a book beneath the counter caught my attention. The cover was red, and bold white letters made up the title: *The Vampire Lestat*. The author's name was just as bold: Anne Rice. I couldn't resist and I picked it up too.

With my purchases neatly concealed in a plain brown bag and my body renewed with fresh blood, I eagerly made my way to the parked RV.

Matthew was ready to go, and I had no sooner closed my door when he stared the engine and pulled away from the parking spot.

I turned on the little light above my head and curled up in the seat. For the next several hours I read Lestat's story. It was an absorbing tale of remorse and morbid accounts of his life. But it was told with splendid candor and witty bits of humor that held me captive page after page. I was devouring the words at an alarming rate, and as I read the last sentence on the last page I closed the book and saw the time was 4:38 A.M. I had conquered a five-hundred-and-fifty-page novel in little more than three hours.

"Did you enjoy it?" Matthew asked.

He didn't need to tell me, I just knew he had already read it.

"Is it true? Do you think Lestat and the others are real?" I asked.

"Have you ever seen his videos on MTV? Have you ever heard any of his songs played on the radio?" he asked.

I didn't like being answered with questions, but I had to admit I had never heard of Lestat before.

"That doesn't make it unreal. Maybe this Lestat just has a good imagination," I said, wanting to believe in it.

"I think the one with the good imagination is the author, and it is an entertaining piece of fiction, but nothing more," he said.

"But she knows so much about vampires."

"Maybe she is one, maybe she knows one," he said.

"You're an old fart," I said. He had completely ruined the magic for me.

"Well then, I'm an old fart. Believe what you want," he said.

The RV began to slow and Matthew exited off I-95.

"Where are we?" I asked.

"Just south of Fredericksburg, Virginia. There is a small campground nearby. We'll stop for the day."

The sky to the east was beginning to turn pale gray and I was beginning to weaken with oncoming sleep.

"Matthew, are you sure we will be safe?"

"You go on back. I'll be along as soon as I get us into our camping spot. Believe me, we will be perfectly safe."

"Are you certain?" I asked.

"Ainjul, I'll be the one sleeping nearest to the door. If anyone happens upon us, they will get me first, and they won't *get* me so you are quite safe. Go on now," he said, and motioned for me to leave.

Just as I squirmed back into the compartment and nestled myself against the far wall the RV stopped. I heard voices and then we began to move again. Sleep was closing on me but I was still aware when the RV stopped again and the droning hum of the engine ceased. I listened while Matthew secured our private little fortress on wheels and then felt him slide in next to me. The latch clicked shut and we were sealed together in quiet darkness.

CHAPTER SIXTEEN

We were on the move again. When I joined Matthew up front the landscape had changed dramatically. He had the windows open and the fresh cool country air reminded me of home.

A road sign sparkled in our headlights: Philadelphia fifty nine miles.

"Matthew, my folks live in Pittsburgh," I said.

"I know exactly where they live. But my farm is in Berwyn, and unless you have any objections I want to stop there first. I had a Trakehner stallion imported yesterday and I'd like to see him. Any objections?"

"No," I said. Another day or two wasn't going to make any difference.

"Good. I have a surprise there for you too," he said.

"You didn't buy me a horse, did you?" I asked.

"Not exactly."

"You didn't buy me a horse *farm?* Did you?"

He laughed. "Ainjul, do you think I'm made of money?"

"Well, you're not exactly Mr. Poverty," I said.

"I've been wise enough to make my money work for me. There was a time when I was very poor. That was right after my father's death. During the year of the Great Plague and the following year, 1666, the year of the Great Fire, Father lost most of his money. There was a deep depression among the wealthy aristocrats during those years. We were lucky in the respects that we did not lose our property. Tellingham is still in my possession, and always will be," he said.

"How did the Great Fire start?" I asked.

"There have been several conjectures about that. The evidence was unclear though it is known that the fire broke out near London Bridge."

"Nothing as simple as Mrs. O'Leary's cow kicking over a lantern like the fire in Chicago?"

"No. Nothing as straightforward as that story. Many believed it was set by the Divine Hand, and in many ways it was a great blessing. The plague was literally obliterated by the fire. London was so infested the year before that the dead rotted in the streets and the stench blew for miles. The fire sterilized the land. It was unfortunate so many lost their homes.

"The vampire who made me boastfully claimed he started it to wipe out the hundreds of inferior English vampires. But he was arrogant and foolish, much like Lestat, and I never believed his tale. It simply wasn't logical to me that he did it. Had he been a mortal man claiming this same story I may have believed it. But the fact that he was not, and the fact that he had to have started it at night proved my theory that any vampires in London would have been able to flee."

I understood Matthew's reasoning. If a mortal man wanted to go to such lengths to destroy all the vampires in London the fire would have been set during the daylight and all the vampires would have perished in their deathly sleep.

"The whole city of London burned?" I asked.

"The statisticians estimated between thirteen and fourteen thousand homes, and nearly ninety churches, including St. Paul's Cathedral, were leveled. Father told me after sunset he could see the orange glow in the sky."

"You weren't in England then, when the fire hit London?" I asked.

"No. I turned fifteen in June of 1666, and the time had come for my education to take me to Europe. It began in Montpellier, a university town in France. I was there when the Great Fire swept London. I stayed there for several months before my tutor took me to Italy and Central Europe. Education was reserved for the upper ranks of society in those days. The European tour was the grand finale, the final polish to my training. It was thought that in Central Europe one could acquire a greater facility of foreign language and social experiences. Any young son of a noble family was schooled in the polite arts: dancing, fencing, and conversation. I was an eager and well-disciplined student. I believed I was going to be something and go somewhere in my lifetime. But my dreams died with my father. I was to be nothing more than the fourth Earl of Tellingham."

"You make it sound dreadful. To me it would be romantic," I said.

"Romantic? I think you have a good case of the Charles and Diana syndrome. At seventeen years of age the last thing I wanted was to be shackled with the responsibility of running the estate. Everything I did was scrutinized by others. Every change I implemented was laughed off to my youthful folly. But the final laugh was on them because most of what I did became fashionable. I was a man before my times."

Matthew hit the turn signal and slowed the RV. We pulled off the main road and entered Ridley Creek State Park.

I knew why we were stopping. My hunger was ready to be nurtured and Matthew's sense of timing again astonished me.

He stopped the RV and reminded me to be discreet, no kills.

My instincts led me to a secluded spot on the edge of a large, dark lake. A young man and woman had pitched a small tent under an alcove of pine trees. Their campfire was nothing more than glowing embers and they sat upon the ground, sipping beer.

It wasn't hard to lure the man away. I snapped a few twigs and the young woman began to get scared and sent him to me. I drank just enough not to harm him and then spat some of the blood-saliva mixture upon the wounds. His mind, already mellowed by the beer, was easy to control and I pushed him into a deep sleep before taking his partner.

She was harder to let go, and I had taken too much of her blood. She buckled in my arms before I realized this, and I reluctantly withdrew. Some victims affect me this way, and I don't know why, it is as if their blood is sweeter with life. But I was sure she would be all right when she awoke.

Before I left them, I carried both of them into their tent and zipped the double sleeping bag around them. They would never remember anything, except for a peaceful night together.

When I got back to the RV, Matthew was stretched out on the little couch reading my *Newsweek* magazine. He looked different, but he hadn't fed, and then I noticed his tan. His skin was bronzed, the white luminescent color completely hidden.

"Found a couple of drunks to dine on," he said, not looking away from the magazine.

I had forgotten that they had been drinking until he noticed and then I began to grow increasingly warm. I wasn't drunk, but the alcohol in their blood was doing something inside me.

"Matthew, why did you do that?" I asked.

He turned a page in the magazine and said, "Do what?"

"Stain your skin?"

"Oh, I forgot," he said, and closed the magazine while standing up. "These northerners expect us southerners to be tan. I'll help you," he said.

He led me to the bathroom and retrieved a small jar of bronzing cream from the vanity.

"Pull your hair back," he instructed.

I pushed the loose strands away from my face and felt him begin to apply the cream. He used upward, sweeping motions, and gently massaged the golden color into my skin.

After my face had been covered he turned me around and tilted my head down to do the nape of my neck. Then he carefully concealed my ears and worked on down my throat. When he began to unbutton my jumpsuit and push the collar away I stopped him.

"I can finish," I said, holding his hand away.

"Make sure any exposed flesh is covered," he said, and handed me the jar.

He left me alone and climbed back into the driver's seat. The RV began to move.

I sat down upon a chair near the couch and worked the bronzing cream into my chest. When I finished with that I rolled up my sleeves and did my hands and arms, clear up to the elbows because I was in the habit of pushing my sleeves up. I started to screw the lid back on when I noticed the whiteness of my ankles and quickly smeared some color there too.

"Do I pass for a southerner?" I asked as I joined him.

"You pass for a tourist. No one will believe you're from South Carolina with the midwestern twang," he said.

I turned to watch that scenery flash by my window. The country road was bordered by thick cornfields. Farms and vintage stone farmhouses dotted the landscape. Everything seemed so pristine and perfect. The smell of the earth was fertile and rich. There was real dirt in those fields, not hard red clay and sand like the dried ground of the South.

We crossed a narrow covered bridge. The stream below was a bubbling brook of freshness. Mortals may have missed such scents, but a vampire's senses miss nothing, and it was pure joy to breathe in the delicious smells. There was no heavy humidity to dull the night fragrance, no thick decaying marsh scents to burn in my sinuses. This was country I could dwell in forever; I found it hard to believe Matthew preferred Charleston.

The road curved sharply to the left and then back again to the right. At both turns a farm building sat solidly only a foot or two from the blacktop.

"Why did they build those barns so close to the road?" I asked.

"Ainjul, those barns were here before the road. In this part of the country most back roads were once cow paths. In the advance of progress, they simply paved them."

The RV began to slow as we climbed a steady hill. The cornfield on my right ended and stone-and-rail fence bordered the birm. The hill peaked and leveled a bit but we continued to slow.

A green light from the turn signal flashed quietly before Matthew prepared to turn. The fence split and now graced both sides of an endless gravel driveway. A rustic sign was mounted between two old wagon wheels. It read: Eclipse Equestrian Centre.

"Your place, I presume," I said.

He didn't respond. He had slowed to a speed that I could've walked faster than and was looking the place over, studying and surveying it.

The pastures on either side of the drive had recently been mowed, I could smell the heady freshness of cut grass. The drive wound into a thick patch of woods then over a little stone bridge and up a slight incline. Even in the darkness the sprawling barns and arenas ahead had a postcard quality. I didn't notice the house until we were almost on top of it. It was a huge, foreboding fieldstone colonial. I counted four chimneys and eight symmetrical windows across the front of the second floor.

"Matthew, this is beautiful," I exclaimed, overwhelmed by the character and period charm of the place.

"I thought you would like it," he finally spoke.

The driveway made a big circle in front of the house, and in the center stood a flagpole surrounded by various flowerbeds. Three smaller drives led off the circle, like spokes from the hub of a wheel. One led to the stadium-sized riding arena, one to the newer large barn, and one to the old stone-and-board bank barn that must've been built the same time the house was.

Matthew pulled around in front of the house and cut the engine.

A light came on over the front door.

"Ainjul, there is no one here like Steven or Delores. None of these employees know what I, we, are. In fact, they know very little about me, which is the way I want it. The trainers and instructors here are competent and reliable. They do what they are told to do."

"I understand," I said.

He pulled a dark pair of gloves from his coat pocket and began working his hands into them.

"In any case, they know I'm a wealthy young man. Some may question you as to your relationship to me. I leave it up to you to tell them what that relationship is."

"Kind of putting me on the spot, huh?" I said.

"I didn't want to be so bold as to presume what our relationship is," he said quietly.

The front door opened and a young woman stepped out. She was tall and slim, outfitted in a pair of canary riding breeches and a baggy Penn State sweatshirt. The breeches only covered her leg to the mid-calf, and the bare flesh above her well-worn tennis shoes was naturally tanned.

"David, Mr. Trenton is here," she called back through the open door.

Matthew got out of the RV and was crossing in front of it when she started to hurry over and greet him. But then she saw me and the big smile on her face faded.

A wiry little man appeared in the doorway. His faded blue jeans, scruffed cowboy boots, and wrinkled straw hat immediately struck me as out of place on this farm, but he approached Matthew and the two of them shook hands warmly.

So that's what the gloves were for, I thought.

"Mr. Trenton, it's good to see you again. I hope your trip up here went well. You made good time," David said.

I closed the RV door and walked over to stand beside Matthew.

"Brie arrived early this morning and has settled in nicely," David continued.

"Good. That is why we stopped. I'd like to see him," Matthew said. "Ainjul, this is David Waldorf, my trainer, and Sandy Kelly, an instructor."

"Awngel." Sandy repeated my name the way Matthew pronounced it. "Are you French?"

"American," I said.

Already she was threatened by me. Every gesture and movement she made showed me she had the hots for Matthew but now she had an adversary.

293

"So you're a college graduate now, Ainjul?" David said.

"Yes, I graduated last year." I answered his question and looked to Matthew. Something was going on here. Matthew was repressing a grin, and his green eyes sparkled mischievously.

David said no more but turned to lead us to the old barn.

Two bright security lights illuminated the barnyard. Moths fluttered in and out of the open glass globe, casting fleeting shadows against the bright white barn wall. David slid the big door open and the horses nickered quietly. He stepped inside and turned on the interior lights.

The center aisleway was swept clean. The ceiling was low, and huge ancient beams supported the loft above.

"Sandy, will you get his halter please?" David asked.

We stopped in front of a large box stall. The brass name plate on the door read: Bastiaan Brie. The stallion was a huge (I guessed he went 16.2 hands easy) dark bay. There were no white markings on him and I thought he looked rather plain, but the gentle look in his large brown eyes gave him character.

Sandy opened the stall door and went in to halter the giant. Brie walked right up to her and lowered his head, ready to accept the halter. She slid the lead shank through the brass ring on her side, ran the chain up over his nose, and snapped it on the opposite side. He led quietly out of the stall.

"What do you think, Ainjul?" Matthew asked as he ran his gloved hand down the big bay's leg.

"You sure won't be cutting any cattle with him. He looks kinda klutzy," I said.

David laughed, and Sandy gave me a look of shock.

"He looks fine. When will you start to campaign him?" Matthew asked.

"I think he'll be ready for the Pennsylvania National in October. There are a couple of local A-rated shows next month and I'll see how he goes there first. With his pedigree and manners I don't see any reason why he wouldn't be booked full for next year," David said.

Matthew stepped away from the horse, and Sandy led him back into the stall.

"Will you be staying long?" David asked.

Matthew looked toward me before answering.

"No. I just stopped in tonight to see him. We'll give Ainjul a tour of the farm but then we must go. Ainjul is anxious to see her parents but we will be back next week," he said.

"Your parents live around here?" David asked.

"They're in the Pittsburgh area," I said.

"Turnpike is just five miles down the road. It's a straight shot from there," David said.

From the opposite side of the barn a horse began to paw at the stall door, demanding some of our attention.

"Ole Pops misses you," Sandy said to Matthew.

"Ainjul, this is the stallion I told you about," Matthew said, and took me by the hand to lead me down the center aisleway.

I flashed Sandy a quick smile and she hung back.

The black stallion pranced around his stall, stopped in front of us with his head and tail held high, and snorted loudly.

"God, Matthew, he's a real beauty," I exclaimed.

The stallion circled in his stall again and gave a little playful buck. Every muscle on his powerful legs was defined, every subtle movement seemed restrained. I was captured by his spirit and bold prowess.

"He's showing off. Under saddle he's docile and obedient. He gives you his all over every course," Matthew said.

The nameplate on his stall door read: Coup de Grace.

"Why did she call him Pops?" I asked.

"It's a nickname. He's got a reputation for popping over the most treacherous obstacles. As long as I have owned him, he has never once refused a jump."

Pops came closer to the bars that held him like a prisoner in his cell. He curled his upper lip back and pushed his nose up into the air to smell us. I had a feeling he knew what we were, but he certainly didn't act afraid, and he certainly wasn't going to tell anyone.

"Come on, I'll show you the rest of the place," David said.

Matthew lingered a moment longer, studying his stallion with fierce pride before joining us.

The night air had a crisp chill to it, and I wasn't sure if it was because I was still so warm from the tainted blood I had feasted upon or because I had grown accustomed to the hot Carolina nights.

We entered the new barn, and when David flicked on the lights all the occupants let out an expectant whinny. The new barn didn't have the charm of the older one but it was just as neat and the fresh smell of pine shavings and horses was marvelous. Most of the horses settled down and just a few let out soft little nickers.

But there was something so familiar in those last few nickers that I instinctively headed for the sound. Again I heard the high-pitched, soft call. It was unmistakable. I had owned that mare for ten years and I knew her voice as well as I knew my own.

I ran down the corridor of stalls on the left, searching each briefly for her wide, white blaze. At last I found her, in the last stall waiting patiently for me.

My eyes flooded with tears but I was still able to read her nameplate upon the stall door: Fan Sea Free.

"Sea B., how did you end up here?" I asked her.

I was sure she recognized me, though any knowledgeable horseman would dispute this fact. I hadn't seen her in four years but she looked just the same as she looked the day they came and loaded her on the trailer.

"Are you surprised?" Matthew asked.

"How could you do this?" I asked him, and my voice was filled with emotion that he mistook for sadness.

"I thought you would be happy," he said.

"Oh, I am happy. But how did you . . . I sold her to a little girl out in Ohio. How did you end up with her?"

"The little girl, Tammy was her name if I recall correctly, was a student here at the time. I sent her to the Quarter Horse Congress that year and arranged for her to stop and try out your mare, and of course buy her for me.

Just because your parents wouldn't foot the feed bills while you went off to college didn't mean I wouldn't," he said.

"Thank you," I said, and turned to embrace him.

"Ainjul, don't let those tears spill or the bronzing cream will streak," he whispered lightly in my ear.

He let me go and handed me a clean linen handkerchief. I carefully dabbed my eyes.

"You better go in and get reacquainted with her, she's been waiting a long time to see you again," David said.

I opened her stall door and stepped inside. She came over to me, and I offered her my hip as I had offered for so many years. She dropped her head and began to rub against me until she got so rough she was squeezing me between her and the wall. I gave her a few friendly slaps on the neck and she walked over to her feed bin and started pushing the salt brick around inside.

"Mr. Trenton, if you can spare half an hour I have some paperwork I'd like to go over with you," David said.

"A half hour won't throw us too far off schedule. Is that enough time for you to spend with your mare, Ainjul?" Matthew asked.

I nodded.

"Come up to the house when you're done and we will get back on the road," Matthew said.

They turned and began to walk away. Not more than a minute had passed before Sandy appeared at the stall door with some brushes in her hands.

"I thought you might like to brush her," she said, and handed them to me.

I was careful when I took the brushes from her outstretched hands. I didn't have a pair of gloves, and even though my earlier feast had warmed me it was never enough to displace the unnatural temperature of our bodies.

There was no need to brush her. She was receiving excellent care and her coat was clean and polished, but I did it anyway, just to be with her again.

"Mr. Trenton is something special, isn't he?" Sandy asked.

Here it comes. The barrage of questions. I didn't answer her.

"Where did you meet him?" she asked.

"In Charleston," I answered.

"Oh, I thought maybe you were high school sweethearts. But of course that can't be, he's from England, isn't he?"

"Originally, yes." I pulled the brush through my mare's long tail.

"He's pretty young to have so much wealth. Did he inherit it?" she asked.

"You might say it's been in his family for years," I said, and smiled at her.

"He always comes here alone. I mean, he's never brought a girlfriend with him before. Are you his girlfriend?" she asked.

"Not exactly," I said, and watched the tentative expression upon her pretty face relax.

"Then you must be his sister. You look so much alike."

I thought about this possibility, but the portrait of Maria loomed in my memory and wavered there as if demanding I not assume her role.

"Actually, I'm his wife," I said, and practically bit my tongue in two after the words slipped out.

Any hope she had to put a claim on him now faded but she took the news like she had already figured it out.

"You're a very lucky woman. I knew a good-looking guy like him, with money and all, wouldn't last long. I'd die to have a man like him."

I began to laugh at her last remark. I couldn't help it, and she looked at me with a surprised expression.

"I'm sorry," I said, and stifled the laughter for a moment. "But if you had seen him the way I saw him that first night, well, he was a real monster," and more laughter came from me in sporadic bursts.

Her look was one of perplexed innocence, and I managed to stop my laughter.

"I'm sorry," I apologized again for my unusual behavior. "I get a bit punchy when I'm tired."

Sandy made herself busy sweeping up a few pine shavings that had leaked under the stall doors and sprinkled the edges of the already-swept aisleway.

I was finishing saying hello to my horse when I heard the car horn. The half hour went by quickly, but since I didn't have a watch I really wasn't sure if it was half an hour.

The horn blared again, and I gave my horse one last hug before closing the stall door and hurrying out of the barn.

The headlights of the RV cut a wide path across the pasture. Steam was rising off the gentle, sloping hill, and in the mystical gray mist I saw three mares with foals at their sides.

The horn tooted again, impatiently, and I ran across the gravel drive.

The engine started as I closed the door, and we pulled around the circle in front of the house and onto the main drive.

Matthew's sharp profile was softened by the glow from the instrument panel of the dash, and I watched him silently for a long while.

During our journey he had begun to let go of his past and I yearned to learn more. Experience, however, told me to be patient. Elijah had also told me this, in his letter, and though I might throw questions to him, he only would reveal that which he was ready to reveal. I wondered if he would tell me now, about the one who made him, and about his beloved sister.

"Matthew, we are married," I said, and watched the corners of his mouth slip upward into a smile. "Did you marry when you were mortal?"

"No," he said, and the smile faded.

"Was there someone special? Someone you had hopes of marrying?"

"No," he said again.

"You bought my mare to buy my love, didn't you?" I asked.

This time there was no answer.

The crunch of gravel beneath the tires gave way to a steady whine when we pulled onto the paved road.

"You've come close to succeeding," I admitted to him. "But I cannot truly love someone like you. You remain a mystery to me, and since you won't share your past with me I simply cannot trust you. When are you going to share that past?''

''I told you once before we will both know when the time is right,'' he said.

''Matthew, how patient must I be? When will the time come?''

''I think very soon now,'' he said. He looked at me and I felt something, something special, something secret, something shared. But this feeling passed in a moment. ''Ainjul, you did very well with David and Sandy,'' he said, changing the subject.

''What do you mean?''

''It takes skill and cunning to act human. You do very well at repressing your new abilities.''

''I wasn't acting. I am still human—in a way. Elijah told me to never let go of my human self because it is a human world.''

''And that was a lesson I instilled in Elijah,'' Matthew said.

We weren't able to travel very much longer before the threat of a new day sent us under cover. Staying awake until the sun was on the brink of spilling over the horizon was one thing Matthew and I had in common. Even though I usually succumbed to the sleep before him, I knew it wasn't much before. Why he awakened so much earlier, I didn't know, but I figured in my mind it was due to his age.

We took the exit for Mount Hope and there found sanctity amid a row of eighteen wheelers at a truck stop. I was still not able to share Matthew's sense of being safe, but we had come to no harm yet.

The next evening I awoke to the hum of pavement beneath me. But there was something else, something so familiar that I wasn't able to discern it until the grip of sleep completely loosened.

A mortal had been brought into our mobile lair, and even now I could smell the fear. Matthew was up to his games again. Above me the bed moved, just slightly, but I felt it. Knowing Matthew's habits and preferences, I already had formed the image of his latest victim in my mind. A young girl, always he took the fairer sex, and I was certain she would be bound and gagged, maybe naked too.

I crawled from my hiding place. The scream I expected to greet me did not pierce the peaceful night. When I looked upon her, she was sleeping, but it was far from a natural sleep. Matthew had fed upon her, and a red splotch of color against the smooth curve of her neck was the only trace that remained from his moment of passion.

She was a ragged-looking thing, perhaps fourteen or fifteen years old. Her hair was the color of autumn wheat, permed at one time and now frizzy and unkempt. Her blue jeans, faded and well worn, had a rip in the left knee and dried blood still clung to the torn fibers there. The baggy Busch T-shirt was stained with grass and axle grease. At first I thought she was a member of a motorcycle gang but the longer I stared at her the more I was convinced she was one of those milk-carton kids, last seen in some respectable little town and now sorely missed by her family.

No ropes bound her and there was no gag to muffle her screams. Under the pale lids and beneath the long soft lashes, her eyes danced wildly. The fear coming from her was from her own mind and I watched, fascinated, while the nightmare took her and wondered again why I never dreamed.

The interior of the RV was lit suddenly by a flood of blue-white light. Like lightning the light flashed through the darkly tinted windows. The rapidity of glare confused me, but when I walked up front to join Matthew I saw that we had entered one of the several tunnels on the Pennsylvania Turnpike.

"Where did you get her?" I asked as I sat down in the passenger seat.

"I picked her up just after sunset. She was hitchhiking," he said.

"Will we make Pittsburgh tonight?" I asked.

"That is why I picked her up. We won't lose any time tonight while you hunt. There are at least three liters left in her, enough to give you a substantial meal."

"What's that supposed to mean?"

301

"Simply that last night you didn't take nearly enough to fulfill yourself. You're rather withdrawn and peaked looking."

"I'm all right. I feel fine," I said.

"Feeling fine and looking fine are two different things. I don't want you to walk through eternity looking like some monster just thrown up from the bowels of the earth. Especially not now, not now that you are my wife," he said, and laughed softly.

"I'm sorry about that. I'm sure I've put you in an awkward position," I said.

"Quite the contrary, my dear Ainjul. You've done me an honor, especially where Sandy is concerned. There is no need to be sorry, I am humbly flattered," he said.

"Well then, I'm the one in the awkward position. I mean, I'm stuck with you now," I said.

His grip tightened just a bit on the steering wheel, and for a brief instant I perceived his thoughts. But like a flicker of flame in a breeze his thoughts drifted away and he sighed.

"When you feel the need to take her, finish her," he said.

I nodded. The hunger wasn't awakened in me yet, and I was quite content just sitting with my legs propped up on the dash and feeling the thick stuffing of the seat give beneath the pressure of my spine.

Bong would've enjoyed this long journey. I pictured him now, head hanging from the window with his tongue out and spittle flying from his great jowls in the wind. It was the first time I thought of him since he had been destroyed. And I did miss him. He had been the perfect hunter, and the perfect companion. Immortality, however, had no meaning for him, for he was dead.

"Matthew, do you know what excites me the most about being immortal?" I asked.

His shoulders shrugged, but he didn't say anything and maybe this was because he didn't find immortality exciting anymore, or maybe he found it strange that I found it exciting. I turned around in the seat so that I was facing him and told him.

"I always wanted to be around to see the time when man

finally set out on the greatest conquest of all. I want to see man colonize space. I want to watch him stretch out into the heavens. I want to go there too, if I am able. Do you think we could travel in space?"

"I have no idea whether or not we could travel in space. I'm still trying to get over the clutter of power lines everywhere, space isn't very often on my mind," he said.

"But don't you want to go, when they go? Don't you want to look down upon our planet and see it the way God sees it, the completeness of His creation?"

"If man should seek to dominate space, and dominate it he will, for man is a creature of conquer, the last thing I can imagine is our kind spreading our evil across the cosmos. What entitles *us* to do that?" he asked with every bit of seriousness.

"I'm speculating, of course, but did you ever think *our* kind came from out there?"

"No. I've never had that thought," he said. He glanced at me. The look upon his face was keen with interest. "You are the product of your time and I am the product of mine. Where your thoughts send you into what will be, mine hold me with what has already been. Technology has driven man away from one darkness but into another. Before I can seriously think about outer space, I must see inner space. By this I mean the spiritual world, the world of good and evil. The world of God and Satan. Before man stumbled upon nuclear fission the interpretation of Revelations was an all out fight between good and evil. Now scholars confuse the real meaning with the material world they have created. Revelations isn't talking about a war that man is going to control. The rules are going to be bent, the unreal will become real. All hell will break loose upon this planet when Lucifer is usurped from his dominance here. I think more about my role then than I ever think about outer space."

"So you still believe in God and Satan? Tell me, have you ever met the devil? In all the nights you've stalked alone, have you ever even just glimpsed him. Don't you think if you were a product of him, a tool to be used later for his sake, don't you think he would show himself?"

303

"Ainjul, we could talk about this forever and never solve a thing. My point is that you are different from me. Every aspect of you is a glimmer of the innocent wonder of this time. Everything for you is possible. You are a refreshing ray of light in my dark world, and every moment I watch you makes me glad for what I did, glad I brought you into immortality, for whatever it holds," he said.

The letter Elijah had sent me and some of the things he had told me before I met Matthew made me aware that Matthew really had "captured" me to end his loneliness. For, if immortality can mean anything, then certainly boring could be a metaphor. And Matthew had grown bored with existing, this was evident to me by little things he did, such as playing with his victims.

"Was it true you wanted to die?"

"Did Elijah tell you that?" he asked.

"I think his exact words were, 'Matthew wants Matthew dead.' "

"Before you were born, yes, I was ready to quit. There was no point in continuing. I had gained all I sought to gain. I had gone everywhere I wanted to go. What was left to do?"

"But you don't understand, that is the very point of it all. With everything you've acquired you can do anything," I said.

"No. Ainjul, it is your concepts that are not understandable. You think that wealth buys power. But when you've had all that for hundreds of years you start to ask yourself, what else is there?"

"I can't comprehend any of what you say," I said, giving up. I felt he had put me in a precarious position, telling me that I was his reason for continuing.

"Don't carry the burden for my existence upon your shoulders," he said, reading my very thoughts. "I never meant for you to do that."

"Well, let me ask just one question," I said.

"And what might that one question be?"

"What is the true reason you made me immortal?" I asked him.

He was quiet for a few minutes, but I knew he was thinking about the real reason, not trying to dodge my question. I hoped to hear something other than, "Because I was lonely," or "Because I loved you." In the dark, twisted catacombs of his memory the true reason was buried and I wanted him to reveal it, not so much for my sake, but for his as well.

"It is a hard question to answer," he spoke at last. "There are so many reasons, selfish perhaps, maybe even arrogantly evil. But the real reason, well, the real reason is because you looked so much like my sister."

He stopped. The look of "I knew it, not her again" was on my face, and he studied me with those crisp green eyes before continuing.

"You've been quite astute in your observations. She has had a powerful hold on me. The real reason I brought you into my life, my immortal life, was to rid myself of her, if it could be done. Maybe I even did it to spite her. She did so much want immortality."

"You talk about her like she is real. Can you see her spirit? Is there something about our preternatural existence that allows that?" I asked.

"She is real, but only in here," he said, and lightly tapped his finger to his forehead. "And in here she dwells forever. Nothing I have tried has loosened her memory, nothing. So, you see, it was indeed a selfish reason I brought you into immortality. But you are her very essence and perhaps the key to set her memory free," he said.

Words again. Elijah's words. I was the key to his past and his future, he wrote those words to me. I felt as if I had become part of a mystical struggle, an integral part.

"Thanks for the truth," I said, still thinking about what had happened between them to keep him a prisoner to her memory.

"I may be the embodiment of evil, but I am never a liar," he said.

I had to take time to digest the things he told me. It always came back to *her*. And yet she was no more than ashes in the earth now. I looked over at my vampire companion, my maker, my friend. Yes, he was a friend. How could he not be with all the things he had done for me?

Something was different about him, and as the cool air from the vents blew the wisps of hair around his face I saw the difference clearly. By telling me the reasons behind making me a vampire he had already released a part of her. The very aura about him had lightened and he glanced over to me and smiled.

But all these things began to lose focus within me. The passion that my very existence now revolved around surfaced hot inside my soul. As I thirsted for knowledge about him, I also thirsted for the gift of life. I said nothing to Matthew as I walked to the rear of the RV. I was going to take the milk-carton child and be done with it so I could think with a clear mind.

But as I stood over her I couldn't do it. She was Matthew's victim. I just couldn't take her, not yet. The need was there, but I would wait a little longer.

Twice the urge to take her hit me and twice I got up and left the passenger seat only to return without feeding.

"May I ask you something?" Matthew said.

"What?" I said with an uneven edginess to my voice.

"Why do you practice self-denial?"

"What are you talking about?" I said, and squirmed against the seat.

"Many times I've seen you put yourself through this agony. You're a young vampire and you need to feed nightly. I can no longer even count the nights you haven't taken enough or haven't taken any at all. I just wonder why you do it?"

"It isn't right, I mean taking her. She's your victim," I said.

"For the love of hell, Ainjul, take her. I give her to you," he said.

"But she'll be dead and I don't want to touch her after she's . . ."

"You've got a big problem with death," he said.

"Well, we both have our peculiarities, don't we?" I countered.

306

"Yes, we both have our peculiarities. Take her, I can't stand to watch you suffer so."

And I was suffering. The fire inside my veins was driving me to her. Only the power that is the mind held me back. At last I surrendered to my instinctive urges, and when I drank I drank deeply until the last heartbeat faded away and the blood became nothing more than air. The very vein from which I feasted began to work out of her body, that's how deeply I pulled from her. And when I was done she was dead. And as always I was repelled from the death like it was searing flame. I did not look back once I left her. Her gift was in me and I was renewed.

Before I sat down beside Matthew I saw the exit sign. We had only three more miles to go. A very different feeling enveloped me, a feeling of being more vulnerable than I had ever been.

Home was so very near.

CHAPTER SEVENTEEN

"Dawn is near. We cannot stop tonight," Matthew said.

The uneasy feeling which spread as each mile brought me closer home eased. I wanted, but didn't want to go there.

"There is time to just drive by, if you would like." he said.

I nodded. *It's only a house, for God's sake.* A thousand butterflies reawakened inside my gut, and for a moment I thought I might throw up the blood I had feasted on. *But it's not just any house, it is my family's house. And my memories are within the confines of those walls.*

"Matthew, I don't know if I can go through with this. It's painful for me already and we aren't even there," I said.

"Ainjul, for your own good you really must do this. Once you see that all is well and all has returned to normal you can let them go and be what you are," he said.

A vampire! What would they do if they knew? If I dared confront them with the truth and prove, beyond a shadow of a doubt, what would they do? And why am I even thinking such ludicrous thoughts. They must never know. It is better that they think me dead. Yet all would never be normal, how can it when a mother or father loses a child?

Suddenly I was angry. I vented my anger at the source.

"If you want to drive by, then damn it, drive by. You are the one who forced all this upon me. Damn you to hell anyway," I said, but my voice cracked with emotion and I ran from him, and from the truths inside myself.

If he drove by, I never knew, for I crawled into our

cramped storage space and willed the sleep to take me. But it cannot be summoned up so, and I squeezed my eyes tighter and tighter until my head began to pound from my efforts.

Finally I began to calm myself and take stock of what was really bothering me. The fact was simple to see. I would be here long after all of my family, and their families, passed on.

Mom told me once how she felt after her mother died. She said that the door was now open, that her death would be next. And though she told me this with great seriousness, I found comfort in her words. In my mind, still fresh with youth, I knew the door would not open for me until she was gone. Though I never could picture myself old, and what young mortal can, I never in my wildest dreams thought I would go first. What words of wisdom was Mom speaking now?

Matthew was near. The RV had stopped but the engine still idled. Above me the bed covers rustled. He was disposing of our poor milk-carton child. Would her parents ever know of her death?

You wanted to come home. You wanted to find Grandma's treasures. Don't cop out now.

Sleep began to descend over me, heavy like a lead barrier. For now I could hide beneath its shield. But what of the thousand tomorrows?

The foreign sound of an aluminum door being closed pulled me away from the blackness. Matthew had returned, and I listened to his soft movements. The RV moved off again, but not very far, and then he was sliding in beside me and securing the brass lock of our hidden vault.

His hand found mine and he squeezed it tightly, reassuringly. But I had no energy to return this subtle gesture of kindness. My mind was already slipping into the dark void of emptiness.

Another day passed without incident; nobody disturbed us. After inching my way out of the storage compartment I eased the panel back into place and ran my hand along the tongue and groove seam. The match was perfect; the piece looked like solid paneling.

The RV was empty. Matthew must've gone out to feed or to secure another victim for me. In either case I was alone and glad to have this time to myself in order to mentally prepare for my family encounter. But the longer I sat and thought about it, the more I began to stew in all the what ifs, and finally I had to get up and do something to occupy my mind.

It was my intention to go into the bathroom and get a cloth to dust with, but when I glanced at myself in the mirror I found something more pressing to take care of. The bronzing cream had rubbed off in places during my sleep, and my skin was splotched with white and ruddy brown patches.

I filled the sink with water and tore open a box of Caress soap. The foamy lather turned an instant brown as the stain washed off my hands, and I had to drain the dirty water from the basin before washing my face.

While the water ran over the washcloth, and just before wringing it out a final time, I studied the soft white luminescence of my clean skin. As always, I was fascinated by the strange beauty of it. Even mortals were attracted to it, like a moth to a flame, and I wondered how long it would be until the fine smoothness of Matthew's skin became mine.

I reached back to tighten my long ponytail, but when I pulled the hair apart the rubber band snapped. Long strands of hair fell around my shoulders and I was the image of Maria. I combed through the curls with my fingers. The door of the RV opened.

"Ainjul, are you ready to go?"

I stepped from the bathroom. Matthew had also washed the stain from his skin and he had changed his clothes. Tonight he wore a red-white-and-blue long-sleeved polo shirt and a pair of navy slacks. His appearance was crisp and correct, and I was the wilted flower by his side.

"Listen, about last night. I'm sorry, I'm just nervous. I didn't mean to blow up like that," I said.

310

He ignored my apology but not to spite me, simply because I didn't need to give him one.

"I've rented a car," he said, giving me the once-over. "You've got some stain on your collar."

"Give me a minute to change and we'll go," I said, and turned toward the closet where our clothing was hung. I heard the door open again, and when I glanced around Matthew was gone. In less than a minute I slipped into a pair of black jeans and a kelly-green sweatshirt. I sat down on the bed to tie the laces of my sneakers. The waistband of the jeans dug into my stomach. Can vampires gain weight? I wondered.

The people door on the side of the RV made a tinny sound when I closed it, and I jiggled the handle to be sure it was secure.

Matthew revved the engine of his rental car a few times and I thought he was hurrying me until I saw the car. It was an old battered Ford Pinto. The areas of body not marred by dents were patched with pink Bond-O. The passenger door was so crumpled that the edge stuck out a good inch from the doorframe. I had to yank hard to get it open. The engine was idling roughly and Matthew pumped the gas pedal a few more times before shifting into first gear.

"Matthew, this car definitely isn't you. Where did you get it? Rent-A-Wreck?"

"I got it from the kid in that camper," he said, and pointed to the left. "He said it ain't pretty but it'll get us where we want to go."

"Well, I hope you didn't pay him much, this thing is a genuine Bond-O bomb."

We pulled away from the campground and the car backfired a few times when we picked up speed, but it continued to run.

"I thought we should have something inconspicuous. The neighborhood isn't one of Ferraris and Mercedeses," he said.

He was correct in his observations. Most of our neighbors owned Chevys and Fords, but none were in this state of decay.

"I think you've gone overboard. This piece of junk is going to be noticed just as much as a Ferrari."

"Do you think so?" Matthew asked.

"I know so."

Not only was the car a heap, the interior reeked of marijuana. Out of curiosity I slid the ashtray open. Lying among the ashes was a roach clip and a few crumpled EZ widers. The kid must've had a recent party in here. I closed the ashtray.

"How are we going to get in the house?" I asked.

"Leave that to me," he said.

"But if my folks are in the house, we can't just waltz in, can we?"

His smile was one of boastful confidence, and I knew he had been in our house before, many times.

"How?" I asked again.

"It's quite simple. You could dart right in front of them and they wouldn't see you, not really. How many times did you sense someone looking at you and glance around to see no one? How often did you just catch a glimpse of a person in the corner of your eye but when you looked again the space was empty?"

"Are you telling me that was you?"

He shifted down and turned right into our subdivision. Except that the trees and shrubs had grown larger, the neighborhood looked as I remembered.

"Remember the night you couldn't sleep so you turned on your stereo and played with those funny ESP cards all evening?"

"My God, you were in my closet!"

His smile grew into a devilish grin, and he nodded.

"Dawn was soon upon me and I had to get rid of you so I could escape. Since it was quite clear you weren't going to sleep, and since I was quite tired of listening to that same album over and over again, and since you were so good with those cards, I just slipped the notion in your head to concentrate on the closet door. Of course I opened it, you weren't telekinetic, but it scared you enough to make you leave and then I made my escape."

312

"I really believed I moved the closet door. I never played with those damn cards again. That was so creepy, and you're a creep for doing that."

Matthew pulled the car off the blacktop road and stopped near the creek where I had played during the hot sultry days of my childhood. He cut the engine, and it coughed and sputtered a few times before quieting, then he was out of the car but I sat a moment and stared up the street.

My house was the one on the corner lot. Dad always hated the location because so many times people cut through the yard instead of staying on the street. I still remember the night he flattened the tires of one with two-by-fours pegged with nails. Despite the thunderous blowout, the car twacked away and we never did find out who it was.

Tonight the house was dark. I'm sure Mom and Dad hadn't gone to bed yet. They must be away but where and for how long? I didn't want to get caught up in the attic when they returned. I wasn't as confident as Matthew about this. Perhaps he could dart in front of them, but I knew I would hesitate just a split second to see them and in turn be seen. Would they think me a ghost?

"Ainjul, are you coming?" Matthew asked, leaning into the window.

I pushed against the door, calling upon my vampiric strength to force it open. Metal groaned upon metal and then with a sudden lurch the door popped open and I was unceremoniously dumped at Matthew's feet.

"Told you I was a klutz," I said, taking his offered hand.

Matthew kept a tight hold upon my arm and we moved among the shadows the way only those of our kind can move. No mortal would detect us.

We circled the house once, and I was able to sense that indeed the place was empty. We entered through the back sliding glass door. The lock was simple enough to open. Maybe as a mortal I wasn't telekinetic but now the energy confined in my brain was unleashed and again I felt that nothing was impossible.

The familiarity of the house demanded that I linger but I overrode this desire and moved like an ethereal wind into the upstairs hallway. The narrow steps leading into the attic were cluttered with things Mom meant to take up. Some of these things were mine. Already she was stored my memory. I picked my way over the treasures and felt the stuffy warmth envelop me as I climbed higher.

Without thinking, I pulled the string of the overhead light, and the single yellow bulb illuminated the room in bronze hues that added to the attics mystery. I headed straight for the corner where Grandma's things were stored.

"What are you looking for?" Matthew asked.

I had completely forgotten he was following me. He had moved so quietly.

"Nothing in particular, just some things," I said.

"I could help, if I knew what you were searching for," he said.

"I'm searching for knowledge," I said, and picked up one of the boxes. I eased it carefully to the floor and sat beside it.

Matthew sat down on the floor beside me and watched while I rummaged through the first box.

"Are you glad they aren't here?" he asked.

"Yes. No. I don't know. Look at these," I said, pulling a stack of old journals from the box. The date on the top one read 1861. I had already found something.

The tiny book was bound together with string, and I turned the pages carefully. On some pages the ink had faded and looked almost like pencil but most of the writing was clear and precise.

Matthew took the book from me and began to read aloud.

" 'Monday Evening, March 4, 1861. Although this day more temptations assailed me than almost any other to my recollection, and everything seemed as though it was sent to provoke, this has been a remarkable day both to me and also to our country.

" 'To me because it is my birthday. Thirty-four years ago it pleased the Lord to call me into being—a poor wretch—only born, as it often occurs to me, to be a trouble to myself. I am often surprised that I am permitted yet to live if I look back to the past and see how often I deserved to be cast away as an unfruitful tree, but O! that my soul might glorify my kind Father and friend who has kept me in the hollow of His almighty hand and provided for me now during thirty-four years.

" 'This has been a great day in the history of our country as it is the day that our President takes his seat—or takes it upon himself the required oath as the chief magistrate of our Union. Abraham Lincoln of Illinois was inaugurated today as President. It is my ardent prayer that God may endow him with power and wisdom from above, as well as all those who sit in council to make laws, and may it please God to grant that rumors of civil wars in our U.S. may soon no more be heard, that peace and good will may reign throughout all our borders, that the Kingdom of Christ may grow and blossom as the rose, and the Kingdom of Satan be overthrown. Amen.' "

"Was he a preacher?" I asked.

Matthew closed the book and handed it back to me. "A self-proclaimed preacher, yes. He tried very hard to lead a righteous life but like so many others before and after him, he was flawed by his own human weakness."

I had another book in my hands and opened it to Thursday Evening April 20, 1865.

" 'Notwithstanding the favorable news of our army which we still hear, and the hope that this Hell-born-rebellion may soon fully crumble to the dust, yet my heart feels remarkably sad and cast down during this week so far, because I am compelled to record the horrible assassination of our worthy President of the U.S., Abraham Lincoln, on last Friday Evening, the 14th, he was shot through the head, by an assassin, while sitting along side his wife in the theatre, in a private box.

" 'My ability fails to express my feelings on this subject. I hope his blood so treacherously shed may yet be avenged, by the utter rout and destruction of all Rebels, North and South.

" 'At the same time another assassin attempted to kill Secretary Seward. When I last heard he still lived, but had three cuts in his throat.' "

"Tell me you didn't do it," I said.

Matthew laughed quietly, and shook his head. "Ainjul, as a rule I generally dine on women."

"I've noticed that," I said, and watched him fall silent.

"You're searching for information about me, aren't you?" he spoke again.

I kept my head down, buried in the old style of writing and the somber tones of the journals.

"You won't find anything in these. These are the writings of your great-great-grandfather on your father's side of the family. The only records your grandmother ever found about her lineage was that two brothers came to America from Wales where they fled in haste as they were to be hanged for stealing horses."

"Horse thieves in my, our, family. You're joking."

"I'm dead serious," he said, and grinned.

" 'Tuesday P.M. May 18, 1880,' " I began to read another entry. " 'It becomes my most painful and solemn duty to record the death of my dear and much beloved wife, Sarah Jane. On Sunday evening she again commenced to go back rapidly, suffered much by coughing and by being too weak to expectorate which troubled her. She spoke much during the night of her hope and assurance of dying in the Lord. Her earnest prayer and longing of her soul was to be delivered and to go home to Jesus.

" 'At about 4 o'clock A.M. on Monday she remarked, "O! Sam, I am so sick," I asked her "Shall I waken up the children," she replied, "Yes, call them up and I will give them goodbye and then I will go home to my Saviour." I called them all up as soon as I could and all stood around her bed, weeping and lamenting bitterly, but she begged and said, "Do not weep for me. I am going home," and now calling each one to her side she gave them her right hand bidding them good-bye.

" 'At about 5 o'clock we all thought she was dying and I thought she was gone, but as we were all lamenting bitterly she again commenced to speak, would ask things and answer everything properly if asked. But how she now, from this time till about 4 o'clock P.M. did pray and longed to go home was almost past enduring to hear. Her constant prayer was, "O! my Saviour take me home. Come. Come. Come." She would frequently say, "O! Sam, do you think it takes long yet? Do you think I am near over? How soon do you think Jesus will take me home?" When I would assure her that it would not be long anymore, that Jesus would take her home when God so willed, she would say "O! yes, when God wills, not my will. O! yes, I will wait till Jesus comes." Once she said, "What time is it," when I said, 'Almost nine," she replied, "So late and I am still here."

" 'Thus she labored till about 3 o'clock in the afternoon when she became happy, her soul overflowed with thanks and praises to God for what Jesus had done for her remarking, "I thank my God that he has still preserved my senses, that I know what I am doing and that I yet can praise my God." After this she became very weak, and laboring much with her breath, she fell into a sleep as it appeared, but her lips were still moving and one could well see that she was speaking, and that she wanted to say, "Come, my Saviour, take me home," and that she just repeated every breath either the word, "Come, come, come," or "Take, take, take." When thus laboring I would ask her, "Is your Saviour still with you?" she would with an audible whisper say, "O! yes."

" 'At about 5 o'clock she awoke suddenly, and looking around the room she said, "But now I must get up," looking somewhat bewildered, but directly appeared and spoke quite composedly, and requested to be assisted to private matters. After which having been attended to she said, "I am so hungry." (She having not eaten anything for twenty four hours.) When soup was brought she, with a pleasant smile in her face, asked, "Naomi, are you done?" when Naomi said "yes," she said, "Then you feed me." After she had eaten about her regular meal, she became more calm, more like taking a natural sweet sleep, was no longer troubled with coughing, her breath appeared to be easier, but was short and became shorter and shorter till 15 minutes after 3 o'clock this morning when she breathed her last, and her spirit took its flight and a happy soul was released from its earthly tabernacle.

" 'Whenever, during this apparent sleep, I asked her, "Sarah, is your Saviour still with you?" she would nod assent with her head, and with an audible whisper say, "O! yes." This answer she gave me just fifteen minutes before her last breath. I am unable to write my feelings but would only say my soul feels glad to know that Jesus can make a dying bed soft and sweet, and that He will not forsake His children who trust in Him, no, not even if they are going through the valley of the shadow of death.' "

I closed the book and gently placed it back in the box. These words, written so long ago, spoke of love and life, death and misery and of hope. I felt like an intruder, an evil intruder of this gentleman's past. I glanced at Matthew. He was watching me, and his expression was one of solemn composure.

"We walk the valley of the shadow of death," he said.

We are the shadow of death, I thought.

As if to exemplify our evil, the passion within me began to surface and I needed to take nourishment.

"Matthew, I have to go. Take me away from here," I said.

"But you've just begun your search," he said.

"Now, I have to leave now," I said, and stood up and looked down upon him.

He nodded, understanding my needs, and rose from the floor with such smoothness and fluidity I was taken aback again at his power and his masterfulness of what we were. Caught in time, he was forever the boy-man, and I stared at the way the light danced among his wavy dark hair and the way his very skin absorbed the light and threw it back out. He almost glowed, and this alone was pure beauty, and I would have bathed in his light but the hunger tore inside me with such unexpected force that I gasped out loud.

"Hurry, I have to get out of here . . ."

A door opened downstairs.

"God, Matthew, they've come home." My voice was shear anguish. If there had been a chance for me to sneak about and not be seen, it was gone because I couldn't control my preternatural abilities and the hunger. I just couldn't.

"Ainjul, calm yourself. It is not your parents," Matthew said, stepping beside me.

"How do you know?"

"I know their scent. Listen to what your body is telling you. How many are in the house?"

"One," I answered, aware of the lone mortal. And I knew more, she was a woman, and she was watering the plants. The fresh scent of damp earth mingled with her warm aroma of life and blood. "She'll kill them, the plants, I mean. She shouldn't water them this late."

"You understand now, don't you?" he said, and smiled at me. "The ability is within you but you've constantly tuned it off and relied upon those inferior human senses. There is a time for such senses, when you mingle with humans, but never when there may be danger. This is what makes me so superior to others of our kind. They all do what you have done, they refuse the magic of the night."

"There is no magic," I said.

"No magic? You can stand before me and tell me there is no magic? My blood is within you and any knowledge you seek about me is in my blood, but you've never learned to focus inward and release that knowledge. I tell you now, think about me and about the one who made me, think hard and you will see pieces of my past."

"Matthew, there isn't time, there is a woman downstairs and we are trapped here," I began to plead with him.

"Then go downstairs and take her, drink up the delicious gift she harbors, and then come to me and tell me again there is no magic."

"No," I said. It was impossible for me to take a victim in my parents' house. I would not defile the loving atmosphere with my evil.

"Do it, Ainjul," he said.

"No," I repeated firmly.

"Then I shall," he said, and moved for the door.

I cut him off and pulled his hand from the doorknob. But

319

his determination was no match for my weakness. He was in command of the power, and I was being tormented by human frailty.

"Why are you doing this to me? Why must I take her in this house? There is a world of victims, why here and now?"

"Because you are so very close to the brink of truth. Here is where you can let go of the human compassion and now is the time for you to do it or I can never share myself with you. And what I have to share is indeed unique. But you will never gain access to me until you fully let go of being mortal, or the madness will take you."

"Matthew, please, I don't understand. I have accepted what I am, I even enjoy it. Isn't that enough? What else can . . ."

"Go, take her," he ordered.

In defiance of him I turned away and he was off, down the stairs and out of my reach. I had to go after him. Whatever this moment was, it was very important to him, I sensed that as keenly as I sensed the woman. But still I could not comprehend.

He lied to me. The one who earlier told me he was never a liar had lied. I found him nowhere, but I did find the woman. She was putting the green plastic watering can back under the kitchen sink.

But had he really lied? Or was he giving me this chance to take her before he went through with his threat?

The woman straightened up and closed the cupboard door. I glanced around the room, searching for Matthew. The woman began to turn and I began to dodge back into the laundry room but suddenly I stood very still in the doorway and let her see me.

Her eyes grew wide with primitive terror but she did not scram. I knew her and she knew me.

"Angela, you're . . ."

"Dead, Mrs. Anson, I'm dead," I said. Quickly I locked upon those disbelieving brown eyes and drew the fear away from her.

She came to me, though I must've commanded her to do so. The very essence of her life pulsed before me, and when

320

she reached out her arms toward me I embraced her and the passion to consume her reared up inside me.

The soft blue-gray curls of her hair smelled of recent perm solution, but once her blood flowed into my mouth all my interests were washed away with the lust of the feast and we became one.

As powerful and demanding as that lust is it never was enough to make me lose touch with what I was doing, and I took only enough to drown the fire of hell welling within me and then I let her go. But before my lips left the warm tenderness of her skin I pushed the blood-saliva mixture upon her wounds with my tongue and lifted her into my arms.

I carried her into the family room. She moaned against me, and once her eyes flickered open and she looked into mine. I suggested she sleep, and I pushed the suggestion deep into her mind and she immediately went limp.

After placing her body gently on the couch I propped her head upon a pillow and covered her with the old afghan my grandmother had crocheted over ten years ago.

My fingers traced the supple contour of her cheek. The skin was so smooth and so soft with age, and I knew where I had felt skin like that before.

"Was it such a terrible thing to do?" Matthew's voice whispered behind me.

I stood up, and turned to face him.

"Get away from me," I said.

"Not until you search within you for the beginnings to the answers you seek," he said.

Our eyes locked upon each other. Like the night on the Battery in Charleston, when he stood with his arms around his bleached blond victim, I felt and saw images coming from him. But his words were true, they weren't coming from him, they were inside me. All this time they were in me. And I began to concentrate on them, bringing the pictures into clear focus.

The night air was cool, and a mellow fog rose from the ground. I was flying, no, I was riding a horse over the mist-shrouded land. Ahead, the dark outline of a ruined abbey appeared. I stopped. The pounding of the horse's heart beneath the saddle leathers rocked me and I could smell the sweat, lathered into a white foam along the horse's neck. I jumped off and let go of the reins, and the horse reared in terror and bolted away from me. But there was sadness in my mind and I couldn't focus on the fear of my mount. Then I saw him, a ghostly figure of white among the black ruins of stone. But when I strained to see him clearly he was gone, and the sadness again swallowed my thoughts. I tried to understand this sadness, focus on the source of it, but I couldn't. I walked under the great stone archway. A cold chill swept over me, and then it happened, the attack. Immediately I pulled away from the images that were too real and too painful to reexperience.

"Are you satisfied now? Did I pass your little test?" I asked him.

"Yes. I thought after you had taken Bong's blood you would realize the magic, but you didn't. It is important for you to understand because the time is coming when I will give you all of my past," he said.

"So you're sure I won't leave you now?" I asked. He had originally told me he would not share his past with me until the time came when he no longer feared losing me.

He started to say something but then tensed visibly. I tried to listen to what he heard but the images of the old abbey played inside me.

"They're coming home," he whispered.

"What about Mrs. Anson?" I asked, looking down upon my sleeping victim.

"She is going to be fine. Leave her there. Do you want to stay or do you want to go?"

"I want to go but first I want those journals," I said, and ran upstairs for the attic. I gathered up all the journals I could find and shoved them into an old empty hat box. Their car turned into the driveway, and I flew downstairs to join Matthew. Together we exited via the sliding glass door but after we reached the cover of woods at the edge of the backyard I stopped.

"Here, take these to the car. I want to see them, but I want to do it alone," I said.

"Ainjul, I don't think you should go back in the house, not with them there. Your emotions are too . . ."

"I'm not going in the house. I just want to see them, that's all. Please go and let me do this alone," I said.

He nodded and left me and I waited and watched and one by one the lights in the house came on as Mom or Dad made their way back to the family room.

I melded myself into the shadows and approached the house.

Mom's voice, clear and sweet and remembered, filtered from behind the glass door. I hung back along the curtain edge and held my breath as I looked in on them. Mom looked the same, but Dad had lost weight and I hoped it wasn't because of me.

"Oh, Marie," Mrs. Anson moaned. "Angela was here, I saw her."

Dad's posture went visibly rigid.

"Shirley, Angela is gone. You just had a dream," Mom said.

"No, it wasn't a dream. She was right there and she told me she was dead. I touched her and she was cold, like death."

"Shirley, it was just a dream, a bad dream. This house just brought her memory back for you, that's all," Mom said.

Yes, you foolish old woman, I was just in your dreams, now please drop it, I thought.

"Have you been hitting the hard stuff, Shirley?" Dad asked, and his tone was rude.

"Cliff, that's enough. Can't you see she's had a bad fright?" Mom said.

Dad turned away from them and walked over to the sliding glass door. I moved back along the siding of the house and flattened myself there. The door opened, and I grew fearful that he would step outside, but he only reached into the night to pull the screen shut.

I moved back into position so I could see them again.

323

Mom was helping Mrs. Anson to stand. She was weak and complaining of being dizzy but she finally stopped repeating her ghost story.

"How is Lizzy, and the baby?" she asked.

"They are both doing beautifully. Lizzy's depression has finally been lifted. I was so worried about her after Angela . . ."

"Marie, I'm so very sorry. I should've never said anything to you. But the dream was so real," Mrs Anson said.

"She's dead, for crying out loud. Shirley, Angela is dead. Can you please let her memory rest in peace." Dad's voice was angry but filled with emotion, and I felt his loss.

Mom helped Mrs. Anson out of the room and Dad took off his jacket and sat down to read the paper.

I was surprised to find the roles reversed. I really thought Mom would be the one grieving, but clearly it was Dad who had yet to accept my "death." And my sister's baby? I had forgotten she was pregnant. I still heard the excitement in her voice the night she stopped at my apartment and told me. And now the baby had come. The time had gone by so quickly.

I waited and watched just a little longer. Dad flipped through the pages of the paper. His face was obstructed from my view but I found his large hands comforting to watch as they fingered the edges of newsprint. When I was sure Mrs. Anson had time to get home, and after I saw Mom come back into the family room, I left them to find Matthew. Yes, they were still my family, but I was distanced from them forever.

Matthew was standing along the bank of the creek, tossing stones into the water. He appeared so human in his mannerisms I could not help but wonder why he had been so adamant that I let go of my mortal senses.

"I'm ready to go," I said.

"Are you all right?" he asked me.

"Yes."

"And your parents?"

"They are fine, as fine as can be expected," I said.

"Do you wish to stay here longer?"

"I said I'm ready to go. I don't belong here anymore. I am no longer a part of their family."

"I'm sorry you feel that way. You will always remain a part of their family. Always," he said.

He walked over to the battered Ford and yanked the passenger door open for me. I pulled it shut as he walked around and climbed behind the wheel.

"Matthew, do you suppose that when they die and go to heaven and don't find me there, do you suppose they will know what has happened to me?"

"They might think you've gone to hell," he said with quiet seriousness.

"That would be so painful for them. I don't think there is pain like that in heaven. If I died and went to heaven and found out that someone I loved had gone to hell I would be miserable. God wouldn't allow those feelings to spoil the happiness of heaven, would He? Do you think they would learn then what I have become?"

He thought a moment and started the car.

"Your thoughts are very complex, and very strange. I haven't ever thought about the rewards of heaven in that light. It would indeed be a terrible torment to go there and find your loved ones in hell, but someone has to go to hell, do they not?"

I didn't answer him. I didn't want to think about it, though I might like to corner a minister or priest and question him about these matters.

"My sister had her baby," I said to change the subject.

"Yes. I know. A little boy," he said, and reached into his coat pocket and withdrew a small, framed picture.

"Matthew, you stole this," I said when he handed it to me.

"He reminded me of someone," he said.

My gaze lingered on the picture. Before I uttered the next question I knew the answer.

"Why are there so few women vampires?"

"Women are creatures of great compassion. They nurture life within them and bear great pain to bring that life into the world. They are not, in my opinion, killers."

325

I stared into the tiny cherubic face of my sister's baby. I had always loved children but never was able to picture myself as a mother. On more than one occasion I had felt alienated by this. As a mortal I found myself strangely disenchanted with these feelings but now I understood that my lack of wanting what the majority of women wanted only shaped my destiny to become the killer I was now.

"Many women have been given immortality, many women have succumbed to the compassion of their victims. A woman vampire can be consumed by this mixture of feelings and a madness soon overtakes them and they can no longer endure our world," he said.

"And so they die," I said.

"Yes. They die."

"Then Debra and I really do share something," I said.

Matthew looked over to me. "Don't put yourself in the same class with her. You are far superior to her in every way."

The hatred in her eyes reflected in my mind, and I wondered when she would make good her threat. When she did move to take Matthew, would I stop her? But this was absurd because Matthew would never have her, still her words echoed in my mind.

"I'm going to take him away, if it takes forever I will do it. I'm going to take him away."

CHAPTER EIGHTEEN

During our journey back to Berwyn I became completely absorbed in my great-great grandfather's journals and wasn't much company for Matthew.

Through weekly accounts I relived the life of another, and what a hard, miserable life it told.

A first son died in infancy, then a daughter was born and also died in infancy. There were three more sons and another daughter, and nearly every month I expected them to die also. If they weren't sick with one ailment it was another.

Life revolved around his church and even I was convinced that he was a lowly sinner in God's eye. His continual tone was one of sadness and melancholy; I often wondered if the man ever had cause to be happy.

He managed to make clear his feelings on the Civil War and yet twice he bought his way out of the draft.

And it wasn't soon after his dear beloved wife was in her grave that temptation drove him into the arms of another woman and they were secretly married in the next county to avoid scandal.

But for all his hardship and disbelief that God allowed him to remain on earth, his was a long life for a man during those times. The journals covered a span of sixty years, he was in his eighties on the last entry.

I wished Matthew had known him, but he told me he only saw him on two occasions and he was every bit the upright, stern individual the journals portrayed him to be.

After stacking the small books in the hat box I became aware of a deep admiration for the man. If nothing else had come of his existence, these records held an account that he lived. And to be so faithful in writing, I was awed by this alone. How many people could keep it up for sixty years? I imagined the evening entries must have become habit.

I sat back against the passenger seat and swam in the memories I had just read. But unconsciously the memories shifted, and again my mind replayed the eerie scene that night at the old abbey. Only this time, when the vampire attacked, the image played one scene further and I felt the life blood being drained from me and I gasped out loud and forced myself back to reality.

"Ainjul, what's wrong?" Matthew asked.

"You've infected me. This so called magic that is in your blood won't leave my mind alone."

"Because it is a part of you now, and now you begin to understand the underlying power in our blood."

"But it doesn't make sense. The memories are yours.' How can they have become a part of my mind, part of my brain?"

"Ainjul, you try too hard to find a logical explanation for something that is not logical. We are the blood. The blood is us," he said.

"So any vampire blood I take will reveal such experience? Why then is there nothing of Elijah in me?" I asked.

"I told you before, he only carried my blood to you," Matthew said.

"That's bullshit. You would've had to drain him first. Did you do that?"

"Of course not. If I had, wouldn't he have been a duplicate of myself? Think about it. My blood was simply older and stronger than his, and more readily accessible. Like oil and vinegar separate in a jar, my blood was on top, ready to be received, fighting harder for new life," he said.

I thought about it for a minute and still it didn't make any sense. But then we were supernatural creatures, the laws of the mortal world did not bind us. It was just that my mind sought too desperately to understand.

"Why then am I not a duplicate of you, if all the vampiric blood in me is from you?"

"Because, Ainjul, you had and always will have your own identity."

"But you just told me Elijah would've been a duplicate of you if you drained him first?"

"Yes, but because he is a vampire," he said.

None of it made sense. I looked at Matthew and asked, "And just how did you become so knowledgeable about this?"

"Years of thought and years of experience," he said.

"So you really *don't* know. It's just what you've grown to accept," I said.

He thought a moment, then turned and glanced at me. "You are free to form your own thoughts and opinions," he said.

"I wish there was a book or something," I said.

He laughed softly. "That would indeed be something. A vampire encyclopedia or a vampire medical reference. Then the entire world would find out about us, and in today's world they would fight to obtain what we have."

"I seriously doubt it," I said.

"Then you underestimate mankind," he said. With that he leaned forward and pushed a cassette into the player, and for the first time since meeting him I heard Matthew's kind of music, and I was totally unprepared.

It was Springsteen, old Springsteen, the Boss from my high school days, and Matthew was singing with the same pitch, the same guttural voice, the same wild enthusiasm.

His mimicry was so believable I could close my eyes and think Bruce sat right next to me in the RV. But the strange part was that the music was magic, like Matthew's blood was magic. Every mortal has experienced this special magic, the way an old song heard again can bring past memories into clear focus. I knew exactly where I was and what I was doing the last time I heard this song. I could even smell the sweet smoke of dope in the air.

Matthew continued to sing, song after song. His mood was high, I had never seen him like this before. I wondered where it was all leading, but dare I interrupt his little melody?

The RV slowed and we exited the turnpike at Somerset. Time had come to feed, and by the rowdy mood of my companion I was prepared for another cat-and-mouse game with victims.

We pulled into a gas station-grocery store. While Matthew filled the dual tanks I went inside to look around. The young man behind the counter struck me as oddly out of place in this Mom and Pop store. His hair was bleached white, cut in a flat top that stood, moussed stiffly, a good inch straight in the air. From the ears back, the hair was dyed in a rainbow of brightness, pink, purple, and finally red. But the oddest thing was the lime-green braid hanging almost to his waist. I wanted to pull it to find out if it really was his hair, and he must've seen the look on my face because he finally stopped rearranging the snack-sized Lays potato chips and spoke.

"You need help with something?"

"A bag of ice," I said. It was either going to be ice I sucked on, or him.

He made his way from behind the smoky gray glass counter and led me to the back of the store. A plume of frozen air fell from the freezer door when he opened it.

"Big one or little one?" he asked.

I was fascinated by his earring.

"Big one or little?" he repeated.

It was a gold snake. Its mouth was biting into his earlobe, the sharp little fangs actually pierced his skin. The body was jointed somehow and it seemed to coil slowly when he moved his head.

"Earth calling the beautiful lady. Big bag or little?"

"I'm sorry. A little bag." I said. Oh how I would have loved to let him feel my fangs, and I was nearly ready to move in on him when an older woman came from behind the storeroom door.

"Greg, you've got a phone call back here," she said.

He handed me a small bag of ice.

"How much?" I asked.

"For you, it's on me," he said, and winked.

"Got any cups?" I asked.

"By the Mister Coffee machine on the counter, next to the register, help yourself," he said.

Then he was gone, and my chance for a hot meal was gone

330

with him, but it didn't really matter, I could subdue the feast for a while with the ice. I walked to the counter and helped myself to a styrofoam cup and headed outside as Matthew came in.

"Ainjul, we aren't stopping again tonight," he said, and it was a warning to me that if I intended to deny myself this opportunity I would suffer for it.

"Fine by me, I'll be all right," I said. I clutched the bag of ice a little tighter and smiled at him.

I turned away from his disapproving glare. He said nothing else and I heard the bell on the glass door twinkle when he closed it.

Come to think of it, he had never spoken to me of the water incident at the convention. Of course too many things had happened to me since then and it probably slipped his mind, or maybe he decided to try some for himself and found it really did no harm.

In either case, I filled my cup with cubes and stuffed the remainder of the bag into the small refrigerator.

I settled into the passenger seat and popped an ice cube into my mouth. Funny thing about being a vampire, my lower body temperature caused the ice to melt too slowly and I found myself pushing it wildly back and forth across my tongue and the roof of my mouth to hasten the watery flow.

Three ice cubes down and still no Matthew. I tipped the cup and let the spoonful of cold water slide down my throat. Ahh, how it quenched the fire in my gut!

I was leaning against the door, when it opened I fell right into Matthew's arms.

"You drive for a while," he said.

His touch was warm, his breath scented with blood. He pushed me back into the RV and I climbed into the driver's seat and looked at him. Again there was a tired expression in his eyes and an almost withdrawn look upon his face. Whenever I took blood it renewed me, but his body suggested an opposite effect.

"You didn't take the punk kid, did you?" I asked.

His smile was slow and tired.

"I usually take women, Ainjul. Their skin is so much nicer,

331

and their terror so much more exquisite. And old women, like old wine, have years of experience in which the terror can ferment.''

"You are an absolute fiend. You didn't kill her, did you?''

"No. I required very little,'' he said.

I started the engine and pulled away from the little store. Bruce was singing loudly, and after I turned onto the main road I turned Bruce off.

"Matthew, how come the blood affects you this way?'' I asked.

"My age perhaps. I often don't need much, and then when I take it my body needs more time to assimilate it. I am weary after the feast, but don't mistake weariness for weakness,'' he said.

"Your look is deceiving.''

"Quite,'' he said.

I slowed the RV and rolled down the window to take the ticket from the man in the toll booth. There was very little traffic and I had no problem merging back onto the turnpike.

We traveled in silence. Matthew dozed off a few times and I found it very hard to believe he wasn't weak. But within an hour he began to transform and clearly he looked younger and revitalized.

Per Matthew's instructions we spent the day in a campground near Breezewood, and when I awoke we were on the move again.

We arrived at the Eclipse Equestrian Centre just shy of midnight, and I grew fearful of my demanding hunger. Would I be able to repress it when Matthew's mortals greeted us, and where would I find a victim tonight?

The windows on the left side of the house were lit, as were two windows in the center of the second floor. But when Matthew cut the engine nobody came outside.

I started to open the door and felt Matthew's hand upon my shoulder.

"We forgot our tan,'' he said.

"Nothing like blowing our cover,'' I said, and followed him into the back. For the next several minutes we smeared bronzing cream on each other and prepared ourselves to assume the roles of southerners.

Unlike Matthew, I was sweating like a pig, and the cream wanted to smudge instead of blend into my skin.

"I told you that damn water isn't good. You won't find me perspiring like this, ever," he said, and reapplied the cream to my forehead and upper lip.

"Well, excuse me. I wasn't aware vampires weren't supposed to sweat."

He screwed the lid back on the plastic jar, and it made a cracking sound and split under his force.

"Are you ready?" he asked, and slammed the jar upon the table.

"What in the hell are you so moody about? I'm the one who should be moody. I'm being consumed internally and I just might take a bite out of one of your precious employees."

"If you are suffering it is your own fault. Control it."

I drew in a deep breath and followed him outside. Something was wrong. A foreboding presence drifted in the air, I sensed it and I knew Matthew was sensing it too.

We entered the nineteenth-century fieldstone house. From the outside the building was large, larger than Matthew's home in Charleston, but the interior was chopped up with many rooms, tiny and quaint. I expected to find another treasure trove of antiques but most of the pieces, although keeping with the period charm, were reproductions.

Someone was in the house, upstairs, taking a shower. The water pipes creaked and groaned between the pine-paneled walls. It was a sound that belonged in this old house, and while I followed Matthew the sound followed me. All too suddenly the water upstairs was shut off and one loud clunk vibrated within the walls, then silence.

Matthew stopped in front of me but my focus was on the sounds and I inadvertently walked right into him, smacked my nose against his shoulder blade, and the sharpness of the pain brought a flood of tears that spilled down my cheeks.

"Damn it, Ainjul, look what you've done," he said, and wiped the tears from my cheeks showing me the bronzing cream smeared across his fingers.

"Well, I didn't mean to. I'm sorry," I said while feeling my nose.

"Go outside and fix yourself." His command was abrupt.

I turned away. As I feared, my nose began to bleed but the blood trickled down the back of my throat and the taste fired my hunger. I walked away, muttering to myself about the uncaring attitude of my friend and about my throbbing nose.

After reapplying the cream I took a few extra minutes to stifle the flames of hunger before I dared venture back into the house. But when I approached the front door, it opened and David stepped outside, car keys jingling in his hand.

"Good evening, Ainjul," he said.

God, the warmth eminating from him, and the smell of his blood coursing internally was delightful. I swallowed hard and fought the urges to take him.

"Are you going out this late?" I asked.

"Yes. Mr Trenton is expecting a visitor soon and he asked me to leave. There is an auction tonight in Devon and the horses weren't to sell until 11:30 anyway, and you know how slow those things go. I'll probably be there the rest of the night."

"Who is Matthew expecting?" I asked. He had said nothing to me.

"A woman stopped in late last night. She said she was from Florida and a good friend of Mr. Trenton's She wanted to stop by tonight and surprise him, but I know Mr. Trenton well enough to know he doesn't appreciate surprises. Think her name was Debra," he said.

"Debra!"

"You know her?" David asked.

"Yes. I know her," I said. So, she had been trailing us. Was she going to step forward now and take Matthew?

"Well, I better be going. It was nice to see you again," he said.

We turned away from one another. He walked toward the Jeep Cherokee wagon and I walked into the house and closed the front door.

The floorboards creaked above me, and I headed upstairs to find Matthew but we met on the stairway.

334

"She's coming to make good her threat," I said.

"She is already here," Matthew said, and brushed by me.

I reached out to stop him but he was already out of my grasp so I began to follow him. He moved swiftly through the house, searching each room for her.

"Matthew, I think she is really dangerous," I said.

He laughed softly but it wasn't his usual laugh. I heard what, a twinge of fear, or anguish?

"What are you going to do?" I asked.

"What do you mean?"

"Are you going to destroy her?"

He stopped, turned on the lights in the family room, and then looked at me.

"No."

"Well, I think she's going to destroy you, or try to," I said.

Again he laughed, and this time it was definitely a nervous laugh.

"Matthew, her threat was real. You didn't see the look in her eyes. She's mad. She wants you. She wants to be like you and be with you."

He walked over to the large picture window and pulled the drapes open. The back floodlights were on but beyond the perimeter of light the woods were dark and even we weren't able to see her, if she didn't want us to.

"What are you going to do?"

"We will wait. If she wants to see me so badly she will have to come to the house." He stepped away from the window.

Outwardly he was being cool but I sensed the tension within him and I too knew the danger. I didn't like this game. Never had I been threatened by another immortal, and I wasn't sure, if it really came down to a fight, which of us would lose. I paced across the thick brown carpet and glanced out the window each time I passed. My gut feeling was that I would lose. I was the young one, the inexperienced one. It didn't matter how many times Elijah spoke of my strength. It didn't matter that the old "Master's" blood was within me. All that mattered was the impending conflict, and I imagined it play by play, three of hell's creatures fighting to the death, three immortals for whom death would not come easily.

335

The clock on the fireplace mantel chimed. The tune was "Auld Lang Syne." One o'clock and no Debra. I was still pacing the floor.

"Ainjul, will you please sit down," Matthew said.

"I can't. This is killing me. What does she want, what is she going to do?"

"We won't know until she comes to us," he said.

"If she is here now, why doesn't she show herself," I said, and my voice was gathering hysteria. Matthew was right. She was here. I could tell too.

A loud bang, then another and another came from the darkness outside. Matthew leapt from the couch the same instant a wild scream pierced the night.

"She's in the barn!" He ran from the room and out the front door.

Another scream filled the night. It wasn't human. It was a horse, and there is nothing worse than that pure sound of animal terror, not a whinny or a nicker, but a true scream of panic.

I ran after him, and once outside my worst nightmare was alive, in living color.

The old bank barn was engulfed in flame. Orange tendrils of fire licked around the open doors and shot upward from the hay loft. The blanket of smoke made an even darker blotch against the starless night sky.

I was frozen to the spot, watching the angry fire but thanking God that she hadn't set the other barn on fire too. But that was my mistake. She knew Matthew and she knew what she was doing. His prized stallion was in there and he was going in to save him.

"Matthew, no," I screamed when he dodged between two arcs of flame.

I ran closer, but the heat was overpowering and my body was beginning to tingle all over. Another wild scream broke above the ghastly roar of fire. Brie came galloping out of the blaze, his mane and tail were smoking but not on fire, and as I jumped clear of him he skidded by and I caught a whiff of his scorched hair.

I had to fight the internal will to keep away from the heat,

336

but I had to get Matthew out of there. *The blood is us.* And now the blood was commanding my body to fall back. Each step closer was a struggle for me.

Then I saw her. She stepped from behind a group of trees and ran in a blur of white toward the newer barn, the one filled to capacity with horses, the one in which my little mare was kept. I was torn emotionally in half. The sounds of my nightmare flooded me. Anxious whinnies and kicking came from the new barn; the aroma of panic poured into the air around me. A loud crackling hiss exploded behind me, and I turned in time to see the fiery inferno of the loft cave in as the old timbers gave way.

A pure adrenaline-forced reaction sent me into the flames. My body was not only tingling, I swear it was beginning to spark, and I pictured myself bursting into flame at any moment.

"Matthew!" I screamed.

The intense heat was swelling my face. I remembered the effect of light upon my hand and now felt my entire body being toasted like a marshmallow. Tears were streaming down my face and I brushed them away angrily.

"Ainjul, get out of here."

His voice was barely a whisper, and I felt it more than I heard it, but at least he was still alive.

"Matthew, you've got to come out, now," I yelled.

"I can't. I'm trapped. Save yourself, Ainjul. Go back."

His words gave me direction, and I jumped over a pile of burning hay bales.

Matthew was pinned to the ground. A beam had fallen across him and small flames were melting the fine fabric of his sport coat. I threw myself on top of him and he screamed in agony, but it was the only way I could smother the flames quickly.

"Get Pops out," he said quietly.

"After I get you out," I said.

"Ainjul, it's too late for me, please save my horse."

I looked down into his eyes. They were almost swollen shut, as were mine. His face was puffed up and his lovely brown hair was burnt in melted clots around his scalp.

337

He began to cough. A little bit of blood came up and he wiped at it feebly.

"Ainjul, please," he whispered.

"Damn it, Matthew, don't you die on me," I said, and stood up over him.

A few more smoldering bales of hay bounced down from above, and I moved swiftly away. My body was melting but my will overrode the pain and I swung the stall door aside so Pops could escape.

But the black stallion was too confused and frightened. The pine shavings beneath his hooves were burning rapidly and he pawed frantically at them, sending sparks into the air around him. I rushed him and threw my arm around his head and neck. A mortal couldn't have done what I was attempting, and I finally managed to pull him out of the stall and into the littered aisleway.

But I forgot the most important thing. I forgot to close the stall door, and even though he was free he wheeled around and ran back inside his box because it was his home and to him it was safe.

Again I went in after him. He was frantic and I hung onto his neck while he reared and tossed me around the walls. My brain took over and I automatically grabbed onto his neck with my hands, forcing great amounts of skin to curl into my palm. He instantly became placid. This was a trick I had learned from my vet. It was the only way I could give my mare injections. By grabbing that handful of skin she would go calm, like magic. Now, like magic, Pops walked out of the stall with me and I steadied him while I nudged the stall door closed with my foot. I steered him away from the fallen timbers and around the burning hay bales. He began to trot and I ran with him, letting him loose at the last moment and slapping him on the rump while screaming for him to get out.

Smoke stung my swollen eyes, and again I wiped the tears away. But the tears were bloody upon the back of my hand and I grew weaker as I fought my way back to Matthew.

"Can you push the beam up while I pull it?" I asked.

"No," he gasped.

I took small, panting breaths of hot air and grabbed onto

the burnt timber. It was like touching a hot iron and my immediate reaction was to withdraw. I placed my feet apart and prepared again. This time I was ready for the searing heat, and as I pulled up on the beam I smelled my own skin being burned.

Matthew screamed again as the weight shifted over his torso and his agony spurred my strength. I heaved the timber and sent it rolling sideway into the aisleway.

"Ainjul, God, the pain . . ."

The old barn creaked again and the back wall began to buckle, but this was good, it was our way out. I shielded Matthew as more smoldering bales fell from above. The shower stopped and I gathered him into my arms. He was so light it was hard to believe. The beam must've crushed his spine, for his legs dangled uselessly, and as I stood I saw the blood-soaked ground. He was badly hurt. The blood loss was too great. But he was alive and he was weeping with pain in my arms.

I leaned into the panels of the back wall. Where the strength was coming from and how much longer I would be able to continue I didn't know, but I felt confident I would get us out.

I braced my feet against the floor and pushed and grunted some more. The plank boards began to bend and I pushed harder until the wall all but exploded and sent me flying into the blackness outside.

I tried to absorb most of the shock as I fell but Matthew's pain was terrible and he moaned wearily before he fell unconscious on top of me.

I dragged him away from the heat. The air was cold and painful on my own burnt skin. But the tingling sensation began to subside and I figured I wasn't in any immediate danger.

Matthew's eyes fluttered open. The contacts had slipped and the blue coloring was shifted to the outer edges of his pupils.

"Take them out," he said.

I reached for his eyes and held the lids apart. The contacts wouldn't budge, and I was afraid to pull too hard because I didn't want to damage his eyes.

"Ainjul, take them out, they sting," he said.

"I think they have melted onto your eyes," I said.

"Pull them off, I don't care what happens, just pull them off," he pleaded.

His eyes watered badly and bloody tears leaked down the side of his face. I waited a moment and tried again. The fresh surge of tears must've been enough to loosen them because this time they did move but I still had to peel them away.

He blinked rapidly and sighed.

"Better?" I asked.

"Yes."

"Are you going to die?" I asked him.

"I feel like I might. Everything hurts, I wish I might die at this moment." He managed to smile briefly before his face clouded again with pain.

"Can I leave you? Will you be okay for a minute?"

"I'm not dead yet. Perhaps in a moment, but not yet." He looked away from me and I followed his gaze to the burning barn, then he looked back into my eyes. "Get her, Ainjul. Kill her if you can."

He had read my mind. I was up and running for the new barn. She wasn't going to start another fire. She wasn't going to live very long.

Good old Pops had forgotten his near brush with death and was teasing a mare. Actually, Pops was the one being teased because the mare was in heat and ready but locked securely away from him. And though the fire still raged outside, the horses in here had already settled down.

Debra was nowhere to be seen. For a brief moment I thought she might've gone back to finish Matthew off, but that was absurd, the last she saw of us was when I entered the blaze. And I knew she wouldn't venture close to the heat, it was hell on my body to do it. If she was watching, and I'm sure she had been, then when she never saw us come out she would think us dead.

On one hand I wanted to go back to Matthew, but on the other I wouldn't feel right until I let all the horses out into the pastures, so if she decided to play another pyro trick the animals would be safe.

I ran to the back of the barn and pulled open the big aluminum door. All the horses would have to go out in this one field. If a few of them got nasty and beat each other up, well, it was better than being burnt to death.

In his lovestruck mood, Pops was hard to catch, but finally I got a rope on him and locked him into a paddock outside. My mind kept going back to Matthew. Would he be dead when I got back to him? I ran back inside the barn and pulled the double front doors closed behind me. Then, one by one, I opened the stall doors and soon was forcing all forty-eight animals outside.

My mare was the last one out, and as she galloped off into the darkness I pulled the door closed. The only one I had forgotten was Brie, and God only knows where he ran off to, probably found his way into the broodmare pasture by now.

I had one more thing to do before going to Matthew. I had to call the fire department. The telephone in the barn office had an emergency call card taped to it and I dialed carefully, told the operator I had a stable fire, gave directions, and then went out into the smoke-filled night.

I kept to the shadows, and kept an eye peeled for any sign of Debra. Somehow I knew she had already left the scene of her crime, but if she believed us dead, then I didn't want her to see me. When I came looking for her, she would really be in for a surprise. And I would look for her.

Matthew was in the same place and position I had left him. Fear froze my heart, he reminded me of Mr. Androgynous lying there so still, so . . . dead.

"Did you find her?" he asked. His voice sounded stronger.

"No. I let all the horses out in case she attempts another fire," I said, and walked closer to him.

"Good," he said.

I knelt beside him. "What can I do to help you?"

"Take me into the hills beyond the property. There is an old mine shaft where we can stay." His voice was growing fainter again.

When I gathered him into my arms he held back the scream but I heard it in the painful wince on his face.

"Which way?"

"Back there, through the woods."

341

I tried to move quickly and gently. Every placement of my feet sent a shock of pain through him and soon I was unable to be so careful as my body began to relent its super strength and weariness engulfed me.

The woods broke into an open field, all uphill.

"How much farther?" I asked.

"Beyond the hill is a stream. Follow the stream to the right. It will take us back into more woods. It won't be much farther from there."

I trudged onward. He didn't answer my question. It could be two miles or ten. But it didn't matter how far it was because I had to get him there.

The stream was easy to find. The water played along the rocks, bubbling and splashing on the journey down from the mountain. In the frolicking sound of playful water I heard the distant wail of sirens and as I continued to walk along the rocky edge the sirens grew louder. The firemen had come. Would they find it strange that nobody was home?

My foot slipped on a moss-covered rock, and for a moment I lost my balance and thought I was going down. I held Matthew tighter and miraculously regained my footing.

"Jesus, Ainjul, it hurts."

"I'm sorry. I know it hurts. I don't feel so wonderful myself. I'll slow down and be careful."

"I think my back is broken. I can't feel anything below my waist. Guess I should be thankful for that," he said.

"Will you heal?"

"I don't know," he said.

I looked down into his eyes. The swelling was going down but he looked terrible. His skin was pulled tightly against his bones. The texture was waxy, the color old yellow. He was deteriorating in my arms.

"Ainjul, promise me something," he said.

"What?"

"Promise me that if I live but am paralyzed, promise to destroy me."

"Matthew, I can't promise something like that."

"Ainjul, please."

My feet were moving automatically now and my brain consciously ignored his plea.

"Ainjul, promise me," he repeated.

Still I ignored him.

"What kind of vampire would I be, bound to a wheelchair for eternity?"

"You will recover," I said, thinking of the many times Bong healed.

"But if I don't. What will I do. How will I hunt?"

"I'll bring victims to you," I said.

"Forever?"

He was being practical. If I were him I would ask the same promise. But I couldn't give him that promise and the reason I couldn't was because I couldn't face eternity without him.

The stream curved up into the woods and the land grew steep and dense.

"Which way now?"

He twisted in my arms and groaned. After looking around he sank back against me.

"Cut right by that boulder and then walk straight for about two hundred yards until you see a clump of three pine trees. The entrance to the mine is just beyond the pines, behind a thicket of rhododendrons."

His direction was superb. Even though the tangled mass of branches concealed the entrance, I was able to slip behind and enter the mine.

For a few hundred feet the mine shaft sloped gently downward, but then the drop became steeper and the blackness down there was too complete. I stopped.

"I can't go any farther, it's too dark," I said.

"You must go farther. The daylight will seep in here. The shaft will jog to the right and when it does there is a natural cavern to the left. The opening is small but we can get through. Take me there."

I walked for a few more feet and stopped again.

"I can't do it. It's suffocating me," I said. And the blackness was. The claustrophobia had me in its clutches and my mind was screaming for me to retreat back into the open space beyond these damp musty walls.

"Ainjul, you must go on. Just get me there and then you can go. There is a little country store four miles beyond the spot where the stream ran into the woods. You can go and get some candles or flashlights. But get me inside."

As he talked, my mind was released from the black grip of fear and I walked farther down the deserted hole in the earth.

"Matthew, keep talking to me," I said.

"We should be about there. Move closer to the wall and feel for the opening."

"Here. I think it is here," I said when my hand slid around the cold stone wall.

"Let me feel," he said.

I pushed him against the wall.

"Yes, this is it. Just help me inside and then you can go."

He pulled himself up into the opening. I tried to steady him and push gently but his moans of pain were too much to bear and I stopped.

"Ainjul, I can take it. Keep pushing me and I'll pull myself in," he said.

"Are you sure. You passed out once already from the pain."

"Yes, I am sure. Push me up."

I held onto both of his useless legs and heaved his body through the hole. I had no idea where he was going or how big the hole was. I couldn't see anything but blackness. His feet were sliding through my arms and then I lost him.

"Matthew, are you okay?"

"Yes. Go now and get some lights. And Ainjul, you better feed before you come back, I need blood."

"I'm going now," I called, and my voice echoed down the mine shaft. "Matthew, you'll be all right, won't you?"

"I'm past the point of death, I think. I would've died by now," he said.

"Matthew, I'll be back," I said, and turned up the slope.

I started running then, and the sound of my feet played around me in an endless echo that pushed more panic into my heart. What is it about the black unknown that terrifies a soul so? What demons were chasing me along the empty corridor? And isn't it strange that I myself was a demon and was still afraid?

344

Once freed from the suffocating black pit, I kept running through the woods. I found the spot where the creek journeyed into the open field and I ran up the other side of the hill. Beyond the ridge I saw lights below. It was a farmhouse and the other building must be the store Matthew told me of. I continued to run for two reasons. I wanted to get back quickly and I had no idea when the sun would be rising.

By the time I reached level ground my heart was slamming inside my chest. The fire had taken an awful toll on my body and I needed nourishment, and I needed a lot of it if I was to share it with Matthew. But where would I find a victim now?

A dog was tied behind the house. He was sleeping and I might have taken him, but I didn't ever want to make that mistake again. I slipped into the shadows and crept to the far side of the two-story home. The wooden stairs creaked under my weight, but not loudly enough to disturb old Fido out back. I turned the doorknob. It was unlocked.

The house was quiet and smelled of, what, strawberries, yes, that was the smell. I crept through the kitchen. The counters were littered with canning implements and a row of jam jars lined the open pantry shelf.

The occupants of the house were in, sleeping, all six of them. I felt them. With quiet speed I climbed the stairs, and one by one I drank from them as they slept. It was so very hard to pull away but I didn't want to kill. Each delirious encounter renewed me. I even took a small amount from the little girl in the crib. And then, full and refreshed, I stole back into the night and broke into the store.

First I found batteries, and then four flashlights. The candles were all the scented kinds, and I mused over the aromas and chose the spicy ones over the flowery scents. In the corner of the store I found camping supplies and pulled a knapsack from the shelf and pushed the supplies inside. As I zipped the nylon bag closed I saw a camp lantern, the kind that burns kerosene, and I grabbed it from the shelf and took five bottles of kerosene to keep it burning.

My return trip was swifter than even I could imagine. Often I am simply amazed by the unlimited abilities of the vampire body, especially after feeding.

345

I reached the mine and loaded the big Eveready flashlight with six batteries, turned it on, and began my descent. The shaft was smaller than I imagined, and the distance shorter than it had been when traveled in utter darkness. As soon as the shaft jogged to the right, I swung the beam to the left wall and found the hole Matthew had crawled through.

"Matthew," I called.

There was no answer and my heartbeat quickened. I pushed the knapsack through and pulled myself up. The beam of light rolled away from me when I let the flashlight go. The interior of the cave was filled with stalagmites and stalactites, like monsterous teeth of some earth-dwelling creature ready to clamp down upon the victims trapped within. The flashlight came to a stop against one of the creature's broken bottom teeth and the beam of light illuminated the body of my friend.

His body remained motionless. His yellowing skin absorbed the light and glowed like a sick lightning bug. I was afraid to approach him. I was afraid he was dead.

CHAPTER NINETEEN

How long did I stand there and stare at his motionless body? And what was the feeling growing beneath the euphoric glow of the feast? Remorse? Fear?

Slowly, very slowly, I approached him. The glow from the flashlight flickered. Was it possible the batteries were going so soon? I knelt down and picked up the large black Eveready. The light blinked off completely but when I jiggled it, it came back to life. The plastic casing had come loose during the roll and I unscrewed it, tightened the bulb, and put it all back together again.

"Ainjul, come to me."

Instantaneous relief flooded me and I began to go to him but I stopped mid-stride. I knew what he wanted. Blood. My blood. He had taken my blood once before and I nearly died. He had destroyed other vampires by taking their blood. Was my trust deep enough to give him what he wanted?

"Matthew, I'm afraid," I said.

"There is no reason to be afraid," he said, and tried to prop himself upon his elbow.

"I've never given my blood to anyone, except Bong, and he didn't really count. He didn't really draw it out of me."

"Ainjul, come to me," he repeated.

Again I stared toward him and again I stopped.

"Will you die if I don't give you blood?" I asked.

"Please, come sit beside me. The time has come for me to tell you my past and I want more than your blood, I want to share something very special with you, Ainjul."

347

I did as he asked.

He reached out and took my hand. His finger traced along the veins of my wrist, sending an excited chill down my spine.

"Have you ever heard of blood brothers?" he asked, still tracing the blue veins.

"Yes," I answered.

"Mortals cut themselves and join the wounds together so their blood will mingle and somehow mysteriously bind them together for whatever reason. Did you ever wonder where that ritual came from?"

I shook my head. It never entered my mind, it was just a thing people did.

"The ritual began in the beginning, as all things do. When the first vampire made the second vampire their blood mingled completely and they were blood brothers. Down through history the exchange of blood became one-sided because, in most cases, the new vampires were hapless victims. Nothing was to be shared from the experience, nothing was to be gained either. You are more than I ever expected you would be and I want to share my experiences with you."

He put his wrist to his mouth and bit down. Then he lifted his arm, stretching it out to me. A thin line of blood trickled out from either side of the puncture wounds.

"Ainjul, take me."

I remembered him telling me we would both know when the time came. But did this mean he would die?

I held onto his wrist and watched the blood ooze slowly around his forearm. There was no hunger, no desire.

"Matthew, you've lost too much blood already. I can't take more from you."

"You begin the exchange. When you are clamped onto me your trust will be complete. I will not harm you."

I looked away from those crazy white eyes and my gaze fell again to his wrist. The wounds were already beginning to close off. I was licking my lips, trying to revive my sated hunger. If I didn't drink quickly, I would have to reopen those veins, and my friend had suffered more than enough pain.

348

While I wetted my lips once more I drew his wrist closer and studied his expression. Though clouded with pain, it was intense and dead serious. When my lips met his skin and my mouth closed over the wounds his expression became one of blind innocence, and I wondered if he knew what we were doing or if his mind had grown delirious.

With the first swallow a blinding rapture overcame me and my body shuddered with delight. His blood, ancient and powerful, was filling me with unspeakable pleasure. His heart beat slow and steady and I was forced to maintain my pulls in rhythm with it.

The cave began to swirl around me. Images exploded within my mind. I closed my eyes and drank deeply. Never had a mortal's blood affected me so. Even Bong's blood was nothing in comparison to the ancient elixir from which I now feasted.

The momentary bursts of images became more rapid. I couldn't actually see them, they just happened, like a part of my brain was being awakened and memories were surfacing in sporadic intervals. In one swift instant I knew Ken and I felt his repulsion at what he had become and I felt his rapture as his blood was drained away. Then another remembrance, and another until my mind was teeming with the life blood of the nameless vampires Matthew had destroyed.

I could hear my own heart beating now, slowing down to match the stronger beat of Matthew's heart. A fiery rush of passion surged within my veins, and I knew at that moment Matthew had taken me.

Drinking Matthew's blood was foreplay. We had now entered the true consumption of each other and our passions rose and fell in explosions of pleasurable torment. The experience was unlike anything I had ever known and unlike anything I would ever experience again.

My memories were being drained away, becoming distant and small. His memories were being pushed in, bold and clear. I was learning everything about him. Everything. I knew Maria intimately. I knew the vampire, Paullinus, that stole mortality from Matthew, and I watched Paullinus die with the same sad horror that Matthew watched him die.

The cycle repeated over and over again. First my memories, then Matthew's until they were no longer separate, until we had truly become one.

We were lying side by side upon the cold stone floor. My left wrist was crossed over my chest to his mouth, his right wrist was against my lips and still we drank. The blood was a current between us, a powerful current that bound us. Neither of us had the strength to break free. An invisible force field held us steadfast while the blood restructured itself. I would never be the same person again, nor would Matthew. We had given ourselves completely.

Even when total exhaustion overcame us we did not separate. Hours passed, perhaps even days passed. Nothing held any meaning except our blood.

Distant thunder crept into my mind. At first I thought it was only a mirage of sound but it increased in strength and fury. Outside a storm brewed. The booms resounded in the valley and echoed down the mine shaft. It was during my quiet listening that I realized we had finally separated from each other.

Matthew's eyes were closed. His face had become full again and his skin was beginning to shed the parchment yellow in favor of stark white. His expression was utter calm. Finally his secret was shared, was known, and he at last earned the peaceful serenity he searched over three hundred years to find.

Maria Abigail Anne. We loved her and yet we loathed her. Our very souls had been touched and tormented by her, but now we could say goodbye to her, forever.

I stood up slowly. My body was in an ethereal state, and I nearly floated as I moved silently across the cavern. His power was now my power. The fledgling vampire I once was had now grown strong wings. Could there be a higher high than this?

The storm beckoned me, and I eased my way from the cavern entrance and let the darkness caress me. The very earth beneath me shuddered with power as the heavens clashed and the flashes of lightning coursed around the manmade tunnel with such eerie brilliance I began to run for the opening.

Fire comes in many forms. Lightning.

I kept running until I reached the edge of the woods, and there I stopped to watch nature perform. The sky was alive. Each time the blue-white streaks bolted to earth I saw more than lightning, I saw colors, day colors, illuminated but briefly in the darkness. A giant network of currents webbed across the southern sky, and for nearly a minute it was daylight and the beautiful greens of the valley cried out to me. Like the first night when I tasted blood, things around me were new and I wept silently while nature tantalized me with her awesome power.

Matthew had awakened.

I hurried back into the mine. His body was healing and his strength returning. This was known to me by instinct, blood instinct. When I reached him he was sitting against the shallow curve of a stalagmite.

"Matthew, what have we done?" I asked, sitting down in front of him. I drew my knees up to my chest and hugged them with my arms. My question was stupid, I knew damn well what we had done.

"We have set Maria free and now I will tell you the complete story of her, and of me," he said.

"But you don't need to. I have experienced it through your gift, I have lived your past."

"I need to tell it. I need to hear the words aloud. Please bear with me," he said, and then he began.

"Maria was my older sister. Hers was a fiery spirit and indomitable soul. I loved her more than I loved my own mother, for it was always Maria with whom I shared my time.

"When we were young we were inseparable. I think this came about because Mother was very ill during my early childhood and Maria assumed her role. Since I was a small child Maria often was my protector but she was always my teacher and her fondest lessons were those of the fairies, the little people of her private dreams.

351

"Her very favorite game was to be the good and just fairy Queen Titania and I was her King Oberon. You see, she really believed in fairies and told me many, many times that they were genuinely little people, shadows of mankind, miniatures of humanity.

"The most important fact she taught me about fairies was they could only be seen during fairy time, after midnight but before morning when Venus shone bright in the sky. And of course they were immortal, and if they chose to they would befriend mortal children, carry them off and make them immortal too by dipping them into their 'virtuous well.'

"Maria believed in this so strongly we spent most of our childhood roaming Tellingham during the predawn hours, searching for them and searching for immortality.

"Though I never saw a fairy, strange things occurred which were presumed to be caused by them.

"During the summer of my eighth year our neighbors to the south, the Colleton family, were blessed with a baby boy. We heard he wasn't a healthy infant and when he was brought to church to be baptised Maria told me what he was, a changeling, a puny, wizened, half-witted child. I still see his face, the wrinkled, aged face of an old, old man, not a fat pink baby face. Maria said that the fairies crept in and stole the real Colleton baby and left this ailing brat in his mother's arms.

"This was serious thought for a young boy's mind, and I believed the changeling story for nearly two and a half centuries before I learned of genetics and saw what inbreeding can cause."

Matthew fell silent for a moment. There wasn't enough time for him to continue his story.

Sleep was closing in on both of us. But it was a weird sleep. Neither of us actually lost consciousness. My body was limp and unmoving, sending me back to the nights I spent out of touch with it. But when I had been paralyzed in Matthew's bed I could feel, and now my body was completely closed off to sensory perception. The hard rock beneath me wasn't there, the air around me wasn't there, yet it was but I wasn't feeling anything. I imagined this was how some people felt when they experience an out-of-body experience but I never left my body. I was entombed in it, but I never left it. In some manner my body had shut down for the day, and after I realized this I noticed that my heart and lungs were no longer working either.

Had I been alone I would have been terrified, but I sensed no fear from Matthew and this helped me remain calm. My mind drifted in and out of blood visions. Everything was Maria. Her image, though surrounded by the images of so many others, was the strongest. I focused on them, understanding the terrible burden of guilt Matthew had carried with him throughout eternity. There was nothing in those visions, however, showing me her strange fascination with fairies, and I wondered why Matthew had started her story there.

I finally fell into a light sleep, and for the first time since becoming a vampire I dreamed and my dream was the perfect nightmare.

I was a vampire in my dream and I was with Matthew and Elijah. We were in the past, and inside an old-time meat store, the kind where carcasses of dead animals hung about. Some still carried feathers and fur, but others were skinned and plucked and hung obscenely naked from the large meat hooks.

I must've just become a vampire because Matthew and Elijah were waiting for me to take my first human. They walked to the far side of the store while I approached the butcher.

The big white apron he wore was smeared with blood and the smell was driving me to madness. I glanced back once at my mentors and they smiled and nodded approvingly. Mr. Butcher brought a knife down with a tremendous whack and the hind quarters of a rabbit slid away from the body. He looked across the counter at me and was about to speak when I lunged for him.

He tried to bring the knife up but I grabbed hold of his arm and flicked it to the side. The movement on my part was barely movement at all, but his wrist snapped and he screamed as my teeth sank into his neck.

His blood flowed fast and I swallowed large amounts before I realized he was changing. His screams had turned into animal growls. His jaw was being forced against my ear and I felt his hot, panting breath and heard the sharp click of fangs.

I couldn't withdraw, the blood was holding me to him, but in the corner of my eye I saw what he was becoming— a werewolf!

In self-defense I closed my hand around his muzzle. I knew dogs couldn't open their mouths when their jaws were clamped shut, and I prayed now that werewolves couldn't either. I was suddenly aware, and suddenly horrified, that if he scratched or bit me I too would be a werewolf, and I was already a vampire and I didn't want to be both.

Then my mind demanded to know if drinking the blood of a werewolf would turn me into one, and when I couldn't supply it with an answer I withdrew from his vein in utter repulsion.

Laughter echoed in my ears. Matthew and Elijah were having a grand time. I held onto the monster's muzzle and turned to look at them. Matthew had a gun. Elijah handed him a silver bullet. One shot, perfectly aimed, hit the monster between the eyes, and his skull shattered and pieces of his furry scalp splattered across my face. He let out a final shriek of death and slid from my grasp.

Matthew and Elijah continued to laugh and I saw another silver bullet go into the chamber of the pistol. I heard the shot and felt the bullet tear into my chest.

"Ainjul, are you all right?"

Matthew's voice pulled me away from the butcher shop. "Ainjul?"

"Yes, I'm all right. I just had a nightmare," I said.

"The werewolf?" he asked.

I sat up and rubbed my hands across my forehead and temples. My head was pounding.

"How did you know?" I asked.

"It's every vampire's nightmare, to drink the blood of a werewolf and then be forced to become one," he said.

"There's no such things as werewolves," I said flatly.

"Or vampires," Matthew added.

"Yeah, right," I said.

"Ainjul, light the lantern and bring it over here. I want to continue with my story," he said, and pulled himself into a sitting position against the far wall of the cavern.

"Matthew, are your legs any better?"

"No. If in a few days they still do not mend, keep your promise," he said.

I busied myself with the lantern. I had never made the promise and I wouldn't keep it if I had. He was going to be all right.

"Where was I?" he asked.

"The changeling child," I said, moving closer to him. The lantern gave off a dull glow against the rock formations. I sat down opposite him.

"Yes. He died three months after his baptism and we attended the funeral. The coffin was so tiny and I remember thinking what an awful thing his death was. He never got a chance to live and now he was gone. Maria only said that it was too bad the fairies didn't immortalize him.

"Fall arrived and I was sent away for my first taste of formal education. Father shipped me off to be a boarder at the Westminster School and it was there that I began to learn how deeply I loved my sister. I never spoke of this with my chums, they would've chided me terribly, but I missed her very much.

"Among my studies I was introduced to art, and I excelled in it and I loved it. The teacher saw my ability and nurtured it, and for a special gift I made a miniature sculpture of Queen Titania for Maria. When I was shipped home for Christmas I was so excited to give it to her that I nearly burst with the anticipation.

"But Maria was different when I got home. She had become a young woman. After she opened my gift she told me it was cute and then she put it away. I was crushed. I had wanted so badly to please her and she simply put it away, in the box, not even a spot on her shelves was reserved for it.

"I went back to school heartbroken. My studies became boring, I had no enthusiasm, even my art teacher noticed it. Time and time again my instructors reminded me that my father paid good money for me to attend Westminster and if I didn't continue to excel I would be dismissed from school.

"But none of this mattered to me. All I wanted was to know what changed Maria, and why we had grown apart. She was my very best friend. Oh, I had some friends in school, but none shared the things we had shared.

"Finally I got my answer. My father was invited to school and he came up to the dormitory where I lived with five other young boys. His look was grave, but I saw the deep caring beneath his facade, and as he sat down upon the foot of my bed I began to cry. He circled his arms about me and comforted me, the first time he had ever done so, and then he told me why Maria was so cold to me at Christmas.

"Simple jealously. Maria wanted to go to school. Maria wanted to learn about the world. Maria wanted more from life than to be someone's wife and someone's mother. But Maria wanted things she could never have and she was simply jealous that I, the second born, the first male child, should have so much more opportunity from life than she would.

"By the time I was sent home again Maria was her old self and I guessed Father must have had a talk with her. We were the very best of friends for the entire summer. We played our games and I tried to teach her all the things I had learned at school. She desperately wanted to learn to speak French and I would sit for hours and repeat words over and over while she said them back to me.

"She seemed happy and content, and it wasn't until the school term was ready to begin, and I was packing to leave, that she became distant and moody once more. Now I was only ten years old, and she was thirteen, but I had matured somewhat during my time away from home and I boldly confronted her.

"It was then that she confided to me things she didn't even dare share with our mother. She had begun to menstruate and she had hid it for four months from Mother. The reason she hid it was because she didn't want Mother to know she had become a woman. As it was she feared that at the most she had only three years left until she would be forced to marry. Girls married early in those days, and Maria simply wasn't ready to give up her childhood. She told me quite frankly she never wanted to marry and never wanted to have children.

"Ainjul, she should've been born in this century."

I nodded in agreement. Maria would've thrived in the eighties. I pictured her as a preppy young executive, maybe she would even have her own company.

Matthew leaned his head back against the stone wall and closed his eyes. A glimmer of tired pain crossed his face. His hand went to his hair and he was about to grab onto that lock again but it was no longer there, and his hand gently brushed the burnt stubble. He opened his eyes and continued.

"I went back to school but I wasn't there for very long when I was called home again. Mother had died. In a crazy way, Maria was elated by this event. Mother was the one who would've married her off.

"She told me after the funeral that now she could remain free until at least eighteen, maybe even until twenty. Just before I set off again she came to my room and quietly told me that when she did marry it would have to be to someone as special as me.

"I was flattered. I had often thought the same thing. Maria was so lovely, I too wanted a wife as beautiful and vivacious as her."

Matthew stopped talking and stared at me for a long time. I knew what he was thinking, I was her very image.

"Ainjul, I need to rest," he said.

He needed more than rest, he needed blood, and though he didn't ask me to I got up and started out in search of it.

"Matthew, I will be back as soon as I can," I said.

"You better tell David that I am all right. And Ainjul,

call Steven and tell him what has happened, but don't let him come," he said.

I climbed through the cavern opening and lowered myself into the mine shaft. Of the several things I needed to do, one of them was hunt Debra. Somehow I knew she was still around, it was as if I sensed her.

By the time I made it back to the horse farm I was certain Debra was still lurking about.

Only a partial stone wall remained of the barn and the air was heavy with smoke aroma. I crept carefully around the burnt pile of rubble. In order to contain the fire a bull-dozer had been brought in and the timbers and hay bales were pushed into a smoldering teepee.

I stayed glued to the shadows. Our RV had been moved and I saw it parked near the arena under the bright glow of security lights. Before I dared to meet with David I had to get in there and make myself tan.

I hesitated against the metal treads of the bulldozer and looked for the best passage across the wide gravel drive. It was then that I saw Debra. The bitch was coming out of our RV.

I waited until she wound her way behind the large barn and then I moved in blinding speed. But I didn't go after her, not yet. I would take care of first things first.

After double checking the flimsy trailer door to be sure it was locked, I found the jar of bronzing cream and began to smear it on myself in the dark. My skin felt okay, the puff-iness had gone down, but just to be certain I was passable I dodged into the bathroom for a quick look in the mirror.

Everything looked all right. My hair was a little singed on the ends but otherwise I had come out of the fire in fine shape.

A scream, high-pitched with terror, pierced the night. I ran outside just in time to see Debra gallop away. She was heading into the woods in search of us.

The scream brought David from the house but I was ahead of him and thankfully I reached Sandy first. As I feared, Debra had taken her but she was alive and she was rambling on about vampires. I took hold of her. The cold-

358

ness of my touch filled her with new terror but I locked onto her gaze and firmly told her there were no vampires. She calmed down. I hoped my little hypnosis would convince her for the duration of her life, but I've never known how long the messages I've sent into mortal minds remained with them.

While I still held her in my gaze I released my fangs from their resting place and carefully dabbed her wounds with the bloody saliva. Her wounds closed just before David entered the barn.

"Ainjul, what in the hell is going on? Where is Mr. Trenton? What happened here last night?" His questions came in a breathless rush.

Sandy slumped back into the chair, unconscious.

"It was Debra. She set fire to the barn. Please, saddle my mare for me, I have to go after her before she . . . ." I shut up. I wasn't about to tell him the truth and I wasn't a very good liar.

"I better call the police," David said, and stepped toward the office phone.

"David, wait," I said, and when he turned to look at me I caught him in a power hold and pushed a barrage of images into his mind. I had underestimated my power, however, and he wheeled backward holding onto his head.

He stopped and leaned against the wall. I was blowing it. The new strength Matthew had given me was unharnassed. I had to learn control.

"I'll saddle your mare," he said, and looked up at me. His expression was ghostly. Had I short-circuited his mind?

David walked out of the office and closed the door behind him. I waited and watched him through the glass panes. He was walking like a zombie might walk, his brain was doing what I had commanded.

While David was gone I picked up the phone and dialed Matthew's home on Legare Street. It amazed me that I just knew the number, like I had always known it, but I never did before. The phone rang over twenty times before I hung up. There was nothing else I could do except go after Debra. I'd have to try and reach Steven another time.

David led my mare to the office. The blank look upon his face was gone, replaced by a bewildered stare. He handed me the reins, and as I jumped into the saddle he started to say something, but I again locked onto his gaze and this time gently reassured him Mr. Trenton was fine.

Then I was off. My little mare was anxious and she shied once before I urged her faster into the woods. The ride was pure exhilaration. She responded to me in a way I'd never experienced. Together we raced between the trees and I found myself hanging onto her neck, my head bent low to avoid the branches above. When we reached the spot where the stream cut across the meadow I saw Debra. She had gone the wrong direction and was trotting across the crest of the hill.

When my mare saw the other horse, she let out a shrill whinny and jumped the stream, running in Debra's direction. I pulled her back. Though at first my plan was to attack her directly, now I thought of a better plan. If she wanted Matthew then I would lead her to him. And when I was certain she had seen me I dismounted and walked with my horse into the woods.

I could feel the pounding of hooves as she rode toward me, but I was shielded from her view by the dense forest cover. I tied my mare to a tree and hurried farther into the woods, closer to the mine.

With quiet agility, I climbed into a large pine tree and perched myself so that my mare was visible.

Debra did not disappoint me. She rode up to my horse and dismounted.

"Show yourself, Ainjul," she called out.

I remained still, waiting and watching for her next move. Something moved off to our right. Debra backed away. I sensed fear coming from her and it silently made me happy. Then I turned among the branches and concentrated on my voice. When my words came out they sounded as if I were in the mine shaft.

"You've destroyed him. If you mean to destroy me, come, I have been weakened by the fire and wish to die."

She tied her horse next to mine and slowly walked in the

direction of my voice. It was my plan to get her in the shaft. She would never get by me, she would never get out alive.

Matthew had been alerted to our presence. He was moving in the cavern, I could feel his pain as he crawled along the cold floor, his legs dragging uselessly behind him. We were communcating somehow, through our shared blood I imagined.

"I have no quarrel with you, Ainjul," Debra said.

I threw my voice deeper into the mine shaft and it echoed back eerily.

"Can you help me?"

Her pace quickened. She wasn't about to help me. Malice floated from her with such strength even the youngest vampire would've noticed her intent. But I waited and watched until she passed the point of no return. She slipped behind the large rhododendron bush and entered the mine.

I jumped down from my perch and landed quietly upon the thick ground cover of brown pine needles. With deliberate care and vampiric speed I moved in behind her.

The ability Matthew had given me melded me into the black walls of the mine. I think she sensed me but when she turned around to look she did not see me; even though she looked directly at me I was invisible to her. I had gathered three centuries of experience in one night and I nearly laughed out loud at her awkwardness.

"Debra."

It was Matthew's voice, cool, calm, and almost inaudible. She stopped, and her fear index rose tenfold. Her head cocked to one side and then to the other trying in vain to find the source of the sound.

I felt Matthew's silent wish for me to bring her closer to him, and I focused my voice again down the shaft.

"Debra, bra, bra," it echoed around the darkness.

Her posture relaxed a moment. She was thinking she obviously heard wrong before. It was just me in the mine. She started forward again, and as she moved into the glow of our cavern lights I followed.

"Ainjul, where are you, you, you."

She reached the turn in the shaft, and at that instant Matthew slid down from the cavern entrance.

"Matthew! But you're dead." Her gasp was strangled with fear.

"We are all dead, Debra, and you've forgotten that to destroy an immortal is not so easy," he said.

Debra backed away from him but only a few steps. He was in tremendous pain and his legs would not hold him. He began to slump against the wall and she moved a little closer.

"But you've been wounded and now I have the advantage," she said, and reached for him.

I moved in behind her and caught her up in my arms. I pulled her elbows back and dug my knee in her spine, forcing her off balance and holding her there.

"Tell me one thing before I destroy you, Debra, tell me why you did this," I said, forcing her closer to the broken body of my companion.

"I don't owe you an explanation," she said.

I forced my knee harder into her spine, threatening to break it as she had broken Matthew. She began to thrash wildly but my hold was too strong for her and she stopped and began to weep.

"You owe me," Matthew said.

"Will you let me go?" she pleaded.

"Tell me why you did this to me!" Matthew demanded.

"Because," she shouted. "Because I wanted your gift and your status. Because it wasn't just enough to be immortal. I had to be queen among our kind as you have been king. And I knew you would give it to her," she said.

She went limp against me and I made the mistake of letting up on my hold. She immediately flung her body away but my grip was still on her arm and we both pulled with such instant ferocity that her arm ripped from the socket. The sound was like pulling the drumstick from a turkey. A loud snap and then a long sucking noise. The muscles of her detached arm twisted spastically in my grasp, and I threw it onto the ground in disgust.

362

She fell back, blood spurted from the hole in her shoulder, and she grabbed the torn ends of tissue and moaned.

Matthew was quickly on top of her, forcing her tightly against the wall.

"It's time to die, Debra," he whispered lovingly, and then he took her.

She didn't struggle long. He thirsted badly and he took her quickly. And I watched with horrified fascination as her body began to age and her skin began to shrivel.

Steven's description was correct. She was being sucked dry. Was this how Ken and Bong looked? Nothing remained but a dried husk. I had done this to Bong but I never looked at him after I had finished. Now I moved closer and saw the way her lips peeled back from her jaw and the way her eyes sunk into their sockets. She was withering away, like the wicked witch of the west when Dorothy threw water on her, Debra was becoming nothing.

Still Matthew drank.

The skin of Debra's slender arm turned ashen gray and began to flake away. Her head tilted further back. The once soft suppleness of her neck was now a stringy mass of tendons and her nose sunk back into the nasal cavity.

I wanted to look away but something held me there. Her cheekbones appeared, glints of bone. The weight of Matthew's body crushed her and I heard the brittle splinter of her rib cage as he sank closer to the floor.

At last the deed was done and he pulled away.

"Ainjul, I'm sorry you had to witness that," he said.

I looked away from her decomposed corpse to him. He had changed. His hair was growing even as I watched. The look of sickness had been lifted.

"Matthew, what is happening to you?"

"Her blood was old and it is healing me. You must take her body and burn it."

"With what?"

"Take some kerosene and the matches. Drag her deeper into the mine and set her on fire."

"Matthew, I can't."

"You must. If I could do it I would but I am still not

363

healed. You must do it quickly. She didn't want to die. She will fight it.''

I looked again at her remains. How was it possible for her to fight now? But for a brief second I saw movement. Her torn arm, still plump and alive, was lying beside the crumpled body, and I swear the hand flexed.

Matthew saw the movement too, and he snatched the arm into his hands. It twisted violently, the hand flexing and fingers curling to strike out at him, but he managed to plunge his fangs into the tender flesh and soon the arm withered away in his grasp.

"Quickly, Ainjul. Do as I say."

I reacted swiftly. Matthew's urgency and the ghastly animation of her dead remains pushed my fear of death away. I didn't want her to come back. I gathered the remaining bottles of kerosene and a pack of matches and then tried to pull her body away from our cavern entrance. But this was a near impossible task. Pieces kept falling off, and I had to stop and gather them up before moving her corpse farther away.

"That's far enough. Douse the body and set fire to it," Matthew instructed.

I poured the kerosene over her hair and her skull. I tried to saturate her clothing and most of the bones and flesh that remained. Then I lit the match and stepped back. I held the match to the entire book, and as all the matches exploded in flame I tossed it upon her.

The smell was sickening. The flames danced along her legs and coursed up her broken ribs. I don't know if it was just an illusion but I swear she moved beneath the blanket of fire and I moved away.

"Is she truly gone?" I asked.

Matthew reached up for my hand and pulled himself erect. He stood in front of me, and beneath his pain I saw a tired expression of loss.

"Yes. She is gone."

CHAPTER TWENTY

"Is a vampire's death always so horrible?" I asked.

"Yes. Even when you are prepared and ready to die, the blood fights the final consumption. But let's not dwell on this, I want to continue my story," he said.

He leaned against me for support and walked beside me to the cavern.

"Your legs have mended," I said.

"Almost. There is still pain."

I helped him up into the cavern entrance. Before following him, I glanced back to the fiery remains of Debra and shuddered. It was an awful way to die. I wanted to live forever.

Since I had last been in the cavern, Matthew had arranged and lit some of the candles. A hint of cinnamon drifted in the air. The soft flicker of the flames danced among the stalagmites and stalactites.

"Did you get hold of Steven?" Matthew asked.

"No. Nobody answered the phone. I'll try again later, if you'd like." I sat down near the kerosene lamp, opposite him.

"Perhaps tomorrow," he said.

We stared at each other in silence. I was waiting for him to begin the rest of the story, but he was just looking at me, remembering, perhaps.

"Do you hunger?" he asked.

"No."

"You won't have to feed quite so often now," he said.

"And you?" I asked.

He smiled. "I will have to feed more often than I did before. But we will rise up and sleep at the same time."

"I thought we would be duplicates of each other but that's not so, is it?" I asked.

"Yes and no. There was a point while we drank when our blood and our minds were equal, but after that brief point we again began to live separate lives. We have shared everything we had to share and from this point on we will each form and retain our own memories."

"Have you done this before?" I asked.

"No. Paullinus told me of it. Before he died he shared his knowledge, verbally. This exchange of blood is sacred and can only be done between the strongest vampires. This is one reason why I had to be sure you were strong enough, Ainjul. If you weren't madness would consume you as the memories of everything I have known flooded your mind."

"I don't understand this and yet I do. I only wish you would have told me sooner," I said.

"I'm sorry I kept this knowledge such a secret but I had to be sure of you, Ainjul, and when you risked yourself in the fire for me I was certain. I didn't want it to happen under such circumstances, but most things that are special in life never happen as we plan," he said.

He fell silent again and just watched me. I wasn't doing anything in particular, except thinking about Maria. The harder I thought and replayed the memories he had shared, the more I found pieces missing.

I knew, for instance, that he planned an elaborate wedding for her and I knew she married, but why wasn't there a memory of him being there? I saw the brief image of a baby and felt heartsick, but I couldn't understand why or whose baby it was. But most of all I knew Maria wanted to become immortal and Matthew very much wanted her to, but something had gone wrong, and when he went to grant her the wish it never occurred, she never became a vampire. Black empty slots interrupted his memories.

"You were going to give Maria immortality but you never did, why?" I asked.

"Don't you know?" he asked.

"There is nothing there. Pieces are missing and I can't find the answers, I can't put the whole story together."

"How much is missing?" he asked.

"Well now, that's a stupid question. I'd have to tell you all that I know and then you could tell me what's missing."

"Must've been in the blood I lost," he said thoughtfully. "Then I have more of a reason to continue with the story."

"Please," I said.

He collected his thoughts and then began again.

"My education continued, as I've told you before, and when I reached my fifteenth year I eagerly anticipated going to Europe. Understand that throughout the years my love for Maria only deepened. What I really hoped to gain by leaving England was to loosen the unnatural hold that bound me to her.

"It was sinful, my love for her. I knew it but nothing could force that love away. Before I climbed into the carriage she kissed me goodbye. But her kiss was more than a sisterly kiss, it was filled with passion and that was when I learned her feelings were very much like mine.

"My tour of Europe was to last three years but Father died during the second year and again I was forced home. Despite the adventures and the lessons my tutor instilled upon me I was unable to shake my love for Maria. It wasn't that there weren't other young ladies, because there were many, but always I compared them with her and not one of them lived up to her image.

"I was seventeen when I became Earl of Tellingham, Maria was twenty. When I arrived home I was startled by her beauty."

He stopped and gazed at me a long time.

"God, you look just like she did then," he said.

"Well, you're not exactly a dog, you know."

He laughed quietly.

"I was quite handsome then, guess I still am. Anyway, I had my share of fair maidens begging me to marry them. Though Father's estate was nearly out of money, I still inherited his title and his property and I was probably the most eligible bachelor outside of the court. Maria too had her share of suitors, but for us the pressures to be married were off. I had the estate to run and Maria had more years of freedom.

"Then the gossip began. Neighbors whispered about the unusual attraction we shared for each other and they wondered just how the young earl and the young lady lived. We had done nothing wrong. We kept to ourselves. But still the rumors of our unwholesome relationship circulated.

"It was then that I decided Maria should marry. We had lived together for five years and for five years had been tormented by things we wanted from each other but could never dare have.

"Maria was twenty-five, hardly the age for marrying. All the men her age had already taken wives. Though she had grown more beautiful, she was in all respects past the age of becoming a bride. But I was adamant that she should marry, and when I told her so she flew off in a wild rage.

"Due in large part of the success of my horse-breeding venture I had managed to build a small fortune and I had a rather sizable dowry to give away with her but still no offers came. Maria was relieved.

"Then, in the summer of 1673, Lord Colleton's wife died and he came to me asking for my sister's hand in marriage."

"Is this the same Colleton, the one with the changeling child?" I asked.

"Yes. He was the child's father. He was forty-one years old, short, fat, and balding. He had a son my age and a daughter who was sixteen. He certainly wasn't what I intended Maria to marry, but on the other hand he held quite a bit of property, and with his and Maria's dowry combined the marriage would bring them wealth.

"At first Maria was dead set against such an arrangement, but at last I convinced her. It wasn't that Lord Colleton was a bad person, he was quite amenable, but he was old. It was this fact that finally won her over, for I convinced her he would not live very long and she would come out of the marriage with a substantial estate.

"To prove his intentions in marrying my sister, Lord

Colleton agreed to have a settlement paper drawn up stating exactly what she would inherit. Together we sat down with her and finalized the marriage. The wedding would take place in September, only two months away.

"Since she could not have the man of her dreams I wanted to give her the wedding of her dreams. With a few bribes, I managed to acquire the court tailor and seamstress to design her gown. The wedding was to take place in our garden, followed by a large banquet after the ceremony. I think invitations were delivered to everyone in the village. I even had one sent to King Charles and Queen Catherine. The king would not attend, but Her Royal Highness, the queen would.

"This alone elated Maria. But the final pièce de résistance was the portrait, and even though she had to sit for the painter I did not allow her to see it until the eve of her wedding.

"In the weeks that followed we prepared for the event with near frenzied haste. I don't know how we managed to get everything done. After my father died I had to let nearly half of our servants go but now I called them back. Everyone was excited. Everyone except me. Underneath my cheerful smiles remained loneliness. I was about to lose the only woman I had ever dared love.

"As had become habit, I often went riding after dinner. I always rode my stallion and my destination was always the old ruins of the abbey on the edge of Tellingham. I didn't know it then but *he* was watching me for several nights before *he* took me. But I'm getting ahead of myself.

"By the eve of her wedding every last detail had been completed, and after I dismissed the house servants for the evening I went upstairs to present Maria with the portrait. As I hesitated outside her bedroom door I heard her weeping softly and at that moment I almost walked away. My facade of happiness was weakened, and now I all but crumbled with emotional strain. I had to comfort her and I had to maintain my composure for one more day. After she left the estate I would allow myself to swoon in misery, but not until. I knocked lightly upon her door and waited.

"It took a few minutes for her to open the door, and had I not heard her weeping I would have never known. She had managed to pull herself together and she greeted me with a warm smile.

"She was genuinely pleased with the portrait. She began to ramble on and on about how much she would cherish it when she grew old and her beauty faded. I tried to make light of her comment but she turned toward me and I still recall her exact words. She said to me 'I never found them, Matthew, and now the magic is gone.' I knew she meant the fairies."

"Matthew?" I interrupted.

"Yes."

"She never loved her husband, did she?"

"No. Though she did grow quite fond of him over the years. He was a good man and he showered her with favors. But she loved me as I loved her. We were separated but also united.

"Then it happened, and to this day I don't know which of us initiated the act, but the magic between us awakened and we unleashed our pent-up passions and loved each other. We consummated our sins that night and forced ourselves to tie a knot of secrecy around our dirty deed. I can't say we didn't care, because we both knew it was wrong, but we were possessed with each other, totally. It was only after the fact, when she lay quietly beside me, that she told me she would never be sorry for what we had done and now that her truest desire had come to pass she would be able to endure an arrangement where there could be no love.

"As for me, it was my first and my last encounter with love. There had never been nor would ever again be another. It was my punishment.

"I waited for her to fall asleep, and then I left her and went off into the night. I rode my stallion hard, punishing him as I wanted to punish myself.

"When I reached the abbey, I jumped down from my mount and he reared in surprise and galloped away into the mist. I wanted to be alone. I wanted no more contact with

370

people. I had been hurt by life and I simply waited while misery swallowed me.

"Had I been in my senses I might've seen *him*. *He* was stalking me, and as I passed beneath the remaining stone arches *he* took me.

"In my confused state of mind I thought he was the devil and this was my true punishment, and I didn't fight him until it was too late to fight. His rapture became my rapture. His love was my love. And when I finally realized it, his death became my death.

"I was lying upon the grass among the rubble of broken stones when I first really saw him. He came to me like a dark angel. His hair was as black as a raven and his eyes were the snowy white of a dove. In stature he wasn't a big man but the power emanating from him was enormous.

"He sat down beside me and cradled my head in his lap. While his fingers brushed the hair from my forehead he spoke."

" 'Now it is time to die,' he said."

"I was very weak, and I closed my eyes and waited for death to take me and then I heard him laugh."

" 'Not your death, young master Trenton, my death,' he said."

"Before I chanced to open my eyes again, he pressed his arm to my mouth and his blood trickled into me. Instantly a strange new fire burned in my soul and I clamped onto him and began to drink, knowing not what I consumed nor what it was doing to me. Perhaps I was naive. I had no idea of what a vampire was.

"The longer I drank the stronger I became until he was no longer holding me, I was holding him. Somewhere, a voice inside me told me to pull away, and though it was the hardest thing I had ever done, I did. He fell from me moaning that I continue, urging me to take him completely.

"But the bond of blood between us was broken and I backed away from him, horrified. Not only had I committed a sin against God this night, now I had also committed sin with a demon.

"I turned from him and ran. I ran from him and from

371

myself. I ran away from all the world and when I reached the edge of the forest I realized I hadn't been running, I had nearly flown.

"Finally I stopped and collapsed upon the ground. There was no denying it, I was different, changed somehow, in league with Satan, I thought.

"Then he appeared before me. So quietly and magically I swear he just appeared from thin air.

"I looked at him a long time. He too had changed. He had become older and shrunken, more evil looking than before, and at last I asked him if he was a fairy."

" 'Is that what you believe me to be?' I recall him asking me."

"I didn't know what he was but he did something to me and now I demanded he tell me. He stepped closer to me and I backed away, crawling along the dew-ridden ground. He stopped and smiled slowly.

" 'I have given you immortality,' he told me."

"I was stunned and I shouted at him again, asking how he could do this to me and why. It was then that he told me."

" 'I am Paullinus. I am a vampire, as you are now. I gave my immortal blood to you, the only mortal I ever felt worthy enough to receive such a gift. I have never made another like myself, and I hoped when you took me you would drink from me until I perished. I am old and I want to die.'

"Old. If he was thirty I wouldn't have believed it, even in his shrunken stage, and I told him so. Then, quite seriously, he told me he was born in the year 25 AD. He boastfully proclaimed he was an ancient and I should be flattered that he chose me to be a recipient of his blood.

"I did not believe a word he spoke, and I asked him to go and leave me in peace. I wanted to be alone.

"He laughed then and told me I would have eternity to be alone. He said he had underestimated my innocence and repeated again and again that until I fully understood what I had become he must stay with me, and he warned me that if I ever chose to pass along the gift of everlasting life I too must stay and be sure the young vampire I created understood.

"He reached out his hand to me and at last I took it. For if I truly had become a vampire I needed him to teach me.

"I'm sorry I failed you in that respect, Ainjul. There was too much pain and too many memories of her, when I created you."

So far, the things Matthew had recalled did not surprise me. I had witnessed all of these things in our union of blood. What did surprise me was the incredible depression that I was sinking into. The more he spoke of his beginning, the more I found it hard to believe he could continue so long.

Matthew leaned forward and took off his blackened Rebok shoes and began to rub his feet.

"They itch. I must be healing," he said.

I wanted to ask him so many questions, but I waited for him to continue. He would tell me all of it, I was certain.

He put the shoes back on and drew his legs up underneath him, sitting cross-legged as I sat. And then he began again.

"My first night as a vampire was wondrous. Paullinus told me his history and I was held in awe of every detail. During Claudius' reign, in 43 AD, he was recruited into the Roman legions. The only requirement to become a soldier was that he be a Roman citizen and that he could read and write. In return he was offered a regular wage, an assured career, and even provision for retirement, things that were rare indeed in the ancient world.

"He met the requirements and set sail for Britain along with three other legions. By 47 AD the Claudian armies all but occupied Britain. During this time his legion was subjected to surprise attacks and ambushes. It was during one of these nightly raids that he was speared and left to die upon the battlefield. In his delirium he saw a cloaked man glide among the dead and he watched this man until finally he was approached. The man was bearded and saintly looking, and he thought it was the angel of death. But it was a vampire, searching among the spoils of war for blood not yet dead. And it was here that Paullinus received immortality.

"I tried to press him for further information about the one who made him, but he would say nothing except that after he had a taste of blood the vampire left him on his own, to discover for himself the ways of the undead. This is why, I presumed, he was so adamant about making me understand before leaving.

"He remained alone for centuries until at last he decided to mingle with the co-inhabitants of the world, the mortals. For a brief period he delighted in bringing about the rise of Maglocunus of Gwynedd, the tyrant ruler of Wales. He boasted of making Maelgwn, as he called him, a ruler blessed with might and power, steeped in malice and evil. I think the year was somewhere around 550 when this occurred.

"After his made ruler was slain, he again became the lonely wanderer of darkness. He witnessed the fall of the Roman rule, and the birth of the British Empire. He knew kings. He watched kingdoms rise and fall and rise and fall again.

"He told me he was a legend. He said other vampires sought him, wanting to know if he truly existed, and wanting the secret of surviving for so many ages. But he shunned them and told me to do likewise. He walked with mortals. He used mortals. He trusted mortals. When I asked him why he simply told me he knew he was always superior to them. And then he told me that never had a mortal threatened him, but on five separate occasions he had been mortally wounded by his own kind.

"This story was fantastic to me then. Over the years I have lived, I have adopted much of what he related to me that first night. After all, if he survived all those years, he was doing something right!

"I learned also that I wasn't chosen haphazardly. He had watched me for years. He had followed me and Maria through the fields while we so desperately sought immortality. He told me he had even followed me to Europe. He thought of me as his son, and he only had to wait before he

374

passed on his gift. And then he damned Maria, saying she interfered with my personal development, telling me she was demented. I felt as if a cold hand had reached out and slapped me.

"Maria was different, yes. But she was not demented. I argued with him angrily, and finally he gave up and told me that if it was my wish to pass immortality to her, so be it, but she would not survive. She had always been wrapped up in her own special world and if given immortality she would grow mad and die.

"Again I demanded he tell me why, but he remained silent. Then the sun began to rise and he took me deep into the forest where we took shelter in a cavern, very similar to this one."

Matthew looked around our little underground crypt. Outside, the sun was rising. The candles around us were melted down to waxy puddles.

"Ainjul, I must rest. Tomorrow I will tell you the end of the tale," he said.

I needed rest too. Everything was bringing the images into a fresh resurgence within me. I understood why this exchange of blood could only be shared among the strongest. His memories, my memories flooded me. If I weren't strong, madness would indeed befall me, it was so much to comprehend and so much to keep straight.

Sleep folded over me, but not a dark sleep of nothing. Again dreams filled me. I was reliving the past. Even his emotions had become mine. But my dream this day was not of werewolves or of Maria, my dream was of being burned alive and sinking into a fiery hell where Debra waited.

A far-off whinny woke me. Matthew was just stirring from his slumber too. We sat up at the same time and looked at each other with a special understanding.

Another whinny filtered into our cavern.

"Damn. I forgot the horses." I stood up and started out.

"Ainjul, wait. I'll come with you," Matthew said.

I turned and watched him get up. He was still in pain but his legs moved freely.

"Are you sure. I can do it and then come back for you," I said.

"Just go at an easy pace, I'll keep up. I want to get outside."

He followed me up the mine shaft, and when we reached the pines where I had left my mare, both horses were gone.

Another whinny echoed from the valley. The horses, left to fend for themselves, had obviously wandered downstream.

"I'll go get them and come back," I said.

Matthew leaned against the trunk of a pine and nodded.

It didn't take me long to spot the horses. But they weren't unattended. David was leading them across the stream and back toward the farm.

I ran down the hill, calling out to him and waving my arms to catch his attention. He saw me and pulled up.

"David, I'm so sorry. They got away from us. We had them tied but they just wandered away," I tried to explain.

"I've been looking all day for you. When you didn't return I thought the worst had happened. Then I found them wandering the hills. I've been worried sick about . . ."

"Listen, I'm really sorry," I said.

"Did you find that Debra woman?" he asked.

"Yes. Matthew had a talk with her. Seems they had an old disagreement but it's all over now."

David gave me a skeptical look. "Where is Mr. Trenton?"

Now I had to lie. My mind formulated a story, and I looked him in the eye when I spoke.

"We are camping, up in the woods," I said, and pushed the idea deep into his brain. "We were just getting ready to come back when I saw the horses had gotten away."

I walked over to my mare and took the reins from David's hand. Then I mounted her and grabbed onto the horse Debra had taken, leading him away from David.

"We will be back later. Mr. Trenton will talk with you then. Go home, David," I said.

He got that blank zombie look again and did as I commanded.

I found Matthew sitting along the stream. He had taken off his shoes and socks, rolled up his pants, and was soaking his feet in the cold current of water.

"Can you ride?" I asked him.

He nodded and slid back from the water. While he put his socks and shoes back on I watched the crest of the moon rise above the treetops. It was a large, full moon. Somehow I felt it pull on me, like earth's gravity had changed by the closeness of it.

Matthew stood and took the reins from my hand, then he turned and studied the saddle for a minute.

"Ainjul, you'll have to help me up. My legs aren't quite strong enough," he said.

I quickly dismounted, gave him a leg up, and then climbed back aboard my mare.

He urged his horse into the stream and I followed. We walked side by side. His mount kept trying to nip my mare in the face, and finally Matthew leaned forward and smacked him in the cheek.

"I succumbed to the sleep of the dead and Maria was married," he said.

He reined his mount to the right, up the grassy slope.

"When night fell again and I awoke I was consumed by the thirst, and by anger. Paullinus had chosen the worst of nights to instill immortality upon me, and I told him so.

"I wanted to go to Maria, but Paullinus had other things in mind and he would not let me leave. It was this night that he told me all about the changes I would undergo and instilled upon me the magic of our blood. He kept me inside the cavern until the thirst was so terrible I no longer could control it. Then he came to me and offered himself once more.

" 'Finish my blood. Grow strong with my ancient power and live forever,' he told me."

"It was his plan to stop existing, and my hunger was such that I was able to take his life away. I took him and I finished him. Every drop of his ancient blood was now my blood. After it was over I was filled with remorse, but as he

377

wished, I dismembered his remains, burned them, and scattered the ashes among the forest.

"I understood what it was to be a vampire. I also understood what it was to be alone. But before the sun rose again and forced me to sleep, I went to Maria. I owed her.

"She was easy to find. Somehow I knew where she would be. The garden was still decorated, but the large arrangements of flowers were now wilted. She was alone. She had been crying.

"When she saw me she came running but I backed away from her embrace. I didn't want her to touch me, I didn't want her to feel the coldness of my skin. I had no explanation to give her, and it was Maria who began the conversation.

"She was so worried. My horse had returned and her new husband had sent the servants out in search of me. The guests attending the wedding weren't particularly surprised that I had ridden off. Everyone knew of our feelings. She alone managed to pull off the event, and with subtle flair.

"She endured her husband's touch on her wedding night because she thought only of me. And then she laughed and told me they didn't get as far as we had because her husband was simply exhausted and fell asleep upon her breast.

"I remained silent, letting her continuous talk soothe the wounds we had created. After she quieted she stared at me a moment and finally asked, 'You found them, didn't you?'

"I nodded but said nothing more.

"She approached me then and this time I did not withdraw. She touched my face and grasped my hands and then she asked me to take her to them.

"I told her no. When she asked why, I told her that they weren't good fairies, but demonic creatures and I had been consumed by them and had in turn consumed them. It was my penalty for pulling her into sin and I could not take her to them. I had to let her go. I had to roam the dark hours alone.

"But before I left her I told her that if she ever needed me, all she had to do was call out. I would hear her and I would come. I left her then, dawn was fast approaching.

She did not try to stop me, she was stunned. And she did not call me for a long, long time.

"I became the creature of night. I moved away from my village and found a hiding place in the ruins of another abbey. During my transition the smell of death clung about me, and I was convinced it was indeed my punishment, especially when my genitals began to shrink away. This was something Paullinus had not told me, and I knew it was my penance for my sin with Maria. It wasn't until much later that I learned all vampires lose their manliness in this manner, and I know Debra told you of this," he said.

If vampires could blush, I'm sure I would have. Matthew saw my embarrassment and offered an explanation.

"Vampires procreate by blood. Reproductive organs are no longer necessary. There is never a sexual attraction as there was when we were mortal. Passions are shared by blood alone," he said.

"But you saw Maria again," I said, changing the subject.

"Yes, I saw her again. Eight months had passed before she called me. Her voice was distant but instinct pulled me to her. The closer I came to her the more I felt her pain and her fear. We met again in the gardens of Tellingham, now sorely overgrown and uncared for.

"She was sitting along the weed-strewn flowerbed, rocking back and forth, cradling something in her arms. The smell of blood was all over her and I was afraid to approach. But she saw me and with weak steps walked over to me. She held the thing away from her breast, nearly dropping it in my arms.

"It was a baby. It was *our* baby. A son," he said.

Matthew reined his horse away from me and stopped.

The image of the baby flickered in my mind and I felt the despair he must've felt when he held the baby so long ago.

"The baby was not but a few hours old, if that. It was an unhealthy, deformed little thing. Premature, wrinkled, and already showing a blue cast to the skin, he was dying in my arms.

379

"Maria demanded I fix him. She did not know what I had become, but she knew I was no longer just a man. When I told her I could do nothing she told me to take it away. She began to speak nonsense. She was mad with fever and pain. She told me she had hid the pregnancy from her husband because she knew it was our child growing within her. Her husband had never loved her.

"She explained of how she would deceive him, of ways she would make him drunk on wine and make him think he had loved her. I guess women can do these things?" He stopped talking and looked over to me.

"If Maria said she did, then I guess she did," I said as I tried to figure out for myself what she had done.

"Well, I took the baby away, and in the quiet darkness I sat with him until he died in my arms. Then I wrapped the blanket around his pathetic little body and I buried him next to my father's grave. I wanted to say a prayer for him but only curses came from me. I cursed God silently and then I cursed him aloud. I shouted up to the heavens and demanded to know when my punishment would end. God no longer would look upon me, I knew that, and Satan was sitting in hell laughing, I felt that.

"For weeks after, I rested in my hidden tomb and I mourned. I mourned for the baby, I mourned for Maria, and I mourned for myself. The thirst tried to make me rise up but my very soul had been depleted. When at last I did rise it was with evil vengeance. In the months that followed I killed ferociously. I made no attempt to hide my victims. I left dead everywhere and a new kind of fear spread among the villages.

"I think what I was doing was trying to get caught. I wanted someone to find me and put an end to my torment. And someone did find me, but not a mortal, another vampire found me.

"I awoke one evening and he was there. The only thing he said to me was if I continued to carry on in such a rampage I was a threat to all of our kind. He never threatened me. He didn't say that others would try to stop me. But he did tell me if I could not handle living through the generation of mortals in which I was born, I should leave and go across the sea to the new land.

"I never saw him again but I am eternally grateful for his advice. It was too painful, remaining in England. In the year 1674, I bid farewell to England and to Maria and set sail for the New World. I stole away on a ship bound for Charles Towne Landing and it was there that I made a new life for myself."

Matthew stopped talking and rode along the timber line in front of me. It wasn't the end of his story. I still did not know why he refused to give immortality to Maria. I knew he went back to England, at least once, and saw her again.

We were heading back in the direction of the stable. I urged my mare into a trot and pulled up alongside of him.

"But you went back," I said.

"Yes, I went back. In the spring of 1681, Maria called me again. I don't understand how she, a mortal, could call me over such a tremendous distance, but I knew she wanted me, so I went.

"Before I rode to the Colleton estate I stopped by Tellingham and I was surprised to find that the grounds and the house were being maintained. I spent a few minutes in the barn. My stallion and most of my broodmares were there, in fine shape, some with new foals at their sides.

"Then I felt compelled to visit the graveyard. As I knelt beside the tombstones of my father and mother, brother and sister and son, I knew I was stalling for time. Maria was calling me, even now, and I was scared to see her again. She would be thirty-three years old, and I had not aged a day.

"But I did go to her. Lord Colleton greeted me at the door and showed me upstairs to her bedroom. Three beautiful little girls hid behind him, giggling and teasing one another. They were her children. It was undeniable. The oldest one was perhaps six, the youngest just a toddler. The guilt that held my heart captive weakened when I saw her children.

"Lord Colleton took the toddler into his arms and led the

others away by the hand. When they had all reached the bottom of the stairway I knocked upon the door.

"Maria did not open the door but told me to enter, and I did. She was sitting beside the window in a rocking chair. A thick shawl was draped over her shoulders, a blanket across her lap. She was all dressed up and even had on a hat with a very fancy spray of feathers. A thick blue veil of lace covered her face.

"I thought she had just come back from an evening out, but she quietly told me she knew I was coming and she was watching from her window for my arrival. As she talked she did not turn her gaze from the window, she did not look upon me.

"Finally she said she knew what I had become. The stories of vampires were popular in England now, partly due to my frightful escapades. At that moment I knew why she called me. She wanted to be immortal. She wanted to join me and live through the centuries. And I wanted it too. To be with her forever. To share a new passion with her.

"As I walked across the polished wooden floor to her, the boards beneath my feet revealed no footsteps. When I stood in front of her chair, I startled her. She looked up, and beneath the veil I felt her awe of me. I reached forward to remove the veil and her hand caught my arm, stopping me.

"All I wanted was to gaze upon her beauty, to witness the gathering grace of age that must've flourished in her. But she wanted the gift of everlasting life, and she roughly demanded I give it to her now.

"I was about to comply. My fangs descended from their sleeping bed and the fires of passion began. But when I bent closer to her, something compelled me to rip the veil, and as I did her hands went to her face and she cried out in surprise.

"She had been stricken with smallpox. She had been scarred badly. The craters were still reddened. Nearly every inch of her beauty was hidden beneath the pits. I could not give her immortality, not this way. She would hide herself for eternity. I had come too late.

"She began to yell at me, making demands, threatening

that she would hunt me down if I did not grant her this wish. But still I refused. And then she told me she hated me, from the day I first went off to school she hated me, from the day I forced her to marry she hated me. When she gave birth to that thing she despised me and now she told me she loathed me.

"Paullinus was correct about her. Even if I had given her the blood, she would have gone mad. She was somewhat mad already. An immortal part of me died then. I understand that now," he said.

We reached the outskirts of the pastures, and our horses began to trot back toward the barn. Matthew pulled his mount to a halt and dismounted. I did likewise.

Matthew handed me the reins of his horse and motioned I take them into the barn. He turned away from me, walked stiffly across the grass, and stepped up to the front door of the large fieldstone house. He was going to feed some logical story to David, and I knew we were going to be leaving shortly for Charleston.

After I unsaddled both animals and put them away for the night I went to our RV and waited. Matthew was gone more than an hour, and I was just about to go in and see what was up when he came outside. I watched as he shook hands with David and then crossed the drive.

He opened the door and motioned that I move over and do the driving. He looked so tired and so frail but he also looked relieved.

Neither of us said anything. We were each busy with our own thoughts of Maria. Perhaps an hour of silence went by, maybe more, maybe less. We had reached I-95 before he finally spoke.

"Eternity could be wonderful if you found someone special to share it with," he said.

"I think so," I said, and smiled at him.

"Ainjul, do you think my punishment is over, truly over?" he asked.

"Yes," I said.

"Then I suppose it is okay to admit that I love you," he said.

"Yes, I suppose it is."

Matthew and I remained in Charleston for three weeks before we boarded a ship bound for England. It wasn't a fancy cruise ship, it was an old cargo ship, but for me it was the perfect ship.

We left the docks of Charleston at noon. Both of us were sealed safely together inside a special crate. By evening we were well out to sea.

We were going home to bid a final farewell to the images of Maria. We would live at Tellingham and for a while, anyway, become reclusive creatures as we were meant to be.

I remember standing next to Matthew and feeling the gentle sway of the ship. The steel railing surrounding the deck was cold beneath my palms. The sun had set but the brilliant reds were still visible and swept the vast expanse of the sky to the west.

My journey was just beginning.